REPREHENSIBLE
CONDUCT

BY D.H. SEILER

PAGE PUBLISHING, INC.
New York, NY

First published by Page Publishing, Inc. 2016

ISBN 978-1-68139-191-5 (pbk)
ISBN 978-1-68139-192-2 (digital)

Printed in the United States of America

PROLOGUE

The stranger sat in the shade of an umbrella on the far side of the pool, reading the same newspaper page he had read for the last hour.

He was wearing dark sunglasses, expensive creased tan slacks, a Hawaiian silk shirt, sandals without socks, and an Indiana Jones–style hat. His well-tanned body was in decent shape—not too heavy, but not muscular in the sense of a body builder. He had thick black hair showing below his hat. Under his shades his eyes were constantly moving, almost devilish, while his head appeared to be facing the newspaper in front of him.

From his seat, he could see the beach, as well as the expansive hotel lobby and the exit door to the pool. His hour-long wait finally paid off when she walked through the door to the pool area.

The young lady was about twenty-five years old and wearing a yellow two-piece bikini, a large floppy hat, designer sunglasses, and expensive fashionable flip-flops, and she was carrying a large stylish tote bag. Her tanned skin glistened when she came out of the shadows and reached the Florida sunshine.

Her yellow two-piece bikini was generously full on top, and her bottom was solid without an ounce of fat. He noticed her cheeks didn't bounce when she walked, but held firm. Her body was partly God-given and partly earned. She worked out constantly in the hotel spa, as well as at her local gym when she was home.

He knew this because he had spent many hours following her. He had had a hand in kidnapping her mother a year before. He was one of a handful of people who knew Mrs. Angela Pinata was being held in captivity.

He looked closely at her daughter as she walked through the pool area. She was covered by a fashionable, transparent sarong that was probably imported from somewhere in Europe, which would upset her father if he knew. Her father was Joseph Pinata, the president of the International Truckers Union. She was beautiful and would fit comfortably on the finest beach the French Rivera had to offer.

She walked with the grace of a model—chin up, posture erect, and with long, soft, leisurely strides. She gave off a natural grace that those in the upper class tried so hard to convey, while she did it effortlessly.

You could tell by just looking at her that she was someone who was well-to-do, someone with a privileged upbringing. Even though her father was a union man, he was financially far above the working middle class that he represented.

Sophia Pinata could show people that she was someone of importance without saying a word. She said it by how she carried herself. Sophia knew she was gathering attention while appearing to be oblivious to her surroundings and everyone there.

He watched her as she walked off the pool area and onto the hot white sand of the beach. He knew she was heading for one of the sun shelters reserved for the special guests of the hotel.

The area was roped off and guarded by the pool boy or, in this case, the sand boy. He was only about sixteen, skinny, with messy long blonde hair, a tuft of hair on his chin, and long flowered surfer shorts. He was the epitome of Mr. Surfer Dude.

He was more interested in checking out the rich girls than holding off the unwanted sun worshipers. He never missed a step from the time she left the hotel through her grand entrance and exit to the pool area. The kid was lost in her beauty, body, and graceful gait.

He was startled when she spoke; his well-tanned face turned rosy as she said, "Hello there, young man, how are you doing this beautiful morning?"

He stuttered as he tried to sound cool in his reply. "I-I-I'm wonderful and now that you're here, I'm even better."

"Slow down, tiger. I don't think you're my type. Besides, I have a husband in the hotel who is pretty protective of me. He's also very big and strong. I don't think you want him mad at you."

He gathered himself, smiled, and said, "I put two fresh towels and a pillow on your patio lounge chair, and there's a fresh cooler of ice and bottled water inside your canopy shelter as well. If you need anything else, just give me a yell. I'm here to serve you."

She set her bag down and grabbed a book from inside, removed her hat, and sat on the chair. She looked up to the skinny little surfer dude and said, "Thank you for setting this up for me. If I do need anything, I will be sure to call you."

He had a wide grin on his face and then walked the fifty feet to stand at his post. He would be checking on her—or more appropriately, he would be checking her out—throughout the day.

She put the pillow on the back of the chair and swung her long slender legs up out of the sun and settled in for a day of reading and relaxation. The warm Florida sunshine was all the therapy she needed to clear her mind.

The stranger waited until the little display with the boy was over and she was settled into her chair. He stood up, dumped the newspaper in the trash barrel, and walked slowly, unnoticed, past the sun worshipers around the pool.

As he walked up to the reserved sand area, the young man actually stood up from his chair and put his hand up, indicating that the he must stop. "This is for special guests only, sir."

The stranger hesitated for just an instant, trying to decide if he should slap the little surfer dude or go easy. He decided to go easy: less attention that way.

He reached into his pocket and produced a gold room key card indicating his stature within the hotel. He was a special guest too. Gold room key cards indicated that you were staying on the top floor in one of the hotel's finer suites. He had the card; he didn't have the room.

The boy lowered his hand and gave a sweeping semi-bow, allowing the stranger to pass. The man smiled a crooked smile and said, "Thanks, kid," as he handed him twenty bucks and said, "Go get a Glenlevit single malt scotch whiskey on the rocks for that lady over there, and be careful, it's expensive." The boy looked up at him and said, "I'm too young to serve alcohol."

"Then go find someone who is old enough and have them bring the drink," the man snapped. "And be quick about it."

The boy dropped his gaze and softly said, "Yes, sir." He turned away and raced toward the hotel.

The stranger walked over and stood just outside the shelter Sophia was sitting in. He waited a moment, looking at her long legs, and then sat down next to the bikini-clad young lady. He glanced over and asked, "What are you reading?"

She looked up at him and said, "It's just a suspense novel, nothing too heavy. I get lost when I'm reading. It's a great, relaxing way to spend your day."

"From where I'm sitting, just watching you makes me relax."

She felt the iciness in his tone and immediately became alert. "I like days like this because I'm alone and nobody bothers me."

"I'm just, you know, just trying to be neighborly," he replied with a smile on his face but a threat in his voice.

She was smart enough to know when to be firm when men hit on her. "I told you I wish to be left alone," she retorted. "So please let me read in peace."

With an icy edge to his voice, he asked, "Is everyone in your family an asshole or just you and your daddy?"

She flashed a quick look at him and quickly reached for her bag, but before she knew it, he had her by the wrist. He twisted it back hard until she let out a shrill scream that was muted by the crashing waves washing ashore. He swung his legs around, grabbed her mouth, and pulled her face close to his. She could smell alcohol on his breath as she looked into his eyes. An immediate stab of fear ran though her body. His eyes were glassy, unfocused. *Evil* would be the best way she could describe them.

"You listen to me, young lady. You tell that daddy of yours that he either starts doing as he is told or all he will find of you is this pretty little yellow bikini." He smiled a nasty grin as he gave her a small kiss on the left side of her face to send her a message. He felt her start shaking and saw fear in her eyes. He smiled and slowly removed his hands. "You've got a fantastic body. Too bad you look scared shitless. How does it feel?"

She just stared at him, not uttering a word.

He continued, "I personally hope that he doesn't listen, because it will be my distinct pleasure to remove this little yellow bikini of yours, and oh, what a pleasure it will be."

He slid his right hand down to her bare belly. She grabbed his hand and said, "No, you get your hands off me, you pig." She said it with conviction on her face.

His left hand came up in a flash, and he grabbed her throat and squeezed. He cut off her airway, and terror came across her face. He held her until she started fighting wildly. He patted her belly and removed his hand and smiled. "That's just a sample of what you'll get if your daddy doesn't listen. The boss already told me that you will be mine if he screws up. Maybe not today, sweet thing, but perhaps real soon. You keep thinking about that, little lady. I will be out there somewhere, just waiting for your daddy to screw up, and then, you will be mine whether you like it or not. I can't wait to get my hands on those big tits of yours. How about a little feel right now?"

He reached for her, and she slapped his hand aside and said, "You keep your fucking hands off me, you bastard."

The stranger stood up, laughed, and said, "I ordered you a Glenlevit on the rocks. Hope you like it. It's my favorite. Besides, I thought you might need it by the time I was done. Enjoy it and the rest of this beautiful sunny day. The drink's on me, honey."

With that, he was gone. She was shaking so badly it was an entire minute before she could move. When she finally stood up, he was nowhere in sight. An older man, a waiter, was almost upon her, carrying a drink on a tray.

She asked, "Did you see that man who just left here?"

"I'm sorry I did not," the waiter replied.

"How did you not see him when he was just right here?" she screamed.

The man shook his head, dropping his eyes as if he lived a life of servitude, and said, "I'm sorry, ma'am, but I do not have my glasses on today. I've misplaced them somewhere. Here is the drink that you ordered."

She felt remorse for yelling at the old man. "I'm sorry for yelling. I was upset. I think I really do need something to calm my nerves. At least the man has good taste in whiskey," she said under her breath.

The old man asked sheepishly, "Is everything all right, ma'am?"

She was terrified about what had just happened, but decided not to say anything. "Yes, everything is okay. I've had a rough morning."

He handed her the drink and said, "Would you like your change, ma'am?"

"No, keep it," she said with a calm voice. She took the drink and said, "Have a nice day, sir."

He did a little bow and left. She sat down and reached for the emergency radio that she was told to always have on her person. All she needed was to hit the emergency button, and help would have been there within minutes, but she had been shaking so badly she wasn't quick enough.

The shit would hit the fan if her husband, Thomas, or her father knew about what had happened, but if she told them, she would have to hear their wrath, and she would never have time to herself.

For the past twelve months, her mother had been missing. Her father told her that she had run away because she couldn't stand her life with him any longer, but Sophia didn't believe it for a minute. Someone had taken mother, and she was sure she was still alive. Her father had hired a private detective a month after she disappeared, but to no avail.

Since the moment of her mother's disappearance, she had had to manipulate her husband to get even a minute alone. Her father insisted on it, and her husband fully endorsed the position. She thought about her mother again and whispered, "Mother, please come back. I need you so much."

She thought about the threat the vulgar man had left her with, but she would say nothing and hope the dirty, smelly pig would someday be sorry that he had threatened her. She thought she would talk to her husband about this, but not right away. He would be upset and would want to put a tether on her, but at least he wouldn't treat her like she was a child, like her father would.

They had talked about this very thing happening. The more she thought about it, the more she considered that maybe she should tell him. But for now, she would be ready if this ever happened again. She needed this time alone. It was her time.

She took a drink of the single malt Scotch whiskey and felt its warmth as it flowed down her throat. This could still be a good day.

With that, Sophia Pinata Sharpe closed her eyes, took another sip of the Glenlevit, grabbed her book, and lay back down on the lounge chair.

ANGELA'S KIDNAPPING

TWELVE MONTHS AGO

Angela walked the streets of Miami with her head down, struggling with the decision she had come to. The emotional abuse of the last five years of her marriage had come crashing down upon her in the last week.

Joseph Pinata, her husband of thirty-five years, was the president of the International Truckers Union, and she knew deep in her heart that the union had become his first love, or so it seemed.

The neglect she dealt with was something she had accepted as a fact of life, but in the last five days, it had become crystal clear to her.

She had received pictures of prostitutes entering his suite, not once or twice, but many times over many days. She knew of the excessive gambling and the late-night parties he had in his hotel suite, but the prostitute thing was too much for her to bear.

When they had come to Miami for the contract negotiations, he insisted they have two separate suites. His excuse was he needed to use one as his office. He claimed he had private meetings and consultations with his staff.

She knew of the unending flow of money her husband kept hidden in a private safe in the suite she was forced to stay in alone. There was never any explanation as to where the money came from. He claimed it was his retirement fund.

Her decision was not without pain, but she knew it was inevitable. She couldn't tolerate the disrespect she received from Joseph and the people who worked for him.

They all knew. She felt their disrespect in the air when she walked into a room, the wives laughing behind her back and the men refusing to even speak to her for fear of saying something that would piss off her husband, their union president.

She and Joseph had not made love in over a year; there was no affection, no caring, no love shown, none of the things that made up good marriages. The few friends she had begged her to leave him and to take everything she could from him.

The problem she faced was that through it all, she still loved him in a kind of sick fashion. Even weirder, she felt he loved her too. There was just this space between them that he had built over the past year.

The unending pressure of his job and the constant emotional battles he fought on a daily basis had worn him down to the point where he didn't function as the man he once was. The real Joseph Pinata was hidden deep within him, but where? Why had he fallen so far?

As she continued her walk, she came to a corner and decided to turn right. Since she didn't have a destination in mind, it didn't really matter. As she turned the corner, the bright sunlight hit her directly in her eyes, blinding her for a brief moment. She looked down and covered her eyes with her hands. Instantly, she felt a hand grab her from behind, while another shoved a rag into her mouth. She could do nothing to get the unseen man to release his grip, or even to scream. He carried her to a car that had just screeched to a stop. The back door opened immediately as he handed her to another man inside the car.

She tried again to scream, but the hand and rag stuffed in her mouth stifled any sound that may have exploded from deep within her.

They forced her to lie on the floor with a foot in the middle of her back. One of the men said, "Relax, lady, we're not going to hurt you." She felt the pressure on her back subside, as if he was showing her he meant what he said.

She managed to look up at the window and saw nothing but black. All the windows must have been darkened, because no light was penetrating the vehicle.

A thought came to her, *Joseph, what did you do now?*

All of a sudden, a smelly rag was placed over her nose, and she found herself struggling for air, and at the same time, a sense of calm came over her as she could feel herself drift off into a deep blackness.

CHAPTER ONE
....

My name is Sean MacSween. I'm a representative for the International Truckers Union. We were in Miami Beach, negotiating the three-year contract with a conglomerate of trucking companies across the United States.

I was walking along the shore of Miami Beach. The beautiful beach enhanced all my senses—smell, taste, sight, and even hearing. The constant low din of the waves reaching the shore drowned out any other sound or sense that I had. Soon, the smell and taste of salt would permeate every fiber of my being, especially when the warm morning sun gave way to the early afternoon heat.

The breeze coming off the ocean was a constant, always blowing inland, slow and steady regardless of meteorologist predictions. I felt the familiar sticky feeling of salt on my hands while sensing the acrid taste in my mouth.

The air was so thick with salt that the clean smell gave way to a physical feeling like smog inhaled freely into my lungs. I wondered what my lungs looked like after all these walks I'd taken along the shore for the past twelve months. Coal miners get black lung. Would I get sea salt lung?

I knew the beach of white sand would soon fill with the day's sun worshipers, mostly with white, pasty, almost powdered-looking skin. It was Sunday, and all the new snowbirds from the north would appear like magic.

They would descend toward the beach to claim their three-by-six-foot personal property for the day. They had to get the perfect spot, and don't try to infringe on their space. They could be very protective of their spot.

You could always tell the new northerners; they were the ones who first appeared with stark-white skin in the morning and searing red skin in the afternoon, and then a sickly burned appearance at the day's end.

The bronze suntanned veterans stood out, with their leather skin that hung loosely even where it shouldn't and the deep-set wrinkles in their faces that screamed for mercy from the sun.

I was baffled why anyone with half a brain would allow themselves to burn their skin to such a leather-like coating. Obviously, they cared little about the threat of melanomas. One old lady was so leathery brown she had a constant smile that wouldn't go away.

Where I was walking, the dry sand grains were hot and soft, beckoning me to lie in their warm, comforting arms. My body ached, so I almost gave way to the urge. The smell of alcohol that oozed from every pore of my skin gave off an offensive odor that I knew could almost overpower the ocean's salty spray.

As I slowed the pace to catch my breath, I could feel my sweat-soaked union T-shirt that read "ITU: International Truckers Union" cling to my body.

I have always kept myself in good shape, though you wouldn't know it by how hard I was breathing. I had been big since I was a kid. I stood six foot two when I was only fifteen years old. I started lifting weights when I was eighteen and still have a large muscular chest and a flat-ridged abdomen. At thirty-six years old, I was a solid 220 pounds. There were tiny love handles emerging around my sides, but at least I saw them. I figured most men were expected to have some, but I had tried to prevent them for as long as I could.

It would all catch up with me in due time. That I knew.

I had been told more than once that I carried myself with the graceful flow of a confident man. I never knew what the hell that meant. I walked like every other man in our family.

I grew up in an Irish family, in an Irish community. My hometown is Detroit, Michigan, and

I lived in a blue-collar neighborhood. The Irish came to the west side of Detroit in the mid-nineteenth century. The move to the United States was prompted by the devastating potato famine that plagued Ireland in the 1840s.

Most of the Irish in Detroit came from County Cork, Ireland. So the area they settled in Detroit was known as Corktown. Half of the west side of Detroit had, at one time, been of Irish descent. In Detroit, Corktown originally reached from Third Street, about twelve blocks from the Detroit River, west past Michigan Avenue to Grand River.

The neighborhood has gotten smaller with each passing decade. Today, there are fewer than two thousand people in the greater Corktown area. Corktown is listed on the National Register of Historic Places and is designated as a City of Detroit Historic District. Shamefully, the area has become a victim of urban decay.

There are some, mostly the old folks, who try to maintain their Irish traditions, but still, the alliance with the old country is slowly dying. Young people just don't seem to care.

I look like an Irishman. I have light reddish-blond hair with a very small touch of gray on the fringes and deep-set green Irish eyes. My mother told me that my green eyes would someday be a magnet for women and get me into big trouble. I never was lucky enough to find a woman who found me irresistible enough to stay longer than a few months.

That is, until I rediscovered Riona. I fell in love with her when I was fifteen years old. Trouble was, she didn't know it until I was almost thirty. Although I was thirty-six, I still looked closer to twenty-six. At least I thought I did.

Even with the past five years of stress my job had laid on me physically as well as mentally, I had somehow been able to maintain my youthful face, a face that told a lie. I figured it had to be family genetics or some other unknown force. I surely did nothing to help my state of being.

I was always intense. I drove myself not for some particular goal—it was just the way I was. I was like the duck you see on the pond, calm on the surface but peddling like hell underneath.

Although my name is Sean, my friends called me Irish. I am a national representative of the International Truckers Union almost by default. My old man was a union representative—that is, when he was sober enough to make it to work—so it just seemed the right thing for me to do.

I was raised in the old school mentality with the belief that it was my duty, not my job, to help our union brother and sisters. Some days, the old trade union ideologies of respect and concern for others seemed to be nothing more than a ghost from the past.

That's not the way I wanted to be viewed, or remembered. It's a part of my being, the creed I live by, to be here for my union brothers and sisters. I know it sounds like a pipe dream, but it's the way

I want to be seen, even with a huge defect in my character: I drink. I drink a lot. The problem is not just that I drink too much—it's that I drink when I know I shouldn't.

Lately, I'd been angry, and I felt somewhat betrayed by the leaders of our union that I love so much. I, and many other union faithful, had spent our working careers busting our asses to improve or, at the very least, maintain the standard of living our members fought so hard to achieve.

The entire last year had been spent negotiating a contractual settlement for the International Truckers Union, our members, and the companies we worked for.

As I continued my walk, I took off my T-shirt and laid it on my left shoulder. God, my head pounded. My breathing was labored, and my body ached as I struggled through the dry, hot, white sand beach at the ocean shore. I seemed to be losing one step for every two I took.

This morning, with the oppressive Miami heat and humidity, my body ached everywhere. The idea that I could treat my body like I had the previous night was nothing more than a brief flash of insanity. I had them every once in a while. They just came out of the blue.

I squinted to help block the sun's glaring rays. I'd left my shades sitting on my bed stand in the hotel room. They weren't doing much good there on the beach. I had been thinking of other things when I left the room for my morning walk.

The night's booze, only three hours of sleep, and the fleeting memory of a fight made it one hell of a morning. The nausea in the pit of my stomach, along with the morning shakes, tremors, or whatever the hell they were called left me feeling vulnerable and weak. I hated that feeling, but it was becoming all too familiar.

My public persona is one of self-confidence and control. Only I know how vulnerable I really feel at times. I am also like the shark, always moving. If a shark stops swimming, he dies. It's that simple. He will either sink to the bottom or float to the surface. The same thing would happen to me if I continued living the way I had been.

Any sign of weakness was buried deep within me even before I walked out the door in the morning. I was always strong. At least, I hoped to appear that way—not just physically, but mentally as well. I was too proud to let this inner persona of weakness appear in public.

It wasn't as if I was a weakling or unsure of myself. It's just a part of me, a weakness I didn't want known or revealed. Lately my self-confidence was being buried behind alcohol all too often. I like a good drink. I just shouldn't drink twenty a night.

Only Riona knew that part of me. She opened herself to me, and I trusted her more than any other person in my life. She allowed me to liberate the daily demons. She was strong— stronger than I was in many ways, and wiser in a simple, naive fashion.

Riona and I had been together for nearly six years. Neither making demands on the other, living separate lives, but always there when needed. Marriage had never been discussed, but we, or at least I, never felt the need or the desire.

While I fought my daily battles within myself, Riona always had that easy manner about her. She was quick with a smile that made her Irish eyes sparkle, and she had a calming warmth about her that was so natural.

This morning, I felt like I had been hit by a truck, but it wasn't just from the booze. Fights within the union negotiating team were not that uncommon. The night before, I had decided to give my opinion on the union's strike, whether anyone wanted to hear it or not. My opinion was probably enhanced, most likely, by the ton of alcohol I had downed.

I hadn't necessarily needed the liquid courage, but it certainly loosened my lips far more than it should have. There was a general consensus that most trade unionists were considered strong-willed in one way or another, almost arrogant. It just came with the territory.

When it came to the union doctrine, I felt I was as smart as anyone, and I wasn't afraid to let anyone interested hear my opinion.

International Truckers Union president Joseph Pinata's personal bodyguard took offense to what I said, and he told me what I could do with my opinion. Although I was no slouch, I did use to be the Golden Gloves champion in Michigan.

Wisdom would have brought a much different ending to the otherwise crazy night.

I knew I took the worst of the fight, but did land a few punches that rocked Tony Wetherby back a step or two.

Tony was hired a couple years back by Joseph Pinata, mainly because of his reputation. He was always in the wrong place at the right time. Trouble seemed to follow him wherever he went. Although he didn't seem like a bad guy, personally, he did have an edgy streak at times.

His official title was executive assistant to the president. His face was one that told many stories. Adolescent acne scars covered his cheeks, along with a large crooked nose that must have taken more than one good punch. He had scars on his face and a cauliflower ear. He was a former professional light heavyweight boxing champion and had worked for the president of the Teamsters Union for the previous five years.

Mr. Pinata made him an offer he couldn't refuse, which was probably the money and freedom to act any way he felt was necessary to do his job. The freedom was the most alluring part of the job offer for Tony. Word around the union was that Mr. Pinata had to rein him in from time to time. He walked around like he was the man to be reckoned with, like he was afraid of no one.

Unfortunately, my ribs ached enough to remind me that I possibly should have kept my opinion to myself. It wasn't the first time nor would it probably be the last. Maybe I was just a stubborn, thickheaded, slow-learning, dumb Irishman with beautiful green eyes. That morning, they were puffy beautiful green eyes.

Although I was the Golden Gloves champion of Detroit at seventeen, I was better known on the streets as someone to avoid. The streets in Detroit were rough, and you had to fight or stay indoors your entire life. Fights happen, and I usually got the better of anyone who cared to try, but there is always someone better. Always.

Since I was young, I'd drunk alcohol. It tamed the one fear I had, which was insanity. The last few years, it had stopped even doing that. I drank to stop feeling the way I felt when I was sober. That's why most alcoholics drink and only alcoholics know what that feeling is. It cannot be explained.

I was told by a friend who has been involved with Alcoholics Anonymous for years that there are three things that can happen when you are an alcoholic: you get sober, you go insane, or you die.

"Take your pick," he said.

What an option. I told him thanks.

He said, "I'll be here when you want to make that decision."

I couldn't get that out of my head. Soon, real soon, I had to decide to go and see him.

This morning, since I'd woken up, I'd been thinking about taking on Tony Wetherby again. That's insane thinking. Doing the same thing over and over and expecting different results.

If I fought him, it would have to be on my terms, which would be sober, not pickled with alcohol. With a clear sober head, the fight might turn out differently. I kept thinking it would be interesting for sure.

I felt a smile creep onto my face and knew it was another one of my brief but frequent moments of insanity. I had them quite often too.

The night before, I'd let a few drinks turn into another night of binge drinking. It was the fourth night in a row that I had drunk more than most people thought was humanly possible.

Like so many other mornings, I asked myself why, but I knew all too well that alcohol was something I couldn't control. The thing is, I knew this thickheaded brain of mine had taken on many issues and mastered them. Why not my alcohol problem?

I forced myself to walk every morning regardless of what I did the night before. If I drank heavily, the walk then became a self-imposed punishment I used as penance for my actions. I never missed a moment of work and was very responsible. I told myself I had to get over this, and I meant it.

My Irish Catholic heritage came with the idea that drinking was part of the culture, part of life. Every Irishman drank. It's just the way it was. A little ale at fifteen turned into a lot of ale at twenty, and for some, it was uncontrolled drinking at thirty.

I told myself I didn't care if people looked at me with distain because of my alcohol problem, but

I was kidding myself. I judged myself more harshly than anyone could possibly judge me. I knew the demon inside me better than anyone.

I had to learn to live with him, cage him somehow, some way. I had to consciously get a handle on the beasts and demons inside me. The experts said that the desire to quit was the first step in recovery. Maybe there was hope.

In the last three months, my drinking had made it more evident that the beasts were caged, but the door was unlocked, and they could come out with vengeance. My drinking seemed to have reached an all-time high, and my daily struggle seemed nearly impossible to handle.

There was no question in my mind what I was, and now it had gotten to the point where the whole world knew.

Alcohol was a problem in my life and had been growing for the last ten years. That morning was not the first time I'd told myself I had to find a way to get control of the liquored monster inside that had taken over my body and my mind.

This was not morning-after regrets. It was reality. Excuses were for the weak, and I couldn't allow myself to accept defeat at the hands of alcohol like my old man.

The tight grip of humidity and heat once again seemed to close around my body. The sweat running down my back and chest felt like an internal cleansing of my soul. It actually felt good to sweat, like a release of the anxieties I lived with each and every day.

It would be extra hot that day. The morning's weatherman warned of the pending insufferable heat and humidity. It was going to reach ninety-four degrees and 98 percent humidity, preposterous even by Miami Beach's standards. The ocean was beautiful and tranquil most of the time, but that morning, the burning sun was just too much too much to bear.

Back in my hometown of Detroit, weather changed every day, even every hour, but in the summer, ninety-four degrees was a rare exception, not the rule. What I hated about Detroit was the frigid, abrasive, intolerably long and sunless winter days.

As I continued my walk, I unconsciously veered into the moist, cool firm sand of the beach. I turned and walked back up to let the heat ooze between my bare toes as the sun burned its way through the grains of hot dry sand.

I loved to walk along the ocean shore in my bare feet. There was something relaxing about the warm sand next to the crashing ocean waves. Troubles always seem to wane under the radiating warmth of the sun, sand, and water.

The breeze coming in off the ocean brought with it the ever present smell of fish, the taste of salt, and the sandy grit from the beach.

As I walked on, I watched the last few veteran morning walkers with their headphones over their ears and their arms swinging like pendulums. They were oblivious to everything and everyone around them. Their only purpose now was to get off the beach; the northerners were invading the south once again.

It didn't make sense why all the older folks—the Q-tips, FOPS, fucking old people—came south to avoid the ice and cold of winter, and as soon as the heat rose, they ran back to their apartments and the cool air-conditioned rooms.

As I continued my walk in front of the multimillion-dollar high-rise hotels, the bikini-clad young ladies caught my attention. Unfortunately, sometimes older ladies who still thought they had it caught my attention in a different way. They thought they still had it, but many had lost it years before they even knew it.

Although I walked each morning as a physical and mental necessity, the bikinis were an added bonus that I thoroughly enjoyed.

I watched the visible heat waves rise over the ocean water, dancing like silk scarves blowing in the wind. The little terns that ran along the beach chased each wave looking for some remnant that would become their breakfast. These little terns spent their entire lives running back and forth with each wave that came ashore. They constantly ran twenty feet toward the ocean and then twenty feet away from the next wave.

Unlike the Arctic terns, these little guys migrated forty-five thousand miles each year, farther than any bird or animal in existence. I read that somewhere. Shit like that amazes me.

Seagulls float in the waves, waiting for something, anything, that resembles food. Then they fly around, looking for someone to toss a morsel of food onto the sand. When that happens, ten seagulls dive in unison for one tiny scrap of food.

A few years ago, I was trying to catch some bluegills, so I baited a hook with some bread and threw it out in the water. A seagull dove for it, and sure enough, I had the damn thing hooked. What a sight that was. It took two of us to hold the bird down long enough to get the hook out of its mouth without hurting him. It was quite a hoot.

I had my route figured out. A walk to the Marriott and back to my hotel was exactly five miles. A trip I had made every morning for the previous twelve months. That day, walking in the sand made it seem more like ten miles.

CHAPTER TWO
· ·

As I reached the Marriott and was about to turn around and head back to my hotel for the final two and a half miles of my struggled walk, I heard a woman's shrill, piercing voice calling my name through the ocean wind.

"Irish! Hey, Irish, wait up. I need to talk to you."

I looked up and saw Jennifer Marks jogging toward me. Other than four secretaries, Jennifer was one of only two female representatives on the actual international union negotiating staff. The men outnumbered the women twenty to two.

This was not done by accident; quite the contrary. When openings on the staff became available, whether from retirements or individuals discharged for lack of support of union president Joseph

Pinata's agenda, new appointees all came from the local unions.

Only local union officials, who have continually backed our president's wants and needs, were appointed to the international staff. The trouble was, 95 percent of local union officers were indeed men.

Women were not taken seriously by our egotistical president, regardless of what they had accomplished for their local unions, how smart they were, or how dedicated they were to the union and its membership.

It was well known that our union president, Joey J, the pet name many on the staff used behind Mr. Pinata's back, had little respect for women. Women were just another tool he used to project himself positively to the unsuspecting public. Basically, he didn't give a damn about women or minorities. His public persona appeared to have women and minorities as a high priority, but the reality was far different.

Although everyone on his staff knew, nothing was ever said. They were all afraid of reprisals. It was just an easier life if you kept your mouth shut and let the injustice continue.

The way I was put on the international staff occurred almost by happenstance. I was vice president and bargaining chairman of my local union. Our local union president was a man who I respected more than anyone I ever knew. For years,

Charlie took care not only of our local union, but many of Joey's problems as well.

He was the one man who Joey looked to for guidance. He respected Charlie like a father and would give him anything he asked to a point. Joey couldn't intimidate him, and actually never tried as far as I knew. When Joey asked him for help, he knew Charlie's advice was golden.

Charlie had been involved in the union for over forty years, and for the last ten, Joey had tried and tried to get him to accept a position on his staff. He always said his local union needed him more than Joey did. He was a quiet man with a tremendous mind and persona that drew people from all walks of life.

One day, Charlie called me into his office for a little chat. When he said he wanted to chat, you knew you were in line for a little direction and guidance. He floored me when he said he wanted me to join the international staff. He said Joseph Pinata needed a man like me who would fight for our members.

I asked how I could get on the international staff. Joey had to appoint me, and he didn't even know who I was. He said leave it to him. I didn't ask why me, or what I could do to steer Mr. Pinata in my direction. I just said if he thought it was necessary, then I would do it. Within a week, I got the call from Joey's office.

A month after I took the staff job, Charlie had a heart attack and died. It was devastating to me and so many who knew him. The day of the wake, over a thousand people passed in front of his casket to pay their last respects. It was the first time I cried since I was eight years old. I loved the man, still miss him.

The day of the funeral, Joey was supposed to meet with the president of the United States, but he called to say he couldn't make it. He told me that Charlie was more important. During the funeral, Joey actually had tears in his eyes. I was amazed. Joey had feelings. It was the only thing I ever saw him care about other than himself.

Positions on the International Union staff were treasured by anyone active in the local union or regional union offices. The wages were enormous, the benefits were unsurpassed, the travel was first class, and there was a daily expense account for everyone on the staff.

Our union president was a devious man who was well-versed in the necessities of life. He was self-righteous, egotistical, and a paranoid loner who somehow still had members begging for a position on his team.

I didn't know what a dick he really was until I had worked for him for a few months. I had to admit I liked the wages, the benefits, and the work I was given. I had to help local unions when they had contractual problems.

It was a very positive work life and I believed, like most staffers, that all the bullshit was well worth the trouble. At first I wasn't totally sure, but I stayed.

It didn't take long to see that Joey used people however he wanted and he took anything he desired. It baffled me how he attained the position of president of the union, and what was even stranger was why Charlie would want me to be here.

I knew I could walk away any time I wanted, unlike others on the staff who let the fear of losing their jobs be the motivating factor in their lives. Joey was a bully, plain and simple, and very difficult to work for. I saw how he looked at Jennifer, and it wasn't as a respected member of his staff. He had one desire for her, and it had something to do with a bottle of wine and a bed.

When Jennifer came near, it was obvious that something was very wrong. Whenever she was angry or nervous, she had a funny habit of moving her jaw back and forth, like an irritating twitch, and today, it was oscillating relentlessly. Poker would never be her game. She could be read like a book.

Jennifer was usually very striking in her appearance—neat and well groomed, clothed with a casual dress style that she turned into an elegance that most women would die for but couldn't pull off.

I have noticed that some women would let their petty jealousy prevent them from becoming close friends because of some other woman's beauty. My old man wasn't always the sharpest knife in the drawer, but he told me one day that if you locked twelve women in a room, in an hour you would have six groups of two. But if you locked twelve men in a room, in an hour you would have two games of poker.

Jennifer was thirty-four years old, about five foot seven. She had beautiful olive skin, long dark curly hair, and large supple but firm breasts—at least they looked supple and firm to me. She had big brown bedroom eyes and a beautiful smile with bright white, almost florescent teeth.

She was shockingly beautiful, smart, and confident and had a personality that did nothing but enhance her beauty inside and out. She had a radiance about her that no one could or would dispute.

Today, her appearance was far from fashionable, but she could still exude a graciousness lost on most women. She was wearing a green rumpled union T-shirt that read, "A Woman's Place is in Her Union," and a pair of red shorts that had the letters for the International Truckers Union, ITU, on the front and butt.

I had noticed the union label the first time I saw her wear them on the beach. I would occasionally tease her that I couldn't keep my eyes off that label. Jennifer and I had become good friends over the last year. It was just a working friendship, and nothing ever transpired between us. I had Riona, and she said she had a man back home.

She was a good union representative in her own right. She took her job seriously, with more self-confidence and dedication to the union than most of the men on the staff.

Her beauty did nothing to take away from her competence. It did bother some of the old guards who were intimidated by someone so beautiful. For the past year, I'd seen what a great trade unionist she was. She deserved to be treated with respect.

As she came near, I was surprised at how upset she was. This was not the Jennifer I knew. I asked, "What's up, Jen?"

"That son of a bitch! I can't believe the arrogance that bastard has," Jennifer blurted out. Jennifer looked sweet and innocent but had a tongue of fire when she was angry, and obviously, someone had pissed her off about something.

"Who are you talking about?"

"Joey J, who else?" she yelled through clenched teeth.

I knew that Jennifer disliked Joey, but she never openly cursed him. By the look on her face and the tone of her voice, Joey must have somehow really overstepped his boundaries.

She shook her head and rolled her eyes and said with as much rage as possible, "Oh god, I am so angry. Last night, I went to the big mandatory contract settlement party, and I drank my usual one beer and was about to leave when Michael Ferrier came up to me and said Mr. Pinata wanted me to come to his hotel suite, that he wanted to talk to me about something. Michael Ferrier, now there's another worthless piece of shit that can kiss my ass."

Michael Ferrier was Joey J's personal aide, another executive assistant and general suck-up.

Joey must have had a dozen administrative assistants. Everyone on the staff knew he was nothing more than an errand boy, a gopher, and a snitch. Everything he heard went straight to Joey. He was Joey's ears.

Jennifer took a deep breath, collected herself, and said, "So anyway, I went to Joey's hotel suite to see what he wanted, and he was sitting there, playing poker with Matthew Simms, Luke Coletta, and two other men I had no idea who they were. My god, I couldn't believe how much money was lying on the table. There must have been two . . . three thousand dollars in the pot. Where do these guys get the money to play with such high stakes?" Jennifer shook her head in bewilderment.

Jennifer always had a habit of changing the subject or losing her train of thought in the middle of a sentence. It was like her mind was ahead of the mouth that was always trying to catch up.

She continued, "As soon as I got there, they finished their hand of poker, and of course, ol' Joey won the pot. Anyway, he asked everyone to leave. He said he was going to call it a night. He asked me to wait in his outer room until the table was cleaned of all its trash." She took another deep breath, trying to calm herself. "He must have put the money in his personal safe because I didn't see it when he called me back into his room. I'm not sure, but I guess I should have felt honored that he allowed me inside to his royal abode."

I could tell that she was more upset than any time since I first met her. I said, "Jennifer, please calm down and tell me what words of wisdom ol' Joey bestowed upon you to make you so pissed."

"I've never been so humiliated in all my life," Jennifer said with a mocking tone to her voice. "Joey told me that he's had his eye on me for a long time and thought that maybe we could get to know each other a little better. I asked him what exactly he meant by that, and he said, 'You know exactly what I mean. Now that this nasty strike business is about over, I was thinking the two of us could really get to know each other in a more personal way.' I couldn't believe my fucking ears. He actually expected me to jump in the sack with him, that slimy son of a bitch. Damn, I hate him so much."

Tears formed in her eyes and rolled down her cheeks one after another as she spoke. I always brought a hankie with me when I walked in case I got some sand in my eyes, so I offered it to her and asked in my best fatherly tone, "What'd you tell him?"

"Well, I lost it and told him it would be a cold day in hell before I ever let him get his slimy hands on me. You're not going to believe this, but he actually said, 'You do know what this could mean for your career, don't you?'" At that point, Jennifer broke down, crying.

She let her face fall against my chest, so I patted her on the back and told her to calm down, take a deep breath, and just try to relax. I felt like a big brother. She did as I suggested, and after a few more deep breaths, she was more under control.

"I can't believe what I said after that," she said as she looked up at me.

I smiled down at her and said, "Oh my god, what words of wisdom did you tell poor old Joey?"

Jennifer retorted, "Poor ol' Joey my ass. I said 'You arrogant bastard, I'm not one of your high-priced, low-classed whores. If you want to get laid, why you don't get one of them, or better yet, why don't you get Michael Ferrier in here. I'm sure he'd do anything for you.'"

While trying to suppress an out and out gut-wrenching laugh, I asked, "What'd he say then?"

"I don't know. I ran out of his suite in tears. Damn it, I hate it when I let someone get me so mad that I cry. It must have made his day seeing that. That idiot Ferrier started laughing when he saw me crying. I should have punched him right in his nasty little grin." Then she lowered her head and really started weeping.

I knew it wasn't funny, but I couldn't imagine her telling mighty Joey J what he could do with his idea. Jennifer really had more balls than any man on staff. I brought her chin up, made her look at me, and said, "Stop, there's no crying in union business." Then, she really let it go. I felt sorry for her. She was too nice of a person to be treated like this.

Then, Jennifer looked up and said, "What are you smiling about? This isn't funny! I thought you were my friend."

"I'm sorry, I am your friend, but I was just imagining you calling big ol' Joey J a fucking arrogant bastard. That must have been quite a sight. I'm proud of you."

"Get serious, Sean. I need your help. This could be the end of my job, my career. I don't want to get fired over something like this."

"I'm sorry, Jennifer. I know this is serious, and I know that Joey probably will not let this go unless we force him to. He won't tolerate anyone talking to him that way, even if he was wrong for doing it. He's pissed that you didn't take him up on his offer."

"Oh, you haven't heard the rest. This morning, about six thirty, there was a knock on my door. Michael Ferrier, that little piss ant, was there, and he said Mr. Pinata had a permanent assignment change for me. He was transferring me from my Ohio district to Texas, and if I didn't like it, I could quit or come back and reconsider his offer from last night, whatever that was."

Jennifer worked out of the union office in Cleveland. Most staff representatives worked in their home state except when called for contract negotiations. On occasion, they would be transferred out of state, but rarely, and not without their approval.

"What'd you tell Michael?"

"I slammed the door in his face, and he yelled through the door, 'Enjoy Texas.' He's such a pathetic little prick," she said. "Do you know what this means?"

"Yeah, I know perfectly well what this means. You pissed off Joey J, and either you become his personal prostitute, or he makes your life miserable."

"I have a home and family. I can't just up and move to fucking Texas and leave everything behind," Jennifer spoke as tears continued cascading down her cheeks. "This is so unfair. I can't believe it. If I sleep with the pig, I'm no better than one of his sleazebag whores. I've never done anything to deserve this."

I gently grabbed her arm, pulled her to me again, gave her a friendly hug, and said, "Calm down, I'll talk to a few people and see what I can do."

"You can't tell anyone about what I said to Mr. Pinata."

"Don't worry; you know you can trust me. I think I can figure out a way to handle this without letting anyone know what you said and without pissing off Joey even further. I have an idea how we might be able to keep your job in your home region too. Whatever you do, don't tell anyone else about this. Right now, it's just between you and me, right?"

She answered, "Yeah, I haven't told anyone but you."

"Good. Let's keep it that way for a while," I replied. Jennifer was a very nice person and didn't deserve shitty treatment like this. "Joey hasn't said anything to anyone that you know of?"

"Not that I'm aware of, but who knows, Joey or Michael could have bragged to someone about it. I don't really know. The slimy bastards might get their jollies off by telling someone. Hell, Michael Ferrier may be blabbing right now. I don't know."

"Just calm down, get ahold of yourself, and stay cool. Let me work on it. Maybe this can be taken care of quietly. I'll see what I can do. I'm sure Joey J would not want anyone to go public with this situation. He can't afford to have a public sexual discrimination suit against him just as the contract negotiations are almost over. It would be a political disaster for him."

I think my response had a calming effect on Jennifer—her breathing eased, her twitching jaw slowed from rapid to fast, and the color returned to her face. She knew she could trust me. At least it seemed like she trusted me.

I had to be careful too. If I jumped into this with both feet and got burned, I could find myself working back in Detroit, or perhaps, if I pissed off Joey to the max, I might be living at the bottom of the Detroit River. Who knows? "Are you okay now?" I asked Jennifer.

"Yes, I do feel a little better. Thanks."

I touched her elbow and turned back in the direction of our hotel, saying, "Come on, let's head back to the hotel. I've got some people I need to talk to. We will have to trust a couple of our union brethren if we expect to get Joey J to change his mind. But don't worry; I will be careful about who I talk to and what's said. I'll let you know what's going on as I get things figured out."

Jennifer looked up at me and said in a genuinely concerned voice, "Oh, by the way, you made another ass of yourself last night. You know you shouldn't drink so much. It doesn't fit your personality. You turn from Dr. Jekyll to Mr. Hyde after a few drinks, and besides, why in the world would you take Tony on in a fight? That was really dumb . . . valiant but dumb."

I had no answer for her. So I didn't try to justify my crazy life.

"You're lucky he didn't really hurt you. I think he let you get a few punches in. You're not a kid anymore. Think before you open that mouth of yours. Maybe it'll save you from future embarrassment and injury."

"Wait a minute. He didn't let me get in a few punches; that was pure skill on my part. So thanks for the advice, but I already know it all too well. If you think I look dumb from your viewpoint, you should see it from my eyes. I think I might have a couple of broken ribs, too. It hurts just to breathe. I'm going to go over and see Tony this morning."

"W-w-what?" she stammered. "Why the hell are you going to see him?"

"I don't want him to think there are any hard feelings. Besides, I don't want him to think I'm afraid of him or anything. Maybe I'll even have another go at him," I said with a wide smile.

"You're crazy. You know that, don't you? Maybe you should let this drop for a while. Tony is not the nicest guy in the world."

"Yes, that's probably true. I *am* crazy, but I was a lot crazier last night when I had all that liquid courage in me."

"Sean, there's nothing wrong with getting help for that kind of problem," Jennifer said gently as she stared up at me. "You know you look pretty rough this morning. Your face is red, your eyes are puffy and bloodshot, and I can smell the alcohol like its oozing from your body. You're gross!"

"Thanks for saying that. I appreciate the blunt honesty." I smiled down at her and continued, "I know my drinking is definitely a problem, and I know it's gotten out of hand recently. I intend to do something about it very soon. I really do." I flashed her a deadpan look on my sorry Irish face and then said, "You know you look a bit shaky this morning too."

"I didn't get much sleep last night, thanks to Joey, and besides, it wasn't because I drank three gallons of alcohol and got into a fight with a bully. I'll bet you have a bigger headache than I do."

"No question about that. Anyway, let's drop this for a while and get working on your little problem. We have to get on that immediately," I replied as I felt a little shame creep into me.

As we started walking back to the hotel, I stopped and suggested to Jennifer that she wait five or ten minutes before she followed. It wouldn't look good if we were found coming into the hotel together from the beach, especially since Jennifer's eyes were still red from crying. I didn't want one of

Joey's boys telling him that Jennifer went running to me for help.

I was pissed that Joey would stoop so low. Everyone knew that Joey openly used high-priced whores, but to say something as crass as he did to Jennifer was even lower than I expected him to go. Joey was beginning to get careless. I would file this in the back of my mind for use at a later date.

CHAPTER THREE

· ·

When I reached the Royal Crown Executive Hotel, I found my new sandals next to the bench where I had left them. One morning about two weeks earlier, I had left my old pair there; when I returned, my sandals were gone, but there was a thank-you note written in the sand. There is nothing better than a polite crook.

Ever since then, I'd been checking out everyone's feet hoping to find my missing sandals. I was like the dog smelling butts looking for their own. It became the case of the mysterious disappearance of the worst-looking skanky sandals in modern history.

I had had them for almost ten years. Who the hell would be so sick as to rip off my old, ugly, stinky sandals? Guess it takes all kinds in this world to make it go around.

Later, when I told Jennifer about the unfortunate case of the missing sandals, she said they probably just walked off into the ocean to die a respectable death. She thought that was cute, and I had to agree.

As I was brushing the sand off my feet, a long black limo pulled up to the curb in front of the hotel. Three of Joey J's boys—goons, bodyguards, administrative assistants, or whatever you wanted to call them—exited out the limo's side doors.

I felt a twinge of anger in the pit of my stomach, wondering why the hell the union always had to stay at the classiest hotels available, use stretch limos, and eat at the best restaurants in town. Joey needs to have his head examined. That kind of wasteful spending of our union members' money had to stop sooner or later.

It's a wonder that someone hadn't reported this to the Federal Labor Board. I wished it would happen soon, though it would be too bad that when Joey went down, he'd drag many others with him, probably me included. Some of the staff was totally innocent of his illegal or questionable activities. It wasn't up to them; they stayed wherever Joey decided to stay. To make it even worse, the union executive board and regional directors stayed in suites and used limos.

Living like that every time we traveled seemed to violate the members' trust. They were getting screwed–not in a good way–and didn't even know it. What a shame. Joey, the egocentric prick, didn't give a shit about anyone; his comfort was all he cared about.

I had these pangs of guilt growing inside me, knowing our union funds could just as easily be spent on something much more respectable, like health care for our members while they were on strike.

Everyone on our union staff, me included, was living the so-called good life. I wondered what our membership would say if they saw the scene of the limo letting out their union officials that I had just witnessed.

For the past year of the strike, the membership was literally trying to survive day to day, week to week. Deciding whether to buy food, pay to heat homes, pay taxes, clothe their children, get their prescriptions filled, or even to seek medical care when illness hit. All the while, our union staff not only lived well, we lived royally.

The Crown Royal Executive Hotel is the most expensive hotel in Miami Beach. It has a plush lobby, four high-end restaurants, indoor and outdoor pools with poolside bars, a day spa/sauna, and a workout center. This has been a bone of contention with the staff. It was surely the good life, I'll say that.

Why Joey insisted they stay at a hotel like this was quite obvious. His egocentric lifestyle fed on this like a famished jackal on a dead zebra. It was blatantly wrong and a totally unethical use of union funds. It's kind of like my aunt who was a lush, but no one dare say anything about it. Aunt Kiley was supposed to be viewed as this nice little Irish nana who knitted and never said shit, when in reality, she was this foul-mouthed, ale-drinking, ass-kicking, gun-carrying babe. Everyone just looked the other way.

Staying at a hotel like this wasn't illegal, but it definitely was unscrupulous. Limos are not illegal, but they are unethical. Fancy restaurants are not illegal, but again—unethical. These thoughts kept bouncing around in my head so much that I felt like I was getting punched to death from the inside out. It was driving me crazy.

My old man said he went through this too. He was not only a drunk, he was a drunken union representative, but also a history buff and a union history buff. If you wanted to know anything about the union's history, you went to my old man.

His real love was American history. In his eyes, Thomas Jefferson walked on water. I think ol' Tom was a tea sipper, unlike my old man, who was a lush. Jefferson was the third president of the United States from 1801–1809. He never did things the way everyone else did. He paved his own way and was also a man of his word.

Most people don't know, or choose to forget, that if we had lost the War of Independence to Great Britain, all of our heroes—our forefathers, the fathers of our nation—would have been hanged for treason. That includes the most famous—George Washington, Thomas Jefferson, Ben Franklin—you name it, they all would have been hanged by the neck until dead.

I could never figure out why my old man was so fascinated with Jefferson. They had nothing in common. The history books say that Thomas Jefferson said, "When the government stops representing the people, it's time to get a new government." He thought it was the same thing with the union: when we stop representing the membership, it's time for new leadership, time to go, time for the membership to step up.

For the last few years, I had developed a habit of talking with my dead father. It was the best relationship I'd ever had with him. That's because I asked the question, and I supplied the answer. We never had a confrontation, unlike in real life, where he was always right.

Back when I was a kid, I always lost our arguments. Today, it's different. I win all the time. Too bad he had to die before I could win an argument, and he could realize just how smart I am.

I closed my eyes and turned my face to the sun; the warmth seemed to drive my guilt deep within me and soothe the anger that was engulfing me. I knew I should do something to get this union ball rolling, but what? Who could I trust? I was treading on thin ice just looking into Jennifer's problem. If I started anything that even remotely looked like an investigation into Joey's union lifestyle, there's no telling what I could be faced with or where my lifeless body would come floating up.

Appeasement was the course everyone took, regardless of their beliefs. It was better and safer to placate Mr. Pinata than to confront him. This policy, along with horrible union politics, was causing the union to self-destruct right before our very eyes.

Promoting political friends, and even their family members, to positions of power was a standard tactic in the union. Take care of your friends and family, and they will take care of you. Family was almost always a sure bet.

The fundamental idea of forming a union was workers banding together for their common cause. It gave workers a stronger position to fight for improving wages, benefits, and working conditions. Finally getting a voice in the workplace caused a dramatic change in the work life for the middle class throughout the nation.

The sit-down strike of 1937 in Flint, Michigan, by the fledging United Auto Workers Union, against General Motors, was necessary in UAW President Walter Reuther's mind, and in the minds of the union leaders everywhere.

Near the same time, he also led a strike in Cleveland, Ohio's Fisher Body plant and declared that they would not settle the strike in Cleveland until a national agreement with GM was reached. It wasn't actually a secondary boycott, which the government made illegal with the Taft-Hartley act, but it was close to it.

The UAW leaders learned that GM was going to move all of their press dies out of the Fisher Body

Plant in Flint, so they ordered their members back in to occupy the plant. The workers took control of the plant on December 30, 1936 and occupied it for forty-four days.

At that time, General Motors was the largest and most powerful corporation in the industrial world. The workers stopped working and sat down in the auto factories. They refused to leave, and they refused to work until GM recognized the UAW as the bargaining agent for the workers. They boarded up the doors and windows and would not allow anyone in or out until the strike was settled.

A Michigan state court judge ordered an injunction demanding the workers leave the plant. The National Guard was called, and they were ordered to surround the plant. They used tear gas to try to force the workers out, and even threatened the use of firearms, but the strikers stayed, sealing the doors and forcing the hand of General Motors and the National Guard.

Then Michigan governor Frank Murphy called off the National Guard, and acted as a mediator to force the two sides back to the bargaining table. On February 11, 1937, the two sides reached an agreement. It was a one-page document that recognized the UAW as the exclusive bargaining agent for the workers. Today, the contract is made up of hundreds of pages. All the union wanted from the first strike was recognition of the UAW. In the next two decades, membership grew from a few to five hundred thousand members.

Even with all the financial problems caused by the lengthy strike, Joey J still insisted that his staff stay in the hotel suites, or at the least, in the best rooms available. The hotel gave the union a break on the cost since we had been there so long and the hotel had so many rooms, but the suites at the Royal Crown Executive still started at 250 bucks per night and went up from there.

Some of the staff refused a suite even when offered because they felt guilty living so extravagantly. Hail Mary. There is a God!

Of the forty-five people on his staff, fifteen were in suites, and the other thirty were in regular rooms. The cost was nearly seven thousand dollars a day just for rooms. The daily expenses for everything from food, phones, cars, limos, and recreation added up to an additional two thousand a day. Altogether, nine thousand dollars of union funds were being paid out legally for the negotiating staff every day of the strike.

In its nearly three hundred days, the strike had cost the union $2,700,000. That was incredible. The thought made me sick.

We had been holed up in the Royal Crown Executive Hotel since negotiations restarted. It took only a few moments for simple old me to calculate the unbelievable cost of these negotiations. I wonder how many of our members figured this out. It sickened me at the thought.

As bad as those figures sounded to me, it made me more nauseated when I reminded myself that Joey J and all the union staff officers were getting our wages paid every day while the striking members received little or no compensation for their struggle. Joey's attitude was, "Hey, our members are struggling. Pass the beer nuts."

Those of us lucky enough to be on the negotiating ITU staff were not on strike like the regular rank and file members. The negotiating staff worked for the union, not for the companies that we were striking. We got paid for every day of the strike, seven days a week.

Our staff had to sacrifice nothing at all, while the striking members sacrificed everything. I truly felt we were no better than the company CEOs that were publicly chastised by the union.

The union's general fund was getting dangerously low, and that was the motivating reason Joey finally found that elusive settlement of the strike he publicly claimed to be fighting for all along.

The trouble was, the settlement was always there, waiting to be embraced. But it took both sides to settle a strike and up until now, only one side was willing to find it—and for some unknown reason, it wasn't the union.

CHAPTER FOUR

I felt very cautious about who I should talk to regarding Jennifer's problem. My first thought was to find Thomas Sharpe, the top PR man for the union. He wanted to be called Thomas, not Tom, because his father's name was Thomas, and he told me his dad was one hell of a man.

Thomas was always trying to get Joey J to hire more women, African Americans, Hispanics, or any other minority out there. He not only felt it was good PR, but he truly believed that the union should be more diverse, a true cross section of today's society.

A couple of weeks earlier, over a few drinks (he drank Coke and I drank scotch on the rocks—good scotch), he had told me that it was a personal goal of his to make the union staff a real conglomeration of people in the ITU. He said that minorities made up 18 percent of the workers, so the staff positions should be filled by 18 percent minorities.

I knew that getting 18 percent quality minority workers would not be difficult, but I asked him if he thought minority members should get a position just because they were minorities. I didn't feel that it was justified to give a person a job because of their race, and that especially included white people. I wish we could take the question of race out of all job applications everywhere.

Thomas didn't feel that it would be a problem finding qualified minorities. He too believed there were plenty of talented minorities who would be a tremendous asset to the union staff. The most important benefit the union provided was equal pay for all workers, regardless of their race, color, sex, or religious affiliation. That is something to be very proud of, in my book.

Thomas Sharpe was a great guy and a good union man. We got along real well. I liked his ideas, his principles, and the fact that he wasn't afraid of Joey J. He supported affirmative action, but he had an ongoing battle with Joey, and he told me he would never give up the fight.

I suspected that someday soon, some big corporation would snatch Thomas up. In the previous year, he'd already been approached by two smaller companies, but he declined. He told me he wanted to stay until this strike was completely put to bed.

He was too smart to be in the job he had with the union. It seemed to me that Thomas would be the best candidate for president of the union once Joey was out of the picture. Thomas was getting about sixty-five thousand a year for the job he was doing, and that's peanuts compared to what he could earn out in the corporate world, especially with his brain.

The thing Thomas had going for him—or maybe not, depending on your viewpoint—was being married to Joey's daughter. Thomas and Sophia were dating before he took the job offer from Joey. Unfortunately for him, many people thought he got his job because he was Joey's son-in-law.

The only time I ever saw Thomas mad was when one of the staff guys had too much to drink and mentioned to him that he thought nepotism was alive and well in the ITU. Thomas got up, walked over to the man, and commenced to slap the snot out of him. The guy was too drunk to defend himself, and I suspect Thomas was a little tipsy also.

I had to give it to Joey; he was pretty smart in grabbing a guy like Thomas to handle the PR for the union. He must have known he would get a rash of shit by hiring his future son-in-law. Frankly, he just did not care what other people thought. Joey needed a good PR man to help get his foot out of his mouth on a regular basis, and Thomas was the man to do it.

Joey J hated the idea of being forced to hire minorities and became especially irate when someone mentioned affirmative action in his presence. He would never let anyone tell him who to hire.

For all intents and purposes, Joey J saw to it that affirmative action was a non-entity in the ITU. In Joey's mind, it was a dead, done, and buried issue. He believed in the old adage, "Do as I say, not as I do." Fortunately, Thomas kept hammering at Joey about hiring minorities until he finally saw the relevance and personal benefit for himself.

He would have his staff fight like hell if there was a discrimination grievance for one of our members, and he made sure it got publicity in the papers and the TV news. He made a big show to the public that he would fight to the death to stop discrimination of any kind to any of our members.

Joey would make sure the few minorities he had on staff were placed where they were in the public eye, but they were never given a chance to perform up to their abilities no matter how smart or how dedicated they were.

At the previous national convention, one member stood up and addressed the lackluster situation of minorities and women on the union staff. He pointed out that of the three thousand members attending the national convention, there were fewer than one hundred women and four hundred minorities.

After only a few minutes, Joey had had the speaker's microphone turned off and told him his time was up and to have a seat. The man was booed off the floor by a large majority of members as a show of support for Joey.

It was the greatest group ass kissing I had ever seen in my life. Even some minorities and women stood up and booed the man. Go figure. I thought, *What the hell is this? Why are these minorities applauding?* It was disgusting. I asked one black woman why she was applauding, and she said that she had been instructed to do so.

The union brother at the microphone knew he would never see another national convention. Arrangements would soon be made to not only ensure he never set foot in another convention, but also that he would never hold another local union position. The long arm of the union president reaches far and wide.

It didn't matter that Joey was leading us to a dead-end. I remember my dad thought that a quote from Golda Meir fit Joey perfectly: "Let me tell you something that we Israelis have against Moses. He took us forty years through the desert in order to bring us to the one spot in the Middle East that has no oil." Joey was our Moses.

CHAPTER FIVE

....

knew I wasn't going to solve all the union's problems by bouncing them around inside my brain; it was giving me a headache. I had to get busy working on Jennifer's problem.

I looked at my watch and saw that it was eleven o'clock. I thought I could still catch Thomas in his room. When he was not in meetings, he was always in his room working. He had a bank of computers and was constantly in contact with the all the different local unions of the International Truckers Union.

His wife, Sophia, was always bugging him, in a good way, about working twenty-four hours a day. They had a great relationship, and you could tell they loved each other a great deal.

Although Thomas was only thirty-five years old, he had plenty of credentials for the job. He graduated as valedictorian from Stanford's Business School and got his masters in economics from Columbia. Stanford and Columbia produced the brightest, and Thomas didn't take a back seat in the smarts department to anyone.

I reached into my shorts pocket and retrieved my pack of smokes. I lit up my first cigarette of the day, took a long drag, and held it deep in my lungs. I let it sit for a bit and exhaled far less than I took in. I always wondered what happened to the rest of the smoke. I was afraid to even guess.

I dialed Thomas's room, but there was no answer, so I called the hotel operator and asked her to page Thomas Sharpe to the hotel courtesy phone.

A moment later, I heard, "Mr. Thomas Sharpe, please call the hotel operator. Thomas Sharpe, please call the hotel operator." Within minutes, the courtesy phone on the wall next to me rang.

"Hello."

"Hey, Irish, this is Thomas. What's shaking?"

"I've got a little issue I think you may be interested in, and I need some face-to-face time so I can explain what's going on."

"Why don't we meet for lunch and we can talk about it?" Thomas said. "How about meeting me in that little café near the south lobby?"

"Well, this is kind of a private matter. I don't think we should discuss it in public."

"Why don't we meet in my suite in about an hour? I'll have some lunch brought up," Thomas offered.

I hesitated just for a second and then said, "It's as good a place as any. See you then. Thanks."

I hung up the phone with a little trepidation. I believed, in the back of my mind, that all conversations in Joey J's office and all the other upper staff's offices were being secretly taped. I really put nothing beyond Joey. I simply did not trust him. I was paranoid about his paranoia.

If I could throw my paranoia out the window instead of letting it occupy half my brain, I would sleep easier at night. Just because everyone was staring at me didn't mean I was paranoid. I still wondered, though, if Joey was secretly taping his staff's rooms.

That would be pretty sick with all the crazy things that go on in hotel rooms. I believed in the old adage, "If you aren't doing anything wrong, there is nothing to worry about."

I had about an hour to kill before I had to meet Thomas. Maybe I had enough time to find Henry Rodriguez, the union director for the Texas region, and Johnny Graves, the director for the Ohio region.

I figured if Jennifer was being transferred from the Ohio Regional Office to the Texas Regional Office, each of the regional directors would be aware of what was going on. It made sense, but then, Joey does not always do things that make sense.

The regional offices would help to get this ball rolling. At least I'd find out if Joey was really serious about a change of venue for Jennifer. Maybe

Johnny didn't want to lose Jennifer, and maybe Henry didn't know he was getting someone from outside his region.

Sometimes that's not acceptable to the directors. Usually, both regional directors have to mutually agree with a change like this.

So knowing Henry the way I did, I thought he would be easiest to reach. I called Henry's hotel suite, but like Thomas, he wasn't in. I was just going to call the hotel operator and do the page thing again when I saw Henry and his wife enter the lobby of the hotel.

Henry never traveled without his wife. They were both in their early sixties and had been together for more than forty years. I liked Henry from the first day I met him. He always had a smile on his face, a warm handshake, or an affectionate hug for the ladies. He was well liked by everyone on the staff.

Henry was a huge man, standing six foot two and weighing well over three hundred pounds. He was proud of his Hispanic heritage and fought as hard as he could to improve the way of life for everyone, especially minorities. He felt it was his duty to speak for those who couldn't be heard.

Joey J had promoted Henry to the Texas Regional Union directorship only after constant urging from Thomas Sharpe. Right after his promotion was announced, Thomas confided in me about how pissed he was at Joey.

Apparently, Joey, the bastard that he is, had said to Thomas, "What the hell, go ahead and promote the Mexican. We probably need a token minority on staff to make us look good."

What he got was not a token, but a dedicated and compassionate trade unionist. Henry's union roots were seeded deep in his family. His father and three brothers worked in a union-represented shop, so union idealism was ingrained in him from an early age. Working in a union shop and then as a union officer was a natural progression in his life.

As I approached Henry and Maria, I stopped and turned around when I heard screeching tires and a woman's scream outside the hotel lobby. As Jennifer stepped off the curb, she heard the roar of an engine and squealing tires as a vehicle leaped forward like a young stallion to gain instant speed. She barely had enough time to turn her head to see a truck heading directly for her, her reflexes nothing more than a feeble attempt to jump out of the way.

She heard a snap and felt her ankle break as it hit the grille, then blacked out as her head hit the windshield and formed a spiderweb of cracked glass. She was thrown out of the path of the truck, just far enough to avoid the rear tires.

I turned back and said to Henry, "Wait a minute, I need to talk to you, but I've got to see what happened outside first." I proceeded out of the lobby front doors. People were running toward someone lying on the sidewalk as a black Ford pickup truck was obviously getting away as quickly as possible.

I looked down and immediately recognized Jennifer in her green rumpled T-shirt and red shorts lying on her side with her face down on the pavement.

I yelled, "Someone call 911!" and then I rushed to her side.

A woman who looked about fifty, wearing a one-piece red bathing suit, red sandals, and dark red-framed wide-angle sunglasses and carrying a large beach bag came running up to Jennifer.

"Don't move her. I'm an RN, and I've worked in an ER for thirty years. We have to keep her as still as possible, but first, we have to carefully roll her over, so she's flat on her back. We need to check her airway, and that way, we can also keep her in a more stable position."

She turned around to a man and woman watching the scene and asked, "Could you two please help us roll her onto her back?"

In unison, they both said, "Sure."

"Now, what we are going to do is roll her on my command. I will secure her head and neck." She looked at me and said, "You take care of her legs, keeping them straight. You other two," she said, looking at the man and woman, "I want one of you to hold her pelvis area and the other to keep her arms close to her body and her chest secure. We are going to roll her in one fluid motion. I will count to three, and we will all turn her at the same time."

The RN secured Jennifer's head and neck with her tightly rolled towel, and checked her breathing.

Jennifer had a large bruise on her face, with the swelling already beginning to close her left eye.

The nurse said, "Okay, is everyone ready? On my count, we will roll her on three. One, two, three, roll."

In one fluid motion that would make any paramedic smile, they rolled her onto her back.

Holding onto Jennifer's head, the RN looked up and said, "In my beach bag, there are two more towels. Roll each of them up tight, and we will use them to keep her head still." The man reached around, grabbed the beach bag, and took out the two towels. He rolled them up and gave them to the nurse, who placed one on each side of Jennifer's face and held it in place.

I looked down at Jennifer and noticed a large gash on her left thigh that was oozing with bright red blood, and her left ankle, which was twisted into a grotesque position with purple swelling infiltrating the normal tissue.

As the nurse was holding Jennifer's head still, she felt a huge lump on the back of her head. Looking at me, she said, "Pull each eyelid up one at a time so I can check her pupils."

I reached down and did as directed. The nurse looked at Jennifer's pupils and saw that both contracted in the bright sunlight. "Both of her pupils are reacting to the light stimulus, so that's a good sign."

"What does that mean?" the other man asked.

"When a patient has a head injury that causes bleeding inside the skull between the dura mater and the brain, the pressure from the blood affects the ability of the pupils to contract like they are supposed to. It's called a subdural hematoma, plus numerous other things can be going on inside the brain."

Jennifer was breathing but was unconscious, and overall, she was nonresponsive. I took a handkerchief out of my pocket and applied gentle pressure to the wound on her thigh to slow the bleeding.

"How could this have happened?" I asked the nurse quietly as I was shaking my head in disgust, saying aloud what I was thinking. I looked around and asked, "Did anyone see what happened?"

An elderly gentleman wearing an oversized straw hat, paisley Bermuda shorts, white socks, and brown loafers stepped up and said in a shaky voice, "I saw the entire thing. She stepped off the sidewalk on the other side by that pillar, and as soon as she did, that truck came at her like a bat out of hell, like he was trying intentionally to hit her. I couldn't believe my eyes. I yelled at her, but it was too late."

I asked him, "Did you get the license number?"

"No, sir, I didn't think about it. Sorry. I do know that it was a black Ford truck, three-quarter ton, four-wheel drive."

"Did you get a look at the person driving?"

"No, I'm afraid not."

"Did anyone else see anything at all?"

No one responded but just stood looking down at Jennifer lying on the sidewalk and shaking their heads.

After a few silent minutes, I heard the shrill sound of the ambulance siren heading our way. I looked up and saw Henry.

"Is there anything I can do to help?" asked Henry. The nurse asked him to move the people back and keep the drive clear so the ambulance and police could get in unabated. Henry did as asked, took charge of the area, and nobody argued with him.

As the ambulance came to a stop, a white BMW slowly pulling out of the parking spot caught my eye. The man who was driving wore dark sunglasses and a New York Yankees baseball hat. He never took his eyes off Jennifer as he passed. He slowly left the scene with a smile on his face—no, not a smile, a sneer.

That pissed me off so much I yelled, "Hey there, stop! Goddamn it, I said stop." He stepped on the gas and quickly sped away. I couldn't make out the license plate number. If I hadn't been holding pressure, I would have run after him.

A man wearing a white shirt with "Paramedic" embroidered on it jumped out of the back of the ambulance. He assessed the area and immediately reached in and grabbed a cervical collar.

"Hold her head while I put this on her."

I looked up and saw another man with "EMT" on his white shirt bring a wooden backboard and lay it down next to Jennifer. The paramedic checked her carotid artery for a pulse and then shone a small flashlight into both pupils. The EMT put a ridged splint on her injured ankle and a bandage on her thigh wound.

With the nurse and me helping, in one motion, we rolled Jennifer onto her right side just as the nurse had instructed us a few minutes before. The EMT slid the backboard next to her, and then we rolled her back onto the board in one smooth motion.

The paramedic and the EMT strapped her securely onto the backboard, with extra padding and straps to better secure her neck and head and a pillow under her knees. The paramedic placed an oxygen mask on her face and said, "Let's set it at ten liters." The EMT was already reaching for the oxygen tank, turning the flow up to ten liters. They obviously had worked together for quite a while, each anticipating the other's move without asking.

"Pupils are equal and responsive to light stimulus, B/P 148/88, pulse 96 and regular. Respirations are 24," stated the paramedic. The EMT was writing the stats on the run sheet. "Let's load her up and get going. We're taking her to Miami General Hospital Emergency Room."

Henry and I helped them lift the backboard and set it on the gurney. Just as we were loading her into the ambulance, a Miami police car with lights flashing pulled into the hotel drive. The officer got out of his car, left the lights flashing, and went directly into the ambulance to check on Jennifer's condition. He emerged from the ambulance a few minutes later and asked, "Did anyone see what happened?"

The elderly gentleman stepped up and repeated his story to the officer.

"Does anyone know the victim?" asked the officer.

I replied, "I know her. Her name is Jennifer Marks."

"What's your relationship to her?" the officer asked.

"We both work for the International Truckers Union, and our entire staff is staying here at this hotel," I told the officer.

"Does anybody else know her?" asked the officer.

"I know her. I work with her too," replied Henry.

"Is there a place where we can talk?" asked the officer.

"Sure, there's a small meeting room just inside," said Henry.

The officer turned to the elderly witness and the RN and asked them to stay for a few minutes so he could get their names and formal statements. Henry turned to Maria and asked her to call Joseph Pinata and Johnny Graves to tell them what had happened, and that he and I would stay to answer questions for the officer.

I led Henry and the officer into the hotel and into the small meeting room to the right side of the hotel lobby.

"My name's Officer Bishop, Donald Bishop. Can I have your names, what you know about Ms. Marks—or is it Mrs. Marks—and what your relationship is to the victim?"

Henry volunteered first, "My name is Henry Rodriguez, and I work for the International Truckers Union as the regional director for Texas. Jennifer works for the union out of the regional office staff in Ohio. I only know her casually and just met her during these negotiations."

"Is she single or married?" Officer Bishop asked.

"You know, I'm not sure," Henry replied.

"She's married," I answered.

"What's your name?" Officer Bishop asked, turning to me.

"I'm Sean MacSween. I work for the International Truckers Union, out of President Pinata's office. I've known Jennifer for a little over a year now. We met at our union regional conference last summer in Michigan. She's from the Ohio ITU region, and I'm from the Michigan ITU region. Our staffs sometimes work together on certain regional issues concerning the union."

As Officer Bishop was writing, he said, "From what the witness says out there, it sounds like this may have been intentional. Do either of you know anyone who might want to hurt her?"

Henry shook his head and said, "No idea at all. As far as I know, everyone speaks highly of her."

Officer Bishop turned to me and waited as if to say "Your turn." All the things Jennifer had told me just a few minutes ago were running through my mind, but I didn't think it wise to share those with him just yet.

I looked directly at Officer Bishop and lied as sincerely as I could. "No, I don't know anyone who would want to hurt her. Like Henry said, she is well-liked by everyone. It baffles me. She's a great person and an excellent worker."

"So you don't know why anyone would want to hurt her? Is that what you're saying?"

"Yes, that's exactly what I just said. I just find it hard to believe this was done intentionally."

"Why do you say that?"

"I don't know. It's just that I've never heard of anyone who was even remotely angry at her, about anything."

Looking me in the eye, Officer Bishop asked, "If you and Ms. Marks are working, why are the two of you dressed like it's a day at the beach?"

"We had a long day yesterday, and Mr. Pinata decided that everyone should take the morning off and start fresh at noon. We just came back from our walks. She went her way, and I went mine. Why would you ask?"

"I'm just curious. That's all," Officer Bishop replied. "Who is this Mr. Pinata you just mentioned?"

"You've never heard of Joseph Pinata?" Henry asked.

"Are you talking about *the* Joseph Pinata, president of the Truckers Union?

"One and the same," Henry replied.

"Okay. Then yes, I have heard of him. He's been on the news a lot lately, hasn't he?"

Henry replied with a wry smile, "Yup, I guess you could say that."

He looked directly at me and asked, "How long will you two be in Miami?"

"We had hoped to be out of here by the end of the week."

"So both of you will be here for another few days or so?"

"That's right," replied Henry.

"If you have to leave before that, could you contact me before you do?" Bishop asked. "I may have to turn this investigation over to our detectives if it's determined to be an intentional hit-and-run injury. It could even be attempted homicide, which is out of my jurisdiction. So if you think of anything else, don't hesitate to call our office." He handed both Henry and me one of his cards and said, "I'll be in touch."

He turned and walked out to continue his interrogation with the elderly man, the nurse, and anybody else who might have seen something.

CHAPTER SIX

In the ambulance, Jennifer awoke to the chilling sound of the siren blaring overhead. She felt the oxygen mask on her face, the rigid cervical collar around her neck, and the safety straps holding her body tightly to the hard backboard. She looked up and saw the paramedic holding his stethoscope, listening to her lungs.

"Well, hello there, welcome back to the land of the living. My name is Harold, and I'm a paramedic. We are taking you to the Miami General Hospital Emergency Room. Do you remember what happened to you?"

Jennifer thought for a moment, and then it all came back to her, the screeching tires of the truck and the smile on the face of the driver. "A black truck hit me. Why did the truck hit me?" Jennifer asked.

"I don't know, but right now, we need to get you to the hospital so the doctor can check you over," Harold said.

"I remember I tried to jump, but he hit my leg, and then, I don't know what happened," Jennifer offered.

The siren slowed to a low drone and then stopped completely. "Here we are," said Harold. "You just stay real still, and we will get you out of the ambulance and into the emergency room."

The back door of the ambulance opened, and Jennifer felt them pull the gurney out and then lift her up, the legs unfolding and dropping to the floor. They rolled her into the hospital through the automatic doors.

The movement caused her to become nauseated. She could smell the pungent odor of disinfectant and rubbing alcohol as they entered the hospital. A woman in surgical scrubs met them just inside the hospital door.

"Hello, my name is Pat. I'm one of the triage nurses. Can you tell me your name and what happened to you?"

"Yes. My name is Jennifer Marks, and I guess I was hit by a truck."

"Where exactly do you hurt?"

Jennifer never felt nor had been aware of any pain up to that point. She then became aware of her body and realized her face was swollen so much that her left eye was almost completely closed and painful as hell. The pain in her left leg and the left side of her chest surfaced at the same time.

"My face, the left side of my chest, and also my left leg are very sore," replied Jennifer. Then she added, "I have a terrible headache, and it's hard to take a deep breath."

The paramedic, Harold, said to the nurse, "Pat, I triaged her at the scene as well as on the way here. Her vitals are pretty normal for what she's been through, B/P 148/88, pulse 96, and regular, respirations 24, pupils are equal and reactive to light stimulus. However, I do detect an irregular rale in her left chest, mostly the lower lobe area."

"Thank you," said Pat, the triage nurse. "We'll take it from here."

Jennifer looked up at the nurse and asked, "What's an irregular rale?"

"That's an irregular sound in your lungs. It may be possible that you injured your lung too," the nurse replied.

"We will get the doctor here right away to see you. Do you have any neck or back pain or numbness in your arms or legs?"

"No numbness anywhere, and my back feels okay. I can't tell about my neck with this goddamn collar so tight," Jennifer responded.

"Are you allergic to any medications that you know of?" the nurse asked.

"No, nothing that I'm aware of," Jennifer responded weakly.

They rolled her gurney into a small room with the word *Triage* stenciled in large letters above the door. Another nurse came in and started taking her blood pressure and pulse, while still another started cutting off her clothes and covering her with a hospital gown.

A moment later, another woman in surgical scrubs walked into the room. She was about five foot four, with blond hair tied in back in a makeshift ponytail, and she wore dark-rimmed glasses. She had a spotless complexion and a warm smile.

"Hi, my name is Dr. Myott. I'm the ER physician today. I'm going to be in charge of your treatment, but since you were struck by a truck and hit your head, I'm going to have Dr. Miller, a neurologist, take a quick look at you. He happens to be here in the ER now seeing another patient. He will also take a look at your spine to make sure everything is okay there."

She took out her stethoscope to listen to Jennifer's lungs and asked, "Can you take in a deep breath for me?"

Sharp pain prevented her from doing so, and for the first time, Jennifer became fully aware of the possibility of serious injury. "I'm sorry I can't. It hurts too much."

"Where's most of your pain?"

"The left lower side of my chest and in back around my rib area."

"Do you feel short of breath?"

"I didn't until you asked me to take in a deep breath. Now I feel like I need to take in a deep breath, but I can't. It's like I can't get enough air." A worried frown came onto Jennifer's face. Now she was scared.

"We will check that out as soon as Dr. Miller sees you." Dr. Myott quickly examined Jennifer's face, eyes, ears, nose, left thigh, left ankle, and her reflexes in both arms and legs.

"Start an IV immediately. Get AP and lateral x-rays of her cervical, thoracic, and lumbar spines before you move her off the gurney or do any other x-rays. Have Dr. Miller look at those, and if he says they are okay, get some x-rays of her ribs and sit her up and get an upright AP and lateral chest. We will get her skull and left orbit after that. We also have to get a CT of her head and chest. Get her to x-ray as soon as Dr. Miller is through with his neurological exam."

A few minutes later, Dr. Miller came into her room. He was young, almost too young to be a neurologist—at least that was Jennifer's first impression. He looked more like a high school physics student.

He had short and slick black hair parted on the right side, black horned-rim glasses, and about six pens sticking out of his white jacket pocket. "Hello, I'm Dr. Miller, and I'm going to check you over for a few minutes and make sure all your neurological functions are normal. Is that okay?"

"Sure," said Jennifer, not really knowing what neurological functions were.

He examined her eyes, ears, nose, and reflexes in her arms, legs, and feet, much the same as Dr. Myott had a few minutes earlier. He held his index finger in front of her nose and told her to follow it with her eyes the best she could. He moved it right, left, up, and down.

"Did you black out when you were struck?"

"I guess. The first thing I remember, after I was hit, I was in the ambulance coming to the hospital."

"Are you nauseated and did you throw up after you woke up?"

"I was a little nauseated when we were coming into the ER, but that has gone away."

When he was done with his exam, he said to the nurse, "Everything looks normal neurologically. Get the x-rays Dr. Myott ordered—just her spine— and let me check them. If those are normal, then you can move her for the rest of the x-rays. I'll be at the desk writing notes. Let me know when they're done." He looked back at Jennifer and patted her hand and said, "Everything looks normal so far, so try to relax. I will be back to talk to you as soon as I see the x-rays. We will take good care of you." He turned and walked out of the room.

Dr. Myott immediately returned to the room and said, "We need to get her into x-ray stat. I want those AP and lateral x-rays of her cervical, lumbar, and dorsal spine ASAP. After Dr. Miller checks them and he says it's okay to move her, here's an order for an upright AP and lateral chest x-ray. We need to see if there are fluids present in her left lung. After I see them, get these."

She handed another order slip to the nurse. The nurse looked at the order slip and said, "I will get this to x-ray right away, Doctor."

On the slip were orders for skull and left orbit x-rays. The nurse asked, "Do you want these before we get the CT of her head and chest?"

Dr. Myott said, "Since you already have her in x-ray, get the skull and orbits. Then take her for the CT, but do not delay. This is very important. The x-rays of her left leg and left ankle can wait until after we check her head, spine, and lungs thoroughly."

Jennifer felt the sting of the needle as the nurse started the IV in her right hand. She watched as she taped the IV tubing onto her hand, then her arm, and as she opened the valve to allow the fluid to run into her vein.

She wondered what it was that was flowing into her bloodstream. "What medicine are you giving me?" Jennifer asked the nurse who was smiling down at her.

"It's not a medicine. It's just fluid to keep your vein open, so when we do give you medication, we do not have to worry about starting an IV in a hurry. We do it routinely in all trauma cases."

They moved her gurney directly into the ER x-ray room, next to the x-ray table. There were two technologists, a young man and a young woman, who told Jennifer to lie as still as possible. Jennifer knew it wasn't possible, but both technologists looked to be about sixteen.

The young lady was the first to speak and said, "Hello, my name is Ronda, and he's Todd, and we will be taking a few x-rays of your spine."

"Everyone calls her X-ray Ronda," Todd interjected.

"That's just Todd. We try to ignore him as much as possible," X-ray Ronda said with a smile.

Jennifer responded as best as she could with the neck brace still hindering her ability to speak. "Do whatever you need to, but why do they call you X-ray Ronda?"

Ronda smiled again and replied, "Before I became an x-ray technologist, I used to work in the office in the x-ray department, and when I answered the phone, I would say, 'Hello, this is X-ray Ronda speaking.' Some of my co-workers thought it was cute, and it just stuck with me."

Jennifer tried to nod her head but couldn't, so with her teeth clenched and the cervical collar still tight around her neck, she said, "That's a cute story."

X-ray Ronda positioned her for three x-rays from above, one each of her cervical, dorsal, and lumbar spine while Todd yelled, "Hold your breath, then you can breathe."

Next, they brought the x-ray tube away from the table and lowered it to table level and aimed it sideways at Jennifer's lower back. X-ray Ronda positioned her for the lateral views of her spine, one each laterally across her upper and lower back. Then X-ray Ronda came into the room wearing a lead apron. She said, "For the next view, I am going to gently pull down on your arms while Todd shoots the next x-ray. It's a lateral view of your neck."

After the x-ray was taken, Jennifer asked, with clenched teeth and rather mystified, "Why did you pull down on my arms?"

Todd had come into the room first and said, "We need to get a close look at your seventh cervical vertebrae to make sure there isn't a compression fracture. We need to get your shoulders out of the way of the spine."

Jennifer said, "Okay," not really understanding what he was talking about, except what he said about a possible fracture of her neck. Could she actually have a broken neck and become wheelchair-bound for the rest of her life?

She instantly felt her mind race and her anxiety level increase rapidly as she wondered for the first time if she had a spine injury and could be paralyzed. She went from high anxiety to terror in a moment. Her heart rate increased immediately, and her breathing came in quick gasps, in spite of the pain in her chest.

She had been told three times that she must lay perfectly still, especially her head and neck. She thought, 'to hell with that.' She couldn't resist the urge to move something, so she first moved her right toes, then her left, and finally, the fingers of both her hands. That brought a wave of relief.

She could still feel her hands and feet—she wasn't paralyzed.

X-ray Ronda told Jennifer that she was going to show the x-rays to Dr. Miller, and if everything was all right, they would be right back to take a few x-rays of her chest.

Jennifer's mind wandered as she lay on the table, trying to figure out what had happened. She remembered, as she walked up to the hotel, that a black truck was parked, with the motor running, about a hundred feet away and facing the entrance to the hotel.

The next thing she remembered was hearing the screeching tires and seeing the truck coming directly toward her. Even though it was just an instant, the vision of the driver's face was still vivid in her mind.

He had a thin face with a pencil mustache, a crooked long nose, long, black, greasy hair that was plastered to his head, and a smile that looked more like a sneer. Why was he smiling? She couldn't get the vision of his face out of her mind.

After a few minutes, X-ray Ronda and Todd returned, and Ronda said, "Dr. Miller says your spine is fine, so we are going to get three x-rays of your ribs, and then we will sit you up and take two x-rays of your chest. We can also take that cervical collar off, which will make you feel much better."

They slid her off the gurney onto the x-ray table. Jennifer was relieved that her spine was okay. At least she wouldn't be paralyzed, and that was a huge relief.

While she was lying flat on her back, X-ray Ronda brought the x-ray tube back up and over her body. They took two x-rays, one high on her chest for the upper ribs and one lower on her chest for the lower ribs. Each time, she went through the "take in a deep breath and hold it, you can breathe" routine. To get a better view of her lateral ribs, she was then turned up 45 degrees to her left side.

Both Todd and X-ray Ronda came into the room and helped Jennifer sit up for the x-rays of her chest. Once Jennifer was sitting upright, she felt tremendous pain in the left side of her chest that got even worse when she tried to take a deep breath.

"Do I have to sit up?" Jennifer asked X-ray Ronda.

"Yes. It's necessary to determine if you have fluid or blood in or around your lungs. It's very important that Dr. Myott knows the condition of your lungs," X-ray Ronda replied.

With Todd holding her arms, Jennifer sat upright with her back against the upright film holder, and then with her left side against it and her arms above her head. Next, they took x-rays of her skull and orbits.

When they were done, they laid Jennifer down on the table and then moved her back onto the gurney. The orderly came for her shortly afterwards and pushed her back into her room in the emergency department.

A few minutes later, Dr. Myott came into her room and said, "It appears you have injured your left lung. You have what we call a pneumothorax.

You have punctured the lower lobe of your left lung. We need to get a CT scan of your chest and head, and then, we will need to put a chest tube in your lung to drain the fluid. It's a simple procedure, but it's quite uncomfortable. We can give you something mild for pain to help you tolerate it, but we can't put you completely out because most pain medications reduce respirations, and we need you to exchange as much air as possible. I don't want you to worry. You are going to be just fine. I have called the thoracic surgery resident, and he will be here by the time your CT is finished. He's very good at putting these chest tubes in place."

"How did my lung get punctured?" Jennifer asked.

"It appears that you have three broken ribs that were pushed into your lung," said Dr. Myott. "It's quite common in chest injuries."

"Will it heal okay?" Jennifer asked.

"Normally, if we can get the fluid out of your lung, it will heal just fine," Dr. Myott replied. "Don't worry; we'll take good care of you."

She turned to the nurse and said, "Give her the small dose of morphine I ordered. Give it to her through her IV, then get her to CT right away. I need both a chest and head CT. You need to stay with her and monitor her vital signs. Get Donna to set up room 4 for a chest tube insertion. I will be in the triage room, checking another patient. Also, where is the oxygen mask? I want her on an oxygen mask at ten liters at all times."

The nurse responded, "The x-ray technologist must have taken it off for the x-rays and didn't put it back on. Here, Jennifer, let's put this on so Dr. Myott is happy." She grabbed the oxygen mask and put it over Jennifer's mouth and nose and stretched the elastic over her head.

"Just let me know when the CT is done," Dr. Myott said as she left the room.

CHAPTER SEVEN

• •

After Officer Bishop had left, I turned to Henry and said, "I am going up to the hospital to see how she's doing. Could you do me a favor?"

"I'd be happy to. Just say it, and it's done."

"I'm supposed to meet Thomas Sharpe at noon for lunch. Could you call him and tell him what happened and that I'm going up to the hospital?"

"Sure, no problem. Consider it done," replied Henry. He could tell I was upset. He put his hand on my shoulder and said, "I'm sure she will be all right. I've heard that Miami General is the best hospital in the South. They will take great care of her. Do you have a ride to the hospital?"

"No, I don't. I was going to catch a cab," I confessed.

"There's no reason to do that," Henry replied. Handing me his keys, he said, "Here, take my car. It's parked out front, the red Chevy."

"Thanks, Henry. I have to go upstairs and change out of these shorts and t-shirt," I said as I grabbed the keys and walked toward the elevators.

By the time I got to my room, my head was beginning to pound once again. I needed a drink, but it was too damn early in the day. Shit, I swore off booze today, I reminded myself. Instead, I lit up another cigarette and thought a lot of good my morning walks did me if I kept smoking these cancer sticks. I felt the slight tremor in my right hand as I held the cigarette to my lips. It was becoming more noticeable every day.

Twenty minutes later, after a shower and a change of clothes, I left the hotel and saw Officer Bishop still talking to the elderly gentleman who had witnessed the accident.

The old man looked quite upset and was talking fast and waving his hands and arms as he spoke, trying to explain what had happened.

Must be Italian; all Italians talk with their hands, I thought to myself.

As I hurried to Henry's red Chevy, I heard the old man explaining, "I know it was no accident. He veered directly toward her as if he was trying to hit her. He did it on purpose, no question about it. I know he did. He saw her but kept going straight at her."

I got into Henry's Chevy, and on my way to the hospital, I kept asking myself if Joey J would have the nerve to do something so appalling to Jennifer. Would he really try to kill her because she wouldn't give in to him or because she called him a fucking arrogant bastard?

Maybe, but that was just too crazy to consider. I knew full well that Joey was a pig, but a killer? I didn't know. My initial instinct led me to believe Joey was not capable of being a killer, but something inside me, deep in my gut, told me something entirely different. I just couldn't quite put my finger on what was amiss.

Fifteen minutes later, I pulled into Miami General Hospital's ER parking lot. I parked Henry's Chevy in one of the few vacant spots and hurried into the emergency room.

I went straight to the window that read "Initial Triage Office," opened the door, and said to the nurse at the desk, "My sister was just brought in by ambulance, and I was wondering if you could tell me how she's doing. Her name is Jennifer Marks."

The nurse at the desk turned around in her chair and asked, "Are you family?"

"Yes, I'm her brother," I lied easily enough again.

"Our attending physician, Dr. Myott, has checked her out and requested a neurological exam by Dr. Miller, our neurologist. He's examining her now for any serious neck, back, or head injuries.

To this point, all her vitals are normal, so we're just waiting for his report. He should be done in just a few minutes. He was in the ER when she was brought in. I can tell you that she's alert and responsive, but we still have to get x-rays and probably CT scans. So until that happens, we cannot give any assessment on her condition."

"Could I see her?" I asked.

"Maybe for just a minute, but I'll have to ask Dr. Myott. If she gives the OK, I will come and get you. Just have a seat here," she said, motioning to the chair in front of her desk. "I'll be right back."

I sat down as directed, expecting a lengthy wait, but the nurse returned in less than a minute. "I just talked to Dr. Myott, and she said she's stable, but you can't see her until we get the x-rays and CT. In the ER, it's always priorities first," the nurse replied. "When she returns from x-ray and CT, we will be putting her in ER surgical room B. Maybe after that, you can see her."

"What do you mean ER surgical room B? Is she going to be okay? Why are they going to the surgery room?"

The nurse could sense my surprised concern as my voice rose a few octaves and a shocked look came over my face. "Listen, my name is Tammy; I'm the triage nurse, and I will let you know as soon as *we* know anything. I will say, it's too early to tell, but it does appear she may have a broken ankle. But we are more concerned with a possible internal injury to her chest. Once we get confirmation on all her injuries, I will come to get you, and then you can see her and talk to the doctor."

"I guess I'd better call David, her husband. He's back home in Ohio. Jennifer and I are here in Miami on business."

"If you don't want to call him, we would be glad to call her husband. Just give us his phone number," Nurse Tammy offered.

"That's all right. I don't have it with me, but I can get it in a few minutes. I'll call him, if it's okay."

Tammy handed me a card with the hospital ER phone number and said, "Have him call us if he needs anything or has questions. We will be glad to update him as her treatment progresses."

I thanked her as I grabbed the card, turned to open the door, and walked into the ER waiting room. It was full of screaming babies and people everywhere. Instead of sitting, I turned around and walked back outside the room. I grabbed my phone and called back to the hotel.

When the operator answered, I asked to be connected to Ken Cloutier's room. Ken was the recording secretary of the ITU.

I said, "Ken, this is Irish."

"Hey Irish, what's shaking?"

"Did you hear about Jennifer Marks?" I asked.

"No, what's up with her?"

"She was hit by a pickup truck right in front of the hotel less than an hour ago. I'm at Miami General right now. They don't know the extent of her injuries, but they think she has a broken ankle and possibly some sort of injury to her chest and lungs. I don't know exactly what, but I hope it's not too serious."

"My god, that's awful. How the hell did that happen?"

"The police are investigating that right now. Hopefully, they can find out what really happened," I replied.

"What can I do to help?" Ken asked.

"I need her home telephone number and her husband's first name so I can call him and tell him what's going on."

"Sure, no problem. Give me a second," Ken replied.

As I waited, I lit up another smoke, the last of my pack, and thought about who I could trust in the upper circle of the union. Ken Cloutier was a possibility, as well as Thomas Sharpe. There weren't too many I could think of on the staff who would fall into the trustable category. There was always Henry, of course. He was the most honest man I knew.

My thoughts were interrupted as Ken came back on the phone. He said, "Her husband's name is David, David Marks." He then gave me her home telephone number.

I wrote the name and number on my empty cigarette pack.

"Is there anything more I can do to help?" Ken asked.

"Not at the moment, but maybe we could get together to talk about some other issues I would like to run by you. Would that be okay?" I asked.

"Sure, just let me know," Ken said.

"I'll let you go, and I'll give you a buzz either later today or tomorrow and keep you updated on Jennifer's condition."

"Talk to you then," said Ken as he hung up the phone.

I dialed the number Ken had just given me and waited as the phone rang for the fifth, then sixth time. I was about to hang up when Jennifer's recorded voice came on saying, "Hello, I'm not here. You know what to do, so do it."

I was taken aback for a minute. There was something strange about the answering machine message. What was it? Then, the beep in the phone made me remember what I was calling about.

"Yes, ah, this is Sean MacSween. I'm on the ITU staff with Jennifer here in Miami. I'm trying to reach her husband, David Marks."

I somehow felt odd, like something in the answering machine message still wasn't quite right. It suddenly struck me. Jennifer said, "I'm not here" instead of "We're not here." Most married couples commonly say "We're not here."

After the hesitation, I continued saying, "There's been an accident, and Jennifer has been hurt. She's in the Miami General Hospital Emergency Room. She was struck by a pickup truck and apparently has a broken ankle and possible internal injuries to her chest. You can call the hospital at 800-585-6000, or you can reach me on my cell. I will be here until I find out her status, so give me a call. If I get any update, I will call you ASAP."

I left my cell phone number and my hotel room number and hung up. I had a weird feeling. The whole thing made me think something wasn't quite right, but what, I didn't know.

CHAPTER EIGHT

. . . .

walked back inside, looked around the visitor's waiting room, and saw a sign that read *No Smoking*. Not three feet from the sign was a cigarette machine. Now that's irony.

I walked over to the machine and put in five one-dollar bills and punched the button, and a single pack of cigarettes fell to the bottom of the machine. Five bucks for one pack of cigarettes—that's legal extortion.

I grabbed the pack of menthol smokes and walked back outside. I needed some fresh air to go along with my cigarette. Too bad they don't sell liquor in machines. I sure could have used a drink. It was obvious that it was not the day to stop drinking or smoking.

What had started out as a bad hangover day had progressively gotten worse. I should have stayed in bed all morning, but unfortunately, I can't lie in bed and relax. It's just not possible for me. I can't get away from me. Wherever I go, I go. That's been the problem my entire life. I still can't get away from myself.

I leaned against the wall and lit up a smoke. I closed my eyes, took a deep drag, and let the menthol smoke linger in my lungs for a moment longer than normal as I pondered everything that had happened. What a shitty day.

I was lost in my thoughts when I was startled by the slamming of a car door. I looked up just as Officer Bishop and another man were getting out of an unmarked police car. The other man was nearly as tall as me, but thinner. He had an oval face and wore a frumpy gray fedora, a thin, beige short nylon jacket with a yellowish white shirt, and wrinkled pants. He looked like the typical big city detective.

Officer Bishop stepped up first and said, "Ah, Mr. MacSween, this is Detective Jack Casey. He's going to take over the investigation of your friend's accident. Jack, this is Mr. MacSween."

"Pleased to meet you," I said while we shook hands.

Detective Casey had a firm handshake and a warm smile. He was about fifty and had a scar across the bridge of his nose. His face showed other scars from what appeared to be knives or fights, I wasn't sure.

He removed his hat as he shook hands. He wore his hair in a flat-top cut with the sides buzzed. Just by the way he carried himself, I knew he had been through more than one confrontation. He was definitely old school. I liked him immediately.

"Mr. MacSween, you look like shit. Maybe *you* should be in the ER. What happened to your face?"

"No big deal. I had a small misunderstanding last night."

"Remind me to listen closely. I don't want to end up with my face rearranged," Casey said with a smile.

"By the looks of those scars on your face, you've had your face rearranged at some point in your life," I said, also with a smile.

Jack nodded his head and asked, "So tell me, Mr. MacSween, how's your friend doing? Have you heard anything?"

"You can call me Irish, if you like. They think she has a broken ankle and possibly internal injuries to her chest, I'm not sure. They're still running some tests."

"Is she with it enough so I can ask her a few questions?"

"I don't know. They haven't let me see her yet."

"They probably won't since you're not immediate family," Jack offered.

"I lied and told them I was her brother."

"How is it that you two are such good friends?" Casey asked.

"Like I told Officer Bishop, we worked together this past year and got to know each other a lot better during these contract negotiations. No big deal, just friends."

"Do you find her attractive?" Jack asked directly.

"What the hell kind of question is that?" I asked quickly.

"Oh, I've always believed that if a man finds a woman attractive, they couldn't really be friends. The man's testosterone and the women's beauty get in the way of things."

I laughed. "Just look at her and you'll see for yourself. She's quite a looker. Actually, she is very beautiful, but all kidding aside, we are really more like working friends rather than even casual social friends. We've never been out socially. Besides, she's married, and I have someone back home. I don't really know her outside of work."

Jack Casey smiled and said, "So you're not having some sort of clandestine love affair are you, an affair that went sour?"

I glared at him, and my body stiffened up. "Look here, Mr. Big City Cop, I'm willing to answer any questions you may want to ask, but let's get one thing clear—she and I are not lovers nor have we ever been lovers. There is no other relationship besides work and a casual friendship. Am I making myself clear?"

Jack smiled and eyed me with a curious look that said, *I'm just shitting you.* "Do you have any idea why someone would want to hurt her?"

"No, I don't. No reason at all. As far as I know, she's a great gal."

"Has she been in any trouble within the union that you know of?"

"No, nothing that I'm aware of, anyway. Nothing at all."

"Is she well-liked by everyone?"

"Sure, absolutely." I wanted to sound as positive as I could, so he didn't get the wrong opinion of Jennifer.

"Has she had any prior trouble that you know of?"

"Again, nothing at all. She's clean as a whistle."

"You sure she hasn't had any problems with any of your union colleagues? You know, like Mr. Pinata or one of his associates?"

"I don't think so," I replied cautiously, not wanting to let him know about her confrontation with Joey Pinata.

"Is she in some kind of trouble in the union?"

I was finally taken aback and stuttered just a bit before asking, "W-w-what are you getting at?"

"Have you ever met her husband?"

"No, I've never seen him or talked to him. Why do you ask?"

With that, Jack turned to Officer Bishop and said, "You can go now. I will be taking over the investigation from here. You've been a great help, and I appreciate your excellent report on the accident. But I wonder if you could have a written report on my desk sometime this afternoon?"

"Yes, sir. I will have my report along with all the witness statements on your desk no later than three o'clock, if that's okay with you."

"That will be just fine, thank you. You can go now," Jack graciously stated with a voice of quiet authority and a gentle wave of his hand.

I was surprised at the level of respect Jack Casey received from Officer Bishop. It was as if he was in awe about working with the great Jack Casey, whoever he was. It was not the usual boss-employee relationship or officer-to-officer relationship. Officer Bishop had a genuine respect for Jack Casey, and it showed.

Jack turned back to me and said, "Let's go have a coffee. There's a little coffee shop around the corner where we can talk." His request sounded more like a demand than a question.

"Sure, why not," I said to his back, as Jack had already turned and walked away.

We walked half a block down the street into the Nervous Break Down Coffee Shop. It was a little mom-and-pop café with a counter and chrome stools much like an old-time malt shop.

There were five tables and six booths. There were two guys sitting on the stools at the counter having coffee. They were probably discussing and solving the world problems. A young couple sitting close, holding hands and smiling, were in one of the front booths. Other than them and the young lady behind the counter, the place was empty.

I followed Jack to the last booth in the coffee shop. Jack slid into the booth, so his back was against the wall facing the entrance. It didn't take a genius to see that even if Jack Casey had a calmness about himself, he was always in charge of the situation and aware of everyone and everything around him.

The young waitress from behind the counter came over to our table. The name tag on her uniform said Barbie.

I immediately said, "Is Ken working today?"

"No, he took the day off," she said with a big smile. I must have had a puzzled look on my face. She said, "Got you."

I had to laugh, and it felt good. I hadn't laughed in days.

"Thank you, Barbie. I was just kidding with you. It was a great comeback."

"Why, thank you. I'm studying acting at the University of Miami, so I try to say witty things when men flirt with me. Act like I'm serious when I'm just pulling their leg.

"I wasn't flirting with you. I was just making a joke."

She shook her head and said, "It was a flirt. I know a flirt when I hear one. It's okay. I like men who flirt, especially when I put the hammer down." She laughed at herself so hard that Jack and I were soon both splitting a gut too.

"So now that we have that out of the way, what would you two gentlemen like?"

"Just two coffees," Jack responded.

"Would you like cream or sugar?" the waitress asked automatically.

"No, both of them black," Jack Casey said firmly.

After the waitress left, I had to smile, and I asked, "She is so cute. I love kids like that. So tell me, Mr. Jack Casey, how the hell do you know whether I take cream or sugar in my coffee?"

"We've been watching you for some time now. Just one of the little things we picked up."

"Watching me? Why the hell have you been watching me? And who are 'we' anyway? What the hell is going on here? Do you think I had something to do with Jennifer's assault, or whatever it is?"

Without answering, Jack asked, "What's your relationship with Joseph Pinata?"

Now I was really confused. "What the hell does that have to do with Jennifer?" I demanded, as I felt the intensity of my voice rise up another octave.

"Do you get along with him?" Jack asked as he again ignored my question.

I looked Jack in the eye and said, "Wait a minute, let's stop right here. Maybe we should start this conversation over. I thought we were here to talk about Jennifer and the asshole that was driving the truck."

"We are," Jack replied softly in his baritone voice.

With this last elusive reply, I had heard enough. I slid out of the booth, stood, and said, "When you want to be honest with me, I'll be glad to talk, but until then, I'm not available."

I turned, and before I could take two steps from the table, Jack said, "Wait a minute, Irish, I apologize. Please come back, sit down, and let's start over."

I hesitated briefly, but my curiosity got the best of me, so I turned around and decided to sit and listen. I wanted to know what he had on his mind and what this conversation was really all about.

"Okay, I will listen and you talk. If I don't like what I hear I walk away, fair enough?"

"Fair enough," Jack responded.

Negotiating was nothing new to me. I felt it was my field of expertise. After all, I had been doing it for over twenty years of my working life. I had settled arguments when no one else could. One thing I knew about negotiating was I could learn more by listening than by talking. So I let Jack have the lead and reminded myself, *short answers and don't elaborate*.

I waited for a full minute while Jack organized his thoughts. "So tell me, Irish, are you a dedicated union man?"

"Absolutely," I answered flatly.

"How long have you worked with Joseph Pinata?"

"About four years."

"Do you make a good living working for him?"

"Very good. Sometimes I feel it's *too* good." As soon as I replied, I realized I had said too much.

"Why do you say sometimes too good?" Jack asked.

"It's the nature of the job," I replied tersely.

"Are you one of Joey's 'disciples,' as they're sometimes called?"

"I don't know what you're talking about."

"Are you loyal to him and the disciples?"

"What do you mean by *loyal* and by *disciple*?"

"I don't know. Do you just generally follow orders regardless of the consequences?"

"I have done a few things I'm not proud of, but I draw the line on certain things."

"Like what?"

Again, I knew I had said too much. "Well, it all depends on the circumstances. I happen to believe this union and its officers are here for one thing, and that's to serve and protect our members. We are not here for our own benefit like some people on the staff believe."

"Would you like to elaborate on that?" Jack asked.

"No, I don't think now is the time nor the place. Tell me, what do you mean by *disciples*, and why are you asking all these questions? Sounds to me like you're trying to get an inside view of the union. Am I right?"

Jack seemed to know he wouldn't get much out of me and probably never would unless he leveled with me.

"Look, Irish, we aren't getting anywhere here. Let's just lay our cards on the table."

"First, stop calling me Irish. I reserve that right for my friends. I don't know if you're friend or foe. So let's keep it formal. Call me Sean."

He shook his head without saying a word.

I like to look people in the eye when I talk to them. You can read so much by a person's eyes. So I asked him with a deadpan look on my face, "Do you want all fifty-two cards, or just maybe half of the deck?"

As he paused, I guessed that Jack had a gut feeling about me, too. He felt he could trust me. He always let his instincts lead him, and today was no different.

I sensed the hesitation in Jack, so I jumped at the chance to make a deal. It was something I learned many years ago. When the other side hesitates, they're unsure. That's the time to attack.

"So if you answer a few questions of mine, I will level with you. Is that a deal?"

Jack smiled and said, "I'm the cop. I'm the one who's supposed to ask the questions, and you're supposed to supply me with all the answers. That's how this works. You're trying to change the rules." Jack had a big smile on his face.

"Well, I am changing the rules," I said with quick authority. "Let's stop the verbal foreplay. It never turns me on. Deal or not?"

"Deal," Jack said as the smile continued to spread across his face. He seemed to be enjoying this for some reason.

I asked, "Who are you investigating here—Jennifer's accident and her assailant, the International Truckers Union, Joseph Pinata and his associates, or me?"

Jack took in a deep breath and let it out slowly. He was taking his time thinking, and after ten seconds, he said, "I'd have to answer all of them, except for you. We are not investigating you."

"That's good to know. Can I leave now?"

"Nice try. We either talk here, or I take you down to the station, and I do not want to do that," Jack responded.

I asked, "Why did you ask me if I knew Jennifer's husband?"

"Let's just say he has more of an interest in this than just Jennifer."

"Is David Marks really Jennifer's husband?"

"Why would you ask that?" Jack asked sheepishly.

"Aw, come on, Jack. Shit! I don't like it when someone answers my question with another question. Besides, I thought we were putting all fifty-two cards on the table, so cut the bullshit."

"Okay, okay," Jack said as he threw up his hands. "You're right. No more bullshit. And no, David Marks is not Jennifer's husband."

I was satisfied with that for now. I knew my instincts were correct the moment I'd heard Jennifer's answering machine.

"How did you guess that?" Jack asked.

"Let's just say I'm observant," I stated quietly.

"Let me guess. Her answering machine said, 'I'm not here' instead of 'We're not here.' Right?"

"You could be right, but I'm not saying anything until I know you better."

"That's fair enough," Jack agreed.

I then asked in a whisper as I leaned closer to the detective. "What the hell are you investigating here?"

Jack hesitated for a moment as Barbie, the waitress and actress, brought the coffee. I knew Jack would let his own instincts lead him. I always do, and he seemed like that kind of guy too. Besides, he needed me and all the information I had, so trust was the only way he could get.

Jack began, "My name really is Jack Casey, but I'm not a detective with the Miami Police Force. I'm with the FBI. I am the senior agent in charge of organized crime, including labor unions. Our agency, along with the Federal Labor Board, has been investigating one Mr. Joseph Pinata for possible tax evasion, embezzlement of union funds, fraud, extortion, drug trafficking, prostitution, and a whole slew of other seedy deeds."

Jack took a sip of his coffee and continued, "Like I said before, David Shanahan, a.k.a. David Marks, is not Jennifer's husband. He is with the

Federal Labor Board. His office is very interested in Joseph Pinata's elaborate lifestyle, among many other assorted dirty deeds. David is a very smart young man. He's a Harvard graduate and has both a Masters and a PhD. I can't figure what the hell he's doing in this line of work, but he is good at his job and is no one to mess with."

"How's Jennifer involved in all of this?" I asked.

"We contacted her about a year ago, right after she was promoted to her present job with the ITU, while she was in Ohio. We've been watching your entire staff for much longer than that. When we initially contacted her, Jennifer admitted to us that she was sick and tired of all the corruption within the union. She was willing to help in any way she could, but only if we promised not to destroy your union, which we assured her, as I assure you now, that our objective is not to destroy the union but to investigate the leaders at the top, namely Joseph Pinata and his disciples. We have been collecting data from Jennifer, who has been very helpful, but now we need more. That's where you come in. Jennifer told us that you, more than anyone else, could be trusted and that you would have access to more of the information we need."

"Tell me, why are you so hell-bent on getting Joseph Pinata and our leadership?" I asked sharply. "What have they done?"

"Joseph Pinata pissed off the wrong people, and he's made a lot of enemies. Frankly, I'm surprised someone hasn't taken the liberty of putting a bullet in his head. He's what we good guys call a scumbag criminal. Hell, he even defied an executive order from the president of the United States. He single-handedly caused a major recession in this country. The stock market plummeted to its lowest level in ten years."

I asked, "Do you think the market drop was caused by this strike?"

"I don't know, but there are enough important people who think it has, and that is all that matters. You don't go around jerking off the richest and most powerful people in the country without acquiring some enemies. We heard this investigation order came right from the president of these here United States himself. Mr. Pinata made him look helpless, and apparently, he didn't take kindly to that, if you know what I mean."

"How long have you been after him?"

"This investigation actually started with his father, Joseph Sr. We knew he was into some illegal business, but we could never get enough on him to get an arrest. We're hoping Joey Jr. isn't quite as smart as his old man."

"Where's the investigation at right now?" I asked as my interest grew.

"We have a lot of information, but not enough to make an arrest stick. It's all just figures, numbers, and assumptions. We're still digging for hard facts."

"Why are you coming to me?" I asked, even though I knew the answer. I could sense they needed a rat on the inside, and I was most likely their best option.

"Jennifer," Jack said with a shrug of his shoulders as if everyone in the world knew. "She said you were the most honest person on Pinata's staff, and she knew you didn't approve of the way he's running the union. Besides, she said you were one of the few on his staff who really cared about the members in the union and not just yourself. She has given us the names of a few other people we will be trying to get on board besides you, but as you can probably imagine, we have to be careful about who we approach."

"What are the other names she's given you?" I asked, just wondering who might be another snitch.

"Let's just leave that alone until I know I can trust you. Don't want to give up our insider information quite yet," Jack Casey stated abruptly.

Carefully and deliberately, I chose my words, "So you need me to be your mole in the hole, so to speak—the eyes and ears of the FBI. Right?"

"Basically, our investigation is going nowhere. Now, with the possibility that Mr. Pinata may have resorted to violence, we have another avenue to pursue. We need someone on the inside we can trust and who's willing to stick their neck out to help us and to help save their union too."

"Don't give me that crap about saving the union. I know you don't give a rat's ass about saving this union. All your people want is Joseph Pinata's head on a platter. I really don't think our Republican president gives a shit about this union either," I added without remorse.

Quietly, Jack continued, unabated, "Either way, we get the help we need, and you get to help return your union back to the people. It's a win-win situation for both of us. How can we lose?"

"Let me ask you this, was Jennifer intentionally run over because of her involvement with you?"

"That's a distinct possibility," Jack responded hesitantly while nodding his head slowly.

"Did you know that Jennifer and Mr. Pinata had a confrontation last night and then again this morning?" I asked.

"No, what happened?" Jack asked as he sat more upright in the booth.

"Jennifer said Joey called her to his suite and propositioned her, wanted her to spend the night with him."

"What did Jennifer tell him?"

"She called him a fucking arrogant bastard and asked why he didn't get one of his high-priced, low-class whores, and then she slammed the door in his face and left."

"Holy shit," Jack said with a huge frown on his face.

"Do you think Joey did this to her just because she wouldn't sleep with his dumb ass?" I asked.

"I don't know. It's hard to say. We were not aware of the confrontation with Mr. Pinata last night."

I replied to him with hostility in my voice, "Joey is truly an asshole, but even I don't know if he would stoop that low."

"With his ego, do you think he would allow Jennifer to talk to him like that?" Jack asked with a concerned look on his face.

"Who knows? But unfortunately, Joey sent Michael Ferrier to her room early this morning and informed her that she was being transferred to Texas and if she didn't like that, she could come back and renegotiate his offer from last night. Oh, one more thing I forgot to tell you. He told her what this relationship could do for her career."

"That may be helpful to our investigation. It's simple solicitation, but it's still Jennifer's word against his," Jack replied.

"So in any event, I'm putting my neck on the line too, right? I mean, I could be facing the wrath of Joey J."

"He probably wouldn't ask you to sleep with him," Jack said with a smile. "But yes, you would certainly be put at risk. That is a possibility. But if we're clever and you listen to me, no one will ever find out."

"You've given me quite a proposition. Either the union stays corrupted or I help out and maybe I become dead. At this point, I'm not sure I should stick my head out and possibly get it lopped off. That doesn't sound very appealing to me."

"Are you willing to sit back and watch your beloved union go down in flames? You do know how a mess like this could really destroy the image of the union, don't you? I mean, in the minds of the general public, and especially your members."

I interrupted and quickly said, "It's just not that simple. Joey has his finger on the pulse of this union. Every move this union makes is orchestrated personally by him. He's like the conductor of a symphony. Plus, there are people on his staff who like it just the way it is. They don't want to lose their cushy jobs, and frankly, will fight every inch of the way to keep them."

"I didn't say this was going to be easy, but we need more than we have now if we are ever going to bring him down, and you could help us a great deal. If you decide you won't help, you may be caught in the crossfire along with everyone else. We are good at what we do. It is just a matter of time."

"Are you threatening me?"

"Irish, I have learned over the past thirty years that idle threats serve no purpose. I wouldn't have agreed to even meet with you if I didn't feel you were the type of man we could trust. We have done an extensive background check on you already. We will get him somehow, somewhere, with or without your help, and we will bring down every person on his staff if they are guilty too. No threat, just fact."

I sat there for a full minute, stirring my coffee without saying a word, trying to absorb everything he had said. I couldn't take my eyes off Jack Casey. We were locked in a duel of reading each other's minds. I felt the familiar rush of gut feelings that I get when I know something is right. Jack Casey and his investigation felt right. I knew it, and at that moment, I accepted it.

"Oh, by the way, we are putting a plain-clothes officer on Jennifer 24-7," Jack said to break the silence.

"Let me ask you this," I said, ignoring his remark. "If you're so smart and sneaky, how did Joey J find out about Jennifer?"

"Hopefully, he hasn't. Maybe he just can't handle rejection. That's what we are trying to find out. There may be a leak somewhere, and we're checking that out as we speak. Maybe Jennifer somehow incriminated herself without even knowing it. That's the problem we face dealing with amateurs. It's nothing against her. She's a great gal and gutsy as hell. If she has balls enough to stick her neck out for us, we have to take better care of her, and we will. We are thinking about having David Marks, I mean Shanahan, come and stay with her, acting as her husband, just to be safe."

"Oh, that would be a tough assignment," I said with a laugh.

"Anything for the agency," Jack responded with an even bigger laugh.

I looked at him very seriously and said, "Let me say this before we go any further. If you are here just to take our union down and don't give a shit who goes down with it, then I'll have no part of it. This conversation never took place. But if you can assure me, as much as possible, that you'll not drag the union down the tubes with Joey, I could be in. I don't give a rat's ass about Joey. This may sound funny or corny to you, but I love this union and will have no part in its demise. Is that clear?"

"Crystal. It's Joseph Pinata who's taking your union down in flames. It's up to people like you to save it. If you and I do nothing, your union will self-destruct. It's as plain as that."

Without hesitation, Jack reached out his hand for me to take and said, "I give you my word that I will do everything in my power not to let the union crumble. And I will never, ever, ask you to do or say anything that might even remotely compromise this union of yours. I give you my word. That's all I have."

"I guess that's about all I can expect," I said with commitment in my voice.

Jack smiled and added, "You do have to understand that there will be collateral damage. The crimes that Pinata and his mob commit will reflect on the union, at least in the public's eye. There's nothing we can do about that. It will be up to people like you to rebuild your union to what it once was or what it could be."

I waited for a moment, trying to find the right words. "You know, I'm not alone when it comes to members who want to clean up our union. There is a large silent majority that feels the same way I do, even some on our staff. Goddamn Joey Pinata has done more to tear this union apart than anyone or anything."

Jack cleared his throat and asked, "Then it's a deal, right? We get this dirtbag out of the way, and you get your union back. Help us and we'll help you. Maybe we can help you gather the others who feel the same as you, and in the meantime, you let us know who to trust."

I paused for still another moment to think about what I was getting myself into. I knew that Joey J wouldn't go easily. I also knew that his revenge would be second to none. It was a very real possibility that good ol' Joey might even resort to murder.

My anger began to boil. This was a life-changing moment for me, as well as the union. I could almost feel the sincerity that Jack was trying to convey. I had a feeling about him, one that was pointing me in a direction I knew in my heart I had to follow.

I looked up at Jack and said, "I'm in, but don't feed me or the ITU to the wolves. I need your solemn vow that you will not hang me and the union out to dry. Can I get that?"

Jack smiled, and he said, "I give you my word that I will not feed you or the International Truckers Union to the wolves. You have my word on that. It's Joseph Pinata we want."

I took his hand, and before I let go, I asked one more question. "Are you recording this conversation?"

Jack laughed aloud and said, "No, I'm not, but technically, you're supposed to ask before you start the conversation. It looks like I will have to tutor you as we go along, but there will be no extra charge for that."

Jack's demeanor instantly changed to a more serious tone. "Irish, this is very serious business, and I will do all I can to protect you, Jennifer, and anyone else who comes on board, and again, you have my word on that."

Somewhere inside me, I knew that it was the right thing to do. It felt like this was the first time in months that I was doing something for the membership besides being a yes man, a puppet of ITU President Joseph Pinata.

CHAPTER NINE

....

We used up about another half an hour in the coffee shop talking about the union and the problems associated with the strike, and all the while, I was attempting to explain as best I could the intricacies of negotiations.

Afterward, I told him I wanted to get back to the hospital, and then, I needed to get back to the hotel to get some work done. Jack still had questions he needed answering, so he asked if I would be willing to come to his apartment later in the evening so we could go over some things in more detail.

He said he was a great cook and would have dinner ready for us at seven o'clock. I thought a real dinner would be nice. I hadn't had one in months, so I agreed. I wrote down Jack's address and cell phone number on a napkin and left the Nervous

Breakdown Coffee Shop, hoping I wouldn't have a nervous breakdown myself.

I walked out of the coffee shop toward the hospital and into the searing, humid Miami heat. It was god awful hot. I immediately broke out in a sweat. It was definitely not a day to linger outside in the beautiful Florida sun.

The smell of diesel fumes from two buses travelling past made it almost unbearable. The noise and life of the city—horns blowing, people constantly moving, traffic unending, everyone always in a hurry—felt comforting in a strange sort of way. It reminded me a little bit of Detroit in the summer.

As I reached the end of the block, I stopped and turned to watch as Jack hailed an approaching cab. As the cab drove away, I somehow knew I had made the right decision. For the first time in months, I felt good about myself and knew there was no turning back.

I had a good feeling about Jack Casey, and for some reason, I trusted him, probably far more than I should. I was sure that shortly I would find out if my instincts would prove correct.

As I walked through the doors of Miami General's emergency room, I was hoping they would let me see Jennifer. I wanted to talk to her about everything, including her involvement with Jack and everything that had happened since. I just hoped she felt good enough to talk.

My mind was racing. What was going to happen to the union, to Jennifer, to me, and to my job? What if Joey J found out about my involvement with the FBI? Would I be Joey's next target, or would he go after Jennifer again?

Who could I trust? Thomas Sharpe, Henry Rodriguez, Ken Cloutier? At the moment, I didn't think I would trust anyone. It was safer that way. There were just too many unknowns for me to feel comfortable. I needed to have a clearer picture before I stuck my neck in the guillotine.

I thought about Riona. Was I putting her in danger as well? I decided to call her after seeing how Jennifer was doing. No reason to concern Riona just yet, but I had to tell her to keep her eyes and ears open for anything unusual.

As I approached the initial triage office, I saw a different nurse on duty. I opened the door and walked in. She was talking to a young woman who was obviously very pregnant but not in any immediate distress. They were both laughing about something.

I couldn't help but smile and said, "I didn't realize pregnancy was this much fun."

"Oh, we're just ripping on all the men in the world, blaming them for all the misery they put us women through," said the young mother-to-be.

"Just think how boring life would be without us guys causing you all this grief," I countered with a hint of sarcasm.

The nurse looked at the mother-to-be and said, "Can't argue there, can we?"

I said, "Excuse me, but my sister was brought in here about 11:30, and they told me I couldn't see her for at least an hour. I left about an hour and a half ago to get a coffee, and I was wondering if I could see her now?"

The nurse nodded her head and said, "Let me check for you. What's her name?"

"Jennifer Marks."

The nurse got up and walked out of the triage office through a door labeled *ER*.

"Are you about ready to have a baby?" I asked the young lady, feeling stupid for stating the obvious.

"What's your first clue?" she responded with a wide grin.

"Yeah, I guess that was a dumb question," I admitted.

"Boy or girl?"

"We don't know yet. My husband and I are kind of old-fashioned. We want it to be a surprise. My labor pains started earlier today for about the tenth time, and by the time we got here, they quit again."

"Good luck. Is this your first?"

"Yes. We want to have three kids. It would make for a great family, especially when they get older. That way, we won't have to grow old alone."

I felt a strange feeling inside. She had a point. What would it be like for me and Riona if we never had kids? It was the first time that thought had occurred to me.

"Do you have any kids?" she asked.

"Not yet. We really haven't talked about it much."

"You do know your biological clock is ticking, don't you?" she asked.

"Are you nicely trying to tell me I'm getting old?"

"No, but men have a biological clock too," she responded.

I couldn't help but smile, and I asked her, "How old are you?"

"I'm twenty-two."

"You're pretty smart for someone twenty-two."

"My mother says it's the natural instincts of motherhood. I guess having babies makes you smarter. I don't know if that's it, but I've never felt this contented before. This really feels like the right thing to do with my life."

Riona and I hadn't talked about getting married and starting a family. I'd never worked up the courage to actually ask her. I don't believe there was ever a question about loving her. She was the only woman I had ever loved, and I felt she was probably the only one I *would* ever love, but there was always something that stopped me from committing to her. I never knew what that was.

I felt a twinge of shame because I knew she wanted nothing more than to get married and have kids. I never thought about how great being a father could be. My lifestyle simply was not conducive to being a good father or husband.

The young lady's smile brought me back to the present. Then, she said, "If you really love someone, your life cannot be complete until you bond as a family. If that means that you and she are the only family you want, then that's okay. But, and this is a big but, sometimes you have to trust her so much that she will complete your life. Fill it with a joy you never knew existed. But you have to be sure she is the one."

"Wow. That's pretty deep."

"I know it sounds that way, but it's just how I feel. My mother gave me the same speech."

"Sounds like you've got a pretty cool mom."

"I do."

I looked at the young mother-to-be and imagined myself as a father. It brought a warm smile to my face. Someday, maybe that could be Riona and me sitting there. The thought made me feel good. The day was full of surprises.

I looked up and saw the nurse coming through the door. I said to the mother-to-be, "Talking to you has made my day. Thank you very much, and good luck with your baby and your family."

We shook hands as the nurse came through the door. "The nurse in charge wants to talk to you. She will be here in a minute. Just have a seat."

I turned around and sat in the only other chair in the little room.

What's going on now? I wondered

I no more than got that thought out of my mind when the charge nurse came barging into the triage office. "Mr. MacSween?" she said rather loudly, looking at me. I nodded. She said, "Please follow me." With that, she held the door open and let me into the inner office. "Hi, my name's Monica Majors. I'm the charge nurse." She said *charge* with just a little too much emphasis.

She turned her back on me and started walking away. I followed like I was told. We went into a larger office that had patient charts all over the desk and hanging on the wall. It looked like mass confusion to me.

Monica Majors saw me looking at the mass of papers and charts and said, "This isn't as bad as it looks. We have our own system of organized confusion. We don't know how it works. It just does." She seemed to warm up just a little from my first impression. "I don't know how much you know about Jennifer's condition, so I'll start from the beginning. Her spine and head are clear of any injury, and that's good, very good. She has a broken left ankle, which we already set. We put a cast on her leg up to just below her knee. It should heal just fine in six to eight weeks."

I could tell that Monica Majors loved this part of her job. The term *Nancy Nurse* fit her to a tee. I smiled at my own clever thought.

"She does have one major problem, though. She has what's called a pneumothorax of the lower lobe of her left lung. Simply put in laymen's terms, that's where the lung has been punctured and collapsed, and residual fluid has collected that must be removed. Presently, the hospital's thoracic surgery resident is putting in a chest tube, which should drain all the fluid and take care of the problem."

"Is this life-threatening?" I asked, somewhat surprised.

"It could have been if she hadn't gotten medical attention, but no, she should be fine if we don't run into any complications—blood clots, infections, things like that. We usually leave the tube in for three or four days if necessary, sometimes longer. It just depends on how well the fluid drains. We have to keep it in until all the drainage stops. We will be doing chest x-rays twice daily to monitor her improvement."

I asked, "When can I see her?"

"Oh, I would say probably in about another hour or so, I think. She will be pretty doped up from the medication we'll give her after the procedure. She will be in quite a bit of pain. By then, you might be able to talk to her. One thing for sure, she sure has a foul mouth."

"That's Jennifer—never shy for words. Thank you for all your help and info. I think I will stick around for a while. I should go back to the hotel and get some work done, but if there's a chance of seeing her in the next hour, I'll stay here."

Nurse Majors smiled and said, "I think that is quite possible. I would stay if I were you."

"I'll be in the waiting room, then." I turned to leave, but stopped, and asked, "Can you come and get me when she's able to see me?"

"Sure, I'll let her know you're waiting."

Just then, Dr. Myott came into the room. "Are you Jennifer Marks' brother?" she asked.

"Yes, I am," I answered.

"Gee, that's funny. When I told Jennifer that her brother was here, she said she didn't have a brother."

"Must have hit her head during the accident," I said with a smile.

Dr. Myott smiled back and said, "She will be just fine but very sore for the next couple of days. Right now though, she is not a very happy camper, as you can imagine. We are giving her something more for pain now that we have her lung stabilized. It's draining very well, and that's a good sign. Hopefully, she will be in a better mood once the pain meds take effect. You should be able to see her in just a little while."

"Don't let her foul mouth give you a bad impression; she really is a very nice gal." I tried to say it with as much conviction as I could.

"Aw, don't worry," Dr. Myott said with the wave of her hand. "We don't let those things bother us here in the ER. If we took everything personally, we would be out of this business in a hurry."

"That's good to know. I'll be in the waiting room when she's ready to see me. Thanks for everything."

Instead of going into the waiting room, I went outside to have another smoke. Even though it was hot and humid, I found a nice shaded area with a light breeze that felt almost tolerable.

As I was lighting up my cigarette, I noticed that a man was sitting on a bench to the left of the main entry. He was reading a newspaper, or at least, it seemed like it. He never turned the page and was always aware of everyone around him. I wondered if this was the plain-clothes officer assigned to watch over Jennifer, the one who Jack had mentioned.

I had noticed him when Jack and I were walking to the coffee shop and then again on my walk back. I looked at my watch and saw that the man had been sitting in the same place, reading the same front page of the same newspaper for what must be nearly two hours.

As I was watching him, a gust of wind blew open the man's sport coat, and I immediately noticed the stainless steel handle of a revolver sitting in a holster under his left arm. My imagination started going crazy. I wondered if he was friend or foe and thought it best that I check with Jack.

I reached into my pants pocket, removed the napkin with Jack's phone number, grabbed my phone, and dialed his number. I didn't want to find out too late that the gentleman sitting on the bench with a gun was one of the bad guys.

Immediately, Jack answered, "Hello?" He answered as if he was surprised his phone even rang.

"Jack, this is Irish."

"What's up? I've only been gone about twenty minutes. Is there something wrong?"

"Oh, I guess I'm playing detective, but I'm curious about a certain person sitting on a bench out in front of the emergency room. Do you know anything about him, like, is he a good guy or a bad guy?" I was trying to sound as light as possible.

"He's a local off-duty Miami homicide detective we hired until our people can get in place. His name is Bob Lee. It wouldn't be a bad idea to introduce yourself to him. I've already spoken to him about you, so he is aware of your situation. Just tell him that you talked to me and that you are Jennifer's brother."

"Okay, I'll do that. I just wanted to be sure."

"No problem. Call me whenever you need to."

He hung up the phone, and I walked over to Bob Lee, still sitting on the bench reading the newspaper.

"Excuse me, sir. Are you Bob Lee?"

He looked up at me, somewhat surprised. He stared for a minute, stood up, and said in a heavy Southern drawl, "Yes, I'm Bob Lee, and you are who?"

Bob Lee was a large man, stood about six foot four, and weighed a solid 230 pounds. He had olive skin, short, brown hair cut in a flat top, high cheekbones, and soft blue eyes that hid his self-confidence.

"My name is Sean MacSween. My friends call me Irish. My sister is Jennifer Marks. I just talked to Jack Casey, and he wanted me to introduce myself to you since I'll be in seeing her."

"I already know who you are," Bob confessed with a smile. "I asked the nurse. Nothing's sacred, if you have a badge. Please to meet you." He stuck out his hand. I reached out and shook it. He had the firm handshake of a confident man. "So tell me, what's so important about that little sister of yours?" Bob asked.

"I really don't know," I lied once again.

"I was hoping you could enlighten me."

"Hell, these Feds don't tell us anything. They don't think we're smart enough to handle their top-secret agent mumbo-jumbo bullshit. But I'll tell you this, if y'all want to know anything about the city of Miami, you come to me. We might be local yokels, but we're no dummies."

"Well, that makes me feel better. I'd hate to have dummies watching over my sister," I said with a laugh.

Bob laughed too. "Don't get me wrong. The Feds are okay, especially Jack. I've dealt with him before. He's a straight shooter. If someone is after your sister, he will find them. Most Feds are just a little stuffy, that's all, but Jack Casey seems different than any I've ever dealt with. He's old-school, and I like that. He thinks on his feet and is not afraid to ask questions."

I liked Bob Lee right away. He seemed to have a good pulse on life, a sense of humor, and a quick wit about him.

"By the way, does your middle name start with an *E*? You know like Robert E. Lee?" I said in jest.

"Cute, but no. My middle name is Bill, not William, but Bill. It's a Southern thing. You northerners wouldn't understand. When I was a little kid, my friends called me Billie Bob. They always had it ass backwards. As I grew older and bigger, they stopped calling me that for fear I would rip their heads off," Bob Lee said with a wide grin.

I laughed and said, "I really thought it was some sort of Southern law that you boys down here had to have two first names. You know, like Jim Bob or Ken Joe or who knows what."

"Careful or the South may rise up again. I come from a long line of hillbillies. You could find yourself tarred and feathered if you keep talking like that. By the way, do you know what's happening with your sister?"

"I wish I did. It's kind of unsettling when you hear someone tried to kill your own sister. But unfortunately, I don't have a clue what's going on."

Bob offered, "I have dug up a little info about your sis, and it seems like someone mighta tried to kill her. At least, that's the way it looks from what I've found out. Know anything about that, Irish?"

"I wish I did. But unfortunately, I really don't know anything about it."

"Another thing—you know, just in case you forgot—she's not your sister."

"How would you know that bit of info?" I asked, sounding a little surprised.

"I'm a goddamn cop. It's my job to know these things," Bob said with a colossal smile. "You'd better go back inside and see how that sister of yours is doing. They'll be looking for you."

"Good idea, and it's been a pleasure meeting you." We shook hands once again.

As I turned to walk away, Bob said, "Hey Irish, by the way, if you need anything, anything at all, don't hesitate to give me a call."

"I will do that. Thanks a lot."

Bob said, "I have worked homicide for better than twenty-five years, but I've got two or three weeks' vacation I have to use up. Plus, I know a few ins and outs about what happens in Miami. Here's my card. It has my office number as well as my cell. You never know when a local yokel like me can be of service." As he handed me his card, he asked, "Do you have a number where I can reach you?"

"Sure. Do you have another card? I'll write it on the back. I'm not important enough to have my own cards."

He handed me another card, and as I wrote down my cell number, he said, "Remember, I'll be around. You may not see me, but I'll be around somewhere. Murders are down this time of year, so I can help you out. So don't hesitate to call."

As I handed him back the card, I said, "Thanks a lot." I turned around and walked back into the ER.

I went directly to the waiting area. I was dog tired. It had been a hell of a day and it was only half over. I sat down and immediately fell asleep in the cool, air-conditioned room. I must have been asleep for about half an hour when I was woken up by a page deep in my subconscious. "Mr.

MacSween to triage. Mr. Sean MacSween, please come to triage."

I finally realized it wasn't a dream and forced myself to open my eyes. I felt like I had slept for ten hours. Did I just have a bad dream, or was I really dealing with the FBI? It took me a minute to bring myself back to reality.

I walked up to the triage window, and yet another different nurse was on duty. "What's the deal, do you nurses change stations every hour or so?"

"Lunch time" was all she said.

"Did you page Sean MacSween to triage?"

"Oh, you're Mr. MacSween?"

"Yes, I am."

"Wow, you look like a Mr. MacSween," she said with a sly grin.

"What does a Mr. MacSween look like?"

"You. Handsome, reddish brown hair, and beautiful green eyes." I could see her face redden just a hint. I think she was flirting with me. "Anyway, Ms. Marks is able to see you now. Follow me."

She punched a button, and I heard the triage door unlock, and then open. Once again, I walked through. I followed miss flirty nurse down a hall and into an emergency room that was labeled Minor Surgery.

"Here she is, Mr. MacSween," she said with smirk as she turned and walked out the door.

"Cute, but brainless," I mumbled under my breath.

I looked up at Jennifer and was shocked by what I saw. Her face was pallid. Her eyes were red like she had been on a binge for two weeks, like mine had been this morning. There was a tube with red-brownish liquid draining into a bag coming out from under her gown on the left side of her chest. Her left ankle was in a cast and propped up on a pillow. She was awake and tried a wry smile.

"You look like shit," I said with a grin. "I guess you should have come back to the hotel with me instead of waiting, like I suggested. Sorry."

"Hi, Irish. It's okay," she said rather sleepily as she did her best to smile again.

"How are you feeling?" I asked.

"I feel fine except for this fucking tube in my chest, my broken ribs, my lacerated thigh, and this goddamn broken ankle. Other than that, I feel just chipper as hell. Oh, also, my head is splitting with pain. So I'm doing fine. How about you?"

"You need to watch that nasty tongue of yours. My grandmother would get the soap out," I said as I tried to make light of her condition. "Listen, Jennifer, I talked to the doctor, and she said you are going to be just fine. That tube should come out in a few days. Your ankle will be in the cast for about six to eight weeks, but after that, you'll be back to normal. No big deal. You're tough!"

With that, tears came down Jennifer's cheeks and turned into slow, moaning sobs. "Irish, someday I'm going to tell you what's going on. I'm not tough, I hurt like hell, and I'm scared to death.

Look, Irish, you don't know what's going on, but someday, I'll let you in on it." Jennifer sobbed.

"It's too late. I already talked to Jack Casey, and he's told me everything," I confessed.

"What do you mean he's told you everything?" she said in a voice as quiet as she could muster.

"I mean *everything*."

"Really?"

"I'm talking about Joey Pinata, Jack Casey, and the FBI investigation," I whispered.

"How did you get involved?"

"Oh, that was your fault. Remember when you told Jack that he could trust me more than anyone in the union?"

"Oh my god, Irish, I'm so sorry I said that."

"Well, I'm not. Yeah, that and the fact that you're not married to some guy by the name of David Marks. That was quite a scam you had going. If I had known that you were really single, I would have put the MacSween charm on you a long time ago."

"You're such a shit," Jennifer replied, sounding winded.

"Take it easy," I said to her.

"I think I'm going to call Riona and tell her you're hitting on me in my weakened state of mind."

My smile turned to a frown, and I asked, "Why did you tell Jack that I could be trusted more than anyone else on the staff?"

Jennifer ignored my question and asked, "Did Jack think my accident was because of my involvement with him? Does he think Joey is behind this?"

"I asked him that very question, and he said he was almost positive ol' Joey had something to do with it somehow. He is at least going with that assumption. It may just be that Joey is pissed off at you for your outburst last night."

"But do you think he would do this just because I wouldn't screw his dumb ass?"

"I wouldn't think so, and Jack doesn't think so either. That's a pretty severe response just because a guy gets turned down. Maybe he has an inferiority complex. I don't know."

"Then, does that mean he knows I'm helping the FBI? Do you really think Joey would resort to having me killed?" Jennifer asked again with a raspy breath.

"I don't know. I do know Joey never forgets and he never forgives. I just have a hard time accepting the idea that Joey is a killer. I know he's an asshole and all, but I'm still not convinced he's a killer."

"What am I going to do? How can I ever go back to work?" Jennifer asked.

"We're not going to worry about that now. As soon as you get out of this hospital, you are going to fly back to Ohio and take a well-deserved rest."

"Sorry, but the doctors said I can't fly for at least two to three weeks after this tube is removed. Something about barometric pressure and my lung or something. I don't know. I didn't quite understand what he was talking about. I was under the influence of drugs, but I think I better listen to what he says."

"Tell me, Jen, have you talked to anyone about your involvement with Jack Casey?"

"Nobody knows but Jack, David, me, and now you. I haven't talked to anyone about it. I was always too afraid to say anything. I wanted to tell you, but I didn't want to get you involved. I told Jack you were the only one I would even consider trusting."

"Thanks a lot. Now Jack seems to think I can help his cause too. If only the four of us know about your little undercover escapade, why would anyone try to hurt you? Maybe Joey isn't behind this because of the investigation, but then again, maybe you just hurt his feelings when you called him a fucking arrogant bastard, I don't really know. Something just doesn't feel right to me."

"It doesn't make any sense that he would be that angry about last night. It really wasn't that big of a thing," Jennifer gasped. "He could have any one of a hundred different women. Are you aware that he hires professional prostitutes?"

"You mean as opposed to amateur prostitutes? Is that what you're asking?" I countered jokingly.

"Don't make fun of me. It's not fair. I'm under the influence of drugs."

"I call it better living through chemistry. It's probably better to be on drugs than try to be tough. After all, look what kind of effect you have on men. Do you have any other old, wounded would-be lovers that you left in the dust?" I joked.

"Yeah, right, I haven't had a lover in months, probably years, but that's none of your damn business," Jennifer said with as much conviction as she could muster in her condition. It was obvious that it hurt her to talk.

"I was just trying to cover all the bases, Ms. Marks." I rolled my eyes with a questioning look. "What about this David Marks or whatever his last name is? How well do you know him?"

"Let's just say we have been getting to know each other in the past few months. Oh yeah, his last name happens to be Shanahan," Jennifer said, as some color came back into her cheeks.

"Ah, now I'm beginning to see. You and this David guy are a real item, aren't you? Have you been playing house together?" I proudly stated as if I had just found an answer to a mysterious secret.

"David and I have gone out a few times in the last three or four months, but mostly, we talk about the union. He told me that we can make it a real date whenever I can get away from these never-ending strike negotiations."

"So is this thing serious between you two?" I asked with what had to be a surprised look on my face.

"He's a great guy, good looking, smart, has a wonderful personality. There's just not much I can find wrong with him."

"Are you in love?" I asked with a laugh.

"You're just like every other man in the world. A man can go out with a hundred different women and it's accepted, but if a woman goes out with a man one time, she must be in love. Maybe I am, and maybe I'm not. You don't need to know."

"Okay, you're right. So I guess I had better let you get some rest. One more thing I forgot. Just so you know, there is a plain-clothes officer standing watch over you 24-7. So stop your worrying."

I leaned down and kissed her on the forehead and said, "I'll try to get back to see you later. If not today, I will be here tomorrow morning. Oh yes, one more thing, I called your main squeeze and left a message with your answering machine and told him you were in the hospital."

"Ah, thanks a lot, I really do appreciate you and all your help. I just hope you don't get hurt. I hope we both keep our jobs too."

"Yeah, me too. I don't stick my neck out for just any old friends, only those sad and in need of sympathy." I was trying to sound as upbeat as possible. "Maybe when all this mess is cleared up, you and David and Riona and I could get together for a little R&R. I'm looking forward to meeting this David Shanahan. Must be he's a good old Irish lad. He can't be all bad. I think I like him already. See you later. I've got to go."

CHAPTER TEN

left the hospital, jumped into Henry's red Chevy, and drove back to the hotel. The first thing I needed to do was call Riona. I'd only left messages; I hadn't actually talked to her in two days. She would be wondering what I'd been up to.

I wasn't the best when it came to keeping in touch. I hated to think what I'd been putting her through. She deserved much better, but being the shit that I am, I almost had to schedule myself a time to call.

I pulled into the hotel parking lot and parked Henry's Chevy in the same spot I found it. I had the air-conditioning blowing full blast all the way from the hospital, so when I stepped out of the car, the heat was insufferable.

I couldn't figure out how anyone could stand to live in this hot sticky weather all summer. It was just too damn sweltering for me. I felt the sweat running down my neck before I even reached the hotel door. I rather enjoy the changing seasons back in Michigan. That is, until the thermometer dips below zero.

I entered the hotel and made a beeline to the elevator. I rode the elevator up to my floor, pulled out my room card from my pocket, and walked down the hall. I wondered what ever happened to the days when you opened a door with a real key.

The thing I like least about the key cards used in hotels is they don't have room numbers on them. A few nights, after a little too much drinking, I forgot my room number and had to ask the desk clerk what room I was staying in. Embarrassing as it seemed, one night, I was actually in the wrong hotel.

When I got into my room, the message light was flashing on the telephone. I picked it up and pushed the Message button. The voice said, "You have two messages. Message number one." It was Riona. "Hello, Sean. Just feeling a little lonely. Haven't heard from you in a few days. Hope everything is going well. I heard on the news the union may have reached an agreement with the companies. That would be great. I miss you a lot. Wish you were coming home today. Give me a buzz. Love you."

It really felt good to hear her voice. But I wondered why she called me Sean. She always called me Irish. I let that thought go and pondered the young mom-to-be and how she may have touched me in some kind of way.

"Message number two. This is Michael Ferrier. Joseph Pinata wants to see you as soon as you get back. Call his room ASAP."

Sorry, Joey, you can wait. Riona has priority. I'm talking to her first. I dialed my home phone, and after two rings, Riona's voice came on the phone and said, "I'm sorry, Sean and I are not available to answer the phone, so please leave a message." I then heard the ever-present long beep.

"Hi, sweetheart, it's me. Just calling to say hello and make sure you're doing okay. It's nice to hear your voice even if it's only on the recording. God, I miss you. We need to talk. I can't go on like this. I hope to be home by the end of the week. I'll try calling later tonight. I have a couple of meetings, so it may be late. Love you lots. Bye."

I hung up the phone and decided I would take a shower before calling ol' Joey boy. When I removed my shirt, the phone rang. I picked it up and said, "Hello?"

"Hi, Irish, this is Michael Ferrier. Did you get my message?"

"No. I just walked into the room. And don't call me Irish. It's Sean. What was it you wanted?"

"Mr. Pinata wants to see you right now. Come on up, he's waiting for you, Suite 3200."

Not waiting for an answer, he hung up. I said aloud to myself, "I'll be right there, you piss ant. One of these days, brother Michael Ferrier, you are going to piss me off at the wrong time, and I'm going to do a tap dance on your head."

I put on a clean shirt and slacks and ran a comb through my hair as best I could. I was still windblown from my walk this morning and desperately needed a full shower.

I left the room and walked to the elevator where I pushed the up button. As I waited for the elevator, I went over in my mind everything I should and shouldn't reveal to Joey. I hope nobody spotted me having coffee with Jack Casey. I didn't need that trouble just yet.

The proverbial shit would hit the fan if anyone did. If he asked, I would just tell him Jack said he was a detective with the Miami Police Department and was asking questions about Jennifer's accident.

When the elevator came, I pushed the button for the thirty-second floor, the top floor of the hotel. It was no coincidence that Joey was staying up there in one of the executive suites.

Fucking Joey Pinata. I wondered what Joey's penthouse suite was costing his dues-paying members. Probably more than I cared to know. The cost of the room, including room service for every meal of the day and special deliveries of fine wine and expensive liquors, added up to a small fortune that the striking members paid for with their dues.

The trouble was, Joey really felt that he deserved the suite and the other bennies because he was the president. What ego. What a dick.

The elevator door opened, and as I was about to step out of the elevator, I came face-to-face with Tony Wetherby. There was swelling and a large bruise around his left eye.

"Hi, Irish, Mr. Pinata is waiting for you in his suite," Tony said as if nothing had happened last night.

"Thanks, Tony, is he in a good mood?"

"Not today. He's been cranky as shit. I thought he would be in a good mood since the strike is most likely settled, but apparently, he's riled up about something. Be careful, don't piss him off."

"Thanks for the warning," I replied as I stepped out of the elevator and Tony stepped in.

Before the door could close, Tony turned and stuck his hand out to stop the door, saying, "Hey, Irish, I'm sorry I was such a dick last night. I had way too much to drink. I hope you're not feeling too bad. I just went off. I'm sorry it happened. I know you took some pretty good shots to the ribs. How's the breathing?"

"A little difficult but I'll survive. Did I do that to your eye?" I asked, a little mystified.

"Yeah, you have a hell of a right cross. It actually knocked me back a step, buckled my knees. I didn't think of you as a fighter. Hell, I didn't think you knew anything about fighting."

"I did a little boxing in the ring when I was a kid. I was the state Golden Gloves champion, but I also grew up on the streets of Detroit. So in my neighborhood, you had to learn to fight, or you wouldn't survive out there."

Tony smiled and said, "I guess I broke the number one rule, never underestimate your opponent. What the hell, don't worry about a little swelling. It's no big deal. Let's just forget last night happened. Is that all right with you?"

I was surprised, but said, "Sounds like a good deal to me."

As we shook hands, he grabbed mine tight and said, "Mr. Pinata doesn't need to know what happened to your face. I didn't say anything to him about our little scuffle. I think it would be better if he didn't know. That okay with you?"

"I'll just tell him I fell in the tub and hit the spout. He'll never know, unless someone else tells him. Did he ask you about your bruised cheek?"

"No, he never even saw it. He was too angry to look. I do have a pretty swollen cheek," Tony admired, touching his face.

"Don't worry about my face. I didn't like being handsome anyway," I said with a casual smile.

Then I said to him, "Look, I say things I shouldn't when I'm drinking, and you called me on it. That's your job. It's this fucking strike. It's lasted forever. I just feel bad for all of our members who have been fighting to survive this last year. I didn't mean anything by it personally. I hope Mr. Pinata doesn't find out what I said."

Tony smiled and said, "If you were referring to Michael Ferrier, I've already taken care of that.

He won't say a thing. We had a little understanding earlier this morning, a little heart-to-heart talk, if you know what I mean."

I had to smile again and said, "Well, then, I thank you for that big favor, and I'll think twice from now on before I run my mouth."

"Yeah, but you didn't deserve to get a busted rib and your face rearranged."

"That's probably true, but I'm a quick learner, so hopefully, I won't spout off like that again. No hard feelings. Maybe if there ever is another time, I'll do better."

Tony replied, "Let me say this. I was the former light heavyweight champ of the world. You really don't want to keep fighting me. In the long run, you may get hurt. I would rather have you on my side."

I knew he was giving me a warning, and he sounded sincere, not arrogant. "Thank you for the advice. I would just as soon be fighting with you instead of against you too. I'd rather be on your side too."

He smiled and said, "You're quick and you're tough. I would like to count on you to be on my side."

I didn't answer him. I just smiled. We shook hands, I said thanks, and then he let the elevator door close. It almost caught our hands, but we pulled apart just in time. I felt good about one thing: I had actually landed at least one good punch. It brought a smile to my face.

The entire conversation caught me by surprise. Why was Tony being so friendly, especially after last night? Some things just didn't feel right. Tony wasn't usually a friendly kind of guy, but maybe he had gained some respect for me for fighting him as well as I did.

I couldn't figure out why Tony stayed with Joey. He always treated him like shit, and Tony wasn't the kind of person who would take it. The money must be awfully good. I wondered what inside information Tony knew about Joey and his inner circle. He could be a useful ally if he could be trusted, but at this point, that was highly unlikely.

I knocked on Joey's door, and Michael Ferrier opened up. "'Bout time you got here."

"Relax, Mike, you're going to give yourself an ulcer."

"The name is Michael, not Mike. I've told you that a hundred times," he said angrily.

"Hey, Mike, fuck you. I didn't realize you were that paranoid, Mike." I walked into the suite and looked around. I was quite impressed. There was plush, thick, shag carpet; deep dark leather furniture; a wet bar that was well stocked; and windows that went from the floor to the nine-foot ceiling.

The suite was overlooking the Atlantic Ocean. There was a door to the left that was ajar, revealing a bedroom. Next to the front of the window was a telescope. *Oh shit*, I thought; *I wonder if he saw Jennifer and me on the beach this morning*. I felt a chill of paranoia creep up my spine but let it go.

Mr. Pinata had more important things to worry about than who was walking on the beach together.

"Where's Mr. Pinata?"

"He's in his office waiting for you."

"This place has an office, too?" I asked sarcastically, looking around.

"Yes, through that door, smart-ass," Michael said as he waved at the doorway on the far wall.

I walked over to the door and knocked.

"Come on in, Irish!" Joey bellowed.

I walked into the office, and there was Joseph Pinata sitting behind a large mahogany desk in a huge, swiveling, plush leather rocking chair. The desk was bare except for a single telephone. There was another small desk to his right that was covered with papers and documents of all kinds.

"Irish, my man, have a seat. Would you care for a cigar?"

"No, thanks. I don't smoke cigars. Mind if I have a cigarette?"

"Not at all. Go right ahead."

I lit up my smoke and settled into the chair directly in front of the desk. It was as luxurious as any I had ever sat in. I actually felt pretty comfortable even though I was alone with the mighty Joey J.

"Tell me, Sean, how's Mrs. Marks doing? I understand you went to the hospital. Is she going to be all right?"

"As a matter of fact, I just left her, and she is apparently going to be okay. She has a huge tube in her chest, a laceration on her leg, and a broken ankle."

"How bad are these injuries? I talked to Maria Rodriguez, and she told me Jennifer was unconscious and didn't look very well when they carted her away in the ambulance. Is she still out?" Joey asked as he squirmed in his chair and puffed quickly on his Cuban cigar as if he was nervous about something.

"Let me tell you what I know. She is awake and able to talk. She has a broken left ankle, which is already in a cast. There was a large laceration on her leg that apparently had to be stitched up, so that's taken care of. But the most serious injury is to her chest."

"That's a big chest to be injured," Joey said, as he laughed at his own joke.

I ignored the sexist remark and went on, "Apparently, she has broken ribs that punctured her left lung. She has a tube in her chest that is draining the fluid from her lung. The doctor said she would be fine in time, but the next few days, she will really be uncomfortable because of the tube. I guess it's pretty painful."

"Did she say anything about who hit her or how it happened?"

"She said she didn't remember a damn thing. In fact, she asked me what happened. Must have hit her head."

Joey jumped right in, saying, "She's been acting very strange lately. I wanted to talk to her last night about a new assignment I needed her to do for me, and she just blew up. I never knew words like that could come out of anyone as pretty as her. Whew, she really let me have it and for no reason. She's lucky I didn't fire her on the spot, but there are a lot of us on the edge due to these lengthy negotiations, so I let it go. She's a good hard worker. I'm glad I promoted her."

Joey floored me with his sincerity. It was totally unlike him. If I hadn't talked to Jennifer this morning on the beach, I would have no choice but to believe Joey's lie.

"Were you going to assign her somewhere other than her home region?" I asked cautiously.

"There's a local union of mostly women down in Texas that has big problems, so I thought a woman representative would be a wise choice, but apparently, Jennifer has other ideas."

"Was this a temporary position for her?"

"Sure. I figured it would take her about a month to get things settled down, and then she could go back to her home unit in Ohio. Why? Did she say something to you about it?"

I felt myself on the spot. I knew if I told the truth, Joey might suspect me of being in on the investigation, or the very least, he would know Jennifer had told me about his sexual offer last night. If I lied, I wouldn't be able to talk to Thomas Sharpe or anyone else about it. I decided I was getting good at lying, so I might as well keep it up.

"No, she never said anything to me. It just seems strange that Jennifer would get so pissed about another temporary assignment. Hell, you've had her on plenty of temporary gigs before. What's the big deal about this one?"

"Maybe this strike business has gotten to her," Joey said as he took a casual drag on his cigar. "What the hell, that idea is out anyway, what with her injuries and having a tube in her chest and all. How long do you think she will be out of work?"

"I have no idea. Right now, she has to concentrate on getting better. I wouldn't be surprised if she's off work a couple months." I was trying to sound unconcerned. "Is this why you wanted to see me, or is there something else?" I added.

"As a matter of fact, there is something else. Have you ever heard of a man called Jack Casey?"

I was about to swallow my tongue but did my best to not show any reaction. I remained as calm as I could while I looked Joey directly in the eye and said, "No, I've never heard of the man. Who is he anyway?"

"He's just someone trying to cause this union a lot of trouble. You know how there's always someone trying to destroy this union, like the goddamn Republicans in office or the billionaire CEOs that try to fuck us every chance they get. They're all against us, Irish. Don't trust anyone. They will try to divide us any way they can. We have to keep our guard up. These scumbags will resort to anything to bring us down. They are devious bastards, every one of them. I wouldn't trust them with my worst enemy," Joey said as he puffed on his twenty-dollar cigar and blew out a long stream of blue smoke. "Irish, keep your eyes and ears open and let me know if you hear of any rumblings. It would go a long ways toward your career, if you know what I mean—not that your career is in danger, or anything. Just keep your eyes and ears open. You can go now unless there's something you need to talk to me about."

"Nothing other than getting this contract signed and sealed," I said as earnestly as I could.

"Then I guess this meeting is over." With a wave of his hand, Joey was through with me. He picked up the lone telephone on the desk and dialed a number, turned his big leather chair around, and said no more.

Joey, the arrogant prick, was finished with me for the moment, and I knew it. Joey had handled me in his usual true Pinata style. Control the situation, and end it abruptly.

CHAPTER ELEVEN

As I returned to my room, I had more to chew on than I had realized. Was Joey threatening me by telling me my career wasn't in jeopardy when it really was? It seemed like everyone was trying to manipulate me.

Joey seemed very sincere and not at all like I had expected. There was something bothering me, but I wasn't sure what. Tony had said he was in a foul mood, but he wasn't that way at all. Jennifer had said he verbally raped her. Jack Casey had laid things out like the union was unaware of the FBI's investigation.

Maybe that's what bothered me. I had been ready for a confrontation with Joey, but didn't get one. Maybe Tony and Joey were having a feud of some kind. Whatever it was, something just didn't sit right. I was puzzled.

I hadn't expected Joey to even mention Jennifer's reassignment to Texas, but he had brought it up himself. Then his mention of Jack Casey really blew me out of the water. It was like he knew everything Jennifer and I had talked about. I didn't like this. There was something amiss. Something didn't feel right. My gut feeling was talking to me, and I had to listen.

Was Jennifer holding anything back, and if so, why? Jack Casey, who is this Jack Casey? Was he really who he said he was? Did he have some other hidden agenda? What should I do?

I sat up and decided the best thing to do was a little detective work. One thing I learned from my boxing days was to keep your adversary close and know him better than you know yourself. But who were my true adversaries, and who were my true cohorts?

I thought I knew what kind of person Joey Pinata was, but suddenly, I wasn't so sure. I thought I knew Tony Wetherby, but now I wasn't sure about him either. Even Jennifer was a question mark.

Before I could concentrate on Joey, Tony, or Jennifer, though, I would first find out who Jack Casey really was.

Part of my job in the union was to be involved in local, state, and national politics. I had been on the political action committee of the union for fifteen years. The PAC's task was to seek out candidates running for public office and see how they voted with regard to vital union positions.

In return, the union supplied the pro-union candidates with campaign workers and, indirectly, money. The federal laws regulating campaign financing were very restrictive when it came to unions giving money to candidates. Sometimes, campaign funds were funneled underground so as not to draw attention.

Large corporations, on the other hand, were free to lobby and spend millions getting pro-business candidates elected.

Both sides of the bargaining table realized that anything passed into law overrode any agreement signed by the union or the corporation. What could take months, sometimes years, of negotiating could be destroyed with the stroke of a pen in Washington.

In the union's viewpoint, supporting pro-union candidates was mandatory, not optional. Unions lobbied at the state level, as well as the national level. We were constantly hard at work urging legislatures to vote in favor of pro-union issues. The biggest problem was that for every dollar spent in support of pro-union candidates, corporations would spend thousands or millions of dollars supporting pro-business candidates.

The laws passed by the pro-corporation candidates could bring unwanted change to America. Issues like minimum wage, health care, union representation, and in turn, dignity on the job and the health and safety of workers, were at risk on a daily basis.

With one stroke, lives could be changed by laws hidden deep within the passage of bills in Congress that affect workers' lives and those of their families. Pork barrel legislation mostly benefits the rich, at the cost of jobs for the middle class. Unions knew that shipping jobs out of our country could in no way be misconstrued as being good for America.

One of the jobs of the president is to nominate people to serve on the National Labor Relations Board. The board rules on many legal issues concerning labor-management legal problems. If the president is anti-union, the candidates appointed are usually anti-union and so are their rulings.

I had worked on the state, national, and local Political Action Committee for over fifteen years and had acquired a few friends during that time who I thought may be able to help me find out more information on this Jack Casey.

Matthew Tennyson was the Democratic US congressman from my home district in Michigan. We grew up together, and had been friends for thirty years. He had a record of supporting union issues throughout his career. I was sure that Matt could get me the scoop on Jack Casey. If Jack was really from the FBI like he claimed, Matt would know, or could at least find out.

I looked in my little address book and found Matt's private phone number in Washington. I dialed the number and waited as the phone rang. On the fifth ring, a woman answered, "Hello, this is Congressman Tennyson's office. May I help you?"

"Yes, this is Sean MacSween from the International Truckers Union. I was wondering if the congressman was in, and if I could talk to him?"

"The congressman is a very busy man. He doesn't have time to talk to everyone who calls. You will have to make an appointment to see him."

"Listen, Matt and I have been good friends for thirty years. He told me to call him any time I needed to and he would speak to me. Please tell him I am on the line and that it's vitally important that I speak to him. Please at least tell him that much."

"Just a moment, sir. I'll check, but I don't think he will be able to talk to you at this time," the woman said in a snippy voice as she put me on hold.

The hold music came on for about twenty seconds before Congressman Tennyson finally answered the phone. "Irish, give me your number and I'll call you back in ten minutes."

"Sure, Matt. Is there something wrong? You sound distressed."

"Just give me your number. I'll call you back."

I gave him my hotel phone number and hung up. Now what was up? This was getting weirder by the minute. What in the hell was going on with Matt?

After ten minutes, the phone rang. I picked it up, thinking it would be Matt.

"Hello, Matt?"

To my surprise, it was Joey Pinata's voice, not Matt's. "Irish, listen, I just want to warn you that we have very reliable information that it's even more certain the government people are coming after this union of ours. They're pissed about the strike. They are people who want to tear this union apart. I'm calling our entire staff myself to tell them not to speak to anyone about private union affairs. If anyone goes against my orders, they are to be fired immediately. Is that clear?"

"Sure, of course, that's clear, but why does the government want to come after us?"

"That's none of your concern right now," Joey said, just before he hung up and the phone went dead. I heard the click on the other end, and once again, I knew Joey was through with me. Call me crazy, but that was bad timing.

I had a strange feeling that it was a warning more than anything else. Now I was almost certain he had my roomed bugged and my phone tapped.

I would check with some of the other staff to see if Joey actually called them too. Was he really giving just me a warning, was there something more, or was I just getting paranoid? I didn't believe in coincidences.

I had no more than hung up and the phone rang to bring me out of my deep thoughts. I picked up the phone and answered, "Hello?"

"Irish, this is Matt. Sorry about not being able to talk in my office. Sometimes, I feel like my phone is tapped."

"I know the feeling. What's shaking in Washington?"

"Trouble. I needed to talk to you privately, so I'm glad you called."

"Wait a minute. Let me get to a payphone, and I'll call you back in five minutes. Give me the number where you are. I don't want to talk on this phone either."

"All right I've got about ten minutes, so make it snappy. Here's my phone number."

I wrote his number down and dashed out of my room, ran to the elevator, and pushed the down button. The door opened instantly. I pushed L for lobby. It was a non-stop descent. That was a surprise. Maybe my luck was changing.

I went to the payphone, put in my pay card, and dialed Matt's number.

He picked up immediately.

I asked, "So what's going on?"

"I wanted to warn you about what's happening here in Washington, and I've been meaning to call you as soon as I got the chance, so I was glad you called me. There are certain people in the president's inner circle of friends who are hell bent on getting back at that union of yours, especially your union president and his vice presidents. Some of my Republican friends have told me off the record that the president, with some urging from Republican members of Congress, has implemented a special investigation into the dealings of the ITU."

Matt stopped a moment to catch his breath, and then continued, "The word out here is they want Joseph Pinata's balls on a platter, and they don't give a damn who gets in the way. Hell, Calvin Moss, the majority leader in the House, told me personally that they are going to destroy your union if it's the last thing they ever do. This is big stuff, Irish. They have given the FBI a high level of cooperation to get this done. People's heads are going to roll, I can assure you of that."

"I'm not surprised. This strike must have pissed off a lot of people in high places," I responded.

Matt laughed. "You could say that. The strike cost many of the president's biggest supporters millions of dollars, and it cost the president votes, and he doesn't take kindly to that. You guys made him look weak, and he's not going to just let it go. Not a good move, if you know what I mean. Pinata even has other unions pissed off at him, not to mention international conglomerates. The ITU strike affected the whole goddamn world. Hell, the fucking stock market is at its lowest level in ten years. What'd they think would happen, that everyone would just pat each other on the back and say let's get back to work?"

"I know that, Matt. A lot of us have been talking about that very thing for the past year of this strike. We're well aware of the anger and grief it's caused. We just couldn't talk Joey into any compromise. He has a hidden agenda, and nobody knows what it is. This strike's gotten out of hand, and the longer it's lasted, the more powerful he's become. He feels he's untouchable."

"Don't be so sure about that," Matt responded emphatically.

"I called to ask if you knew a guy by the name of Jack Casey."

"Jack Casey? Why, hell yes, I know Jack Casey. Jack's the number one man in the FBI's investigations into organized crime and now, your union. Why are you asking if I know Jack?"

"Well, Jack's been here asking some questions about the union, Joseph Pinata, and some of the union hierarchy. How well do you know him? Is he a man of his word?"

"I got to know Jack during the congressional hearing on organized crime back in 1996. I was the goddamn chairman of the committee, and Jack and I became very good friends."

"Do you trust him?"

"Has Jack come to you for information about Pinata and his bunch of hooligans?" Matt asked as he answered my question with a question. I could sense nervousness in his voice.

"Let's just say I'm trying to decide who the good guys are and who the bad guys are. Let me put it this way, Matt—if Jack Casey tells you something, is his word good?"

"You can take it to the bank," Matt responded resolutely. "Jack's the most honest man I've ever met, a man of his word. He will never double-cross you, ever. He's old-fashioned, loves God and country. He's one of the good guys. He was a colonel in the Navy SEALs. Then he was the youngest person to ever make commander in the SEALs' history. He's the kind of guy who would give his life for his country without hesitation. Trust me! Back when I first met him, we were in a bar having lunch when these three guys were running their mouths about how horrible our country is. He took offense and kicked all three of their butts in about ten seconds. He was impressive."

"That's good to know. It helps a lot. What else do you know about this investigation?"

"All I've heard is that the president is so goddamn pissed he will stop at nothing, and so are some key members of congress. Hell, even some of my Democratic pals who have been your greatest supporters are pissed. They want Joey baby's head on a platter along with his balls, and will go to any extreme to get them." Matt hesitated a moment to collect his thoughts and said, "The political pressure is mounting every day. Plus all the corporate CEOs who have the president in their pockets are crying to get revenge. We Democrats are not always informed about high-level Republican vengeance, if you know what I mean."

"I have one more question for you, Matt. Do you know a David Shanahan? He works for the Federal Labor Board."

"No, I can't say as I do. I'll have him checked out for you," Matt offered.

I'd heard enough to satisfy me for the time being. "Thanks for all the info, Matt. It really helps a lot. Do you think you could let me know if you hear anything new?"

"Yeah, how can I reach you?"

"I'll give you my cell phone number."

"No, no, cell phones are too risky."

"Do you have my home phone?"

"Yes, I do."

"You can leave a message there with Riona. Is that all right?"

"Well, I'd rather just leave a message for you to call me. I don't want a recorded message that could come back and bite me in the ass. Irish, there are not too many people I would stick my neck out for, but you and I go back a long way. But please remember, you and I never talked. I don't want my ass in a sling too."

"Matt, you have my word on that. I would never hang you out to dry. I value our friendship. Always have and always will."

"You be careful, Irish. I don't want you taken down with the rest."

He hung up the phone, and I felt a little better. Matt had never crossed me before, and there was no reason to think he would now. Matt was one of the few honest people in Congress, as far as I was concerned.

CHAPTER TWELVE

returned to my room and took a shower to remove the grime that seemed to blanket my body, and to freshen my mind. The hot water seemed to wipe away the tension. A hell of a lot had happened, and I was pretty exhausted. When I finished the shower, I got dressed and sat on the bed to think. I had about an hour before I had to meet Jack, so that was just enough time to go downstairs to the hotel restaurant and get a beer.

I took the elevator down to the lobby and walked into the hotel bar. The hostess seated me in a corner table that happened to have a clear view of the restaurant entryway. They had Bud Light on tap, so I ordered a tall twenty-four-ounce draft. I lit up a smoke, even though I was supposed to give that up along with the beer. *Maybe tomorrow*, I told myself.

I looked up at the entrance to the bar and noticed Thomas Sharpe walking through the doorway. I got up from my chair and softly yelled, if anyone can really yell softly, "Hey, Thomas, want to join me?"

"Oh, Irish, sure, I'd love to. Thanks."

Thomas walked over to the table and we shook hands. He sat down, loosened his tie, and waved to the bartender, indicating he would have the same as me.

He was medium height, about five eleven, had a full head of dark wavy brown hair. His body was well-proportioned–very muscular, not bulging, but well put together. His complexion was smooth and clean. He had dark brown eyes with rather bushy eyebrows and an engaging smile with bright white teeth. He was handsome in a rugged sort of way and always neatly dressed.

Thomas was a man of confidence, alluring to most women. Sophia Pinata fell for him, and he for her, and that's all that mattered. Joey wasn't happy with him as a son-in-law but had little say in this arrangement. Sophia loved him, and she would not let her father dictate to her who she could love and who she couldn't.

"How's Jennifer Marks doing?" Thomas asked.

"She's pretty sore. She has a punctured lung, three broken ribs, a huge laceration on her left thigh, and a broken ankle—and her face is so swollen her left eye is closed."

"Wow, that's a bundle of injuries for her to deal with. I couldn't believe it when I heard," Thomas replied.

"The doc says she's going to be all right, but for the next few days, she's going to be one sore little puppy."

"That's really tragic," Thomas said sincerely. "How in the hell did she get hit right here in front of the hotel?"

"I guess some bastard tried to run her down." I tried to put as much perplexity in my voice as I could muster.

"Yeah, that's really bizarre. Henry Rodriguez told me the police officer thinks it was actually intentional," Thomas added with purpose.

"Yeah, I know, but why would anyone want to hurt her?"

I looked at Thomas and wondered just how much I could trust him. After all, he was married to Joey's daughter. I took a chance and thought I would press him just a little.

"This sure has been a bizarre week, what with the strike settlement, Jennifer's possible attacker, and now Mr. Pinata calling all his reps to warn them about a possible government investigation into the union. It seems like the week started off great but then turned to shit."

"What investigation are you talking about?" Thomas asked, surprised by the comment.

"Mr. Pinata called me just a little while ago to warn me about a government investigation into private union affairs. He said he was going to call every staff member himself. Didn't he say anything to you?"

"I haven't heard a word," Thomas admitted.

"He probably hasn't gotten to you yet," I said calmly.

"He should have. Hell, I just left his office before I came down here for dinner, and he never said a word."

"That is strange because he was kind of upset when he called me a little while ago. I don't know, maybe you should just let him come to you about it. Wouldn't want him to think I was talking in public about it."

"Maybe you're right. I'll just wait and see," Thomas said calmly. "What was it you wanted to talk to me about over lunch?"

"I heard this morning that Mr. Pinata was transferring Jennifer to Texas, and I wondered if you knew anything about it. It just seemed strange to me that he would want to take a woman off his staff after all the work you did to get him to hire one."

"I don't know what you're talking about there either. I was just in a meeting with him and all the VPs, and nothing was mentioned about transferring anyone," said Thomas, as he shifted his eyes and looked confused. Thomas paused for a moment and then said, "This is a surprise to me. The last I knew, Mr. Pinata was happy with Jennifer. I don't have a clue what you're talking about."

I could sense that Thomas was leveling with me, so I added, "I don't know what's exactly going on either, so let's just let this all lie. Maybe something will develop so we get a clearer picture."

Thomas then asked me, "Did you hear that Joey has hired two bodyguards for each of the higher staff members?"

"No. What the hell would make him do that?"

"I honestly have no idea," replied Thomas with a disgusted look on his face.

I thought now might be a good time to talk this out with Thomas. He seemed very perplexed with his father-in-law. So I took the plunge. "Let me ask you something. Are you happy with the way Joey runs this union?"

"Am I happy? Hell, no. I'm disgusted with him most of the time. He's dragging this union down to its grave while I do nothing to stop him. We should all be ashamed of ourselves for letting him intimidate us to the point that we turn our backs to all the shit he has pulled over the last year or so. I keep hoping someone will step forward and challenge him to stop this stupid strike. He had the settlement we needed eleven months ago. It's like he is trying to destroy this union on purpose."

"I thought I would never hear anyone who felt the same as I do. I am so pissed about letting him tear this union apart at the seams. I want to do something to stop him, but I don't know where to start." I confessed that much to see what Thomas's response would be about Joey, his father-in-law.

Thomas said, "Maybe if the two of us can make a pact to join together to stop Joey, we could possibly entice others to join us. But how do we go about doing that without being fed to the wolves?"

I immediately thought of Jack. But I couldn't possibly tell Thomas about him just yet. I didn't know what liberties I could take as far as recruiting him to the cause. Plus I wasn't 100 percent sure Thomas was serious and not a plant. I would have to talk to Jack about Thomas's interest.

But I had to tell him I had something going as far as saving the union. So I said to him, "Thomas, I need you to trust me for just a little while. I am aware of certain individuals who are interested in reclaiming this union for our members. Can you give me a couple of days to check things out?"

"Irish, I've waited this long to talk to someone about Joey and the demise of our union, so a couple more days really wouldn't matter. I'll wait until I hear from you. I trust you, and I hope you feel like you can trust me too."

"Can you keep this completely between just you and me? I don't think you should even say anything to Sophia until I get back with you."

"I give you my word that I will speak to no one, including Sophia, until I hear back from you."

"Would you be willing to talk to someone if I line it up?"

"Who is it you're talking about?"

"I can't say at this time, but it will be within the next day or so. I have to get ahold of my contact, which I will try to do today."

"You sound like a man with a plan," Thomas said. "Consider me in."

I was amazed. I didn't think Thomas would be this easily persuaded to join our merry gang of mercenaries. Things were developing faster than I had ever imagined.

After our discussion, we ordered another drink and talked about anything but the union. We talked about Riona; Thomas's wife, Sophia; the upcoming football season; the weather; the beach; anything besides an investigation or Jennifer's injuries or transfer. Thomas was uneasy and found small talk difficult, which was rare with him.

After we finished our beers, Thomas offered to pick up the tab. I'm sure he charged it on his room tab. We left the table and walked into the hotel lobby. I quietly asked Thomas to let me know if he heard anything about the investigation or Jennifer's transfer. He said he would and asked me to do the same.

We shook hands and parted ways, but suddenly, I realized I still had Henry's car keys. I turned around and yelled, "Hey, Thomas. Aren't you and Henry staying on the same floor?"

"Yes, we are."

"Can you give him his car keys? He let me borrow his car earlier today to go to the hospital, and I forgot I still had them."

"Sure, I'll be glad to."

I tossed the keys to Thomas and said, "Thanks."

CHAPTER THIRTEEN

David Shanahan stepped out of a Cadillac and into the shade provided by the huge cypress trees that overwhelmed the circle driveway adjacent to the large portico of the white mansion. The shade provided little or no relief from the scorching sun.

He was dressed in a dark pinstripe suit, crisp white shirt, and red silk tie. He looked like the consummate businessman. He carried himself with grace, his head held high and posture erect and straight. From a distance, he looked calm and friendly, until you looked into his eyes, which were those of a hard man–dark, and almost evil-looking. He was a man who never took no for an answer.

He looked forward to the task ahead of him. He would deal with the man inside the mansion the way he always dealt with those who caused problems. He could not show weakness of any kind.

Weakness was how disrespect and turmoil grew within an organization, and disrespect and turmoil he would not tolerate. He had worked too long to let some imbecile ruin things now that almost everything was in place.

The other doors of the car opened and closed as three more men got out, joining him in the Miami heat. Carlos, who was of Brazilian descent, was a huge man, six foot four and 260 pounds. He seemed uncomfortable in his ill-fitting suit that appeared to be two sizes too small due to his huge neck, large chest, and bulging biceps.

The men from the backseat were equally intimidating, but in another way. They had the appearance of well-proportioned athletes, with large chests, narrow waists, and piercing gray eyes that showed no kindness or tenderness—only anger and hate.

Kit and Kip were brothers who were hired for just this sort of problem. They were enforcers who would impose their will on anyone who disagreed with them or the man they worked for.

They were both wearing loose but well-fitted dark sport coats without ties, gray slacks, and white long sleeve shirts opened at the neck. Their black wing-tip shoes were specially made with steel toes.

Kit and Kip walked up onto the large covered portico of the Southern mansion and walked through the double doors without knocking. David followed, while Carlos was the last through the doors.

The impressive foyer was dominated by the huge double-wide marble staircase with thick, Brazilian mahogany rails that must have cost thousands. They walked across the marble floor, directly past the staircase into the large living room. The room was fully appointed with dark leather furniture, a large stone fireplace, and a beautiful ornate chandelier.

In front of the fireplace was a tall, thin man strapped to a wooden chair. He had a long, narrow face, wispy hair, a large nose, and a crooked mustache. He was covered in sweat, with fear written all over his face.

Two men were standing on either side of him, preventing him from attempting a magical getaway. He looked up as the four visitors entered the room and immediately started struggling with the ties that bound him to the chair.

"Hello, Freddy," the man in charge said as he walked up to him.

"Hello, Mr. Shanahan. Let me explain what happened. Please, please let me explain," begged Freddy, with fear dominating his voice.

"I plan on letting you explain how you lied to me about taking care of our loose end. I want to know exactly what happened and why. Why you *lied* to me, you little weasel. You could say your life depends on it, Freddy."

David Shanahan turned away from him and nodded to Kip before Freddy could say anything. Kip took a small step toward Freddy, and with the back of his hand, hit Freddy across the nose, breaking it with little effort. You could hear the bone break, and instantly, blood gushed out all over his shirt as the back of his chair slammed to the floor.

Freddy screamed and cried out, "Oh my god, why did you do that? I didn't even get to explain anything yet." Then he started crying.

"That's just so you know I'm not fucking around," David said with a smile. "You better have one hell of an explanation to satisfy me. I'm tired of your bullshit. You've had enough time, you piece of shit. Where is he?"

Freddy started shaking violently as tears streamed down his sweat-covered face. Kip stepped over to pick up the chair and set it upright. He then proceeded to slap Freddy again, this time, with his open hand. There was enough force to snap his head back, but only enough to rock the chair, not make it fall.

Freddy screamed again. "Please, please don't do this. I'm not a killer. I couldn't kill him, I just couldn't. I made him promise me that he wouldn't say anything. He gave me his word."

"His word!" David yelled. "You don't even know who he is. How can his word be any good, you stupid ass? I have to find him. Where is he?"

It was totally quiet for ten seconds. David could feel his heartbeat rising the angrier he got. Then he said, "Your 'friend,' who you don't even realize could ruin everything. You couldn't control him in the first place. He acted on his own. I told you I did not want Jennifer hurt. He fucking ran her over with his truck, almost killed her, for Christ's sake. Then you lied to me and said he was taken care of. Why should I spare your worthless life? Give me a good reason."

Freddy took two deep breaths, and his shaking subsided a little. "I know I can find him. I will bring him to you. I promise you. He's a member of a gang here in Miami. It takes more than a day. I just need more time, a day or two more at the most. I'll deliver him dead or alive, but I will deliver him to you."

"Why don't you just give me his name, and we'll let Kip and Kit find him?" David said with little remorse.

"I don't know his name. I got him from a friend of a friend. He was referred to me and is supposed to be very reliable. He's a member of a gang. He's not going to go to the police. They hate the police. So you see, you're safe. No one will find out about this. Oh my god, please give me another chance. I will bring him to you if you want."

"You piece of shit. I think I'm just going to kill you. I don't trust you. You're too weak, too pathetic to trust."

Freddy started pleading for his life. "No, no, no. Please let me try. I don't want to die. Don't kill me. Please."

"Give me one reason I shouldn't kill you."

"You need me to find him. Without me, you'll never be able to quiet him. I'm going to help you get him. I promise."

David thought about what Freddy had said and realized he was right. There was no way to locate this guy; he didn't even know what he looked like, didn't have a name or a description.

He decided this was his only chance of locating the piece of shit, so he relented. "I'll tell you what I'll do. I'm going to give you twenty-four hours to find him. When you do, you tell Kip and Kit, and they'll take it from there. You don't have to worry about bringing him to me or killing him. Kip and Kit will take care of him for me. So for the next twenty-four hours, you will have company. Kip and Kit will be here to make sure you don't decide to run off somewhere. You locate our mystery man, and I will call us even. If you can't find him in twenty-four hours, then I'll return and settle this once and for all. Do you understand me?"

Freddy looked relieved and said, "Yes, I understand you loud and clear. Can I have the freedom to leave this house so I can go see my contacts? I need to be free to do my thing so I can find him."

David smiled and said, "Anything you need, just so long as you find this fucking idiot. But remember, my two friends will be with you at all times. I don't trust you, and if you screw me over on this, it will be the last thing you ever do. I am giving you more room than you deserve. You lied to me, and I don't tolerate people who lie to me. It makes me look weak. You have me by the balls. I don't know who this guy is, where to look, or even what he looks like. I need you to do this for me. If you do this, I will call us even and spare your worthless life. Are we clear?"

"I hear you loud and clear," Freddy said, thinking that his life was all but over unless he could figure out how to get away from David's two goons. As soon as he found the man, his life was over. Either way, he knew he was in too deep and that David was too vicious and evil to allow him to live.

"Untie him. Let him use the bathroom to clean up. Then get him some food and clean clothes. He needs to be able to think. Do not let him out of your sight. I don't care if he's taking a shit. One of you has to be with him. Is that clear?"

"Yes, boss," Kip and Kit said in unison.

If they didn't follow his orders to a T, they would be the next ones sitting in the chair by the fireplace. David Shanahan turned to Carlos and said, "Come on, let's get out of here. We have work to do."

They turned and walked out of the room, leaving Kip and Kit alone with Freddy. They knew what had to be done once they located the missing man. Freddy had to die.

CHAPTER FOURTEEN

I walked out of the hotel lobby, and had the valet flag a passing cab for me. I gave him a couple of bucks and climbed into the taxi. I gave the cabbie Jack's address and settled into the seat. Casually, I looked around to see if anybody was following us. Strange, but I had a feeling that someone was watching my every move. I wanted to just wave it off as another personal paranoia.

I went over in my mind the conversation I had just had with Thomas, and it was apparent that Joey wasn't talking to every rep about a government investigation. Thomas didn't know about it, so if he didn't know about it, probably no one else did either. He said he didn't know anything about Jennifer's transfer, and I was sure he was telling the truth.

After ten minutes, we pulled up in front of Jack's apartment building. I paid the cabbie a twenty for a fifteen-dollar fare, got out of the cab into the sticky Miami heat, and walked up to the front door of the building.

It was like any other in the inner city of Miami—dirty red brick, a postage stamp–sized yard with uncut grass, a broken screen door lying next to the narrow sidewalk, and dirty windows that ran down both sides of the front door.

It looked like the last time anyone did any maintenance on the building was back when it was built fifty years ago.

I pushed the button to Jack's apartment, waited a moment, and then heard a buzz and a crackling voice that–I think–said, "Come on in."

I pushed the front door open and walked into the building. The air was cool, damp, and stale, with a musty-smelling odor. It was almost cold—not like temperature cold, but like an odd mixture of cold atmosphere and an eerie feeling that triggered chills. I instantly felt a sense of caution, but I didn't know why.

Even though I knew I should walk up the stairs, I took the antiquated elevator. It was slow and creaked like it was going to free fall any minute. It didn't.

When the elevator opened, I found myself in a hallway that hadn't seen a paintbrush in at least forty years. I wondered why Jack would stay in a place like this. If there was an earthquake that measured even one on the Richter scale, it would crumble to the ground. Jack's floor was musty smelling, even more so than the lobby.

I walked down the hall and easily found Jack's apartment. I knocked on the door and heard Jack yell, "Come in, it's open!"

I walked into the apartment, and it was just about what I would have expected after seeing the lobby, elevator, and hallway.

The room was a combo living room and kitchen. The sparse furnishings included an old worn couch, an even older chair, and two end tables with lamps that had old torn yellow lampshades. There was a small television sitting on a wooden crate. There was a small kitchen table that was covered with pizza boxes, empty beer cans, and a pile of newspapers. The floor had faded and worn gray linoleum. The walls had originally been painted white, but that was many years ago. The place fit Jack to a T—kind of rumpled and disheveled.

Jack yelled from the bedroom. "Make yourself at home! I'll be right with you!"

I yelled back, "I can't. I could never call this place home. It's too fancy for me."

I walked over to the kitchen table and noticed a small refrigerator/freezer with the freezer door removed and the fridge handle turned upside down. A hot plate on the small counter served as a stove.

I removed some papers from a chair and threw them on the floor onto a pile that was already started. I sat down at the table and yelled into the bedroom, "Is the maid on vacation this week?"

"She's on strike. She wanted a raise, but the fucking government couldn't afford it. Then she wanted to join a union, so I fired her ass." Jack laughed at his own joke as he came out of the bedroom.

"Just think, Jack, without the unions, you may be out of a job. Admit it, without unions, there wouldn't be any criminals to investigate, and then you couldn't afford a place like this," I countered.

Jack was wearing a shirt that was too large for him. It was one of those Hawaiian square bottom shirts that didn't require tucking in. It was the type that tourists wear in Florida. In place of buttons, there were pearl-looking snaps every two or three inches, and two wide square pockets on each breast. He had on beige slacks that were too long. They bunched up at his ankles.

"Now that's a fashion statement if I ever saw one!" I said with a wide smile.

"You're just jealous that I not only live in a lush palace, but wear the latest trends in clothing," replied Jack, with a snappy comeback.

I asked, "Are you really going to wear that outfit in public?"

"I have some snooping around to do tonight, so this fits the bill. I'm a tourist."

"A poorly dressed tourist at that," I responded.

Jack asked, "Would you like a beer?"

"After last night, I swore off booze, but after today, I think I'll postpone the wagon for a while longer. Sure, a beer sounds good," I replied.

Jack pulled on the upside down handle and opened the fridge. He took out two beers. "Glass?" he asked.

"No thanks, I'd better stick with the bottle—at least until the maid gets rehired. If she needs a good union representative, let me know. I think I can get her better pay and definitely a better working environment. This place is a health and safety violation waiting to happen. Does Florida have an OSHA department in its government?" I asked.

"Not real sure, but probably not. Hey, listen, this place is only temporary for a few days. I needed to blend in to the community as a regular guy. It's part of my disguise," Jack replied.

"I'm just ragging on you. But Florida is a perennial Republican state, and everyone knows Republicans do not want anything to do with any type of OSHA regulations. They do have an OSHA department, but it's the most inactive of any state in the union. They claim OSHA stifles business growth, and without OSHA, they see a growth in the medical field due to the increase in job-related injuries."

Jack just smiled and opened both bottles, handing one to me. He took a long pull on the beer and set it on the table.

I said, "No kidding, this really is a nice place you've got here, Jack. Makes me want to move out of the high-rise hotel I'm living in, with a view of one of the most beautiful beaches in the world." I was sorry I said that as soon as it came out. I thought of our members struggling while I lived lavishly in the hotel. It made me feel guilty all over again.

Jack said, "Look at it this way. This place has everything: early attic furniture, modern kitchen appliances, and an indoor bathroom that sometimes even works. Plus you can't beat the modern kitchen."

"Where is the bathroom?"

"It's in the master bedroom suite, along with the toilet that flushes about every third time you use it. But enough talk about my plush accommodations. Shall we get right to it?" Jack responded, trying to ignore my sarcasm.

"Before we do, I have to admit something," I said as I sat down. "I checked you out. I have some friends in Washington, and they tell me you're a straight shooter—bad dresser, but straight shooter—and that you could be trusted."

"I would have been disappointed if you hadn't," Jack responded. "Hell, I had you checked out months ago, so that makes us even. So shall we begin?"

"Before we do that, what did you find surprising in my life?"

"I was surprised that you joined the army at age eighteen and were an Army Ranger for three years, and that you spent those three years in Iraq and Afghanistan. I also found out you were decorated four times for bravery and received the Silver Star for your fighting during the last month over there. Didn't anyone tell you that you're supposed to lay low the shorter the time you have left?"

"I missed that class, and nobody told me about it."

"Not too smart, were you?"

"I haven't gotten any smarter since then either."

"Let's get started," Jack said, to change the subject.

"Sure, might as well," I responded.

"Do you have a problem if I tape our conversation?"

"As a matter of fact, I do. I think, for the time being, we should keep this just between you and me. At least until I feel more comfortable. Is that all right with you?"

"Yeah, no problem for now, but at some time in the future, we will have to get this on official record. But I can see your point. We'll just talk. I might have to jot down some notes once in a while as we talk. My memory isn't what it used to be. It's still good, but short. You don't mind, then, if I write a few things down?"

I smiled and said, "Sure, it's OK. I remember my old man told me one time, 'Of all the things in life I've lost, I miss my mind the most.' I think that applies to both of us. So you and I can take all the notes we want. Do you have another sheet of paper and a pen?"

"Sure, I'll get you some." He got up and walked into the bedroom. After a few seconds, he returned with a notebook and pen. He handed them to me and sat down. Without hesitation, he asked, "What exactly do you do for Mr. Pinata?"

"My official title is administrative assistant to the president of the ITU. Wherever or whenever there is a problem, I'm sent in to find a solution, whether it's a strike, a grievance, or difficult contract talks—you know, whatever."

"What about this strike? What exactly is your function?"

"I have been helping with negotiations by doing research and helping write language for the contract."

"Was that your main job during the last year?"

"Well, for the past year, I've been to hell and back, trying to calm the troops. I was constantly sent to many different local unions to give updates on the negotiations. I now have the unfortunate duty to go to some of our small local unions that gained basically nothing from this strike and tell them they have to settle for less than they would have twelve months ago."

"How will they take that?"

"How would you take it? I imagine they're going to go ape shit when I have the honorable privilege of telling them the contract sucks and that they just lost an entire year's wage that they'll never get back. I either do it, or I'm in the unemployment line."

"So the membership will get a little upset?"

"Yeah, they'll get real upset. Hell, I can't tell them they were pawns used by Joey for his own personal benefit and not theirs. We just learned this morning that Joey, being the concerned union leader that he is, has hired two bodyguards for each member of the executive board. He said some members may not understand the intricacies of a contract as extensive as this one. So he wants to keep all of them safe while we're presenting the contract to our members. Of course, I will not be given the same safeguards. I have to face the membership alone." I could feel my blood start to boil.

"Where do you stand on the contract?" Jack asked casually.

I paused a moment to think of the right answer. I knew I had a puzzled look on my face, but then I calmly said, "Personally? Hell, I think we had a better agreement a year ago, before all of the companies lost millions. Now they can't afford a decent wage increase or the job security that they could have had had we settled back then. Joey screwed the pooch for this union and every member in it. I honestly don't know how I'm going to tell all our members just how screwed they are. I dread that more than anything."

We sat there, just staring at each other for almost a minute, when Jack broke the silence. "Where exactly do you stand in regards to Mr. Pinata?"

I asked, "Do you mean my working relationship or my personal opinion?"

"Both."

"I work with him because I have to. He's not the negotiating giant that the public thinks he is. I sit in on most of the meetings. I'm told what to do but not always why or how. I'm never asked my opinion. On the rare occasion when I am allowed to speak, I'm told what to say and I better stay within their parameters."

"What happens if you get caught up in the meeting and get excited about something and give your opinion on the matter?" Jack asked seriously.

"I get my ass reamed after the meeting, and then I'm told to stay out of the meetings for a while. I guess it's a punishment of some sort. It's like getting disbarred from the staff for a short time. It's no big deal. You wouldn't miss much. The real negotiating is done after regular hours anyway. Everyone knows the regular meetings are no more than a dog and pony show for the press," I stressed, with an edge to my voice.

Jack took a long, hard look at me and then asked, "So you think this strike has continued for more than a year just because Joseph Pinata had a personal hidden agenda?"

"Without a doubt," I replied.

"What do you think his personal agenda is?" Jack asked in a concerned tone.

"I've often wondered that myself. I'm sure he has something going on that we mere mortals are not privy to."

"Why do you say that?" Jack asked in return.

Without hesitation, I jumped right in. "I guess it's pure instinct. It's a gut feeling I get when I know something is not screwed on right. I like to keep my ears wide open. I hear a lot of things.

Things that were not okay a year ago, but now, we are begging for them. Most of our members may not have college degrees, but they can add, subtract, read, and write. When they find out this strike was total bullshit, there are going to be some mighty pissed-off union brothers and sisters."

"Would the members know what was offered a year ago? I thought all negotiations were confidential until everything was settled."

"Things leak out. They always do. It's human nature. People talk. They say things they're not supposed to say. This set of negotiations is no different than any others. Shit happens. After a few beers, people start to talk, and the more they drink, the more they run their mouths," I answered.

"I hear you drink a lot. Do you let your mouth run about negotiations when you've been drinking?"

"The funny thing is *I'm* the opposite. I run my mouth about what the union should be getting our members. I have never bragged about all the wondrous things we hammered out for our members. Most of the time, I'm in trouble for running my big trap about something we didn't do or should have done."

"You seem to be moving rather cautiously. How did you happen to get your face rearranged?"

"I opened my mouth last night about what a shitty deal we're getting for our members, and Tony Wetherby took offense and thought he could shut my mouth."

"Looks like he did a good job."

"He was the light heavyweight champ, but you should see him today. His left eye is partially closed, so I got in some good punches."

Jack smiled and said, "Really? We hear Wetherby is a pretty good enforcer, that he's a man to be reckoned with. How did you happen to close his eye?"

"I hit him with my right hand. How do you think I closed it?"

Jack smiled and said, "Just answer the question."

"I used to box when I was young, and I was Michigan's Golden Gloves boxing champion when I was seventeen. I have to admit he obviously got the best of the fight, but if I was sober, I think I could do a better job on him."

Jack just smiled and said, "I will have to keep that in mind so as not to piss you off."

"From what I hear, you don't have to worry about that. I hear you can handle yourself quite well."

Jack just shrugged his shoulders and said, "I have been meaning to talk to you about our situation here; you know, you helping us with this investigation."

"What exactly are you trying to say?"

"It's common knowledge that once in a while, you have a habit of drinking a little too much. We don't want any slip-ups. There could be harsh penalties if the wrong things were said in public. I am more than concerned about you having too much to drink and running your mouth."

"I'm not going to lie to you. I know I have a problem with my drinking. What can I say? That I'm never going to drink again and that I'll be a good boy and be home in bed by eight o'clock every night? I can't do that. I just simply can't, not right now. I will say that I will do my best to keep my drinking to a minimum, stay out of the bar, and avoid any fight that comes my way."

"I suppose that's all I can ask. Look, I'm not judging you. I do know what you're going through. For years I watched my dad fighting with the same demons you have to face."

I said, "Let's just let it go at that. Deal?"

"Deal," Jack responded wholeheartedly.

I wondered if everyone knew I'm a drunk. I suppose if Jack knew if I didn't take cream in my coffee, he would have to be aware of my drinking problem.

"What do you think of Joey personally?" Jack asked to change the subject and stop the silence.

"I think Joey J is a bigot and an asshole with an ego that's beyond human comprehension. His only concern is for himself. He really doesn't give a shit about anyone in this union but himself. He is a pathetic human being. But mostly, he's just your run-of-the-mill bully. Spoiled as a child and still spoiled as an adult, if you really can call him an adult."

"Does the general membership know what he's like?" Jack asked.

"He puts on a good public face, but he still uses people for his own advantage, and people are becoming aware of it. He never shows any respect for women, and to him, they are good for only one thing. Minorities are tolerated only because they help him publicly and politically. If he has no use for you, he will discard you like a sack of garbage. Basically, I think Joseph Pinata is a big bully. That's the best way to describe him."

"How does he keep getting elected if he's such an asshole?"

"He's not elected by popular vote, that's for sure."

"What do you mean?"

"In the International Truckers Union, the international executive board, which he heads, is elected by the delegates at the national convention that's held once every three years. The delegates are elected by each local union and sent as their voice, their vote. The problem with this is even though the delegates have the right to vote any way their local union wants them to, they are told how to vote. So it's impossible to get him out."

"How's that possible? Isn't their vote by secret ballot?"

"Not at the convention. They have to get up to the microphone and state publicly who their local votes for. It's like a guy gets up and says 'my name is John Doe, I'm from local 1234, and our local votes for Mr. Pinata.' It's all in the open."

"That doesn't seem quite fair. It certainly is not the democratic process, whereas in public elections, we get that private vote," Jack added.

"Well, the ITU is not a democratic association. If you vote against Joey and his agenda, your local union is in deep shit. After voting against him, you and your local union will pay in many ways. From that point on, don't try standing up for your members' rights or your local union's rights, or you'll get stonewalled. They cannot get any support from the international union, and they know it. So for political purposes, they do as they're told. It's a hell of a lot safer in this union to do things as you're told."

"Do the members who refuse to be told how to vote ever get threatened?"

"Sure, they do. They would get threatened physically, but along with that, their life could become a total mess."

Jack asked, "What other ways are you referring to?"

"There are many ways to retaliate, and nothing is ever overlooked. Threats can come in many forms. It's not unheard of to see some very good careers spiral right out of sight. Midnight calls to wives have ruined more the one marriage. Propaganda put out to your membership that ruins your union political career or even your job. Your career is short-lived if you buck Joey Pinata's system."

"What about the other candidates? Don't they ever get a chance to win an election?"

"Don't know. There hasn't been any real opposition for probably ten or twelve years. The caucus in power stays in power forever. It's a fact of life. There has never been anyone with enough balls to run against Joey or anyone in his caucus."

"So the members just go along with that?" Jack asked.

"There was a movement a long while ago to have the president elected by popular vote. Three regional union reps and some local unions were behind it, and after it was shot down at the convention, the three representatives were on the outside looking in. One was outright fired, under bogus circumstances. Another was brought up on charges by the Federal Labor Board, and it was rumored that information was supplied by President Pinata's office. It was never revealed publicly. The third one was harassed so badly, he resigned. His wife was given pictures showing him in bed with another woman. He claimed he was drugged and knew nothing about the incident. Even the local unions were made to pay the price for their defiance. One local was put into receivership. All their money was untouchable. Still is to this day. The other two were forced into amalgamated local unions, which took away all their voting power."

"How does an amalgamated local union take away one union's voting power?" Jack asked.

"Amalgamated unions are made up of units from different companies. Each unit has its own bargaining committee and union representatives that are elected by the members within that particular unit. They negotiate a contract with their individual company.

"However, the amalgamated local union executive board—the president, vice president, recording secretary, financial secretary, and trustees—are all elected by the members of the entire local union, which is all the units within the local union. The large units then control the election of the local executive board, and all decisions involving education, training, off-sight union conferences, and so forth need to be approved by that executive board. They just say no to the small units. The small units have no power to do anything."

Jack said in response, "In essence, the large units in the amalgamated local unions control the local union finances, and therefore, the local union. The international union places those large local unions that support their causes in an amalgamated local union so they have enough members in their units to control all the voting results. What happens to the money the small individual units collect from their members?"

"Once they're put into the amalgamated local union, the money is controlled by the local union executive board, not each unit. The idea behind amalgamated local unions is just. More members equates to more money available for training and such. The trouble is, the small rogue units never get their hands on the money after they're put into an amalgamated local union. They are always outvoted. They've, in essence, been stripped of control of their own money," I said, shaking my head in disgust.

"I'll be damned. I didn't know all that," Jack said, sounding amazed. "I've heard that union politics can be vicious, but it almost sounds like a dictatorship."

"You won't convince any of the ITU leadership of that. I believe it's definitely a type of taxation without representation."

"Tell me, are you aware of anything that might be useful to our investigation?" Jack asked.

"What are you looking for?" I asked in return.

"Such as expenditure of union funds that may be questionable," Jack answered.

I thought for a moment and said, "I'm not real sure. I do know he spends a lot of money on extravagant parties, women, booze, private jets, limos, and luxury hotels—that sort of thing—but I'm not sure where he crosses the line or how he hides it in the financial reports."

"Do you know anything about steering companies to sign agreements that may, in some way, benefit him or any of his associates?"

"As a matter of fact, Joey bargained medical coverage for our members with one particular HMO whose CEO is a neighbor of his, even though their premiums are higher. Joey claims the coverage is better and that accounts for the higher costs. But that's debatable by anyone who has seen their health care coverage and was able to compare it with other insurance companies."

I hesitated for a moment to think, and then said, "There is also a company that supplies all the safety glasses and safety shoes for ITU members. It just so happens that the owner of the company is a cousin of Joey's. Nobody knows it but a few of us on his staff."

"That's real interesting. It could be violation of laws regarding collusion. We'll have to look into that. Can I get the names of the people and the companies they run?"

"That's not a problem, and I'm almost sure there are others that benefit from Joey's off-the-table agreements," I said with a sad tone.

"You know, Irish," Jack said, sounding excited, "we find that wherever there is collusion, there are other spicy, illegal activities going on. Extortion is one of them, and racketeering is another. These could definitely be a potential Achilles's heel for ol' Joey."

I asked Jack, "Have you had a chance to talk with Jennifer since she was injured?"

"No, why? Is there something more I should know?" he asked as he got up to get two more beers.

"No, not that I'm aware of. I was just thinking that she needs to be brought up to speed on everything that has transpired."

"I see your point. Hey, by the way, I've got Chinese being delivered any time now. I forgot to tell you that."

"I thought you said you were a great cook?"

"I am, but I don't cook here. This shithole would probably have roaches coming out of the walls and getting the food while it's still in the pan. What do you think all these pizza boxes are doing here?"

I shook my head and felt myself smile. "You do have a point there. This place is definitely not the Ruth's Chris Steakhouse."

I drained my first beer and grabbed the next one from Jack's hand. I took another long drink from the bottle and let his words sink in. I could feel the effects of the alcohol calming my brain and my body. I should have had those drinks hours ago.

Jack sat back in his chair and tried to absorb what I had just told him. "Do you personally know Frank Bartolone, the treasurer of the union?"

"Sure."

"Does Pinata have any access to union funds without Bartolone's involvement?"

"No, I don't think so. At least, that's what it says in the ITU constitution. All financial expenditures by the International Truckers Union must be recorded by the treasurer, Frank Bartolone, and any disbursements—you know, checks that are written by Frank—must be approved by the ITU executive board beforehand. Then, Frank and Joey both have to sign the disbursement checks."

"There has to be a way that Joey is getting his hands on the money he spends," Jack stated loudly.

"If they truly follow the rules, it takes two people to sign for all disbursements. There's no other way to legally handle union money. I'm just not sure that all the money taken in is accounted for. Plus, the union is audited yearly by the Federal Labor Board. You guys should all know this," I said, challenging Jack.

"We do know all that, and we have been over and over the books a dozen times, and we've come up with nothing. So there has to be some way that he's getting to union money or some other money without leaving a trail," Jack answered. After a long pause, I could see his wheels spinning. Jack continued asking, "So what you're saying is if Joey is mishandling union funds, then Frank Bartolone must be in on it?"

"Yeah, I guess it seems that way, but that doesn't mean Joey may not have other means. If you would have asked me a month ago if Frank Bartolone could be involved in something like this, I would have told you you're insane." I paused to think of the right words and said, "If you think about it, all union dues collected are first handled by Frank before anyone else even knows how much was taken in."

Jack's response was calculated. "In your gut, what would you tell me about Frank's participation in all of this?"

I looked into Jack's eyes to answer, just as the door buzzer sounded. Jack got up, walked over to the door, pushed the door button, and said, "Come on up."

"Hey, how would you know that this person who rang your bell is not a mass murderer? You didn't even ask who it was."

He smiled and said, "I guess I'm more trusting than you," as he opened his shirt to reveal a Colt Special Combat Government Chrome .38 Super under his left arm, strapped around his chest. "I have never been mugged by a delivery boy yet, and I eat a lot of delivery food."

We halted our conversation for a minute until we heard the knock on the door. Jack was waiting for him and opened the door with his left hand, leaving his right hand free access to his weapon.

He opened the door to reveal a teenager standing in the hallway holding a stapled-together bag. I could smell the food inside. Jack paid for the food, closed the door, and said, "Clear the table. The homemade food is here."

I swiped the papers and other unknown articles onto the floor, and he set the food down on the table, saying, "Hope you like sweet and sour chicken, moo goo gai pan, egg rolls, and fried rice. Cause if you don't, you're shit outta luck."

"I hate Chinese food."

"Really?"

"I'm just yanking your chain. I love it."

"Shall I get some plates?"

"I would rather eat the Chinese out of the cartons than off one of your dishes."

He opened the refrigerator. "Look, new plates." He took new disposable plates still in the wrapper from the fridge.

"Why do you have paper plates in the fridge?"

"It's the only place I have that the critters can't get to."

"Oh my god, Jack, how can you stand to live here?"

"Its home. What can I say?"

We ate in silence for ten minutes, and when we were just about done, Jack asked, "Has Joey ever mentioned anything about personal investments to you, or has anyone else you know of heard anything?"

"Not that I know of."

"Ever see his home?" Jack asked.

"Sure, but just once. It's a real beauty, must have cost over a million, and it's right outside of Detroit. Plus it's in a great neighborhood. Guess I'm not one of the in crowd. I didn't get offered a revisit pass."

"We know Joey is not divorced, but does he have another particular lady friend?" Jack was determined to keep prodding me for information.

"I have seen him with this one gal quite often. She's about twenty-eight, about half his age, and quite a looker."

"Know her name?"

"No, I've never been introduced. She could just be a high-priced hooker for all I know. I really don't know who she is or what their relationship is."

"How much does he get for salary, expenses, and fringes?"

"His salary is published in the International Truckers Union constitution—about $124,000 a year plus the bennies."

"The what?" asked Jack.

"You know, *bennies*, the daily benefits that are supplied by the union to its officers. When they are on union business, they have expenditures like meal money, transportation, lodging, and other incidentals, that sort of thing?"

Jack nodded his head in understanding.

I continued, "The use of union funds, for those things, is a little less vague. He does have his own driver who he lists as his special assistant. I'm sure there are other ways for him to get his hands on some of the union money, but if I was a betting man, I would look into those other things. He could be getting money for doing special favors, if you know what I mean."

"So what you're saying is, he's using his union position and influence as the union's president to obtain access to money deals," Jack surmised.

"Yep, that's exactly what I'm saying. I really believe that could be happening. I have no proof, just speculation. I do know he has contacts and access and to so many people in high places, it's incredible. Joey seems to live high off the hog for someone making a hundred and a quarter a year. Did you know he's got a summer home on Hilton Head and a condo in Palm Springs? I just don't get it."

"Yes, we've known that for quite some time. Maybe he's just a great money manager," Jack offered.

I asked, "Do you know if he inherited a bunch of money from his old man? Have you checked that out?" I asked.

"Sure we have. But his old man apparently didn't really leave him a tremendous amount of dough. He was a high roller, but we never found a money trail that he left behind when he died. We obtained a copy of his will, and there was nothing mentioned about large amounts of money. Does Joey gamble a lot?" Jack asked as I got up to get another beer.

"Hell, he gambles all the time. He even flew to Vegas during these negotiations just to spend a few days at the tables. That's why we have about six conferences a year there. He plays poker at the high roller tables."

"I didn't know he could afford that," Jack said, shaking his head. "Did he fly there on union business just to gamble?"

"I'm sure he did, but I'll bet there was some union-related reason."

"He must cover his ass real well," Jack said as I handed him his third beer.

"Do you personally know for sure if Joey ever threatened any particular union official physically, or any local union because they went against his wishes?"

"There was one local union president that I had to deal with who claimed he and his family were receiving threatening phone calls because he tried to get the Federal Labor Board to investigate certain contracts negotiated directly by Joey. Apparently, he felt Joey cut a deal with some companies regarding his members' health care."

"What happened to him?"

"He resigned after a few months, and claimed his local union was being discriminated against by the international union. He said the local union was put into receivership and had their financial books confiscated, and that a recall election vote was somehow passed. He won the recall election, but shortly afterwards, he said he'd had enough of the bullshit and resigned. He told me he and his family were threatened many times and his wife became so frightened she wouldn't let their children leave the house. It made pretty good headlines back in Detroit. An investigation was launched by the local police, but nothing ever came of it."

"When did all this take place?" Jack asked.

"That was about three or four years ago, I guess. Something like that."

"Do you remember this guy's name?"

"Sure, it's Peter Hollister. He lives in Detroit, was president of ITU Local Union 1324. It's a small local that represents about six or seven hundred members, most working in the wholesale food supply business. They haul food to the grocery stores and some restaurants. I do know the International Warehousing Union was found snooping around their local union, trying to get our members to leave the ITU and join them," I added with a shrug.

"Mr. Pinata must have loved that. What happened to Mr. Hollister after he left the union?" Jack asked.

"I know for a year he couldn't find a job any-where. Finally, he moved his family out of Detroit and went to Grand Rapids. He's working in a small nonunion shop that makes door hinges for General Motors."

"What happened to the Warehousing Union's attempt at to get the members to leave the ITU?"

"I'm not sure, but word out was that Mr. Pinata got really involved with their local union politics, and then, nothing ever came of the threat" I responded before I took another pull on my beer.

"I'm going to have Shanahan check this out. It was before he started so he probably isn't aware of it," Jack added. "Do you know of any other union official who may have some hidden shady deals going on?"

"Not really. There have always been rumors, but nothing concrete. I'll start doing a little digging and rack my brain into gear, and I might be able to come up with some other things."

"Well, you've been very helpful. I appreciate all you've done so far. I would like you to report anything you hear in your meetings or rumors that are spreading around. Everything can be of value to our investigation."

"This is just between the two of us, right?" I asked, thinking about possible repercussions from Joey.

Jack said, with as much confidence he could muster, "Just go about your normal business, and no one will know we talked. If anything comes up, you know how to get ahold of me. I'll be in touch every day."

"Sounds good to me. So does this mean we're done here?"

"That's all I have unless there's something more you want to add," Jack replied as I got up to leave.

"Not really. Wait. I guess there are a couple things."

"What are they?" Jack asked.

"Today, Joey called me in to his office, which never happens, and told me that the union is being investigated by high government officials. Then, he shocked me by asking if I knew you."

"No shit? Wonder why he would ask that. We haven't been seen in public other than that café where we had coffee. I had men inside and outside the café keeping their eyes open for just such a thing.

I asked, "Who was the guy inside the café who was watching over us? I didn't see anyone."

Jack smiled and said, "Did you see the two men sitting at the counter having coffee? They were ours. What else did you want to ask?"

"When I talked to Jennifer earlier today, she told me that the guy driving the truck was smiling at her when he struck her. Unless he knew her personally or he was just happily going on his merry way, I don't think it was accidental. This guy was either a person from her past, which she cannot believe, or he was hired to do it. What do you think?"

"I think if you ever leave your cushy union job, we could use you chasing bad guys. You seem to have a good head on your shoulders. But yeah, we're sure without a doubt that it was intentional. Irish, I would like you to come by again tomorrow so we can discuss some strategy for our next move. Do you have any time in the morning?"

"It doesn't appear that I do. We have a meeting that should last a long time. But if I happen to get free, I'll call you. How does that sound?"

"That sounds good to me. I look forward to hearing from you."

With that, we shook hands and I walked to the door, but then I stopped. I turned around and said, "It might be my imagination, but I get the feeling that sometimes, someone is watching me. Think it's just normal paranoia?"

"I don't know what normal paranoia is, but just in case, keep your eyes and ears open and don't talk about this with anyone—especially on the phone," Jack said rather loudly.

"Okay, Dick Tracy, I got it." I opened the door, stopped again, and said, "Jack, you are in serious need of a maid. This place should be condemned. You're not actually paying someone to stay here are you?"

"Actually, I don't sleep here, if you must know. So yeah, I hear you. Now get the hell out, and next time, bring a vacuum or, better yet, a maid—a cute one!" Jack shouted loudly.

CHAPTER FIFTEEN

I walked out of the building and was luckily able to hail a taxi after ten minutes. I said, "Royal Crown Executive Hotel, please" as I entered the cab.

As I sat in silence, I could feel the effects of the three beers Jack had given me. That ever- present calmness from the beer seemed to manifest itself more easily than ever. At the least, it took away what I was feeling when I was sober. That's the feeling I couldn't handle— and that is why all alcoholics drink. They can't stand the way they feel when they're sober.

I wondered, as I sat staring out the cab window, why I couldn't feel like that without a drink. It seemed like I had used to be able to, years ago, when I was young and cocksure of myself, but not anymore. There was always an edge, always an uneasiness that I could feel constantly. It never went away. I hated that feeling that I had learned to live with for so many years.

The cabbie pulled up in front of the hotel, and I got out. "That will be eight dollars, please."

I took a ten out of my pocket and handed it to him. "Keep the change."

It was my intent to go straight to my room, but instead, I headed to the bar. It was like a phantom power I couldn't control that steered me there. I was almost powerless to control my own thinking and actions.

I knew I shouldn't have another drink, but when the devil came calling and told me I needed another drink, there was nothing I could do. It was like the opposite of an allergy. It was a craving I couldn't control. It was that mysterious demon that all alcoholics feel.

I told myself to just turn around and go to my room. Instead, my feet steered me onward, onward to another drink. This was insane thinking. It was like there were two people inside my head, arguing about what I should do. How the hell could I stop this madness? I had to overcome it somehow, some way, but this was apparently not the night for that to happen.

I walked into the bar and immediately smelled the lingering stench of cigarette smoke and booze. The jukebox was blearing some blues tune that seemed to set a depressed mood. I saw Ken Cloutier and another man I didn't know sitting at a table in the middle of the bar.

I walked over to the table and said, "Hey, what's shaking, Ken? You have room for one more?"

"Oh, sure, Irish. I thought you might be in here tonight. Have a seat. This here's David Marks, Jennifer's hubby. David, this is Irish MacSween."

David stood up and extended his hand and said, "Pleased to meet you. Jenny has said so much about you I feel like I already know you." David shook my hand with a firm grip.

I replied, "Same here. It's a pleasure to finally meet you. Jennifer has told me a lot about you too. I'm glad to see that you got my message."

David Marks/Shanahan was a very striking man, about thirty-eight, six foot one or two, with a well-groomed, muscular face offset by thick, curly black hair, tanned skin, and dark deep-set eyes that most women referred to as bedroom eyes.

He wore a dark, pinstriped suit but had removed the tie. His firm handshake came with a warm smile. I could see why Jennifer had the hots for him.

"Irish, I really appreciate you calling and leaving me that message about Jenny," David said with sincerity.

"How did you get here so fast, all the way from Michigan?" I asked.

"Actually, I was in Atlanta on business and checked my messages, and then I caught a flight here to Miami right away."

"When did you get here?"

"About two hours ago. I went right to the hospital for about an hour, but they kicked me out so Jenny could get some rest, so I came over here. Thought I might as well use her room. She gave me her key."

"Do you two know each other?" I asked Ken with a wave of my hand.

"No, we actually just met a few minutes ago. Some of the staff were in here having a drink, and he overheard a few of us talking about the strike and asked if anyone knew Jennifer."

"How's Jennifer feeling tonight?" I asked.

"Kind of rough. They've got her drugged up pretty good. I couldn't believe it when you called," David said as he shook his head.

I looked down at David's beer, saw that it was empty, and offered, "Can I buy you another one?"

"No, thanks, I usually limit myself to one a night. Besides, I want to get up early and get back to the hospital. I'm really worried about her. I called her parents and told them. They're really upset too."

"Are they coming down?" I asked.

"Not right now, but maybe tomorrow. I told them I would call them in the morning to let them know how she's doing."

Though I felt like I could sense sincerity in David's voice, there was something a little out of whack. Even if he wasn't her husband, I could tell that there seemed to be genuine affection and concern that showed through, but something else just didn't seem to fit. It was like his sincerity was a put on. It was my gut feeling, and I'm seldom wrong.

The waitress came over to the table and asked, "Can I get anyone a drink?"

"Not me," Ken said. "I'm going up to Mr. Pinata's to play some cards."

"I'll have a Johnny Walker Red on the rocks," I said. "How about one more drink, David?"

"Okay, I'll take another draft."

Ken said good-bye and left. David and I sat in silence, listening to the blues playing on the jukebox. The waitress brought our drinks. I handed her fifteen dollars and told her to keep the change.

There were only four other people in the bar, and they were at the far booth in the corner. The rest of the place was empty.

"So tell me, Mr. Shanahan, what do you think of Miami?"

It was an almost knee jerk reaction as David's eyes instantly grew wide and he sat up straight, all the while trying to act cool to the question that he thought no one would ask.

"How the hell do you know my name?" he whispered as he bent toward me.

"Relax; I didn't mean to surprise you so much. Jack Casey and I have had a few conversations about Joseph Pinata, Jennifer, you, him, and a lot of other things."

David stammered as he said, "I'm . . . I'm sorry you noticed my reaction, but I'm not real good at this undercover stuff yet."

I laughed. "That's pretty obvious. Jack told me you were very intelligent, had a couple of degrees from Harvard."

"I do, but I didn't major in spy, for Christ's sake. I have a masters in economics and a PhD in labor resources."

"How the hell did you get involved with the Federal Labor Board?"

"They needed someone good with numbers and labor policy. I fit the bill. They made me a good offer I couldn't resist, so here I am in Miami with the girl of my dreams busted up in the hospital."

Nodding my head in agreement, I said, "Jennifer is a real sweet gal. It's too bad something like this happened to her."

"No question about that. I feel sick that she got hurt this bad," he responded.

"She's lucky she didn't get killed," I said grimly.

"God, I hope she's going to be all right," David said, with a sad look on his face.

"Tell me, do you two really have a thing for each other, or is that a put on because of this investigation?"

"Hell, yes. After we were done with this strike stuff, I was going to try to get to know her even better, if you know what I mean."

"No shit? That's great," I said, showing true surprise as I took a sip of my drink and wondered if he was truly sincere.

"We do need to talk about some of these other issues," I said, changing the subject.

"How about tomorrow at about eleven? I should be back from the hospital by then," David replied.

"I can't make it then. We have a staff meeting to go over all the issues with the strike settlement. How about five o'clock tomorrow afternoon. Will that work?"

David replied, "That will work well for me, unless something comes up. Let's plan on it."

David finished off his beer with one long pull and then reached over the table and shook my hand as we said our goodbyes. "Well, I'm calling it a night. It was nice meeting you."

I ordered another drink and sat there, listening to the music. David Shanahan was one cool character–almost too cool. There was something about him that didn't sit real well with me. I couldn't put my finger on it, but something was amiss about David Shanahan. Again, my instincts were telling me something, but what?

My second drink turned into my third, then fourth, until I lost count. Before I knew it, the waitress came over to my table and said, "Sir, it's one in the morning, and we are closing now. You're going to have to leave." I downed my drink, got up, and staggered out the door through the lobby and to the elevator.

I pushed the up button, and the door opened immediately. I stepped into the elevator and pushed floor number nine, but before the doors closed, two men stepped in and stood on either side of me without saying a word. I was so drunk I didn't even raise my head to look at their faces.

I was about to turn to the one on my right to say hello, but before I knew it, a fist smashed into the left side of my face and knocked me to the back elevator wall. Another punch quickly landed in my stomach. I felt myself sliding to the floor just as a foot kicked the left side of my ribs. I felt the air escape from my lungs. I couldn't breathe.

"You dumb son of a bitch, you're fucking around with the wrong people. Take this as a warning, or they may find your sorry ass washing up on shore with the fucking seagulls."

I tried to get up on my hands and knees, but another powerful fist landed on my left cheek again and knocked me back to the floor.

"You're not too smart, are you? Better be careful who you talk to and what you say. Do you understand?"

"Fuck you," I muttered. I felt someone grab my shirt and lift me up just high enough that I was able to throw a hard right to the man's balls. At the same time, I felt another punch to my face. That was the last thing I remembered before everything went black.

I woke and found myself lying on the floor of the elevator. I tried to open my eyes, but the lights were just too bright. My left ribs hurt even worse than they did the night before. I managed to get to my knees, where I could grab the handrail and lift myself to a standing position, but not without tremendous pain. Holding the handrail with both hands, I stood still for a minute to get my balance. The combination of the alcohol and the ass-kicking kept the tiny room spinning.

I looked at my watch. It was almost 1:10 a.m. I'd been out for almost ten minutes. I finally looked up to see where I was, and saw that I was on the fifteenth floor. I finally figured out what the ringing that was banging around in my head was—the emergency stop was pulled out, and the alarm was sounding.

I pushed the button back in, and then hit floor number nine once again. I felt the movement of the elevator as it descended. It came to a halt and the doors opened. I staggered to my home away from home, got out the key card, slid it into the slot, and opened the door. I walked in and immediately saw that the entire room had been torn apart.

The dresser drawers were emptied onto the floor and clothes were everywhere, along with stuffing from the mattress. Even the carpet was pulled away from the wall. What the hell were they looking for in my room? I didn't have anything to hide.

I reached into my pocket for my phone and called Jack. It rang three times, and finally, Jack answered. "This better be important. It's one fucking twenty in the morning."

"Jack, this is Irish."

"Why are you calling me at this hour?"

"It seems that I've pissed a few people off. A couple of guys just beat the hell out of me in the elevator."

"When did that happen?"

"About ten minutes ago. I just now woke up from their beating. Then I came into my room, and someone has torn it apart, even slashed my damn mattress and pulled out all the guts. What kind of sick bastard would slice up my mattress?"

"I don't know, but are you all right?" Jack asked.

"You ever get the shit kicked out of you?

"As a matter of fact, I have."

"Then you know how I feel. No, I'm not all right. I hurt like hell. What do you think?" I felt myself taking quick shallow breaths to avoid the pain in my ribs.

"I think you sound just like I did the last time it happened to me. God, I'm really sorry about this, Irish," Jack replied.

"I thought no one would find out. Who the hell did this to me, and why was I targeted? We just talked this afternoon, and already someone is on to me," I said with a pissed-off tone in my voice.

"What did they say to you?" Jack asked casually.

"They said I was fucking with the wrong people and I'd better be careful who I talk to and what I say, and to take this as a warning, or I'll be found washed up on shore with the fucking seagulls."

"Is there anything else?"

"That's all I remember. What'd you expect, that they'd invite me to morning tea and properly explain my situation to me?"

"Did you get a look at 'em?" Jack asked.

"Not really—I'm kind of drunk, and they never gave me the opportunity. I was always on the floor."

"Do you need to go to the hospital?"

"No, I'll be okay. I did manage to punch one of the guys in the balls. In the morning, I'll go around looking for a man with sore balls. Hey, that's a thought. We could go around and look for a man who's doubled over and ask him if his balls are sore. That's a great idea."

"All right, all right, that's enough sarcasm. Maybe you should take a hot shower. It might help. Then just get some rest," Jack offered.

"Yeah, that's a great idea, but my mattress is all over the place," I replied, and hung up the phone.

I took what was left of the mattress away from the wall and laid it on the bed frame. It still had some padding, so I started pushing the strewn filling back into it. After a few minutes, I decided it was enough to sleep on.

I took off my clothes, walked into the bathroom, and turned on the shower. I stepped in and let the hot water wash all over my body. It felt wonderful. The soreness seemed to wane for just a few minutes.

I stepped out and looked at myself in the mirror. What a mess. The entire left side of my face was swollen, and my left eye was almost closed. How would I explain this in the morning meeting? I needed an ice pack, but it would have to wait. For now, I was too tired.

Damn, what a shitty day it had been. I should have gone to bed when David left the bar. *This senseless drinking has got to stop*, I thought, *and soon.* If I had been sober, I could have kicked the shit out of both of those guys.

I went back into the other room, found a pair of underwear, and lay on the bed on my back. I didn't move for a few minutes, just enjoyed the ride, watching the room spin out of control. I hoped what had happened didn't make matters worse for Jennifer or for the investigation. Had I run my mouth too much? How could I help matters if I didn't get my drinking under control?

"Shit!" I screamed out of frustration. Once again, I had let a few drinks turn into another long night of boozing. I was really getting sick and tired of this lifestyle I was living. I could be better than this.

I let the pounding in my head continue for ten minutes before I decided to get up for some aspirin. Whenever I traveled, I always carried aspirin for moments like this.

When I reached the bathroom, the telephone rang loud and clear. Who the hell would be calling me at this time of night? I lifted the phone.

"Hello?"

"Irish?"

"Yeah, who's this?"

"This is Bob Lee. Remember me? I'm the one looking after Ms. Jennifer?"

"Why are you calling me at this hour? It's too late to think about anything."

"It's not late. It's early. It'll be daylight in four hours. Anyway, some guy came by about an hour ago and said he was Irish MacSween, Jennifer Marks' brother, and needed to see her. I might not be too bright, but I realized he didn't look anything like you," Bob said with a laugh.

"What did he look like?" I asked.

"He was about six foot, maybe a hundred ninety pounds, kind of stocky build, blondish red hair, and reddish mustache. He wore a dark sport coat, no tie, and light gray slacks."

"Ever see him before?"

"No, he's definitely not a local," Bob replied, as if he knew everyone in Miami.

"What'd you tell him?"

"I told him she couldn't be disturbed, that she needed her rest, and that the doctors had her sedated. He left, and I followed him out of the hospital. I did get his license plate number as he got in his car and drove away. He was driving a newer BMW. I couldn't tell you what kind; I'm not too up on all those foreign cars. I'm running an ID on it right now."

"Did you call Jack Casey?"

"Sure, but there wasn't any answer."

"What the hell you mean there was no answer? I just talked to him ten minutes ago. When did you call him?"

"About five minutes ago. Why were you talking to him at one thirty in the morning?" Bob asked.

"A couple of guys beat the shit out of me in the hotel elevator. Told me I was fucking with the wrong people and that I didn't know who I was messing with. I guess I pissed someone off. So you're telling me Jack wasn't in about five minutes ago?"

"That's right," Bob replied.

"But he sounded pissed because I woke him up when I called. That doesn't make sense. Are you sure you called the right number?" I asked.

"I'm pretty sure," Bob replied. "Let me get the number I called and see if it's the right one." I waited a full minute before Bob finally returned. "I couldn't figure out how to use this new phone. It took me a minute." He read the number, and it was the same one Jack had given me.

"That's the right number, but I wonder where he was when you called?"

"Hold on a minute, the station is calling. They must have the license tab run."

After thirty seconds, he came back on the line. "The car was a rental, and the person who rented it was a Mr. John Smith. Guess what we'll find if we search *that* name?"

"You'll probably find a dead-end."

"No doubt, but listen—I'm going to let you get some sleep. I'll follow this up just in case it's not a phony name, but don't count on it. Get some rest."

"I agree. I've had enough for one day. I'm going to bed. Let me know if anything comes up."

"Sure, but I'm supposed to report only to Jack, so don't say anything."

"Not a problem. Is there someone replacing you when you leave?" I asked with my own tired voice.

"Yeah, my partner Dominic is here already. So I'll talk to you tomorrow."

I hung up the phone and went into the bathroom to get the aspirin. The pounding in my head had just intensified; I'd have to take a double dose. I took the four tablets, walked back into the bedroom, and laid on my back in the middle of the lumpy mattress.

I had just closed my eyes when there was a knock on the door. I thought, *who the hell is that?*

I got up and slowly staggered to the door, asking "Who's there?"

"It's me, Irish. It's Jack."

Well, now I knew why he hadn't answered the phone for Bob. I opened the door, and Jack was standing there, but he had on dark glasses and a white wig, with a built-in frown on his face. He looked like an old man extraordinaire.

I said, "Wow, you look good. It's an improvement from your original look."

"Funny, Irish, you look like shit too. Can I come in?"

"Yeah, come on in."

223

Jack stared at my face and said, "Man, they really did a number on you. Can you see okay with your left eye?"

"Yes. It's just swollen. My eyesight is fine."

"I had to come over. I'm so sorry this happened to you. I can't figure out how anyone could have found out we were talking. Are you sure you don't have other enemies out there who would do this to you?"

"There are some pissed-off union members, but it seems more logical that they would go after Joey, not me."

"Can I take you to the hospital?"

"No, I'll be okay. I'm just going to have to explain to everyone what happened to me."

"Use the old 'I fell in the bathtub' adage; it works all the time," Jack offered.

"Do you want to see my humble abode? It's a mess."

Jack stepped into the room and took in the disordered condition of my room.

I asked Jack, "What the hell were they looking for?"

"I haven't a clue. What could you possibly have that they went to the trouble of tearing your room apart for? Hell if I know."

"I think it's pretty obvious they're on to you and me. Somehow, whoever 'they' are knows we met yesterday. You have a leak somewhere."

Jack nodded his head and said, "I think you're right. But who could possibly know? I trust all of my agents. This really upsets me, to think one of my people has changed sides."

"Jack, I'm going to worry about this tomorrow. I'm tired as hell. Good night, Jack. Go home and let me get some sleep."

"I'll talk to you in the morning. Have a good night's sleep," Jack said as he turned and walked down the hall.

I shouted, "Yeah, on my lumpy mattress!" I heard him laugh.

I lay back down, and the spinning of the room became a whirling carnival ride that I couldn't stop and couldn't get off. I closed my eyes, hoping that it would subside, but it only got worse.

I had been there so many times, I knew if I could just hang on long enough, it would slow down to the pace of a slow merry-go-round, which would be more manageable; but even that, I was still powerless to stop.

After about fifteen minutes, I finally felt the room slow and the blackness of sleep come over me. I let it engulf me and eased into the darkness, and I slept.

CHAPTER SIXTEEN

• •

The ringing of the phone shook me from my deep sleep. It sounded like an echo that kept coming back. I finally opened my eyes, rolled over to look at the clock, and saw that it was nine o'clock.

"Shit, I'm supposed to be in a meeting at nine," I said aloud as I picked up the phone.

"Hello?"

"Sean, this is Jack. How are you feeling?"

"I don't know. I haven't moved yet. I'm afraid to.

"Well, get up and let's meet for coffee. We need to talk."

"I can't. I have to be in a meeting five minutes ago. It'll have to wait until after. Mr. Pinata will be pissed if I don't show up. We have to wrap up some details on the strike settlement so there's no telling how long it will take. Can we meet afterwards?"

I asked hopefully. I needed to hear what Jack had to say.

"That's kind of what I wanted to talk to you about."

"What—the contract?"

"Yeah, but it can wait until later. I'm meeting with David at one."

"Yeah, I know. He told me last night," I confessed.

"Where did you talk to him, at the hospital?" Jack asked.

"No, I ran into him in the hotel bar. We had a couple of drinks and talked for about half an hour. He's using Jennifer's room since she won't need it for a few days."

"I'll call you as soon as we're finished. Will that be fine?

"Let's meet at my place again?" Jack asked.

"That sounds good. I'll be there."

"If things change and you get out early, call me and come over. I will make myself available all day."

"Will do," I responded as I hung up the phone and became aware, once again, of the pounding in my head. I rolled to my side to sit up, and severe pain shot through my chest. I hadn't noticed pain in my ribs last night, but now, I could hardly breathe.

I walked into the bathroom and gently brushed the taste of blood out of my mouth. I quickly got dressed, grabbed my briefcase, and went downstairs to the main conference room.

I grabbed a coffee from the table sitting in the hall outside the meeting room and walked in. I saw that mostly everyone was there, except Mr. Pinata and all the union vice presidents.

As always, it was okay for them to be late, but if one of the staff showed up a minute late, they would get the infamous Joey J stare. If you did it twice, you would be banned from the next day's negotiations as punishment.

I flashed back to the hundreds of hours spent in this room, talking and arguing amongst ourselves, as well as with the company's representatives. The room was about twenty feet wide by fifty feet long, had fifteen-foot ceilings and two large ornate chandeliers hanging directly over a gigantic table that could sit forty people.

There were microphones and speakers at each seat, so nothing would be missed. Joey had the ability to turn off anyone's microphone if he so desired, even those sitting at the ends of the table. Sometimes, when he didn't like what was being said, he cut them off without a word—embarrassing not only the person speaking, but even members of the companies we were negotiating with.

There were two rows of chairs directly behind the table on each side. On the union side of the table, we always had our three attorneys present, plus our actuaries, who deal with the financial impact the contractual agreements have on our membership and to handle the cost accounting of each segment of the contract. They made sure every piece of the pie was divided properly. Lastly, but most importantly in my viewpoint, were two or three secretaries taking notes on everything that was said. Taping the meetings was not allowed.

On the company side would be at least six or seven attorneys, four or five secretaries, two or three labor relations gurus, workman's compensation experts, benefits experts, health and safety consultants, and five or six people who we never figured out what the hell they were doing there.

The main table, as it was called, was where most of the contract negotiations with the companies were supposed to take place. We all knew differently.

The real talks were held in a small conference room down the hall that held only ten people. That's where Joey and the disciples, a.k.a. vice presidents, met privately with company bigwigs.

The term *Joey's disciples* became popular when Matthew Simms was promoted to vice president. He, along with Mark Palmer, Luke Coletta, and John Graham made up the disciples—Matthew, Mark, Luke, and John.

I actually coined the phrase, and it just caught on. I thought it was pretty clever on my part. The negotiators for the companies were the top labor relations experts around. They were well- educated—all had college degrees, and most had their master's. Education and experience were mandatory, or they wouldn't be at the bargaining table.

Even though everyone on the union side of the table was an elected or appointed representative, who may or may not have a formal education past high school, it wasn't as big of a mismatch as someone might expect.

In my own mind, our experience versus a college education made it a distinct advantage in our favor. The corporate big guns were smug about their so-called intelligent representatives.

Regardless, our people could better relate to the membership and their concerns and problems than someone educated in some sterile college classroom. That was everyone, excluding Joey Pinata.

The union staff may not be as well-educated, but we were proficient with the details. Everyone on our staff had been involved in many different types of negotiations. There is a different approach when you are negotiating with a small wholesale grocery transport company versus a company that transports millions of vehicles.

Transporting material and cars for the auto industry poses many different problems than a smaller transport company would encounter. With larger companies, there tend to be more issues to deal with, and the problems are more complex when slicing up the financial pie.

Every issue in a contract is ultimately affected by money. Both sides know there is only a certain amount of money in the pie, and all negotiations are for is to determine how we divide it up.

The larger companies face issues in a contract such as the need to carve out medical and supplemental unemployment benefits, overtime, health and safety concerns, job preferences, seniority, work rules, and many other issues that seem to take forever to solve.

But a small company cannot possibly afford many of these issues that would potentially cause them to go bankrupt, and the union isn't in the business of draining the lifeblood from the company coffers.

If the company goes broke, our jobs are down the tubes with them. Then we all lose. The school of hard knocks may not give out diplomas, but it produces experts nonetheless.

In order to speak in a meeting with the companies, each union representative at the table had to get permission to speak prior to the meeting, and Joey and his disciples wanted to know what they intended to say beforehand. Sometimes, we were given assignments to present to the companies so we had better be fully prepared or we would get the wrath of Joey J. He kept total control, all the time.

The chairs at the table were reserved for those directly involved in the contract negotiations with the company, whereas the chairs behind the tables were the line of demarcation. They were for the adjunct staff, who were proficient in contract negotiations and there to provide research on the topics at hand and to give advice to those actually sitting at the table. The companies and the union both paid extravagant salaries for their legal and financial knowledge and expertise. The companies usually employed theirs on a full-time basis, whereas the union hired them as consultants on an as-needed basis. Both sides employed full-time attorneys. Many of those present in the negotiation meetings had previously been some of the most powerful local union presidents and chairmen in the nation. Now they were reduced to little more than puppets waiting for Joey to pull their strings.

This meeting would be just for the union. The company was meeting separately, probably doing the same thing. Each person had to get a complete understanding of the settlement language. An incorrect interpretation was not allowed.

Joey expected everyone on his staff to understand exactly what the written settlement meant to the union members.

We would then go back to our home regional union offices, our local union halls, and our warehouses or businesses to explain it to the members; errors of interpretation were dealt with harshly.

We were all told not to interpret the contract language and to say exactly what we were told the intent of the language meant. At this point, the language could not be altered. They either voted to accept it or to turn it down. There was no other option.

If the contract was turned down, both sides would have to go back to the negotiating table and iron out the problems. If both sides negotiated in good faith, a rejection by the membership was extremely difficult to settle.

I sat in my regular assigned seat at the table. Located in front of each chair on the table was a copy of the tentative new contract. Everyone seated was looking through it, hesitating at the high-lighted changes. It was in book form and about two hundred pages long. That meant that it was two hundred times longer than the very first union agreement with General Motors.

I picked up my copy and had started glancing through it when Ken Cloutier said, "Holy shit, Irish, what the hell happened to your face?"

"Slipped in the shower last night, hit my face on the faucet, and then the side of the tub."

"Sure you didn't pass out?" Ken asked with a laugh.

"Feel like I got hit by a truck," I responded as I looked down at my watch and saw it was nine thirty.

I tried to change the subject by asking jokily, "What time does this nine o'clock meeting start?"

"As soon as Mr. Pinata gets here and says so. I guess he was called out a few minutes ago for an important phone call," Ken said, shrugging as though he really didn't know.

I wondered what Joey Pinata would think when he saw my face. I mostly wondered what his reaction would be. Knowing him like I did, I would have been surprised if he showed one at all.

Staff members who were standing and talking started taking their seats. A few minutes later, Tony Wetherby came through the door followed by Joey Pinata, with Michael Ferrier scurrying close behind him.

They sat down just as the four union VPs walked in together—Matthew Simms, Mark Palmer, Luke Coletta, and John Graham.

I studied Joey J closely, waiting for some reaction when he saw me. Joey was concentrating on the document in front of him and didn't seem to notice my swollen face.

"My god, Irish, what the hell happened to your face?"

I looked to my left and saw that it was Matthew Simms who had asked the question.

That brought everyone's eyes to my face, including Joey's. With a grin, Joey said, "Looks like you stood up when you should have shut up."

"No, it was nothing like that. I simply slipped in the tub and hit my face. No big deal. I should sue this place for damaging my handsome Irish looks," I replied with a forced smile.

Joey dropped the subject quickly by saying, "Before we begin, I don't know if everyone is aware of the accident involving Jennifer Marks, but for those who aren't, perhaps Irish could bring us all up to speed on what really happened and how Jennifer is doing."

I was caught completely by surprise. I certainly didn't expect Jennifer to be brought up at this meeting. Everyone turned and looked at me, waiting for my response. I stole a quick look at Joey, trying to get a read from his facial expression, but saw nothing, just as I suspected.

"Apparently, she was struck by a hit-and-run driver right out in front of the hotel. The local police are investigating it as a possible intentional assault, but I have no idea where they are with the investigation. Jennifer is in Miami General Hospital with multiple injuries. She has a broken ankle and some broken ribs, but the most serious injury is a punctured lung."

"Is she going to be all right?" John Graham asked sincerely.

"The doctor said that she will be real sore for a few days, but if everything goes according to plan, they expect her to make a complete recovery."

"Let's pray that she does," John said, with a tone that seemed to express true concern.

"Well, let's get this meeting started." Joey demanded. "Everyone will stand and join in saying the pledge of allegiance?" It wasn't a request. Standard procedure was to begin every union meeting with the pledge.

Everyone in the room stood and faced the US flag in the corner of the room, put our hands over our hearts, and recited the familiar oath. Afterward, we settled into our seats, waiting for Joey to start the meeting.

"I might as well give you the bad news right up front. The contract appears once again to be unsettled. It seems the other side got a bug up their ass this morning, and after taking a closer look, they didn't like it. We tried to convince them that a verbal agreement was reached, and they were required to abide by it. Unfortunately, our lawyers say they are within their legal rights."

A huge groan filled the room, and then it went deathly silent. This was not what we expected to hear. Not a word was spoken; no one moved. You could hear the second hand on the wall clock tick each second away while we waited for Joey to explain what the hell had happened. What could possibly have gone wrong? Was an entire year's worth of work being flushed down the drain?

Henry Rodriguez raised his hand and asked, "What seems to be their problem? This is very unusual. How can they just change their minds? I thought we had an agreement."

"Like I just said, Henry, our lawyers say they are within their rights, and until this contract is voted on, passed, and signed, it is not legally settled. Until then, everything is open for discussion. Now, we are *not* going to let those sneaky bastards dictate to us what is or is not open for discussion."

Everyone in the room was fixated on every word Joey was saying. Stunned disbelief showed on every face. These contract negotiations had already taken their toll on everyone involved. I wondered what the people from the other side felt. Were they hit as hard as we were?

"They only want to renegotiate certain wage and benefit clauses. We told them that if this is the road they're taking, we insist on reopening every clause in the contract. We'll start from square one—the beginning paragraph of the contract."

I was dumbfounded! I couldn't believe what I was hearing. Could this really be happening? Looking around at the faces at the table, I knew I wasn't alone.

After waiting a minute for the information to settle, Joey continued, "They said they just flat-out refuse to start from the beginning. We told them if part of the contract is still open for discussion, then all of it is open. We will not allow them to unilaterally decide what is settled and what isn't. I guess they didn't like how we reacted to their ridiculous position. They got up from the table and said the discussions were over. No further words; they just walked out on us."

"Where does that leave us?" someone at the end of the table asked.

"Due to the devious actions by these corporate bastards we're dealing with, we are officially at an impasse."

The looks on the faces in the room said it all. Where did we go from here? To declare an impasse was akin to being on life support. Someone had to blink, and blink soon. In the pit of my stomach, I somehow knew it wouldn't be Joey J.

Joey broke the uncomfortable silence once again. "We have put a bulletin out to the press, explaining to the general public the type of people we have been dealing with. This will prove that they've been the ones negotiating in bad faith all this time and are the cause of this lengthy strike."

There was complete silence once again. "If the press prints what we sent them, it will prove to the public and our members that this union has been diligently working to reach a settlement during these difficult negotiations, without cooperation from the key corporate players."

What started out as a low din, with everybody talking at once, rose to a level akin to the main floor of the New York Stock Exchange. Everyone in the room knew the news had already leaked out to their members that a tentative settlement had been reached. What could we possibly tell them now? As angry as everyone in the room was, it was impossible to feel the frustration their striking union members were feeling.

The banging of the gavel brought the noise to a halt. "I will not allow this meeting to turn into a riot. Now everyone will shut up and pay attention." Joey's face was flushed with anger.

The room fell silent once again.

"From this point forward, no one is allowed to talk to the press, whether it's the television or the newspapers. You are not allowed to discuss this with anyone outside this room. Complete agreement with this is mandatory. No questions. You will be informed as soon as anything changes."

There were no questions, only blank stares on the faces of the entire bargaining team.

Joey rose to leave, stopped, and said, "We will remain here at this hotel until further notice. I might suggest, to keep you occupied, that every one of you familiarize yourselves with the tentative agreement. When and if this strike is ever settled, we will explain the specifics." Joey turned and walked out of the meeting, followed by his four VPs.

I grabbed my copy of the supposedly settled agreement, put it in my briefcase, and left the room.

CHAPTER SEVENTEEN

. . . .

I made it to my room and went right to bed. I had a lot on my plate, but I needed some more sleep, even a couple of hours. Jack would have to wait. I set my alarm for two hours and immediately fell into a deep sleep.

When the alarm woke me up, I crawled out of bed and walked into the bathroom. I had started undressing for the shower when my phone rang. I finished taking off my shirt and walked back into the other room to get the phone. I picked it up and said, "Hello?"

"Hey, Sean, I'm just calling to see if you're still going to be able to come to my apartment for the meeting?"

"Sure. Why wouldn't I?"

"I heard about the glitch in the settlement and wondered if that was going to alter your schedule," Jack admitted.

"How did you find out about the problems with the contract when I just heard about it myself not two hours ago?"

"The eyes and ears of the FBI are everywhere," he said with a laugh.

"That's fair enough. I should be there in about thirty minutes if I can get off this damn phone."

"All right, I'll see you then."

I hung up the phone and resumed taking off my clothes. I hopped into the shower and let the hot water cascade over me for five minutes. I finished my shower and got dressed, all in about ten minutes.

I walked out of the hotel and into the humid Miami heat, where the doorman waved up a waiting cab. I gave him a buck and jumped in. I gave the cabbie the address, and we headed directly to Jack's apartment.

The ride took about twenty minutes. It should have taken only six or eight, but I noticed the cabbie took the long route so he could get a higher fare.

When we arrived at Jack's apartment, I got out of the cab and paid the fare without complaining. Everyone needs an angle to get along in this world. I thought the cabbie must need the money more than I did. He looked like he needed some new clothes and smelled like he could use a bath, too. I figured it was my way of helping the needy.

I walked up to the front door of the apartment building and rang the bell. I checked my watch and saw that it was still a few minutes before noon, so technically, I was right on time.

I waited for Jack to answer, but there was no audible response, just the proverbial buzz. I pushed open the door and walked into the building, making my way up the stairs and to Jack's apartment.

I walked up to the door and noticed it was ajar. I yelled, "Don't you know it's dangerous to leave your door open? Some criminal might get you."

There was no response. I pushed the door open and instantly knew that something was wrong. The Chinese food containers were scattered about the floor. The nasty table and chairs were overturned, and papers were strewn everywhere, as if a twister had taken up residency.

I called Jack's name again and waited. No response. I took a few more steps in and checked out the small kitchen. There was no sign of Jack. I turned to go into the bedroom when I felt something smash against the side of my head. Everything went black.

After a few minutes, I opened my eyes and focused as best as I could on the dirty ceiling. I felt the swelling on the side of my head. I was getting a little tired of the abuse to my body.

There was an excited voice coming from the doorway. "Sir, are you all right? Sir, can you hear me?"

I raised myself up on one elbow and managed to say, "Yeah, I guess I'm all right."

With that, a man came over and helped me to my feet and into a chair. "Maybe you better sit down for a bit. You look a little shaky," the man said, with concern in his voice.

I looked up at him and saw a tall man, about six foot three, but looking like he only weighed around one sixty. He looked to be about seventy years old, had thin wispy black hair and a very red face. His breath smelled of whiskey and cigarettes. He was unsteady on his feet and appeared to be a little drunk.

The man looked at me and said, "Hi, my name is Alfred. I live down the hall. I heard some shouting—furniture crashing or something, and what sounded like two or three men fighting. I waited ten minutes before I came over. Not much use in a fight at my age, and besides, I've got a bad back."

"Do you know Jack that lives here?"

"Oh, yes. I know Jack real well, ever since the day he moved in. Jack's quite a talker. Always has something good to talk about."

"Is he here?" I asked. "Have you seen him since you heard the commotion?"

"No, I just came in and saw you lying on the floor and thought you must have been in the fight."

"Maybe he's in there," I said, as I pointed to the bedroom. "I'll go take a look."

"You're pretty unsteady. You should let me have a look," Alfred offered.

"No, I'll be okay. You can just wait here in case I need you for something," I said, attempting to get up, but falling backward and down onto the chair again.

"Listen son, sit tight. I will go look."

The bedroom light was on as the old guy walk in. I saw him walk around the end of the bed, where he stopped.

"I've found him," he said as he stooped down next to the bed.

I got out of the chair and asked, "Is he alive?" I staggered into the bedroom. It looked like the same housekeeper that did the rest of the apartment took care of the bedroom too. It was a mess, with clothes scattered about and papers everywhere. I saw two feet sticking off the far end of the bed. He was lying on his stomach. I walked over and confirmed it was Jack. "Well, is he alive?"

"I'm not sure," the old man responded.

I said to him, "Let me take a look."

Alfred stood up and walked past me. I knelt down and checked Jack's carotid artery. I felt a solid heartbeat. I turned him over and asked, "Jack, can you hear me?"

There was no response. Hopefully, he had just been knocked unconscious. I lightly slapped his face and said, "Jack, it's Irish." Still nothing. I turned around to Alfred and said, "Call 911. Tell them an officer is down. Give them the address and his apartment number."

"Yes, sir. I'll have to go to my apartment. It looks like his phone has been ripped out of the wall. Did you say officer down? Is Jack a police officer?"

"Yes, he is. Please hurry. I'll wait here with Jack."

The old man left the bedroom quickly, and a few seconds later, I could hear the sound of his steps fade away as he rushed down the hall.

I looked Jack over, and saw that he had obviously been beaten severely. His shirt was torn half off his body, showing a large bruise on the right side of his chest. Both of his eyes were swollen and he had bruising all around his face, not to mention the blood running down from a large two-inch gash below his right eye.

"That'll leave a scar," I said to myself. I watched his chest rise slowly, so I knew he was breathing.

An instant later, I saw his right hand move toward his face. I said softly, "Jack, just lie still. This is Irish. We have an ambulance on the way. I'll get you a cold cloth from the bathroom. Hold tight." As I got up, I saw his eyes flicker and open just a bit.

I went into the bathroom and grabbed a towel and a somewhat clean washcloth from the towel rack. I rinsed the cloth with cold water and went back to kneel next to Jack. I applied the cold cloth to his face, wiped away some of the blood, and then held pressure to the wound with the towel.

Jack stirred and mumbled, "What the hell are you doing?"

"Jack, you've been beaten severely. Just lie still. The ambulance should be here shortly."

He was starting to become oriented to time and place. His eyes opened fully, and he looked up at me. "I feel like a truck ran over me."

"What happened here, Jack?"

"My doorbell rang right after I talked to you. So naturally, I answered the door. I thought it was the delivery man. I had ordered us some Chinese. When I opened up the door, these two guys were standing there, and one of them was holding my takeout Chinese. I knew right away they were not the delivery boys, so I tried to shut the door and grab for my gun, but the guy threw the food in my face."

I laughed and asked, "You didn't give them a tip did you?"

"Hell, no. I was instantly pissed. For one thing, I was hungry, plus they wasted our food. I punched the guy in the face. The other guy hit me, and the fight was on."

"Looks like they won," I said with a laugh.

"In my younger days, I would have kicked their asses. As it was, I at least knocked both of them down *on* their asses. Unfortunately, I couldn't handle them both. One got behind me and grabbed my arms while the other played tap dance on my face. How bad do I look?"

"You look like a hockey goalie from the 1960s."

"Help me up."

"No, I think you better lie still until the ambulance gets here."

"Why did you call the goddamn ambulance? I'm all right."

"You were unconscious. Plus, by the looks of your face, I should have called the morgue. So shut up and lie there."

"Okay, Mother." He tried to grin, but the pain stopped him from even a little smile.

I asked, "Did you get a look at their faces?"

"Sure, but I didn't recognize either one of them. They were big guys—six foot three—and they looked like they weighed about two-fifty."

"I wonder if they were the same men who paid me a visit." I said.

Just then, I heard the first emergency vehicles. As the sound got closer, it became obvious that there was more than one. Sounded like ten. The sounds grew nearer and then stopped.

"They must be here now."

Jack didn't say a word. He lay very still like he was afraid to move.

"Does it hurt to move?" I asked.

"Hurts to blink, hurts to move, and hurts to breathe."

Within a few minutes, the cops busted through the door and yelled, "Police!"

"In here!" I shouted back.

They came in with guns drawn. "Put your hands up!" one of them yelled.

"I'm holding pressure to a wound."

"I don't give a damn. Put your hands where I can see them."

I let go of the cloth and put my hands in the air as he demanded. I was looking at a young cop who stood over six feet five inches. He appeared to have wild eyes and continued pointing the gun at me.

An older cop surveyed the situation and said, "Check the bathroom."

The young cop kept the gun at a firing position and walked into the bathroom. "All clear." He turned around and again pointed his gun at me.

Without taking his eyes off me, the tall officer said, "Stand up and put your hands against the wall and spread your legs."

I did as I was told.

The older officer frisked me from head to toe. "He's clean." To me, he said, "Turn around. What's your name?"

"Sean MacSween."

"We got the call that there is an officer down. Is that him?" he asked, pointing to Jack lying on the floor.

"That's Special Agent Jack Casey with the FBI, and if we don't do something soon, he's going to bleed to death. He has a large wound under his right eye that is bleeding a lot. Plus, he's been beaten severely. He needs medical attention immediately."

He turned to the young officer and said, "Holster your weapon. I think everything is under control." He looked at me and said, "And you can put your hands down now."

The older officer holstered his own weapon and said, "I'm Sergeant Grier, and this is Officer Derik Jakes."

I knelt back down and reapplied light pressure to the oozing wound.

"What the hell happened here?" Officer Jakes asked in a cocky voice.

"Why don't you ask him? He's awake," I snapped back.

"Officer Casey, can you tell us what happened?"

"I got the shit kicked out of me. What's it look like?" Jack responded.

I jumped back into the conversation, saying, "It's difficult for him to talk. He's in a lot of pain."

"I didn't ask for your opinion. I was talking to Officer Casey," Officer Jakes answered rudely.

Sergeant Grier stepped in and said, "Hold on. There's no reason to talk to him like that. Why don't you go and bring the ambulance crew up here. I'll do the interview."

Officer Jakes reluctantly turned and left the room. Sergeant Grier said, "I'm sorry about Officer Jakes's attitude. He's a rookie and thinks everything is life-threatening. He's still learning and has a long way to go. So, Mr. MacSween, can you tell me what happened?"

"I came here to see Jack and have some dinner. I pushed his buzzer, and someone let me in. I came up here, thinking Jack had let me in. His door was ajar, so I naturally thought he must have left the door open for me, so I walked in. I saw the mess out there and called his name. The next thing I knew, someone hit me alongside my head with something hard. I passed out but came to a few moments later, and I was on the floor."

"Who called 911?" Sergeant Grier asked.

"The fella down the hall. His name is Alfred. He came in and helped me get up."

Officer Jakes had just returned and was listening to what I had to say. "The ambulance will be here in a couple of minutes. This story of his doesn't make sense," Officer Jakes said, shaking his head as if I was lying.

"What do you mean?" I asked.

"Why would someone come in here, attack this man, and then let you in? If they didn't want to be caught, they wouldn't answer the damn door."

"I don't know, Dick Tracy, that's your job to find out, but that's exactly what happened," I answered irritably. "Maybe you should talk to Alfred. He can at least tell you where he found me."

"Take it easy, you two. Derik, go down the hall and find this Alfred character and bring him here. Also, find out if he made the 911 call," Officer Grier said.

"Yes, sir, but that's such a crazy story. I'll see if this Alfred exists."

Officer Jakes left the apartment, and I heard his footsteps fading as he was walking down the hall, much like Alfred's had.

Officer Grier asked Jack if he knew Alfred, and Jack said he didn't. I jumped in and said, "Jack, this Alfred told me that he knew you real well."

"Not that I'm aware of. I never heard of an Alfred living in this building."

The ambulance crew entered the apartment right behind Officer Jakes. I recognized the paramedic as the same one who had come to Jennifer's aid. He looked at me and said, "Hi there, didn't I see you a few days ago?

"I'm afraid you did."

He smiled and asked us to leave the bedroom so they could attend to Jack. The three of us walked out of the apartment and into the hall to talk.

"So what's your relationship with this Jack Casey?" Officer Grier asked.

"I met him at the hospital. I was there seeing a friend of mine who had been struck by a truck right in front of our hotel. Jack was assigned to the investigation."

"Yeah, I heard about that one. So you were a friend of the victim?" Officer Grier asked.

"That's right. We are friends, but mostly, we work together."

"So Officer Casey started asking you questions about that incident, and that's how you came to know him. Is that right?"

"That's right. Then he asked me to come here, so we could talk some more about the accident. He wanted to stay out of the public eye."

"Who's your friend who got hurt?"

"Jennifer Marks. She and I work for the International Truckers Union. Some idiot in a pickup truck hit her right in front of our hotel."

"Why was he helping with a local investigation of a possible hit-and-run? Seems kind of out of his jurisdiction, doesn't it?" Grier asked.

I answered in a much calmer voice. "I don't know. I'm not a cop, so I didn't think to ask. Jack and I just had coffee and talked for about an hour while we were waiting to see Jennifer. The docs were doing tests, and Jack had to wait until they were done so he could talk to her, but he had to leave before we were given permission to see her."

"So he just invited you over for a little talk and dinner?"

"That's right," I answered briskly.

Officer Jakes laughed and asked. "What's going on—are you two gay?"

"Are you a freaking comedian or something? I don't know about Jack, though. He could be, for all I know. You would have to ask him if you're interested."

"Fuck you," Jakes responded angrily. Then he said, "So I asked at a couple of the apartments down the hall, and they said no Alfred lives in this building and never has. So now what's your story, smart-ass?"

"What do you mean there's no Alfred living in the building? That's exactly what he told me. I didn't make this shit up. Jack said he didn't know the guy either."

"That is strange," Sergeant Grier said.

"Look, Sergeant Grier, why would someone let me in the building, keep the door ajar to let me in the apartment, hit me alongside the head, help me up, call 911, and lie to me about living here? That makes no sense."

"Sounds like an outright lie you got caught in," Jakes stated with even more sarcasm.

Sergeant Grier looked sternly at Jakes and answered for me. "This is so odd. He couldn't make up a story like this. I believe Mr. MacSween."

Jakes nodded and said, "I got the phone number of whoever called 911. It was a cell phone. Number's 949-6180, and it was called in at 5:57 p.m."

"Hey, wait a minute!" I said as I took out a piece of paper from my wallet. "That's Jack's phone number. The bastards used Jack's phone to call for help. That's ballsy, isn't it?"

Just then, the ambulance crew came through the doorway, forcing us a little further back down the hall. They had an IV started, and Jack was breathing through an oxygen mask.

He said in a weak voice, "Wait a minute. I want to talk. Sergeant, the men who attacked me were professionals. If they had wanted to kill me, they could have."

As they rolled the stretcher away, Sergeant Grier turned to me and said, "I would like to talk to you some more. Do you think you could come down to the station so we can get your statement on record?"

"Look, Sergeant, there is much more going on here than just an assault. I can't get into it right now, but I will finish this interview a little later, if that's all right with you. I would like to go to the hospital first and make sure Jack is okay. I could come by as soon as I'm done there."

"That sounds fine to me," Sergeant Grier replied.

"You're not really going to believe this shit, are you?" Jakes yelled.

"Officer Jakes, I have made my decision. Why don't you go to the car and wait for me? That's not a question. That's an order."

Jakes glared at me and stormed down the hall to the stairwell and left without a word.

I smiled at Sergeant Grier and said, "Thanks. I will be by your office later."

"That sounds good to me," he replied.

CHAPTER EIGHTEEN

I walked into the ER and went right to the triage office, where I saw the same nurse who was working the last time I was there.

"Excuse me. A friend of mine was just brought to the ER by ambulance, and I wanted to check in to let you know I'm in the waiting room. His name is Jack Casey. He said he wanted to talk to me as soon as the doctors allow him to."

"What is your name?"

"Sean MacSween. He may have called me Irish MacSween."

"I will check with Mr. Casey to see if he does in fact want to see you. Sometimes, I get the strangest stories from people wanting to get in to see someone who is not family. Normally, we only allow family in, but occasionally, when the patient wants to talk to someone who is not related, we allow them to come in. Let me go in and talk to him and the doctor in charge."

"Jack does not have any family here in Miami. I'm the closest thing to family he has. By the way, who is the doctor who's taking care of him?"

"It's Dr. Myott. Why do you ask?"

"I actually talked with her when another friend came in through the ER. Tell her it's Irish MacSween. I'm sure she'll remember me."

"I'll do that."

The nurse left triage and walked back into the patient treatment rooms looking for Jack and Dr. Myott. Instead of going to the waiting room, I stood at the desk, waiting for her, or possibly Dr. Myott, to return.

As it turned out, neither of them did. A different nurse took up residence at the triage desk. She smiled at me and asked, "Are you Mr. MacSween?"

"I am."

"Amy told me to tell you that Mr. Casey is in x-ray right now. When he's finished there, Dr. Myott might possibly come and talk to you. At this time, we do not know the extent of Mr. Casey's injuries."

I looked at her name tag and said, "Collette, I don't know if anyone knows this, but Mr. Casey is a federal agent, and I have to let some very important people know his condition."

"I've heard that line before."

"I'm not kidding. I have to let someone know what's going on. So I'm not playing games here.

You must keep me informed. If you don't believe me, call the Miami FBI any time and ask."

"I will pass that information along to Dr. Myott. I'm sure she will do her best."

She got up from her chair and returned to the treatment area. I wasn't sure what I should do at that point, so I went into the waiting room. It was full of crying babies, a couple arguing, TVs blaring, and the smell of old sweat—a combination that didn't sit well with me. I walked back out to the triage desk and leaned against the wall. I could have fallen asleep standing up. Tension really drained me. I felt dog tired.

I closed my eyes and slipped into a cat nap. A few moments later, I heard, "Mr. MacSween, Mr. MacSween." It was like a voice coming through a fog a long distance away.

I opened my eyes and realized I had fallen asleep standing up.

I returned to the triage desk, and saw Dr. Myott standing there. She said, "Hello, Mr. MacSween." She smiled at me. "So you're back. You've been spending way too much time here in the ER. I hear Mr. Casey is a friend of yours and that he's an agent of the FBI."

"That's right, and I have to give an update as soon as I know anything."

"I don't think you have too much to worry about. Mr. Casey has been beaten up badly, but there are no life-threatening injuries. I had to suture the cut on his face, and he has a couple of broken ribs, but they are not serious. A lot of soft tissue injuries. He obviously has a severe concussion, which could cause him problems if he doesn't take it easy. He must be watched properly for the next forty-eight hours. He will be very sore tonight and tomorrow. If I release him, is there anyone who can stay with him? I don't want him to be alone, just in case something goes awry."

"I'm sure I can get someone to stay with him for the night. He won't like a babysitter staying with him. Will he be able to be released today?"

"Presently, we have him on a couple of IVs. One is an antibiotic, and the other is just fluids. He is quite dehydrated. I will have to see how he responds and also what his scans look like. He is quite adamant that I release him. What is going on with you and your friends? It seems like you're a person to stay away from. All of your friends keep getting injured."

"That's not true. I have a lot of friends who are very healthy. I have just been telling them that you need the business here at the hospital."

"That's very funny, Mr. MacSween. I will let you know more in a few hours. But for now, I would like him to stay and rest for four to six hours to see if his concussion symptoms subside."

"He said he wanted to see me when I got here. Is there any possibility that I do that?"

"I will have to check with him. If he indeed wants to see you, I will have the nurse let you in."

"Thank you, Doc. I appreciate all your help."

"That's not a problem. I'll send someone to let you know in just a few minutes. But do not get him agitated and don't stay long."

"You have my word on it," I responded. Dr. Myott turned around and left. She was a very caring doctor, in my viewpoint. I wondered if she was single. It wouldn't hurt to find out.

I waited for five minutes, and then the RN named Collette returned. "Mr. MacSween, Mr. Casey would like to see you. Please come in." She opened the door, and I followed her into the action area of the hospital ER.

There were multiple patients lying on gurneys down the hallways, nurses running to and from the patient rooms, and a man somewhere down the hall yelling, "I've got to pee. Someone help me! I've got to pee."

X-ray technologists were pushing portable machines into two rooms at the same time. It looked like total chaos to me. I heard Dr. Myott calling for assistance with an intubation in the room with *Surgery* marked over the door.

We walked past and turned left down another hall. She led me to the last room on the right. "Here he is, Mr. MacSween."

I smiled at her and said, "Thank you."

Jack was lying with an oxygen mask over his face. As soon as he saw me, he took it off. He gave me a half-assed smile and said, "Hello there."

"Hello, Jack. You look like shit. You look like you fell out of a window from the fifth floor."

"Thanks a lot. I feel like I fell from the tenth floor. Those guys did a number on me. They're lucky I wasn't thirty-five years old. I would have kicked the shit out of them."

"Yeah, yeah, I don't want to hear it. You got your ass kicked, just accept it. You couldn't handle them." I laughed a hardy laugh. "What did you want to see me about?"

"I got a call this morning from the director, and he told me that they got an anonymous phone tip that there is a man hiding out in Sweetwater who has firsthand information about the attack on Jennifer Marks. Apparently, he says there are some others that are going to be hit next. Obviously, you and I were on that list. The nurse gave me something in my IV to help with the pain, and now I don't know my own name. I wrote the guy's number down on a slip of paper."

"What do you want me to do?"

"Take this." He handed me a sheet of paper with a phone number on it.

"What's this number?"

"It's the guy out in Sweetwater. I also want to know if you would drive me out to Sweetwater tonight. Apparently, he wants to talk about some people inside the union that are being led to slaughter."

"I would, but you may not even be released from here today. I talked to Dr. Myott, and she said she may keep you overnight."

"No fucking way am I staying here. There's too much on the line right now. We have worked for months on this, and I'm not going to let a little pain stop me."

"Jack, you just came close to never waking up again. Don't you think you should listen to Dr. Myott? You're not a kid anymore. You can't bounce back as quick as you used to. Dr. Myott said you are going to be real sore tonight, and especially tomorrow. Not to mention that you may have a very severe concussion."

"Well then, we should go tonight. Tomorrow, I may be too sore. Like you said, I have to listen to the doctor." He tried to laugh but could only manage a little grunt, and then he released a deep, hollow moan. The smile left his face, and he closed his eyes, refusing to acknowledge the pain.

"Jack, listen to me. If Dr. Myott releases you, then I will be happy to drive you to Sweetwater. Are you going to bring any other agents with us?"

"That's the thing. I don't have any agents available. They are all deployed, and I can't pull them off their assignments. I would really appreciate your help. I will make it up to you."

I laughed and said, "How are you going to do that? Make me another home-cooked dinner?"

"Maybe we can go out and get really drunk. Get obliterated."

"I may take you up on that. This danger shit is tough to deal with."

"Bullshit, Irish. You've been involved in a lot of fights and probably all kinds of mayhem. You're not a virgin when it comes to trouble."

"No, but I'm not a kid anymore. Every time I get into a debacle, I swear that I will never do it again."

Jack smiled and said, "Sounds like an alcoholic. Please, God, get me through this, and I will never do this again. Right! What I would really like to do is swear you in as a temporary federal officer."

"What? Are you crazy? You must have taken a gigantic hit on the head. Why would I want to be a federal officer?"

"If you're a federal agent, even on a temporary basis, you have to keep this investigation confidential. So if the local cops ask you questions you are not allowed to answer, you can tell them it's confidential and part of a federal investigation."

"I wouldn't say anything even if I *wasn't* a federal officer."

"I believe you, but they could hold you for further questioning until they get something out of you. At least twenty-four hours."

I thought about it for a minute and knew it sounded smart, so I said, "Okay, if you think it's necessary. Let's do it."

Jack asked, "Raise your right hand." I did as he asked. "Repeat after me. I, Sean MacSween, do solemnly swear that I will defend the Constitution of the United States of America against all enemies, foreign and domestic, etcetera, etcetera, etcetera."

I repeated what he said and asked, "What exactly does the 'etcetera, etcetera, etcetera, mean?'"

"It means that you'll do whatever the hell I tell you to do."

"Oh shit. What have I gotten myself into?"

At that moment, I was officially a federal officer of the FBI. Something I had never dreamed of. There I was, trusting Jack once more.

"I would like you to just hang around the hospital until Dr. Myott releases me. I would appreciate it. Then you can drive us out to Sweetwater. She first wanted me to stay overnight for observation. I said no way. She gave in a little and agreed to four to six hours at the very minimum. I'm pushing for four."

"Okay, not a problem. I will take some time to go up and see Jennifer. Update her on what's happened."

"I wish you wouldn't do that right now. She's scared and jumpy as hell, and this isn't going to help her. Go see her some other time, but let's keep this to ourselves. Are you okay with that?"

"I told her I was going to keep her up-to-date on things, but I guess it wouldn't matter if I kept this one little thing just between us."

"Little thing? I was seeing the bright light. I thought I was dead," Jack said with a little laugh.

I laughed along with him. "The bright light was the lamp that was on the floor next to your face. You probably got scared because of the heat. You thought you were going to hell."

"Why don't *you* get the hell out of here and let me get some beauty rest."

I turned and started to walk out of the room, but stopped and said, "It's going to take more than rest to make that face beautiful, but since you're going to be here for at least four to six hours, I'm going to visit Sergeant Grier. He asked me to come back and see him. It shouldn't take too long."

"Then it's a good thing I deputized you. Now get out of here so I can get some sleep."

CHAPTER NINETEEN

I walked outside into the Miami heat and got into a waiting taxi. I gave the driver the address of the police station and sat back.

"Are you a plain-clothes officer?"

I thought for a moment and replied, "Yes, I am."

The cabbie said, "That's cool."

I answered, "It can be sometimes, but most of the time, it's stressful."

The cabbie accepted that and said nothing further. The ride took about fifteen minutes because of the traffic. We reached the station, and the cabbie told me it would be twelve dollars. He probably took the long way, but I was in such deep thought I didn't notice. I gave him fifteen, got out of the cab, and walked into the station.

At the reception desk, I asked, "Can you point me in the direction of Sergeant Grier's office?"

"Sure, it's down the hall to your right, second door on the right. But wait a minute. Do you have an appointment?"

I showed him the card Grier had given me and said, "He told me to come by today and talk to him. So here I am."

"I'll call him to make sure. He doesn't like people just walking in on him."

"No problem. I'll wait."

He picked up the phone and pushed a button. I heard it ring and then heard Grier's voice. "Hello."

"Sergeant, this is O'Malley at the desk. There is a gentleman here to see you."

"What's his name?"

O'Malley put a hand over the phone and asked, "What's your name?"

"MacSween, Irish MacSween," I replied.

"He said his name is Irish MacSween. You know him?"

"Well, I'll be damned. He showed up. Send him in."

O'Malley hung up the phone and said, "You can go."

I walked down the hall to Grier's office. He was standing behind his desk waiting for me.

"I thought I would have to come looking for you," he offered as a greeting.

"I had some time and thought I might as well use it to come and see you. I figured you would hunt me down like an animal if I didn't, or at the very least, Jakes would come with his weapons drawn."

He laughed and said, "Have a seat. How's Mr. Casey doing?"

"I just left the hospital. He has some broken ribs, and that cut on his face had to be sewn up. The doctor said there's nothing life-threatening, but he's going to be very sore for a few days."

"Are they going to keep him for a while?"

"Not if Jack has anything to say about it. He can hardly breathe or move, but he's still trying to get the doctor to release him."

"He looks like a tough old bird, been around for a while. You can tell just by looking at him. Well, let's get started, but first, I'm sorry to say I have to call in Officer Jakes. It's part of his training. Between you and me, he's such a pain in the ass."

"Do what you have to do. Maybe he's calmed down by now," I offered.

Sergeant Grier tapped a number into his phone, waited a moment, and said, "Mr. MacSween is here. Yes, a minute ago." He put down the phone and said, "He'll be here shortly."

A few minutes later, Officer Jakes lumbered into the office, said hello, and took a seat.

Sergeant Grier said, "This shouldn't take very long. You have already answered most of our questions back at Mr. Casey's apartment."

"What can you tell us about Mr. Casey's assault?"

"I've already told you what I know about that. I came over to his apartment and found him just like I said . . . just like you did."

"What do you know about whatever it is that he is investigating?"

"I'm sorry, but that's confidential FBI information."

"What do you mean? You're not obligated to keep anything you know confidential."

"I'm sorry, but you're wrong on that. I am a federal officer, and I am obligated to keep our investigation confidential."

Jakes interjected, "That's some more bullshit he's laying on us. Since when did you become a federal officer?"

"About half an hour ago. Jack swore me in at the hospital."

Sergeant Grier smiled and said, "Mr. Casey is pretty smart. If you're sworn in, you can't tell us shit."

"Can he do that?" asked Jakes with bewilderment on his face.

"He not only can, but he did," Grier offered.

I slowly looked at Grier, then Jakes, and smiled. "You're an asshole, MacSween," Jakes responded.

Officer Grier raised his voice and said, "Jakes, I told you that if you can't control yourself, I'm going to ask you to leave."

Jakes said, "I'm sorry, Sarge. It won't happen again." To me, Jakes said, "What do you have to do with the investigation?"

"That also comes under the jurisdiction of the FBI. I can't say anything about it."

"What exactly is your job for the Truckers Union?"

"I am an assistant to the president, Joseph Pinata."

"What do you do for the president?"

With a grin, I said, "I assist the president with contract negotiations, as well as our local unions."

"Mr. MacSween, it appears that you are not going to be able to be very cooperative. Is there anything at all you would like to share with us?"

"Really, my hands are tied now that I'm sworn in as an FBI agent. I will say this. There is a lot of pressure on Jack, his fellow agents, and the union. That's all I can say."

Sergeant Grier paused for a moment, and then said, "I would normally hold you for further questioning. I usually have the right to do that for twenty-four hours, but that's not possible with you being an agent of the federal government. I would like to offer our assistance if there's anything we can do."

"I thank you for that. You will have to go to Agent Casey if you want to ask any more questions."

Jakes couldn't hold back any longer. "He's not above the law. We should be able to hold him and grill him until he tells us what's going on and what he's involved in!"

Grier voiced resolutely, "Jakes, shut the hell up and get out of my office. You are required to act like an officer. You are out of line. Now go, get the hell out!"

Jakes turned around and walked out of Grier's office, all the while insisting, "This is bullshit! This is outright bullshit."

Grier shook his head and said, "Sorry about that. We have some serious issues with Officer Jakes that need to be addressed. I'm going to have to go to the captain and talk to him about Jakes's actions. I hate doing that to a fellow officer, but he just doesn't seem to be able to control that mouth of his. You probably should go before he comes back and starts in again."

I laughed and said, "Thanks for everything, Sergeant Grier. I'll be in touch."

I left the station and hailed a cab to take me back to the hospital. I thought it wouldn't be a bad idea to go see Jennifer. I wouldn't have to tell her about Jack. I'd just let her know I was concerned about her and give her whatever update I could on the investigation, within the given limits.

CHAPTER TWENTY

. . . .

I had the cabbie drop me off at the ER entrance. I knew my way to Jennifer's room by now, but only by way of the ER. I didn't stop to see Jack. I figured he would page me if anything changed prior to his self-imposed four- to six-hour deadline.

I got off the elevator and saw Bob Lee standing outside Jennifer's room, which was just a few doors down. He smiled at me as I walked up and asked, "What brings you here at this time of day?"

"I thought I would brighten her day, maybe cheer her up."

"So how is Jack doing?"

"How the hell do you know about him?"

"I've got spies everywhere in this city. Nothing gets by me. So tell me what happened and how he's doing."

"A couple of thugs pretended like they were delivery boys, and when he opened the door, they jumped him and beat the ever living shit out of him. They used his face as a punching bag. Right now, he's being held at Miami General for observation. He's trying to get out after four hours, but the doctor wants to keep him overnight for observation. Jack says he's out after four hours."

"Who is the doctor that's treating him?"

"It's Dr. Myott."

"He should listen to her. She knows what she's doing. That's from personal experience," Bob Lee said.

"Don't tell me someone busted up that beautiful face of yours."

"Nothing like that. Someone tried to take out my liver with a .45 caliber."

"Ouch, that had to hurt."

"Dr. Myott saved my life. I owe her big time. If she hadn't stopped the bleeding in the ER, I would have died."

"You haven't said anything to Jennifer about Jack, have you?"

"No, I wouldn't do that to her. I didn't think she could take any more bad news."

"I see her door is closed. What's going on?

"She's sleeping, believe it or not."

"I think I'll wake her anyway. She needs to know I was here."

"I could tell her when she wakes up," Bob offered.

"No, I want to see her myself."

"Your call," Bob responded.

I opened her door, walked in, and said, "Hey, Jennifer." She didn't move, so I touched her arm.

She practically jumped out of the bed. "What the hell are you doing? You scared the shit out of me," she said loudly.

Before I knew it, Bob was in the room. He looked at Jennifer and asked, "Are you okay?"

"Yes. Irish just scared the hell out of me."

"That's the Jennifer I've come to know and love. The woman of sweet words," I said with a laugh.

"Go to hell. This place is driving me crazy. I can't take much more. How are things with you and Jack?"

Bob interrupted and said, "I'll let you two cats scratch at each other alone. I'll be out in the hall."

"So how are things with you and Jack?" Jennifer asked again as Bob shut the door.

"Things are moving along. Nothing new I can update you on, though. We don't have anything to report on your assault. The local police and the FBI are working hard on it. I just came by to see how you're doing. Are you still in a lot of pain?"

"No, not much now. The doctors are shooting me up with some pretty good stuff. In another few days they are going to x-ray my leg again to see if it's holding together like it's supposed to."

"Do you need anything?" I asked.

"Yes, I would like to see David a little more. He hasn't been here at all today and only for about twenty minutes yesterday. I can't reach him on his phone, either."

"If I run across him I'll tell him to get his butt up here. I also wanted to remind you that the man outside your door is Bob Lee. He's a detective from the Miami Police Department. He's watching you on his off hours. His partner's name is Dominic."

"I know all that. They introduced themselves when they first arrived. That Dominic is quite a cutie. I wish I could take care of *him*," Jennifer said with a laugh, before the pain stopped her.

"You're not in any shape to take care of Dominic or anyone else. You need to rest. I have to take off. Jack has me busy running around doing nothing. Just busywork that, to me, doesn't seem to matter. It's kind of like in the old days—a woman is giving birth, and the doctor tells the husband to boil water. Afterward, he asks the doctor what was the water for. The doctor says it was for nothing, but it kept you out of my way for a little while." I laughed at my own joke much harder than Jennifer did.

I bent down and gave her a kiss on her forehead and turned to leave. She smiled as I looked back at her. The smile was a great improvement from the day before.

CHAPTER TWENTY-ONE

I walked back into Jack's room. He was sitting on his bed without the oxygen mask on his face. He grimaced when he looked at me.

"What's wrong, Jack?"

"I'm having a difficult time standing. I almost fell on my face a few minutes ago. I wanted to try before Dr. Myott came in, 'cause if I fall in front of her, I'll be here for another day, or maybe a week."

"I got a tip a few minutes ago from a very reliable source."

"What kind of tip?"

"It was from Bob Lee. He said that you should listen to Dr. Myott. She knows what she's talking about. She saved his life a couple of years ago. He was gut shot, and it hit his liver. He almost died."

"I have no choice. I've got to talk to this guy. He refuses to come to us. He's hiding out, and he's afraid. He told one of my men that if he's discovered, he's dead within the hour."

"Can't say as I blame him. Whoever he's afraid of sounds like one mean son of a bitch."

"Supposedly, he knows who that guy is. He wouldn't talk over the phone, and even then, he was on the line for about thirty seconds. He asked for me by name, said I was the only one he would talk to."

"Have you ever thought that this might be a trap?"

"I have, but why would they want to lure me out there when they had me dead to rights in my apartment? That doesn't make sense to me. Like I told you before, if they wanted me dead, they would have killed me then."

"Yeah, I guess that makes sense," I answered. "When is Dr. Myott expected to come see you?"

"I asked the nurse about half an hour ago; she said Dr. Myott is sewing somebody's arm up, and when she's finished, she'll come and see me. So I suppose any time now."

"You should listen to her. If you're dead, you can't help the investigation very much. Hey, if you're dead, maybe I'll get promoted to your position. I hear promotions are rapid here in the FBI." I laughed and gave him a soft tap on the shoulder.

"You've got a lot to learn, sonny."

We small talked for about another ten minutes before Dr. Myott entered the room.

"Hello, Mr. Casey, how are you feeling?"

"Pretty good. I've had a little sleep and feel much better."

Dr. Myott looked at me, and I just raised my eyebrows. She said nothing to me, but asked Jack to stand. Jack slowly slid off the bed and stood upright the best he could.

"Can you bend and touch your knees for me?" Dr. Myott asked.

I looked at Jack, and he slowly bent forward, but only about twenty degrees. "My back is a little stiff right now. I don't think I should try that," Jack replied.

"How about if you follow my fingers with both eyes. Your eyes aren't stiff, are they?" Dr. Myott asked with a smile.

She moved her fingers to the right, then left, then up and down. Jack's eyes were slow and always behind the movement of her fingers.

"Can you stand on one foot for me?"

Jack attempted this and almost fell down. I had to catch him. Then, he became dizzy and had to grab the bed.

"Mr. Casey, you show multiple signs that you are suffering a severe concussion. I do not feel you should be released from this hospital right now. We need to do more testing; you need to get an MRI and an EEG, at the very least. It would be very dangerous for you to leave now. There could be more going on with you than we know. Please listen to me. Your life may depend on it," she said with a soft, concerned voice.

Jack shook his head, looked at Dr. Myott, and said, "I just cannot stay here. You don't understand the situation I'm in. I wish I could tell you, but I can't. It's classified."

I broke the thirty-second silence that followed and asked Dr. Myott, "Can you give us a few minutes? We need to talk."

She said, "Sure," then turned and walked out of the room.

"I've got an idea, Jack. Has this guy we're meeting ever seen you?"

"No, all I know is his name. I haven't even talked to him."

"Is there any chance he would know what you look like?"

"I don't see how. Why?"

"Why don't I go meet this guy? You could give me a list of questions and what I can do to help him. I'm sure he wants something, or he wouldn't have called."

"I can't ask you to do that. It could be very dangerous."

I laughed and said, "You think in your condition, you're better than I would be in a confrontation? Hell, Jack, I could kick your ass with one foot. You can't even stand up. Let me go and do your job. I hear you're not very good at it anyhow." I smiled and gave him another tap on the shoulder. He winced.

"I suppose you're right, but don't get yourself hurt or killed, for Christ's sake. It would be my ass."

"I will keep your job in mind and try to stay alive."

I opened the door, and saw Dr. Myott standing a few feet away, writing in Jack's chart. She looked up and asked, "What did you two talk about?"

"I've managed to change his mind. He's staying," I replied.

"Are you kidding me? You actually got that stubborn man to change his mind? I tried for thirty minutes to get him to agree to stay, but he wouldn't budge. What did you say to him?"

With a big smile on my face, I replied, "I made him an offer he couldn't refuse."

Jack yelled from inside his room. "I'm not a stubborn man, Doctor! I'm just dedicated to my job."

She shook her head and said, "That's wonderful. You may have saved his life."

"Give us a few minutes before you take him for testing. We need to talk."

"Not a problem. It will take at least an hour for all this to get in the system."

She left, and I went back into Jack's room, saying, "I told Dr. Myott that you agreed to stay. She was relieved. I think that was a good decision. You're in no shape to confront anyone. Hell, you can't even stand. Now, let's talk about how I am going to go about seeing this guy. Are you strong enough to tell me what I should ask and what I should offer and so forth?"

Jack replied, "Sure, let's get down to business. First, I wish we could get him back to our office so we can interrogate him properly, but I doubt that could ever happen. Sometimes, it takes a well-trained agent to win the trust in this type of situation."

We talked for the next hour. At Jack's insistence, we went over things three times. I felt pretty confident about what exactly my mission was. I need to tape our conversation, ask the questions I needed to ask, and offer him a safe and secure place to hide. My first task was to get him to trust me.

After the hour, I was ready to go when Jack said, "There is one more thing. Here, take this." He reached under his blanket and handed me a Model 637 .38 Smith & Wesson Special and said, "It's loaded; here's another clip, and this is a shoulder holster. God help us if you need it."

"How the hell did you get that in your bed?" I asked.

"I had Steve Hill, one of my senior agents, get it for me. It's registered to him, so don't shoot someone and run for it. He could go to jail," Jack said with a small smile on his face.

"What about you? Don't you need to be armed lying here all by yourself?"

Jack reached once again under his blanket and pulled out a Smith & Wesson .357 Magnum. "I'm going to be just fine."

"I was wondering if I should be armed. I'm glad I have this. I feel safer. I'm not sure that it's necessary, but don't worry, I'll know what to do. I'm not new to guns. I was in combat, if you remember. My dad told me one time that if you draw a weapon, you better be ready to use it. I will keep it in the holster at all times, except to save my own life."

"To pull it out would be the last resort. I don't want you to be gun-happy," Jack said with all the seriousness he could muster.

"Don't worry about that. I'm not the hero type."

Jack said he would have a car ready for me at the hotel, and that I was to call him at seven thirty to find out what car I was driving and any more instructions that may have come up. He gave me the number of our man, and said I was to call him at eight o'clock.

I left the hospital and went back to my hotel. Once in my room, I went into the bathroom to take another shower. I had to be alert and keep my composure throughout the meeting.

After all, I was an FBI agent.

CHAPTER TWENTY-TWO

Once I was back in my hotel room, I took another shower. It helped soothe my aching body and mind. I stepped out of the shower, dried myself, and put on my undershorts. I set the alarm on my phone and passed out on the bed. I had slept for an hour when my phone alarm went off.

I woke up partially, but was still in a sweaty daze. I was dreaming I was in a firefight back in Afghanistan, and I had taken one in my arm. I tried to shoot back but couldn't hit anything. Go figure.

I took another shower to wash off the sweat from my dream. It was not a first. I have had hundreds of combat dreams since I left the country.

I called Jack at seven thirty, and he told me that a black Buick was outside the hotel in the parking lot with the keys under the backseat floor mat.

It was a nervous thirty minutes, but finally eight o'clock came. I called the man. He answered with a sheepish hello, and I said, "This is Jack Casey." Silence for twenty seconds. "Are you still there?"

"Yeah, I'm here."

"Where are you?" I asked.

"That's not important. We aren't meeting here anyway." Once again, he was silent for about thirty seconds. He seemed very fidgety and nervous. His voice was cracking when he did finally speak, saying, "I want you to meet me at Coral Estates Park. You take the Dolphin Expressway west until you get to Southwest Ninety-Seventh Avenue. Go south until you get to the park. It will be about a half mile down on your left. You can't miss it."

I responded, "Not a problem."

"Once you get there, walk on the main pathway until you get to the pavilion. Turn right and walk about two hundred yards to another pavilion, and I will be sitting at a picnic table."

Click. He hung up without saying another word. I hung up the phone, grabbed the holster, put it on, and shoved the .38 Smith & Wesson in place. I put on my jacket and looked in the mirror. I was relieved that I couldn't see the gun. I reached into the night stand and grabbed my flashlight.

I raced to the elevator, and when I reached the ground floor, I quickly walked out the hotel doors and immediately saw the black Buick parked to my right. Further down, I saw two men sitting in another dark vehicle. They were slouched down in their seats.

I didn't hesitate and walked directly to the Buick. I opened the back door and felt under the mat to find the keys. I didn't look at the two men in the other car, but backed out slowly. I put the car in drive, took a causal look in the mirror, and drove out of the parking lot. They followed.

I turned right, and there was the underground parking lot for the hotel. I sped down the ramp and took an immediate right and then a left to get in the outgoing exit lane. I put the car in park and waited. As soon as I saw them, I would put it in drive and get out as quickly as possible.

I waited two minutes, and there was no sign of them. I figured they must be waiting outside. I couldn't let them follow me to where I was meeting our man. I waited some more.

Then my phone rang. Who the hell could that be? I looked at caller ID and saw that it was Jack. I said, "Hello."

Jack answered and said, "There are two men outside of the parking garage waiting in a black Mercedes. I want you to wait another five minutes, then leave."

"Wait, Jack! How do you know where I am?"

Jack chuckled. "I couldn't let you go by yourself. You're not even a rookie. You're less than a rookie. I called off Bob Lee from Jennifer and asked him to follow you. He's going to take care of the two men in the Mercedes, but give him five minutes. And, Irish, never get yourself blocked in at a place like a parking structure, you dummy. Hide in plain sight where there's an escape route."

I answered, "Okay, but who's watching Jennifer?"

"Bob Lee's partner, Dominic. He'll be with her until Bob returns."

After five minutes, I drove out of the parking structure and saw that two police cruisers had their lights flashing and were blocking in the black Mercedes. Four officers were out of their cars with their weapons drawn. They had the two men up against their car and were patting them down.

I left the parking garage and turned onto Northwest Seventh Avenue toward the Dolphin Expressway. I followed the instructions that I'd been given. I looked in the mirror and didn't see Bob Lee following. I hoped he hadn't lost me already.

I drove onto the Dolphin Expressway ramp and went west for fifteen minutes. I turned south on Southwest Ninety-Seventh Avenue, and drove until I came to Coral Estates Park.

I parked, grabbed my flashlight, and got out of the car. I turned on the flashlight and walked to the pavilion. I then turned right as instructed. I walked the two hundred yards to the other pavilion and came to some picnic tables, but there was no sign of anyone sitting at the tables.

I shined my light on the tables and saw a note tacked to the first table. It said, "Go back to the pavilion, turn left, and I will be there."

I did exactly as it was written. When I reached the place, he walked out from behind a large oak tree. He shined a light at me and said, "You're not Jack Casey." Then he turned and ran. He was out of shape, and not very fast. I caught him after few seconds.

I grabbed his shirt, pulled him down, and pinned him to the ground. He yelled, "Please don't hurt me! Please don't hurt me!"

"I am not here to hurt you. Just calm down. I work for Jack Casey. Now calm down."

He did as I asked. I looked at him, and saw his face was bruised and battered. It looked like he had been beaten severely about a few days ago. The swelling was just subsiding. I could tell he was terrified. His eyes darted back and forth like a cornered animal.

"Who are you, and where is Jack Casey?" he screamed.

"I am an agent with the FBI. My name is Sean MacSween. Unfortunately, Jack got the shit beat out of him. He's in the hospital, so he couldn't make it. He sent me instead."

He looked at me with suspicious eyes. "You're not here to kill me, are you?"

"No. If I wanted to kill you, you would be dead already. I'm here to help you and hopefully get some information that will help us with our investigation. I can get you out of here to someplace safe. Would you like that?"

"How can you guarantee that I'll be safe?"

"We can put you in protective custody. No one will be able to terrorize you anymore."

We stayed looking at each other as I held him down. I slowly released my grip to let him relax. He seemed to calm down, and his breathing began to slow.

"What happened to your face?" I asked calmly.

"I was locked in a basement for three days, and they would come down occasionally when they wanted to have some fun and ask me questions. If I didn't tell them what they wanted to hear, they would beat the crap out of me."

I released my grip and let him sit up. I asked, "Where was this house?"

"Not so fast. How do I know I can trust you?" he asked.

"Listen. Could you at least tell me your name?"

He looked around the park as if he was looking to find a place to run and hide in the dark. Then his shoulders slumped, and he said, "My name is Freddy. Freddy Sanchez."

"Okay, Freddy. My name is Sean, but my friends call me Irish. You can call me Irish. I'm here because Jack is in the hospital. He was beaten up pretty bad. I have been with the FBI for less than a year. I'm a rookie, so I'm pretty nervous myself." Hell, five hours is a lot less than a year. He didn't have to know exactly how long. "Most rookies never get to go on an assignment like this unless they're with a senior agent. I'm not here to do anything but help you and not screw up. If I screw up, I'll get assigned to some place in northern North Dakota for the rest of my life. We have to trust each other."

I stood up and extended my hand. He reached up and grabbed it. When he stood, he grimaced in pain. I could sense he was relaxing just a bit. He looked around again as if he could see in the dark. He was still a little nervous.

I broke the silence by saying, "Coming out here, we didn't know if this was a setup, or even an ambush. I could have been the one killed. So you see, we both need to trust each other."

Freddy stared at me for a few moments, and then said, "I don't know, man. If they find me, they're going to kill me. You've got to help me get out of here. I've got nowhere to go, and I haven't eaten for three days. I think they've broken my ribs and who knows what else."

"Well, why don't we get out of here and get you somewhere safe, somewhere they can't get to you anymore. What do you say? Trust me, Freddy, you really don't have any place else to go. Besides, if I wanted to kill you, don't you think you would already be dead?"

"How do I know you're not one of them and you just want to take me back to that house?"

He said "that house" like it was the gates of hell. He was terrified of returning.

"Do you want to stay here? I can just leave, or you can come with me. But if you stay here, they are eventually going to find you. You need to leave with me right now. Come on, trust me a little."

I could see his face softening as he stared at me. Finally, he let out a breath and said, "I guess I don't have any choice. I'll go with you, but can we stop and get something to eat on the way?"

I smiled, and then he smiled back for the first time. I said, "Sure, we can stop, but you have to promise me you won't run. I'll get fired if you do."

"I won't run. I've got nowhere to go."

As we started walking back to the car, I noticed he had a marked limp. I asked, "Why are you limping so badly?"

"Sometimes they would hit me with a lead pipe—never in the same place twice. But when they wanted to be *real* mean, they would use my shin as their target. I don't know if I have a broken leg, but it hurts so fucking bad I can hardly step on it. It's swollen up twice the normal size."

"Here, let me help."

"Naw, I can do it if I take my time."

We reached the far side of the pavilion and sat on one of the picnic tables to give Freddy some rest.

After a few minutes, I asked, "Are you ready to go?"

He replied, "Yeah, I'm ready."

As soon as we stood up, a shot rang out, and I heard Freddy scream as he was slammed to the ground. I hit the ground next to him, pulled my gun from its holster, and turned out my light. I had no idea where the shot came from, but from the way Freddy fell, it may have come from the direction of our car. *Oh great*, I thought, *now we have to get past him to get to the car.*

"Freddy, can you talk to me?" I nudged his left shoulder and he winced in pain. "Freddy, talk to me."

He was breathing hard and gasping in pain. "I've been shot in the left shoulder, goddamn it. Oh my god. You set me up."

"Freddy, stop. I didn't set you up." Just then, another shot rang out and hit the picnic table just above my head. Wooden splinters flew everywhere.

"Now do you think I set you up? Whoever this is, he's trying to kill both of us. We've got to move. Can you crawl?"

"I don't think so."

"Well, you stay here. I'm going to try to get around the other side of him. Keep your head down. Lie as flat as you can." I reached up quickly and grabbed the picnic table, pushing it over onto its side. "Stay behind this table and don't move. I'll be right back."

I got on all fours like I was in a track meet and sprinted as fast as I could. I felt the air of a bullet whiz past my head, missing by inches. I heard the shot an instant later. That was followed by two more shots, but they sounded different. Plus, I didn't feel any bullets whizzing past my head.

I dove behind a shed that was next to the pavilion and felt the skin peel away from my right elbow. I stayed low and listened for an entire minute. Nothing—no sound, no voices telling me to give up, no more gun shots—nothing.

Finally, I heard a voice yelling my name. "Irish, where the hell are you. Did you get scared away by two little gun shots? Don't be a pussy."

I didn't say anything, trying to figure who was calling my name, and then it hit me—Bob Lee.

"Is that you, hillbilly?"

"Damn straight. I thought you knew I was following you. Jack said he told you I was going to."

Then I remembered. "Show yourself, Bob. Walk out in the open so I can see you." I placed the flashlight on an adjacent table, turned it on, and ducked. There were no shots fired my way, so I waited a few more moments. Bob walked into the beam of the flashlight so I could see him.

I took in a deep breath to relax and said, "Bob, you scared the hell out of me. Who was shooting at us? Our man took one in the shoulder, and I think he's hurt pretty bad. We've got to get him out of here as soon as we can."

"Relax, Irish, I just got here," Bob said with a big grin on his face. He holstered his gun and walked closer. "Where's your guy lying?"

"He's over by those picnic tables," I said as I pointed the flashlight in Freddy's general direction.

"Well, let's get him the hell out of here. I'll go get the car and drive it up. I've got a first-aid kit in the back. I'll grab it."

Bob Lee ran back to the car. I heard a car start, and then I saw headlights through the trees. I ran over to Freddy. He was still on the ground, moaning in pain. "Freddy, I've got a friend here. We're going to take you to the hospital and get you taken care of. I'll call Jack Casey to see where he wants us to take you as soon as we get you loaded in the car."

Bob brought the car up off the road and onto the park grass. He slowed, trying to locate us, so I flashed the light to indicate where we were. He drove up and grabbed his first-aid kit as he got out, leaving the car running. He came around and saw me leaning over Freddy.

I shined the flashlight on Freddy, and we saw a pool of blood around his left shoulder. Bob kneeled down and withdrew a large gauze pad from his first-aid kit and placed it under Freddy's shirt on the entry wound. He held it in place as we lifted Freddy to a sitting position.

His shirt was full of blood on the backside. Bob grabbed another large gauze pad and placed it on the exit wound. He then took some roll gauze and began to wrap the two pads to keep them in place. After he was finished, we lifted Freddy and placed him in the backseat of the car.

Bob asked me to sit with Freddy and hold pressure on the wounds. I did the best I could while I called Jack. He answered on the first ring. "How is everything going, Irish?" Jack asked excitedly.

"I've got the package in the backseat of Bob Lee's car. He's been shot in the left shoulder. Plus he's been beaten quite severely over the past two to three days. He's lost a lot of blood. What should we do with him?"

"Take him to a clinic on West Flagler Street. It's about a half mile west of I-96, just past the Miami River. It's called Flagler Emergency Medical Clinic."

"Jack, I don't think you know how bad he's injured. I'm not a doctor, but he'll probably need surgery. We shouldn't mess around at some clinic," I protested.

"Listen to me, Irish. Take him there. They can handle anything. Hell, they removed a bullet from a guy's heart about a year ago. It's not just your average everyday clinic. They specialize in unique injuries, and they keep their mouths shut. No insurance necessary. Take him directly there. I'm sure Bob knows about this clinic."

"All right, Jack. I'll do as you ask."

"Irish, are you in Bob's car?"

"Yes, I had to leave my car back at the meeting place," I responded.

"Come back to the hospital as soon as you deliver your package. I want to know exactly what happened."

Just then, Bob interrupted me, "Tell Jack that I killed a man back there. He was the one shooting at you. Tell him I did not recognize the man, but he was a big guy, about two hundred sixty pounds, all muscle, blond hair, about thirty-five years old. I will go back and pick him up after we deliver this package."

I repeated what Bob had said.

Jack responded, "Tell Bob good work. Why don't you go back and pick up your car. You may need it sometime."

I told Jack I would do as he asked. I repeated the orders to Bob. As we rode to the clinic, Freddy woke up and smiled weakly at me, asking, "Am I going to live?"

"I'm not a doctor, but I think the odds are in your favor. How do you feel?"

"I feel better than when I was beaten back at the house."

"Hey, you never told me how you managed to escape."

Freddy winced in pain but said, "One of the guys guarding me must have felt sorry for me. He brought me a DVR and some movies. That night after he left, I tore the DVR apart and found enough metal in the casing that I could file it down on the concrete floor to make a pick, and then I unlocked the door. I did it after everyone was asleep. I snuck out of the house and ran. I ran like hell." Freddy laughed.

"That sounds ingenious to me. You're pretty clever and rather brave, too. I don't know if I could have done that," I said, trying to get his mind off the pain he was in. "You can relax now. You are going to be in good hands. There's nothing to worry about. So just hang in there until we get to the clinic."

By the time we arrived, there was a team of nurses and doctors waiting for us. There was no one else at the clinic.

They came out with a stretcher and loaded Freddy onto it. I watched as they took him inside the clinic. As soon as they entered, all the lights went out. It was like the Flagler Clinic was no longer open for business.

I looked at Bob and asked, "What the hell?"

He just smiled and said, "Don't ask. We never saw a thing. The best motto is don't see and don't tell."

I just shook my head and said, "What clinic?"

"Exactly," Bob replied.

As we rode back to the meeting place, Bob told me what had happened. He had placed a GPS device in my car and followed me. He was a little late getting there because he got held up by a train. When he arrived, he turned his headlights off and stopped about a quarter mile down the road. As he was walking up, he heard the two rifle shots. He got behind the shooter and told him to drop his rifle, but instead of dropping it, the shooter drew a handgun from his shoulder holster and tried to shoot him, so Bob had to shoot back in self-defense.

He said the only reason he shot twice was because the man was so big one shot couldn't do the job. Plus, he said it was dark, so he couldn't see well enough to make it a one-slug job.

CHAPTER TWENTY-THREE

woke up the next morning and sat on the bed, thinking about all that had happened the previous day and night—Jack getting beat up, me getting knocked over the head, the police involvement, getting sworn in as an agent for the FBI, meeting an informant named Freddy and talking him into coming back with me, then Bob Lee having to shoot a man who shot Freddy. What an assed-up day.

It had been a hell of a day, but I just knew it couldn't get any worse than that. I got up, went into the bathroom, and took a quick shower. I had just finished dressing when the phone rang.

I had a funny feeling that I shouldn't answer it, but curiosity got the better of me. I took it out of my pocket and answered, "Hello."

A woman was screaming into the other end. "Oh my god! Oh my god, Henry has been shot. Oh, Irish, I need you to come to the hospital right away. Can you come? Please, I need you."

She was overcome by crying. It was Maria Rodriguez. "Maria, what happened to Henry? You say he's been shot? Who shot him?"

She took a deep breath and squeaked out, "He was getting out of his car in front of the hotel, and a man got out of another car and walked up to him and shot him in the chest. He fell to the ground, and then the man shot him again."

When she stopped talking, her sobbing and moaning resumed, making it impossible for her to say anything more.

"Maria, I'm on my way. I'll be there in fifteen minutes. Do you hear me?" I shouted. I think she said okay, but I wasn't sure.

I ran down the hall to the elevator, waited two minutes, and rode it to the lobby. I ran out the door, and a taxi waiting right outside. I climbed in, but the cabbie said, "Sorry, pal, but I'm waiting for someone else."

"I don't care who you're waiting for. This is an emergency. Take me to Miami General ER I'll double your fare."

"You got it." He slammed the gearshift down, and away we went.

We arrived at Miami General in about five minutes. It had to be a record time because we practically flew all the way. I got out, handed him thirty dollars, and ran into the ER. Dr. Myott was standing at the triage desk. She saw me coming up to the desk and asked, "Well, Mr. MacSween, what are you doing here?"

"My brother was brought in here because he was shot in the chest."

"What in the hell are you involved in? Every time I turn around, you're here because of someone getting brutally injured. I think you need to talk to the police about this one. Mr. Rodriguez died about five minutes ago."

"Oh no! This is going to devastate his wife and family. Could you show me where they have Mrs. Rodriguez? She called me about ten minutes ago and asked that I come to the hospital. She doesn't have any family here."

"I should just report you to the police myself. You have got to be involved in this somehow."

"Look, Doc, I just know these people. Henry Rodriguez is a coworker just like Jennifer Marks is. I can't help it if they were injured. You just have a suspicious mind. I'm only here to give support. Jennifer's husband wasn't here when she got hurt, and Maria Rodriguez is all alone too."

"Very well. I will show you where Mrs. Rodriguez is. Maybe I misjudged you. I'm sorry. Come with me."

I followed Dr. Myott through the emergency waiting room and down another hallway. Just as we entered, we saw Maria being led down the hallway by a woman in plain clothes and an orderly. Maria was so distraught that she could hardly walk.

When they reached the room directly in front of us, they opened the door and led her to a bed. The two of them lifted her into the bed and eased her head onto a soft pillow. The orderly placed a light blanket over her and left. Maria appeared to be asleep.

"Did she already get something to make her sleep?" I asked.

The young woman was walking out the door, but stopped to turn and face me. I was shocked by her beauty. Her smooth, spotless dark skin, brilliant deep blue eyes, and thick black hair gave her a beautiful aura unlike any woman I have ever seen. She was without a doubt the most beautiful woman I had ever laid eyes on.

She stuck out her hand, smiled, and said, "Hello, my name is Katrina Bernetti. I am the social worker assigned to Mrs. Rodriguez."

I froze as I looked into her eyes. It took me a moment to get a grip. I finally said, "Hello, my name is Sean MacSween. I'm a good friend of Henry and Maria's. She called me about fifteen minutes ago when they had Henry in surgery. Dr. Myott just told me that he died in there."

"Yes, I'm afraid that's true. When we told Maria, she collapsed onto the floor. She didn't hurt herself, but emotionally, she's a wreck. A nurse is coming shortly to give her another sedative ordered by Dr. Myott. It's best if we try to keep her as calm as possible."

Dr. Myott spoke up and said, "I've ordered two types of sedative. If the first doesn't keep her calm, we can give her another that will help her sleep. So for now, that's about all I can do. I have to return to my other patients in the ER."

I turned to her and said, "Thank you for all you've done for Henry, Maria, and Jack–and also Jennifer Marks. I can't tell you how much I appreciate it."

"Not a problem. Perhaps I'll check in with Mrs. Rodriguez if I get a few minutes. Good day."

Dr. Myott turned and left, leaving Katrina Bernetti and me alone. The silence was deafening for the first thirty seconds. Never one to be shy or have a difficult time talking to women, I was, at that moment, speechless.

Finally, Katrina broke the silence. "So you are here just to be with Mrs. Rodriguez in her time of need?"

"Like I said, she called me and practically begged me to come be with her. All she had to do was say it once, and I would have been here in a heartbeat. She and Henry are great people. I think highly of both of them. I worked with Henry directly for the last year and became very good friends with him. We are members of the bargaining team for the International Truckers Union that's been on strike for the last year."

"I've read a lot about the strike. I hear there has been a settlement reached. That's wonderful. It's been hard on a great many people."

"I'm sorry to say that problems have developed with the settlement. We are just waiting to see if something can be done to correct things."

"That's too bad," Katrina said with the most sincere look I had seen in quite some time. I was caught once again by her eyes. She was so captivating. I was in a trance that held me staring deep into her pretty blues.

She smiled and asked, "What are you looking at, Mr. MacSween?"

"You. You are the most beautiful woman I have ever met. I feel like we formed an instant bond of some sort." She smiled. "That's not a line I'm using. I really believe it, Ms. Bernetti," I assured her.

"I think you may be right. I feel drawn to you as well, and that's not a line either, Mr. MacSween," she said, flashing her beautiful smile.

"I have never been this forward with any woman in my life. This is so strange. I came here so full of anxiety because of what happened to Henry, and now all I can think about is you."

"You flatter me, Mr. MacSween."

"Don't call me Mr. MacSween. My friends call me Irish."

"Does that mean I'm your friend?"

"I would hope so," I responded.

"Then Irish it is." She hesitated for a moment and then said, "I have to return to my duties. I am in charge of all the social workers in the hospital. Normally, I don't get directly involved with the patients, but when Mr. Rodriguez died, Dr. Myott asked me if I could help Mrs. Rodriguez right away."

"That was very kind of you, Miss Bernetti. It is *Miss* Bernetti, isn't it?"

"Do you care that much if it isn't?"

"I only have relationships with single ladies no matter how beautiful and instantly infatuated with them I am. I'm not a home wrecker. I will not do that to a family, period."

"That's good to know. I have no respect for any man who would involve himself with a married woman, either."

I smiled my big Irish smile, showing off my bright, pearly white teeth. She smiled back. I felt good, almost relaxed, in her presence for the first time since we'd met.

"Well, perhaps we will see each other again sometime."

"I would really like that. Maybe you could drop by in a little while just to see how Maria is doing. I am going to stay with her until someone in her family arrives. I could be here for quite a while."

"I will be back shortly, but in case I miss you, it was great to meet you."

She stuck out her hand, which I grabbed and held onto. It was soft, warm, and inviting. "Please come back and check on Maria. It's important that we keep a close eye on her."

"Good-bye, Irish. See you later. Thanks for coming to Mrs. Rodriguez's aid."

With that, she left. I kept my eyes on her back as she walked down the hallway.

"Please come back," I whispered.

Never have I been so taken by any woman so quickly. I never believed in love at first sight, but at that moment, I believed I'd just experienced it.

CHAPTER TWENTY-FOUR

M aria was still thrashing about on the bed and mumbling "Henry" under her breath when I returned to her room. She seemed to be in a dream state, but I wondered if she was in fact awake, keeping her eyes closed to prevent the reality of the situation from coming to light.

After Katrina left, a nurse came in and gave Maria the injection that Dr. Myott had ordered. It took about ten minutes, but she finally stopped writhing and fell into a deep sleep.

After the nurse left, I moved my chair into the corner of the room. I closed my eyes. I felt so tired. I drifted off and must have slept for thirty minutes when the door opened. The same nurse came in and said, "We just received a call from Mrs. Rodriguez's son, Roderick, and he said he would be here in about two to three hours. He was imme-diately taking a flight from Dallas to Miami. He wanted to make sure someone was with his mother until he arrived. Are you able to stay?"

"I'll stay until he gets here." I looked over at Maria, who was once again thrashing about. "Could you possibly give her something more to keep her calm?"

"It's only been about an hour since the last injection. I'm supposed to wait at least three hours before I can give her another shot. I will be back in two hours, but if she wakes and is really troubled, call for me and I'll come right back."

The nurse left the room, so I took my phone from my pocket and called Thomas. He answered on the first ring.

"Good afternoon, this is Thomas Sharpe." Thomas is always a gentleman in speech and dress.

"Hey, this is Irish. I suppose you have heard about Henry, haven't you?"

"I have, Irish. What the hell is going on? Why Henry? Who would do such a thing, especially to Henry?"

"I'm not sure what is going on, but I can tell you this. We—and I mean you, me, Jennifer, and anyone else who thinks Joey is destroying the union—better watch what we do, what we say, and where we go. This is not some petty game anymore. Someone is playing for keeps. I have to talk to you about Henry, but not on the phone." I stopped talking and waited for Thomas to say something in return. I wanted to hear his voice again to see if I could tell he was still sincere.

I could hear him take in a deep breath as if he was trying to calm himself. Then he said, "Irish, I never thought anyone would get killed over this. Do you think Joey was behind this? I just can't see Joey killing someone. He's a prick, but I don't know about this."

He sounded real, somewhat forlorn, and his voice was cracking with emotion. I asked, "Thomas, have you heard anything that might make you think Joey is involved?"

"I did overhear him arguing with someone on the phone this morning. I was at his door and was going to go into his office, but I stopped and waited for him to get off the phone. He sounded like he was going to blow a gasket. He really lost his cool. He was as angry as I have ever heard him. He said he was going to do things his way and fuck everyone else. He's done taking orders, and if they didn't like it, they could go to hell. It sounded like someone was pressuring him to do things he didn't want to. Who do you think could have that kind of power over him? He doesn't take orders from anyone."

"I don't know, but we are going to find out. Hey, do you think you could meet with me and our friend a little later this afternoon? I told them here at the hospital that I would stay with Maria until her son arrives. He should be here within the next couple hours. Our friend is really interested in talking to you."

"I would, but it would have to be somewhere private. I have to be extremely careful," Thomas replied.

"How about if I call you back in a few minutes, and I'll let you know where and when we can meet?"

"That sounds good. I'll clear my calendar for this afternoon and evening."

"Okay. I'll talk to you later." I hung up the phone and immediately dialed Jack's cell.

He answered on the first ring. "Hello, this is Jack."

"Jack, it's Irish. Henry Rodriguez has been shot and killed."

"I know. I got a call about ten minutes ago from one of my men. They're already on the case."

"What have you found out?"

"We have a witness who says she saw the whole thing. She's one of the desk clerks at the hotel. She said she forgot her purse in her car and was going out to get it when everything happened. Henry was getting out of his car in front of the hotel, and this man—he was wearing aviator sunglasses, a dark blue jacket, white shirt, and tan slacks—got out of the passenger side of a black Mercedes and walked right up to Henry and shot him twice, point blank. Henry went down, and the man calmly turned around to leave but stopped took off his aviators and shot him once again. She said he then calmly walked back to the Mercedes, and the driver drove slowly away. Sounds like a professional hit to me."

"Did she get a good look at his face?"

"She said she did. She said he was white with a deep tan and tall, six two or three, and had thick black hair. She said she believes she's seen him at the hotel before, but can't remember where or when. She said if we put him in a lineup, she would recognize him in a minute," Jack said eagerly.

"Henry's wife Maria also saw the entire thing. How can someone just do that in broad daylight in front of everyone?"

"I don't know, but I think they're getting desperate," Jack responded.

As I registered the excitement in Jack's voice, I asked, "Did you get a look at the hotel's security cameras?"

"They're trying to do that now, but hotel security says they were down at the time of the murder. Unfortunately, for some reason, they were shut off. The chief of security has no idea why that happened. He said they would have recorded the entire episode had they been in service."

"He has no idea why they were off?"

"That's the strange thing. Immediately afterward, they were back on. He said he's the only person who has access to that particular electrical panel."

"Have you had him checked out?"

"We have. Steve Hill followed up on it himself. The man has been with the hotel security since it opened. Before that, he was at the Carlton Hotel for twenty years."

"We've got to find out who shut that off and why," I added.

"Wait a minute, Sherlock Holmes. We are trying our best to get that information. Leave the police work to us. We are very capable of working this case.

"No offense, Jack. I'm sorry. I didn't mean anything by that. I'm just so pissed about what's been happening."

"No offense taken. I really appreciate all your input. I was just busting your balls now that you're an FBI agent."

"Thanks, Jack. One more thing. Is this woman willing to testify in court?"

"She said she is. I had her put into protective custody. The game changes now. This is no longer just a vendetta for some politicians to get back at the union leaders. As our investigation is evolving, we have reason to believe that Joey is involved with an organized crime syndicate and that, possibly, they are calling the shots and using Joey as a puppet."

"No shit? Well then, I think I might have something for you. I have that person of interest who is willing to talk to you. He might have some information that fits right in with your theory about organized crime calling the shots. Can you meet with us later today? I have to stay with Maria until her son arrives. He should be here within the next couple of hours."

"Absolutely. How about this afternoon in my hospital room. Let's say two o'clock?" asked Jack.

"Okay, it's a date. Hey, hold on a minute. I have a call coming in. I think I should take this. I'll be right back."

I pushed hold and answered the other line, "Hello."

It was Thomas, and he was frantic. "Irish, I just got a call from Sophia's driver. He said she and her girlfriend went into a ladies shop over on Biscayne Boulevard and never returned. He said after twenty minutes, the lady running the shop came screaming out of the store. She said a man came in from the back and pulled a gun out and forced Sophia and her girlfriend out the back door. He told the lady to lie down on the floor behind the register and not to get up for five minutes."

"Goddamn it. I've got my friend on the other line. Let me tell him what happened."

Thomas jumped in quickly and said, "Wait a minute. As soon as I hung up that call, I got another call from some other man who said not to go to the police and that if I wanted to see Sophia and her friend alive again, I would wait in my room until I received further instructions. Irish, I'm not leaving this room until I hear from this guy. So our meeting for later today will have to wait."

I said, "Hold on a second. I need to tell my friend what happened. I'll be right back."

Before Thomas could argue, I put him on hold and got Jack back on the other line. "Jack, that call was our person of interest. It seems that someone's kidnapped his wife and her friend. He was told not to leave his room until he receives further instructions. He says he's not going anywhere until he gets that call."

"Damn, first assault, then murder, and now kidnapping. This is getting real interesting. Tell him to stay put. Tell him to do whatever they want, but to call you immediately and to not leave his room until we get there. Tell him we will come to him. I'm getting the hell out of this hospital. I have to get Dr. Myott to release me. When Maria's son arrives, call me and then go directly to the hotel and stay there. I should be ready to go in about two hours, so I will meet you at the hotel as soon as I can get there."

"What about more security in the hotel?" I asked.

"I will get some more agents in the hotel right away. I called Washington, and they sent ten more agents down. They arrived about an hour ago. Also, I want more men on Jennifer. I'll send two of those agents to the hospital. I don't want anything happening to her. It seems like someone has declared war. We just have to find out who we're fighting."

"I wonder if Joey is behind all of this. He has been really bold the last week or so. Maybe Joey J. Pinata has raised the bar to another level?"

"Call Bob Lee and have him stay with Jennifer right in her room until my agents get to the hospital. I have to make arrangements to get to your person of interest in his hotel room."

"Won't that be kind of dangerous for you to go to the hotel? What if someone recognizes you? Our entire cover could be blown."

"Normally I wouldn't take this risk, but with everything that has developed, I have to talk to him, and that's the only way we can handle it. Believe me, neither you, nor anyone else, will recognize me. I'm a master of disguises. It's one of my many talents. I used to be a makeup artist in college, and I got pretty good at it. It'll be okay. Your job will be to convince our friend to stay put as long as he can and to convince him that no one will recognize me. Tell him I guarantee it."

Without another word, Jack hung up and Thomas came back on the line. I told him, "I just talked to my friend, and he said to stay put. Do whatever they tell you to do but keep us informed and call me immediately. You must stall them if they want you to leave your room. My friend is putting more men in the hotel as we speak. Then as soon as Maria's son gets here, I will come back to the hotel. So we're talking maybe an hour or two at the most."

"He can't come here!" Thomas yelled frantically into the phone. "What if someone sees him come to my room? That would be the end of me and my union job, and probably Sophia."

"No one will recognize him. He said he used to be a makeup artist. He said there's no chance anyone will recognize him if he comes to your room. Plus, it's no big deal if I come to your room. We do that sort of thing every day. You have got to trust him on this. He knows what he's doing. I'm trusting him with my life. I guess we all are. So hang tight. He needs to talk to you as soon as he can."

Thomas was very hesitant but agreed, "Okay, Irish. I trust you, and if you trust him, I will too."

He said he trusted me. Wow, that was scary. I didn't even trust myself, and now I had Thomas laying everything on the line because of me. What the hell was I getting him into?

"Okay, good. I'll see you in a little while. Keep in touch if anything new comes up."

"I will," Thomas replied.

We hung up, and I sat back down in the only chair in the room. Maria was still sleeping, but was unconsciously troubled and starting to get restless again. I wished she could sleep for another week, so she wouldn't have to face the death of Henry. My heart broke for her and her family.

I heard the door opening and turned to see Katrina Bernetti walk into the room. I smiled and stood up to greet her. She returned a tender smile and extended her hand for me to shake.

As we gently clasped our hands together, and she asked, "How is Mrs. Rodriguez doing?"

"She's tossing and turning a lot. It's like she's living this nightmare in a dream. I feel so bad for her. What an awful thing to have to face. Her life will never be the same."

"Surprisingly, people can be given something to help them sleep, but they never go deep enough to block out the reality of such a tragedy."

"I have never really lost anyone who I loved as much as she apparently does Henry. The only person was my dad, and we never were that close."

Katrina responded, "I lost my mother, and we loved each other so much. It was a very difficult time for me. I know what Mrs. Rodriguez is going through."

At that moment, we both looked down and realized we were still holding hands. It felt so comforting to me. She didn't pull away like she was uneasy. She kept her hand there like it was a natural thing to do.

Our eyes met, and we looked deeply at each other. There was a strange calmness, a tenderness that neither of us wanted to lose.

"Irish, why are you still holding my hand?"

"I was going to ask you the same thing—not that I want you to let go. I don't think I'll ever want to let go. This just feels right."

She smiled and I could feel her hand relax in mine. We smiled again at each other, but just then Mrs. Rodriguez let out a deep moan. We released our hands and the moment was gone.

Katrina patted Mrs. Rodriguez's side like she was a mother comforting her fearful child. Whispering to Maria, she said, "The Lord will take care of you in your time of need. I am praying for you along with many others. You need to be strong. God will give you the strength."

I was overcome by her gentleness and care for someone she didn't even know. I knew right then and there that she was special. She was captivating my heart like no one I had ever known.

She turned around and looked at me with tears in her eyes. She dabbed them with a tissue and tried to smile. She was obviously overcome with emotion.

I asked her, "Do you always get this emotional with your patients?"

"It's a weakness that I have. I get too wrapped up with people in need. It just kills me to see so much pain—pain that I see every day."

"That cannot be healthy if you get like this every time a patient is troubled. I don't know myself, but I heard that people in hospitals have to separate themselves from the pain they deal with every day or it will destroy them."

"Normally, I can control it, but this is so tragic, and I am directly involved with her. I was with her when the doctor told her about her husband. She fell into my arms and screamed like she met the devil himself. It was a horrible time for her. I just want the pain to go away. Why does life have to give us so much pain?"

As I drew her near me to separate her from Maria, she fell into my arms and cried. I held her for a full minute, or I should say, we held each other, as she put her arms around my neck and buried her face there. It just felt right. Apparently, at that moment, we needed each other. It was the first time in ages I could hold on to someone who really cared.

We finally let go of each other, and she sat down. I left to go find another chair, and was back in ten seconds as there was one right outside the door. We sat and talked for the next two hours. She eventually admitted that her shift was over because she had come into work early that morning, but she wanted to wait until Maria's son arrived.

The two hours passed too quickly. As crazy as it sounds, we connected in that time like we had been together for years. Finally, she decided to check in with the nurse to see if there was an update on Maria's son's arrival.

I sat there for a few minutes before realizing I had forgotten that I needed to call Jennifer, but before that, I needed to make the call to Bob Lee to give him a heads-up on the situation. I had completely neglected everything Jack wanted me to do. I wanted to kick myself, though I was glad

Jack wanted more security coverage for Jennifer. It relieved a little of my stress.

I pulled out my phone and Bob's card, and dialed his number. After two rings, he answered, "Irish, to what do I owe the honor for this call?"

"Bob, have you heard about Henry Rodriguez?"

"No. Hell, I don't even know who Henry Rodriguez is. So I don't know what happened to him. Enlighten me."

"This is no joke, Bob. Henry is the International Truckers Union regional director from Texas. He was shot and killed this morning right in front of the hotel. Apparently, Henry got out of his car, and a man walked right up and shot him. After Henry fell to the ground, he calmly shot him again. Then the guy got back into his car and drove away. Henry died an hour later here at the hospital."

"No shit? That sounds like a professional hit. Hell, I've only been out and about for an hour. I didn't get to bed until about four this morning. I suppose you want me to keep a closer eye on Jennifer?"

"That's why I called. These people are dangerous. Jack does not want to take any chances. He said he's also sending two more agents over to the hospital, which will take some time. If you could get there ASAP, we would be very grateful. If you see two guys hanging around the hospital or near Jennifer, hopefully, they're the ones Jack sent."

Bob responded quickly, "I'll be in her room in five minutes, and don't worry about me seeing Jack's men. Those guys stick out like a turnip in a strawberry patch. I'll touch base with them, though, as soon as I see them."

"There is one other thing, Bob. Do you know Thomas Sharpe, our secretary for the ITU?"

"I know who he is, but I've never had the opportunity to meet him. Why? What's going on with him?"

"We believe his wife has been kidnapped. She and her friend were taken out the back of a clothing store down on Biscayne Boulevard by some man about an hour ago. Her driver didn't know about it until twenty minutes later."

"Man, you northern boys sure bring a rash of shit to our peace-loving city. Why would she be mixed up in all this?"

"Well, she's not only Thomas Sharpe's wife, but she's also President Pinata's only daughter."

"Wow, whoever is behind this is really stirring that bucket of shit. Things smell pretty ripe about now. These boys don't pull any punches. It sounds like it's time we start throwing some punches of our own," Bob said with a laugh.

I laughed with him and asked, "What the hell do you mean by 'stirring the bucket of shit'?"

"Well, if you put a pile of cow shit in a bucket and leave it alone, after a while, it'll stop stinking. As soon as you stir the shit, it starts smelling again. It's one of those intelligent Southern sayings. We have lots of them down here. If you stay long enough, you all will have them rolling them off your tongues."

"Never know how long I'll be down here. I've met some mighty fine people. I may stay for a while. You never know."

"What happened? Did you meet one of our Southern belles and fall in love?" I just smiled, and he said, "I'll be goddamned. You did, didn't you?"

"A nice guy never tells, but she sure is beautiful."

"Is she someone here at the hospital?"

"Yeah, I just met her today, and we've already talked for almost two hours. She is like a goddess," I said, with emotion in my voice.

"Hell, I know who you're talking about. She's got beautiful skin, black hair, is well-built and sweet as apple pie. It's Katrina Bernetti, isn't it?"

I had to laugh. "How did you know? Am I not the first guy to fall for her in an instant?"

"Don't get me wrong, she's as nice as could be—beautiful and very sexy—but no man has even been able to get her phone number. She will break your heart just like all the others."

"I will get her phone number, and I'm going to have a date before I leave this hospital."

"Well, I'll be hog tied. You must be good with the women. I've never seen her give her number out to anyone."

"I'm not really that much of a ladies' man, but we have a certain draw to each other. She has it, and so do I."

"Well then, good luck with your date, but enough of this. I've got to get my ass up to Jennifer's room."

"Can you stay with her until Jack or I tell you otherwise?"

"Not a problem. I'll head up there right now."

"Where are you? At home?"

"No, I'm outside of the ER reading that damn newspaper. I'm a slow reader. Like all the other Southern boys, I never finished fifth grade, but I think I can find her room. I will be up there right away. Don't worry about her. I'll take good care of her," Bob assured me.

I let out a deep sigh of relief and said, "Thanks so much. I'm going to call Jennifer right now and let her know what's going on and that you will be watching over her real close."

"Okay. Let's get rolling," Bob said as he hung up the phone.

Before I could dial Jennifer's number, my phone rang. Jennifer's ID showed on the screen, and I thought 'how the hell does she know enough to call me just before I'm going to call her?'

I clicked the green button on the phone and answered, "Hello?"

It was Jennifer, but I could hardly tell by her deep sobs. In a shaky voice, she managed to say, "Irish, I just heard. Is it true about Henry? He was such a good man. Maria must be devastated." Then she lost it completely.

I waited through the crying and sobbing until I heard her take a deep breath and let it out slowly. She sounded like she was almost breathing normally.

"Jennifer, it's true. Henry was shot out in front of our hotel. They took him to surgery, but he didn't make it. I guess he lost too much blood. The doctors could do nothing more."

"I can't believe this. Does this have anything to do with our other business? If it does, I have to get out of this hospital right away. They may come after me. I'm a sitting duck lying here in this bed." I could hear the panic in her voice.

"We don't know for sure if this is related." I was lying just a little about the connection, but I didn't want to scare her any more than she already sounded. I continued by making light of the situation. "Besides, where are you going to run with just one good leg? Are you going to hop all the way to Ohio?" Before she could say something back, I said, "Jack told me to call Bob Lee. You remember him? He's the cop keeping watch downstairs who comes and goes. Jack wants to have him spend some of his quality time with you. At least until Jack figures out what to do next. So don't worry, you're safe here in the hospital. Jack is also sending over two more agents to keep an eye on you."

"You said 'here in the hospital.' Are you in the hospital too?"

"I'm not a patient, Jennifer. I'm sitting with Henry's wife, Maria, until her son arrives from Texas. He should be here shortly. As soon as he gets here, I have to get back to the hotel so I won't be able to come and see you. Bob is going to be with you any minute now, so you'll be safe."

"Oh, Irish, what did I get us into?"

"Now's not the time to second-guess yourself," I responded, trying to sound confident. "Everything is going to work out. Jack's people are all over this. Right now, you're safe, and I'm safe, so try to relax. I will get with you as soon as I can. Okay?"

"You and I are okay, but Henry is dead. But if you say everything is going to be fine, I'll wait until I hear from you, but please don't let me lie here without knowing what's going on. Holy fuck, I'm scared shitless."

"I know, so am I. But try not to worry; I'll check on you as soon as I know anything else. Just try to stay calm. Bob Lee is very capable, and he will keep you safe. He should be there by now."

She said, "Wait a minute, someone's at the door." I heard her yell, "Come in!"

Then I heard Bob Lee's Southern voice say, "Hello, little miss sunshine. How are you?"

"I'm scared shitless." That's Jennifer for you. "Okay, Irish, he's here."

"That's good. You're in good hands. Don't give Bob a hard time. He's there to protect you, so be nice."

"I will be nice, don't worry. Good-bye, Irish, and keep me informed."

"Good-bye, Jen." I heard her mumble something to Bob, and I hung up the phone. I sat back down in the chair feeling exhausted.

I looked at Maria and watched her writhing in the bed with a horrified look on her face. My heart broke again just seeing her. I wondered if she needed some more sleeping medication. I was going to call the nurse's station to get Maria something more to calm her down, but my phone rang before I could.

I answered, "Hello. This is Sean."

"Irish, it's Matt Tennyson. How are things with you?"

"I'm not really sure, Congressman. Did you hear that Jack Casey got the shit beat out of him?"

"Yes, it's all over Washington. Jack has a good reputation here. Word gets around fast," he responded.

"Everything has gone to shit since I talked to you. Have you heard Henry Rodriguez was shot to death today, about four hours ago? Some guy walked right up to him as he was getting out of his car in front of the hotel and shot him in the chest. After Henry was down, the guy shot him again. It's been awful here."

"No shit. I hadn't heard about Henry. That's fucking insane. Just what the hell is going on down there? It sounds like a Mafia hit, if you ask me. I've got some information that might help you out too."

"I'm sitting in the ER at Miami General with his wife, Maria. She's devastated. Her son is coming here from Dallas. He should be here any time now."

"Like I said the last time we talked, you watch yourself, Irish. This is some real bad shit that's going on. Anyway, the reason I called is because you asked me to check out David Shanahan."

"What did you find out about our mystery man?"

"This might fit right in with Henry's attack. It seems that Mr. Shanahan has a history of being involved with some very bad people. His dad was involved with the West Coast Mafia. He must have pissed someone off, because they found him face down in San Francisco Bay. That was about ten or twelve years ago. Now it seems that David has been tracked back to the same Mafia family that his dad worked for. His history came to a dead halt about five years ago. He just disappeared from the map. I called my friend, the director of the FBI, Henry Sullivan. I had him do some digging on this David Shanahan. It was very interesting. He did a cross match on his fingerprints, and they matched with a young kid by the name of David Marzetti, who was arrested twenty-two years ago, when he was sixteen, for aggravated assault and murder. He beat the rap by having an airtight alibi, but he was a muscle guy for the neighborhood Mafia's sons. It seems that the men in charge for the Marzetti family had David protect their sons. It appears he was quite a hellion when he was young."

I couldn't believe it. "I thought Jack told me they did a background check on Shanahan, and it came up clear. How did this get by them?"

"It appears that someone inside the bureau presented Jack with a false background check. FBI Director Sullivan's checking into that as we speak."

"Does that mean David has someone inside the FBI who is covering his ass?

"It sure seems that way, but it's not that unusual. Years ago, the Mafia had someone as far up as the assistant director of the FBI on their payroll. As incredible as it sounds, every organization of the government has been infiltrated. So I'm not really surprised."

Matt sounded like this was an everyday occurrence. I had a hard time believing that people could be bought so easily. What happened to serving your country with dignity? Viewing the deceit that runs amuck in the union, though, I guess shouldn't be so surprised.

"Do you have a problem if I talk to Jack Casey about this?"

"Not at all. Though I think he may already know about it; Sullivan said he was going to call Jack right away. I bet this will change the entire ballgame. Maybe Jack will be able to focus his investigation in an entirely different direction."

"That's if Jack can get his ass out of the hospital. He really took a beating. Plus, he's so fucking stubborn. He tries to act like he's still twenty years old."

"Well, if I hear anything else, I will get in touch with you. Don't call my office if you need me. Call me on my cell—it's the only phone that is secure through the federal network."

"Thanks for everything, Matt. If more shit happens down here, I will try to keep you posted. And Matt, one more thing. Try to get some rest. You sound tired."

I hung up the phone and looked at Maria still moving around uncomfortably in the bed. I buzzed the nurse's station. A woman's voice came over the speaker and asked, "Can I help you with something?"

I responded, "Mrs. Rodriguez is thrashing around a lot, and I was told if she does that again, I was to call for another shot to calm her down."

"Not a problem. I will be right in with something."

Two minutes later, a nurse came through the door with a syringe in her hand. "This will put her in a deep sleep for the next three or four hours. That's the best possible solution for her."

I thanked her, and after she closed the door, I tried closing my eyes to get some sleep myself, but to no avail. I sat there watching Maria roll around for about another five minutes, and then she seemed to completely relax into a deep sleep.

For the next hour and a half, I sat there with running everything through my mind, trying to put pieces in their place, trying to make some sense of everything that had happened.

All of a sudden, the door burst open, and in walked a man who looked just like Henry Rodriguez, only twenty years younger and a hundred pounds lighter. He looked at me, then at his mom, and tears filled his eyes. He walked over to Maria and hugged her while she was sleeping.

"Mama, it's Roderick. I'm here, Mama."

Maria opened her eyes. She seemed confused at first until she realized it was her son, and then she started silently weeping. He put his arms around her and just held her for two minutes, not wanting to let go.

Finally, Roderick turned around and introduced himself. "Hi, I'm Roderick Rodriguez. You must be my dad's friend, Irish."

I stood up and shook his hand and said, "I'm so sorry about your dad. He was a great man and a good friend."

He clasped my hand with both of his hands and said, "Thanks so much for not leaving my mom alone. I appreciate your help so much. My dad spoke so well of you. I remember him saying that you were the best man in his union."

"Well, I don't know about that. But I do know your dad was one of the best. He taught me a lot about the union and a lot about life. You were very lucky to have had him as your father."

"We are going to miss him a great deal. He was more than just a father. He was the head of our entire family, not just Mom and us kids, but his brothers and sisters and all their kids. Everyone listened to what he said. They all came to him for counsel. Dad was our leader. He was a gentle man and was loved by everyone."

I listened to Roderick praise his father and wished I could have said the same things about my dad, but I couldn't. Simply put, Roderick was a lucky man in many ways.

I emerged from my thoughts and said, "Listen, Roderick, I really do have to get going.

There is so much on my plate right now, and it's getting fuller by the minute. So if you don't mind, I will leave you alone with your mom. The nurse gave her a shot about an hour and a half ago and said she should be out for three or four hours. She said it was the best thing for her at this time."

I gave him my phone number and said to call if there was anything I could do to help. I turned to walk out the door, and he stopped me by saying, "Help the police find out who murdered my dad."

I said in return, "I intend to."

CHAPTER TWENTY-FIVE

As soon as I stepped out of the room, I dialed Jack's phone. He answered, "Hello, Irish, are you leaving the hospital now?"

"Yes, I am, and I'm heading to my hotel. Are you going to be able to join us there?"

"I told you I would be there, didn't I?"

"All right then, I'll see you when you get to the hotel."

"I will call you, Irish, when I'm leaving my apartment."

"Sounds like a plan to me, Jack. I'll see you in a little while."

I hung up the phone and started walking through the ER waiting room toward the exit when I heard, "Irish, where are you going? I thought you were staying with Mrs. Rodriguez until her son arrived."

I recognized the voice and turned to see her beautiful face. Katrina Bernetti was standing at the triage desk. My eyes went immediately to hers. Her dark, sensuous appearance almost made me melt. For just an instant, it was just the two of us. The rest of the world did not exist. How could this woman captivate me in such a way that I never knew existed?

I walked over to her without touching the floor. At least, it seemed that way. I said, "Mrs. Rodriguez's son got here about five minutes ago."

She flashed her beautiful smile and said, "That was an awful quick flight from Dallas, wasn't it?"

I smiled back and said, "He said he caught his flight immediately after hearing the news." Then without even thinking about it, I asked, "Could I speak with you privately?"

"Sure. Let's go outside and get some fresh air."

I offered my hand, and surprisingly, she took it. We walked hand and hand out the exit doors. I was in heaven.

Once outside, we walked over to the table that Bob Lee occupied so often and sat down. I didn't know what to say because I had never felt this way toward any woman in my life. But calmness came over me as I felt the warm touch of her hand in mine.

"Can I have my hand back?" Katrina asked softly.

I let go of her hand and said to her, "I don't know how to say this to you without sounding foolish, but I just feel there is something special about you. Would you be willing to go out to dinner with me?"

Without saying a word, she leaned into me and gave me a gentle kiss that was no more than a soft brush of her lips on mine. "Don't say any more," she whispered. "I know what you're talking about. I feel it too. I was afraid it was only me and that you would just walk out of my life as quickly as you arrived."

I put my fingers on her lips to stop her from talking more and said, "I do. I have actually felt this way from the instant I saw you."

I felt the softness of her cheek with the back of my hand. I wanted to take her into my arms and hold her, but I didn't. We sat there, holding each other without touching, silently looking deep into each other's eyes.

After a few minutes, I came out of my semi-trance and said to her, "I hate to leave you, but I must. There is so much I have to do. So much has happened. The police will want to talk to me about Henry, and my boss will be wondering what's happened to me." I brought her hands up to my face and softly kissed her palms. "Can I see you later? I would love to go out to dinner with you tonight, but I have no idea what the rest of today will bring. Can I call you if it looks like I can get away?"

"I have a better idea," she countered. "If you can get away, call me and come by my place? I would love to cook for you. I'm a great cook. I know this great Italian recipe that you would love. Then it would be just the two of us, and maybe we can figure out what this feeling is and what we should do about it."

"Sounds like a perfect night. I will call you."

As I stood up, a thought that I've had many times over the last ten years came to me—*why am I giving up my life for the union when normal people go home at night and forget their jobs?* Katrina stood and I pulled her to me, wanting her more than any woman I've ever known.

For just an instant, she gently laid her head on my chest, looked up at me, and with that beautiful smile, whispered, "Not here. This is my workplace. I will melt into your arms later."

She stood on her toes, and our lips softly touched again. She turned to leave, but I stopped her. "Aren't you forgetting something?"

She turned back around to me with a puzzled look and asked, "What do you mean?"

I gave her my best grin and said, "I don't know where you live or what time dinner is being served."

She let out a hardy, flirtatious laugh. "You made me lose my train of thought. You have that power over me."

I smiled. "I hope so," I replied.

She reached into her white jacket pocket and took out one of her business cards and a pen. She wrote her phone number and address on the back of the card, handed it to me, and said, "Here; try to make it by nine?"

"If I'm not there by nine, call the FBI," I said jokingly. If she only knew.

I looked at the back of her card and instantly memorized her address and phone number, just in case I lost the card. I walked to the circular drive of the hospital entrance and luckily found a cabbie waiting for his next fare.

As I entered the cab, I said, "Royal Crown Executive Hotel, please."

The cabbie responded, "You got it, pal."

I wasn't his pal, but I didn't care. In spite of all the tragedy around me, I was happy for the first time in a long while. I felt a murmur of peace in my heart.

I rode the entire way in silence, thinking of Katrina, Henry, Jennifer, Jack, and Joey Pinata. Before I knew it, the cabbie had pulled up in front of the hotel. "That'll be eight bucks, please."

I took a ten out of my pocket and handed it to him. "Keep the change."

It was my intent to go straight to my room, but instead, I headed to the bar to see who was there. I felt the familiar pull of the power of alcohol, but I suppressed it. I still felt the need for a drink, but there was something different this time. I knew I could walk into this bar to see who was there and not allow alcohol to control my thoughts and actions. I felt free for the first time in ages.

The controlling demon in my life was releasing his grip ever so slowly. Under his rule, I was almost powerless to control my own life. It was like the opposite of an allergy; it was a craving I couldn't control. It was that mysterious demon that all alcoholics experience. But at that moment, I was controlling him. I didn't ask how. I just let my heart guide me for the first time in many moons. It felt good.

Instead of the bar, I went straight to my room to wait, and decided to take a short nap. I didn't know if or when I would have the opportunity again.

CHAPTER TWENTY-SIX

· ·

I woke up with a start. The phone was ringing next to my head. When I finally realized what was happening, I picked up the phone and said, "Hello."

"Irish? Is that you?"

It was Riona. I sat bolt upright.

"Yeah, it's me. I was sleeping. You woke me up."

"I'm sorry I woke you, but I just had to talk to you," she said quietly.

"No problem. I thought I would catch a few winks while I could. Is everything okay?"

"Yes and no. I have to talk to you about something, and it can't wait any longer."

"What is it, Riona? You sound like there's something wrong. Is there?" I asked.

"Irish, I have been waiting here for you for the last year. Hoping and praying that someday you would come home. But you never have. It's always that stupid union job first. I'm always second, or even third, for that matter."

I sat there, shocked. The last thing I expected was a Dear John call from Riona.

"I cannot take this any longer. Irish, I've met someone else. He's someone who's here for me. He calls me every day, sometimes two or three times a day. He says he loves me, and I've fallen so in love with him. He's a wonderful man, and he treats me like I'm his queen. He asked me to marry him, and I said yes."

I was stunned. I could tell this was killing her. In all the time we'd known each other, she never wanted to hurt me or make me feel bad in any way.

"Riona, I have been waiting for this call for a long time. I am so sorry that I was never there for you and that I asked so much from you without giving anything in return. You are such a beautiful person, and you deserve someone better than me. What you've wanted, I've not been able to give. I have failed you in so many ways. I'm sorry from the bottom of my heart."

It was her turn to be silent. After what seemed like an hour, but was less than a minute, she asked, "Then you don't hate me?"

"How could I hate you? You were always there for me. I will never hate you. You'll always have a part of my heart. I can only wish you happiness, because I realize I've lost the best woman I have ever known."

I could hear her softly crying into the phone. She took a deep breath and said, "Thank you for understanding and not hating me. Now that I know you're okay, I can move forward. Good-bye, Irish. Remember that I will always love you in a special way."

"And I will always love you too."

She hung up the phone without another word. I sat there on my bed, wondering what lay ahead for me. Was Katrina for real, or was she just a fantasy because of her beauty? Only time would tell.

I got up, undressed, and walked into the bathroom to take another shower. I felt dirty—not physically, but mentally, from everything that had happened. I finished and dressed quickly to wait for Jack's call. I didn't even know if Dr. Myott had released him from the hospital or if he had just left on his own accord.

I sat at my desk and waited thirty minutes before the phone rang. It was Jack, and he sounded like he was ninety years old. His voice was raspy and shaky. "I'll be ready to leave shortly. Give me about fifteen minutes, and then go to your friend's room."

"Wait a minute, Jack. Are you saying that you talked Dr. Myott into releasing you?"

"Let's just say it was a mutual agreement. I said I was leaving, and she said she couldn't stop me."

"Are you physically able to do this? You sound like you're about to die any minute. We don't have to do this right now. Things are going to happen whether we meet with my contact or not. Give it another day."

"We have to act quickly if we are going to get a step ahead. I'm not really as bad as I sound. I'm in character. I look like I'm an old man, a very old man. So to complete my disguise, I have to sound like an old man too."

"Is that why you're grunting in pain?"

"Let's just leave it at as it is. I'll get by. After I talk with your contact, I will go back to my real apartment and rest for the night. That's the best I can do right now."

"Whatever you say, Jack. I'll wait ten minutes and then go up to his room. See you in a few." I gave him Thomas's room number and said goodbye.

I hung up the phone and decided to make some coffee in the pot on my dresser. By the time it was done brewing, it was time to leave. I put the coffee in a travel mug and headed out the door. I took the elevator to Thomas's floor and walked down the hall to his room. I knocked twice on his door and it opened immediately.

In a soft voice, he said, "Hi, Irish, come in. I was beginning to worry. I didn't think you were coming."

"I had to wait for Jack to call before I could leave my room. He should be here in another five or ten minutes. How are you doing, Thomas?"

I could see the strain in his face and body language. His mouth was frozen in a frown, and he was slumped over like a little boy who just lost his favorite puppy.

"I'm getting by, but I'm so worried about Sophia. I couldn't live if she was gone forever. She's my whole life. We just found out that she's going to have a baby. As a matter of fact, she told her father just last night. She was so happy when she found out. Oh my god, Irish."

He couldn't finish. Tears came rushing down his face, and he slumped down onto the sofa and cried. I stood there, not knowing what words of comfort to offer, so I said nothing. I just watched him sob with his face buried in a pillow.

Suddenly I became very angry. How could anyone do this to a good couple like Thomas and Sophia? I wanted to get my hands on them for about five minutes. I would show them what it's like to make someone suffer.

I let my anger boil for a few minutes, but then brought it under control. Anger wasn't necessarily a bad thing for me, because I used it as motivation. If I became angry enough I would do anything to correct an injustice I or someone else had to face. As Bob Lee said, "If you leave a bucket of shit alone, it will stop stinking, but if you stirred the shit, it would smell." Someone was stirring my shit, and I didn't like it.

I let Thomas cry out his anger and frustration without saying a word. Finally, he gathered himself and said, "Whatever I have to do to get them back, I will. Nobody can stop me from saving my family, my unborn child."

I could tell that he was at the end of his rope and would be willing to cooperate with Jack on this investigation to the fullest.

All of a sudden, there was a knock on the door. I pulled out the gun Jack had given me from the shoulder holster and walked over to the door. I waited for a moment, and finally, a weak old man's voice demanded, "Goddamn it, open the door."

I looked through the peephole and saw an old man standing outside. I thought, *what the hell does this old man want at a time like this?*

I opened the door, and he started walking in. I put out my hand and said, "Wait a minute, old man. What do you think you're doing? You can't just walk into someone's room without an invitation."

He stopped and said in a weary old voice, "I'm sorry, I must be confused. This isn't my room. Excuse me." As he turned and started walking out, he stopped, looked at me, and said, "It's me, Irish. It's Jack, you dumb shit."

I laughed. I couldn't believe it was Jack Casey. I said in a whisper, "Jack, I didn't recognize you. What a getup. You look fantastic. Come in, come in."

I looked at Thomas, and he was stunned. "This old man is Jack Casey?"

"One and the same," said Jack.

Thomas looked at me and said, "I don't get it. How could an old man like this still be working for the FBI? Are they real hard up for manpower? I don't feel good about this, Irish. I don't trust someone this old to handle this case."

"Take it easy, Thomas. Jack is not this old," I said, pointing to Jack's masked face.

With that, Jack reached behind his head and peeled off his 'old' face. Underneath was a smiling Jack Casey in the flesh.

"I'm sorry I startled you, but you did not want me to get recognized coming to your room, so I put on this face and walked and talked like an old man."

Jack reached out to take Thomas's hand but winced in pain as Thomas shook his hand. Still with his old man's voice, he said, "I'm pleased to finally meet you, Thomas."

I realized then that he was not putting on the voice, that it was now naturally his. Before Thomas could speak, I asked, "What the hell happened to your voice, Jack?"

"The guys who roughed me up stomped on my throat. The doctor said my voice would probably return to normal in a month or so. But what the hell, it works for me today."

"They could have fractured your larynx and killed you. You're a lucky man, Jack. It looks like they were really trying to send you a message to stand down. Perhaps you should have listened to them."

"It's going to take more than a bruised larynx to stop me. I'm a tough old bird. Besides, who would keep you under control if I stayed in that damned ol' hospital?"

I smiled but said nothing.

Thomas stepped up and said, "It's good to see that you're not ninety years old. I was beginning to get discouraged. I'm glad to see you are at least less than sixty, Jack."

"Not by much, Thomas, but I've got a few years to go before I get there. Shall we sit down at your table so we can talk?"

"Oh, right. Excuse me. I should have offered you a seat when you came through the door. I took the liberty of ordering some snacks, coffee, Coke, and a few beers for everyone."

Jack gave a woeful smile and said, "Wonderful, Thomas. I could use something to eat. The food in the hospital tastes like it was made for the MASH hospital during the Korean War. It's not fit for a dog. I don't know how they feed it to patients."

"Great. There are some turkey on rye and ham and cheese sandwiches, as well as chips, fruit, and some cookies. Please help yourself."

Jack and I helped ourselves to the sandwiches. I filled my travel mug with more coffee and sat in silence while Jack and I ate. When we were done, Thomas sat down with us to talk.

Jack reached into his jacket pocket, pulled out a tape recorder and asked, "Do you mind if I tape our conversation?"

"I would rather we just talk for now. When I feel more comfortable with you, maybe then you can use the recorder."

"Fair enough. That seems to be the standard answer," said Jack, turning to look at me.

He put the recorder back in his pocket and asked his first question. "Do you have any knowledge of Mr. Pinata or any of his so-called disciples taking orders from another organization such as a Mafia family?"

"I do not have any knowledge of that actually happening, but I've always felt that someone was pulling Joey's strings, especially lately."

I jumped in and asked, "Why do you say that, Thomas?"

He looked at me and replied, "You were in the meetings from day one. Lately, he has made some very stupid decisions—decisions that make no sense to me or anyone else at the table, including you."

"I can't argue with you on that," I responded.

Jack came back with another question. "What makes you think someone else is behind this, and it's not just Mr. Pinata caving in after a year of being on strike?"

"Joey doesn't cave when it comes to negotiations. Even if he isn't right on something, he will stick to his guns to the very end."

"Doesn't anyone call him on it when it appears he's just being obstinate? It seems to me like there would be enough people at the table who could gang up on him to make him come to his senses."

Thomas took a long look at Jack and said, "Joey doesn't scare easily, but lately, he's afraid of something. You can see it on his face. He says and does things that are completely out of character for him. Just three days ago, Jim Kennedy, the lead negotiator for the companies, asked Joey if he would be willing to accept the financial package they offered a year ago. At first, he said hell no, but then he took a break and made a phone call. I watched him while he was on the phone, and he was going wild. Whoever he was talking to really pissed him off. When he returned, he had changed his mind and was willing to accept it in its entirety, the complete financial package. It didn't make sense at all."

"That's real interesting. Have you ever overheard him talking about the negotiations to someone who is not directly involved?"

"Not in person, but I have heard him on the phone and wondered who he was talking to since everyone involved with our side of the negotiations was present here at the hotel."

"Let's go a step further," Jack said. "Have you any knowledge that Mr. Pinata has given favorable treatment when it comes to companies dealing with the ITU?"

"What exactly are you referring to?" Thomas asked.

"I'm talking about giving specific contracts that the ITU negotiates for its members to friends or family over other companies that may have better bids, for example."

Thomas hesitated for a moment, thinking about exactly what he should say, then finally blurted, "What the hell. This was going to happen sooner or later. Joey gave the contract for safety shoes to his next-door neighbor. The contract was worth about twenty-five million dollars. Everyone who works in a warehouse or truck has to wear steel-toed safety shoes."

"Was this the lowest bid?"

"No, not by a long shot. Joey tried to justify it by saying they had better quality shoes. The thing is, all the companies bought their shoes from the same supplier in China. He even refused to let a unionized company here in the United States have the contract. It made no sense to any of us on the staff. Do you remember that, Irish?"

"Sure as hell do. I was livid when that happened. Unions are supposed to support other union workers in this country. He expects nothing less, but wouldn't change his mind."

"Are there any others?" Jack asked.

"Unfortunately, there are," Thomas admitted. "The ITU put out bids for safety glasses for all of our members. The contract was worth somewhere in the neighborhood of fifty million dollars."

"Wow, that much?" Jack asked.

Thomas smiled and replied, "You have to figure there are five hundred thousand members, and each pair of glasses cost about a hundred dollars or more. That's fifty million dollars. Anyway, you figure it out."

"Who got the contract? Jack asked.

"Joey's cousin owns a company that manufacturers glasses and has the stores to retail them. Somehow, he got the bid over two unionized American shops and one nonunion American shop with lower bids. Not to mention, there must have been five foreign companies that underbid his cousin by millions."

"What's his cousin's name? Jack asked.

"Frankie Marzetti. Have you heard of the Marzen Eyeglass Company? They have advertisements on TV and the radio constantly. They drive me fucking bananas. There must be something like three thousand stores throughout the country. Frankie Marzetti owns all of those stores, plus four factories overseas that produce the glasses. It used to be the third largest eyeglass company in the world. It's a huge operation, and with Joey's help, they are now the largest."

Jack sat and stared ahead for quite some time without saying a word. Then his face came to life, and he asked Thomas and me, "Have either of you ever heard of the Mafia family called the Sarducci Family?"

We both shook our heads no at the same time. I asked, "What do they have to do with all of this?"

"When you," Jack said, pointing at Thomas, "said that Frankie Marzetti owns the eyeglass company, something clicked in this feeble brain of mine. The Marzetti Mafia family and another one called the Sarduccis made a pact about five years ago. The two families have been in a partnership on some very questionable dealings. Everything from racketeering to extortion and murder. You name it, they are involved in it.

I looked at Thomas and he seemed to be staring off into space, like he was looking into the future. I asked "Thomas, are you with us?" When he didn't answer, I prodded, "Thomas. I asked you a question."

He finally looked up and replied, "Oh, I'm sorry. I was just thinking about something."

I asked, "What the hell are you thinking about that made you look like you were in outer space?"

He replied, "Let me give you a scenario on what I think could be happening. Let's say over the last couple of years the two Mafia families invest millions of dollars in the stock market. Then a little over a year ago, just before the strike, they sell everything they have invested. They still make a great return on their investments because the market is at an all-time high. But that's only peanuts compared to what they'll make later on."

Jack said, "I'm not following you."

Thomas continued. "Let's suppose they figure out a way to make the market crash. Once the crash starts, they wait patiently for it to hit rock bottom. Then after the market bottoms out, they start buying back all those stocks they sold previously. They wait until the stocks regain their previous value, then they sell again and reap enormous profits."

I asked. "How does this involve the union and the problems we're having?"

Thomas said. "It's rather simple if you really think about it. They force the union to strike for an entire year, which causes the national economy and the markets to crash to their lowest level in decades. We have watched that very thing happen over the last twelve months."

"Now that the market has hit rock bottom, they have the union settle the strike, at which time they start a buying frenzy. Now they can take the money they raised when they sold twelve months ago and buy the stocks back. Since the market is down as low as it is, they can buy thousands more shares with the same amount of money they had a year ago. They hold on to these shares until the market rises back to its pre-strike level and sell again, making millions of dollars in profit. It's genius."

Jack had a puzzled look on his face when he asked, "Can you be a little more specific? I think I know what you're saying, but put it into layman's terms."

Thomas said, "Let me give you a clear example. Let's say twelve months ago, before the strike, you were invested in the Acme Bubble Gum Company with twenty thousand shares of stock and each share was priced at fifty dollars. You sell all your shares and your net worth would be one million dollars.

"Now, twelve months later, after the stock market has plunged to the bottom, you take your one million dollars and buy back that same stock in The Acme Bubble Gum Company. But, since you sold the stock twelve months ago, its value dropped to five dollars a share. Now with the one million dollars you had a year ago, you would be able to buy two hundred thousand shares instead of just the twenty thousand you had before.

"If you were patient and waited until the stock rose back to its pre-strike level of fifty dollars a share, your net worth would increase from one million dollars to ten million dollars. Just imagine if they had a couple hundred million invested. They would be filthy rich."

Thomas was getting excited. He sat bolt upright and asked, "Jack, do you have any proof that something like this is happening?"

"We have a special task force that has been investigating corruption by the Sarduccis and the Marzettis for two years now. The head of this task force believes that they have been using intimidating scare tactics on at least ten of the companies that make up the DOW. Do you remember the three killings on Wall Street; two last year and one just a few months ago?"

I spoke up and said, "I do, but there wasn't enough proof to lead to an arrest. I read that the prosecutors found no evidence of foul play in any of the three and ruled them suicides."

"I'm afraid that's true," Jack responded. "However, there wasn't enough evidence to support that decision. One man supposedly jumped out of a window from the fifty-fourth floor, another man slashed his wrists, and the third person died of a drug overdose. All three of those individuals had no mental illness in their history, but all three were ruled suicide. A background check on each of them came up empty. Their families were not only devastated, but taken completely by surprise. They all denied the presence of depression or even anxiety in any of the three men. None of them used drugs or drank excessively. It just didn't add up. All three families are fighting the suicide rulings in court. Plus, there are apparently large insurance claims for each victim, and their families are missing out on the huge beneficiary amounts because of those rulings."

I asked, "What does all of this have to do with Joey Pinata and these negotiations?"

Jack looked at Thomas, and Thomas responded, "If Joey is forced to keep this strike going long enough, it would have a domino effect on practically every financial institution in the country, including the DOW Jones Industrial. With the truckers on strike, the auto industry is completely dead, shipping of every online order has stopped, and every item manufactured here or imported into the country will never get delivered. When everything stopped being delivered, all manufacturing stopped; when manufacturing stopped, people lost their jobs; and when they lost their jobs, they stopped buying. Once the buying stops, the economy takes a nosedive, and the stock market falls sharply. Once that happens, people start bailing out. The stock market values fall to a certain level, and a buying frenzy starts. It would be interesting to find out which individuals sold before the strike started and who is in a buying frenzy right now."

Jack sat there smiling as Thomas gave his dissertation on the events that had transpired and were still happening. "Thomas, I think you may have hit the nail on the head. We may also find out that Joey hasn't done any of this on his own, but was forced to by the Sarduccis and the Marzettis. If we can prove Joey's just a puppet, he may be off the hook."

I said, "Knowing Mr. Pinata as well as I do, I don't think he would let anyone force him to do this without his okay. My guess is he's part of the overall grand scheme."

Thomas interrupted me and said, "It doesn't help us get our union back, but if Joey is innocent, it could shine a bright light on the union after all. We would not be looked at as an evil force by our members. This just might save the union even with Joey still in charge."

Jack let that sink in for a minute, then said, "That could be very true, Thomas. Everything we have been investigating for the last two years could be for naught, but that would be okay if we can nab the bigger fish. The ultimate goal is to get the biggest fish we can catch, and believe me, the Sarducci and Marzetti families are real big fish."

I asked, "So what do we do with this information, Jack?"

"Tell me, Thomas, since you are recording secretary for the union, do you have any way to get a look at Joey's personal financial picture?"

"Not legally, but I could ask Frank to let me review the union's financial books. Maybe he even has some information about Mr. Pinata's personal financials. If he lets me, it would give me an opportunity see what has been paid out to Joey since he became president. Not only that, but Frank does Joey's income taxes for him. Frank keeps everything in a file in his office. I see no reason he wouldn't just give me a key to the file and let me have all the time I need. I could take a peek at Joey's records if Frank leaves me alone for a few minutes."

"Would you really do that, Thomas?" I asked, somewhat astonished that he would even bring up such an idea.

"I told you I was in with you on saving this union. Nothing has changed to alter my position. So yes, I would be willing to do this."

Jack broke in and said, "Thomas, this may take some nerve to pull off. Are you up for it?"

"Are you questioning my bravery, Jack?"

"Not at all, Thomas. I can see that you and Irish are stand-up kind of guys. I wished I had more like the two of you. My job would be much easier."

"So what's our plan of action?" I asked.

"Well, Thomas is going to do his thing with the books. I'm going to go to our financial people and have them check all the principal people on Wall Street and see who sold big before the strike and who is now in a buying frenzy. Isn't that the term you used, Thomas?"

"It is. In investing, always sell high and buy low. It's the best way to ensure a positive profit margin."

Jack said, "After I go to the financial people, I am going to get my team together and refocus our attention on the bigger picture. I will also call our guys on the Mafia task force and see what information they can give me about the Mafia's influence on the union. We have to start building a clearer picture of all of this. I need to see it up on a wall where I can study it. That's the best way for me. Get all the information I have, put it up on a wall, and rearrange it as necessary to make it clearer. It works for me that way. That's all I can say."

I asked, "What about me? What am I supposed to do?"

"Irish, I have to ask you to do something that is rather distasteful. I need you to talk to anyone on the ITU Executive Board who you feel you can trust. I'm not sure who that might be or if there even *is* anyone else, but I trust your judgment on this. You figure out who that might be. We need to find out who is aware of what's going on and how much they know. I don't think you should approach Frank Bartolone. He's too close to Mr. Pinata. I'm hoping Thomas will get the information we need from him by going through those books. But remember, Thomas, the FBI has no knowledge of you looking through them. This is for informational purposes only. We would need a court order to legally look into his personal records, and I don't think we are at that point yet."

"How am I supposed to approach them? Just go up and say, 'Do you know about any illegal operations going on with a Mafia family and the union?'"

Jack laughed. "Not quite that way. Just find out if they know anything about the union being threatened by the Mafia. That's all you really need to know. Not the specifics, just generalities about the situation. We need to find out if anyone else is involved with Joey, or if anyone else is threatened by the Sarduccis or the Marzettis. If more of Mr. Pinata's staff is being held hostage, then who knows how big this really is."

I had one idea I was sure Jack would want to know. "That doesn't sound like such a big deal. I guess I can handle it, but I do have one thing that has been troubling to me. Do you remember that Mrs. Pinata supposedly walked away about a year ago?"

Jack and Thomas both nodded their heads. "Let's just say she didn't walk away, but rather was kidnapped, and for the last year, has been held captive. She could be the leverage that the Mafia families are using to force Mr. Pinata to do the things they want done—forcing him to not settle the strike, but to keep it going to the point that the economy goes into a tailspin."

Thomas jumped at that. "Sophia has been saying for the last year that she couldn't believe her mother ran away. She insists that her mother is not one to run from a fight. She too thinks her mother was kidnapped."

Jack seemed to take that thought in and study it for a while. Then he spoke, "You know, that makes all the sense in the world. That could explain why Mr. Pinata has made the decisions that he has. Why the strike never ends. Maybe Mr. Pinata is a victim too."

I asked, "Do you think you should bring Joey in and talk to him about this? Maybe he needs some help getting out of it. Have you ever thought that everything Joey has done may have been against his will? He may have been forced to keep this strike going."

"My team has thought of hundreds of scenarios, but not this one. But, after what both of you have said, it doesn't seem that wild of an idea. This may be the track we need to follow. I don't know if now is the time to bring Joey in and try to help him get away from the Mafia boys or not. Maybe he's actually a major player, and I will do nothing more than tip them all off."

Thomas replied, "I really think Joey has been acting so out of character that it's pretty obvious that someone is telling him what to do. It was especially evident when he changed his mind on the financial offer from Jim Kennedy, the head financial person for the companies. First Mr. Pinata accepted it, and then he changed his mind. That's not how Joey operates."

"I will have to talk to Henry Sullivan since he's the director. It will probably be his call. There's too much at stake to bulldoze ahead on this. He might have my badge if I called Mr. Pinata and told him we're aware of the Mafia involvement."

Thomas and I both nodded our heads in agreement. Then I added, "Jack, you have both Thomas's and my support on this. Whatever you decide, we are behind you. You know the big picture much better than we do."

"Thanks a lot, Irish. Thomas, I had a lot more questions for you, but I think we have uncovered the beast. Now we just have to capture it and try to free all of the caged prisoners. All right, let's get busy. I will leave first and go to your room, Irish. Give me the key, and I'll wait for you there. Give me five minutes before you follow."

I said, "Wait a minute, Jack. Do you think Sonia's kidnapping was done to put more pressure on Mr. Pinata?"

"It makes sense. It all ties in together. Let's just hope she, her friend, and her mother are being treated well. I'm sure we'll find out soon enough."

I gave him my key. He pulled the mask back over his head and shuffled out the door. I turned to Thomas and said, "Wow, I didn't think we would get this much direction out of this meeting. Are you okay with this, Thomas?"

"I have never been surer of anything in my life. For the first time in years, I have a direction in my life that I like. No matter what happens, I'm okay. I just wish Sophia would come home. This is tearing me up inside. I can't imagine what could be happening to her. If they touch her, I will kill each and every one of them."

I couldn't believe I was listening to Thomas Sharpe. I thought he was a passive person, but I guess I was wrong. I felt sorry for anyone who hurt Sophia. Thomas would get his revenge—that, I was sure of.

After ten minutes, I stood up and said, "I guess I had better get going. Jack's had time to get to my room by now. He's probably anxious to get started." Thomas and I shook hands, and I looked into his eyes. I saw determination. I hoped he saw courage in mine, for little did I know how much courage I needed with what lay ahead.

A few minutes later, I reached my hotel room and knocked on the door. An old man's voice sang, "Who the fuck is there?" Then, he laughed and opened the door. Jack was still in costume and playing up his character. He used his old pathetic voice to say, "Please come in."

I shut the door and said, "Knock off the bullshit, Jack. What are we going to do tonight?"

"I think it's a little late to start anything tonight, unless you want to call some of the executive board."

"I would just as soon start tomorrow morning. I'm kind of tired tonight."

"Cut the crap, Irish. You have a hot date planned for tonight. The last thing you want to do is mess with this shit. Go and have fun on your date, but please keep it low profile. I don't want to have to visit you in the hospital tomorrow."

"Don't worry about me tonight. We are having a private dinner at her house, just the two of us."

"Sounds like a hell of a plan. Enjoy yourself and remember, don't go out in the rain without your rubber boots."

"Very funny, Jack. Thanks for the advice, but I had the sex talk with my old man years ago."

"What words of wisdom did your dear old dad give you about sex?"

"He said it's good. Just some is better."

"Wow, Irish. That just gives me goose bumps. Your dad must have been a wise gentleman."

"You're funny, Jack, but my dad was an asshole. That's the best word to describe him. Good night, Jack."

"Good night, Irish."

I held the door as he shuffled out and down the hall.

CHAPTER TWENTY-SEVEN

I looked at the clock and saw I had thirty minutes to get ready. I practically ran into the bathroom for a shower. I stepped into the shower spray, washed quickly, and rinsed myself and all my vital organs twice, just to be sure. I brushed my teeth and combed my hair. I dried myself and put on a crisp white shirt and soft gray tie, tan slacks, and black loafers. I was nervous. I felt like I was going on my first date.

I slipped on a lightweight dark gray pinstriped sport coat as I walked out the door. I took the elevator to the lobby and walked toward the front doors of the hotel. Passing the bar, I could feel the magic pull that tried to draw me in, but I resisted and practically ran to the taxi stand.

I gave the driver the address by memory and settled in for the ride. I still had the Buick that Jack had obtained for me, but I wanted to be totally detached from everything that had happened.

The driver took me up Biscayne Boulevard and north out of Miami toward Miami Beach. We drove past some high-rise hotels along the beach and into an upscale neighborhood.

As the taxi turned down Katrina's street, I was amazed. The homes were extremely large. They looked like each one was over four or five thousand square feet, and some even larger.

I thought, *Wow, she must be pretty well off.*

We pulled up in front of her home, which was a large federal-style house with a gated drive and fences all around it. It looked like the White House on a somewhat smaller scale—but maybe not *that* much smaller. The extra wide driveway was made of dark red brick and lead to a four-car garage.

Large pillars adorned the front of the home, which had a flat black roof above and behind the pillars. There was an angle in the center that was exactly like the White House. The large white portico was amazing. It stood out like inviting arms welcoming everyone home.

There were huge double doors with four-foot wide stained glass windows on either side. The lawn was a deep, dark green that was illuminated by the exterior lighting of the house. Thick grass was a rarity here in the south. Plus, there was a huge water flowing fountain in the middle of the yard— another feature copied from the White House.

I paid the cabbie, got out, and stood there staring at the house. Who was this girl and how can she afford such a great home?

I walked up to the gate, and it opened automatically. I noticed the cameras move on each side of the gate as I walked up the drive to the brick sidewalk. Before I could knock, the door opened and Katrina smiled at me, saying "I'm so glad you made it."

She was dressed in a short, silky black dress, with white pearls, matching earrings and four-inch heels. She was stunning, to say the least.

She stepped forward and gave me a hug. "Irish, please, come in."

As I walked through the door, an older man, about seventy, stepped up and said, "Hello, I'm Katrina's father, Frank."

"Pleased to meet you, sir. I'm Sean MacSween, but please call me Irish. All of my friends do."

"Pleased to meet you, Irish. Katrina has told me a lot about you. Welcome to our home."

I smiled another big Irish smile and said, "Katrina was very gracious to invite me for dinner. She said she's a very good cook. Is that right?"

"She's the best. Her mother taught her everything about cooking. She is as good, or maybe a little better, than her mother was, and that's saying something, considering her mother was the best cook in our entire family. Her sisters, all nine of them, tried to better her cooking at our family gatherings, but they always fell short."

"That's good to hear. I'm starving. I must say that you have a beautiful home," I complimented her father.

"Thank you very much. It's a great jump from where we started—a one-room apartment for my wife and me in the heart of Chicago's west side. It was a rough neighborhood where only the strong survived. Back then, you had to be smart, or the city would wear you down."

"Well, I grew up in the heart of Detroit. You survived the streets only if you knew how to handle yourself. The gangs ruled if the community let them. The Irish in Detroit were pretty tight. We protected our turf, and kept the gangs on the other side of Woodward Avenue. Hell, I was the Golden Gloves State Champion, but that didn't do much good on the street. It was a totally different game. Out there, you had to be tough and wise. It was a wild, scary place to grow up."

"We have a lot in common, Irish. Both of us had to be strong to survive, and we were. Look how far I've come."

I nodded my head in agreement and said, "You have obviously done well with your life. You also have done real well with your daughter. Katrina is the finest woman I have ever met."

Frank smiled and said, "She takes after her mother completely. Her beauty, her personality, and her warm heart make her virtually a clone of her mother, who I fell in love with the first time I met her. Love at first sight. Have you ever had that happen to you, Irish?"

I looked at Katrina, and as our eyes met, I said, "Only once in my life." I could feel myself blush and was a little embarrassed. Then I noticed Katrina was doing the same.

Frank said, "Why don't we go into the study where we can talk?"

I didn't want to. I was here to see Katrina, not her father. To be respectful, though, I was about to agree, but before I could say anything, Katrina jumped in and said, "Papa, he's here to have dinner with me. You can talk to him some other time. He's mine tonight, and dinner is almost ready."

He smiled and gave in. "Looks like you are in demand, Irish. I have been overruled. If you come around here very often, you'll see what I mean. She always gets her way. I have spoiled my dear child. God forgive me."

Katrina grabbed my hand and said, "Oh, Papa, you are a spoiled man yourself. But tonight, you lose."

She led me down a hall to the left and opened a door to her kitchen. I smelled something that was so aromatic I felt my stomach grumble with anticipation. She led me through the kitchen into what appeared to be a family room.

There was a wood fire burning in a large stone fireplace. A large screen TV hung from the wall and a stereo with Bose speakers mounted on all four walls emitted a soft stereo surround sound.

The music was the velvety voice of Carole King. How did she know I liked Carole King? She was a pop star when my dad's generation was young, but I loved her smooth melodies.

Katrina turned around and gave me a soft kiss on the lips. I pulled her close and felt the electric sensation of her tongue on mine. Instead of resisting, she drew my tongue further into her mouth. I immediately felt myself get hard, and she must have felt it too. She gently pushed her hips into me and moaned.

My heart must have instantly jumped to 150 beats a minute. I thought it might leap out of my chest with anticipation. We stayed in each other's arms for a full two minutes, softly rubbing our bodies together.

When we finally released our hold on each other and took in a deep breath, I smiled at her and said, "Well, hello to you."

She grinned at me and said, "You're obviously glad to see me." Then she laughed and kissed me softly again, then whispered in my ear, "I know I've only known you for a day, but there is something magical about you, something very special. I'm so sorry I said that, but with you, it's easy for me to lose my shyness. I feel safe with you."

I kissed her again and asked, "You don't say that to every guy you have over for dinner, do you?"

"I have never said that to any man, especially not in five years and never in this house. You are the first."

"So your papa won't barge in on us?"

"No, he would never do that. We have too much respect for each other."

"Since we are confessing, I'll tell you that Riona has been the only steady woman in my life, but we are not seeing each other anymore. I thought I loved her, but now, I'm not sure when I compare my feelings about her to my feelings for you. There really is no comparison."

"I've only been serious about one man in my life, so I'm not very experienced. As a matter of fact, John was the only man I have ever been with. But then, he was killed in a boating accident. I lost the only man I have ever felt enough for to give myself away."

"I'm sorry to hear he was killed. By the look on your face, you had a lot of feelings for him," I said with compassion.

"Thank you. I did, but that was five years ago. And if I'm to be honest with you–and I always will be–when I met you, I had never felt this kind of love for anyone in my life. I think you and I have a destiny of some kind. Irish, I cried when I came home today. I was afraid I was never going to see you again. I thought it might have been an infatuation for you, and you would never want to see me again."

Tears began to form in her eyes once again. As I pulled her close and hugged her gently, I felt the warm softness of her tears on my cheek. Her big tears now rolling down my face, I knew at that instant that I loved her more than I had ever loved anyone in my life.

"Katrina, we have only known each other for one day, but I know I'm in love with you and want to spend the rest of my life with you. Your papa said this is the way it was for him and your mother, so if it could happen to them, I see no reason why it wouldn't be the same for us. I hope with all my heart that you feel the same."

"Oh, Irish, I have never wanted to hear anything more in my life. Papa told me that if I truly love someone, I will know it the first time I see him. He fell in love with Mama just like this, just like he said."

"Katrina, kiss me."

She looked up at me and our eyes met. Our lips touched softly, then our tongues, and then our bodies. We held that position, afraid to let go of each other, afraid to lose the moment forever.

Finally, a shrill siren from the kitchen brought us back to the present reality.

"Oh my gosh! That's the smoke detector." She leaped from my arms and ran into the kitchen. I heard her laugh, so I followed her. She was holding a pan in the air and dancing around the kitchen island, laughing. Smoke was coming from the pan. She had obviously burned whatever was in there.

She saw me standing in the doorway and giggled. "This was our dessert. We were supposed to have Italian cannoli. Now we'll have to settle for cookies I made yesterday. Will that be okay?"

She had such a sweet look on her face that I grinned from ear to ear. "It doesn't matter. I love cookies. What kind did you make?" I asked in anticipation.

"Ginger cookies. They're my mother's recipe and very delicious, especially with hot coffee or tea," she responded.

I asked, "What's for dinner? Something smells wonderful."

She smiled proudly at me and said, "First, we're going to have meatball soup. It's delicious. Then, we'll have a small antipasti salad, followed by torta rustica. After dinner, we were supposed to have the cannoli, but now, we'll have cookies."

She seemed to glow with satisfaction because she was proud to be cooking for me. I was caught once again by her eyes. I asked, "What is torta rustica?"

She told me about the ingredients and how it was prepared and said, "It ends up like a pie with lots of spices and pasta. I hope it'll be to your liking."

"I don't know about the food, but you look delicious."

"Careful, Mr. MacSween; what you see is what you may get."

I walked over to her and put my arms around her, pulled her close, and said, "I have a feeling that you taste wonderful." I kissed her ear and then her neck, where I tasted a hint of jasmine.

"I was right. Do you taste like that all over?"

"I guess you'll have to find out for yourself."

We kissed again, long and soft. We melted into each other, just enjoying the feeling. After a few minutes, she whispered in my ear, "Want to see the rest of my apartment?"

"Are you sure about your papa?"

"I'm positive he won't bother us. He's in his study engrossed in some union thing."

"Then show me everything."

She said, "I intend to."

We held hands as she led me down a hall. I could feel her heartbeat in her hand; it was racing almost as fast as mine. When we reached the end of the hall, she opened the last door on the right. As we walked into her bedroom, I noticed the king-sized bed with a soft pink and white canopy and a matching fluffy bedspread.

I closed the door as she walked to the bed. I followed her lead and kissed her, while my hands automatically began discovering her body. There was no resistance. She moved slowly to my caresses.

Our lovemaking was seductive, alluring, gentle, and intense—all at the same time. The pure act of the lovemaking took me to a new height that I had never known. It was like our new-found love emanated through our spiritual connection, as much as by our physical touch, and made me finally realize what spiritual love really is. We held each other and made love for the next hour, which was sixty minutes of the purest form of ecstasy I had ever encountered in my life. Afterwards, we lay spent on the bed. I said to her, "I have never made love like that."

She looked up at me. "I have never felt that way before. I can't even describe it. There are no words to explain such pure love, pure joy. We were one. We came together and stayed together so naturally. Irish, I do love you, so very much."

I smiled down at her and said, "Truly, you are the love of my life. I have never experienced love-making like this. This was more wonderful than I could have ever imagined."

We lay there for half an hour more, just holding each other. *Incredible* is the only word that would come close to describing what I felt. I was right before. I was in heaven.

Eventually, we made it to the shower, and together, we cleansed our bodies from our lovemaking. We finally made it back to the kitchen and had our dinner. Like everything with Katrina, it was wonderful. After dinner, we sat and ate her cookies. I had coffee, black, and she had sweet hot tea. A thought came to me.

"Frank Bernetti. I've heard that name before, but where? Katrina, where have I heard your papa's name?"

"His name used to be in the news every day. He was head of the International Auto Workers Union for over thirty years," Katrina replied.

"He's *that* Frank Bernetti? Well, I'll be dammed. I didn't get the connection. There's been so much written about his accomplishments in negotiating with the auto companies."

I was stunned to hear that her father was that man who was so well thought of. "He negotiated contracts that didn't break the companies, was fair to his members, and helped the companies grow their businesses. It was a perfect resolution for both sides. The company CEOs praised your father like he was a man ahead of his time. He's been placed alongside Walter Reuther, one of the greatest union men of the twentieth century."

"It wasn't always like this. When he and Mama were young, they struggled so much. But Papa was smart. He invested every penny he could into the companies he helped promote. Twenty-seven years ago, he was called to go to Poland to help with the labor strife there. He was instrumental in saving the companies, and even the government, some say."

I interjected, "I read all about that. I even did a paper on the labor movement over there and how it affected their country."

Katrina had tears in her eyes as she said, "The government in Poland was so grateful that they presented him with their highest peacetime award, and along with it, they gave him ten million dollars as a sign of their gratitude."

"Yes, that was news all over the world. Your papa then gave up two million dollars to start an organization that helps the homeless in Chicago."

Katrina added, "That's true, and it's still going to this day.

"He is an amazing man. His strategies are taught at all of our teaching seminars. Some of the major universities that teach labor studies use his messages as their standards in labor education.

Wow! I didn't relate you and him. He truly is a legend in labor."

Katrina sat proudly as I complimented her precious papa. She smiled and said, "Thank you so much for the compliments. I know what you mean. I've heard it so many times, especially when I was a young girl. Everyone seemed to have so much respect for him. I've never seen him get angry. He was always so composed, except for when he used to take me to his office. When he had meetings, he would set me on his knee while he met with his union brothers, and you know how the vocabulary can get out of hand. Whenever anyone would swear, he would rebuke them and scream, 'hold your tongue my daughter is here!' Those were the only times I ever witnessed him getting angry or raising his voice."

I smiled at her and said. "This is incredible. You are incredible. This whole day has been incredible. I'm so glad you invited me here." I couldn't hide my joy from her.

Then she added, "I'm so glad everything worked out the way it did. I have never had a day like this. I've never been with a man like you. At first, I was scared when I saw you were naked, but you were so gentle. You were wonderful."

We sat in silence, looking at each other. Finally, I said, "It's time for me to leave. I have a lot of work to do in the morning and I don't know what might transpire for the rest of the day. If I get caught up in my work, I won't be able to call you.

But don't feel bad—I will call you as soon as I get a free minute."

She gave me her saddest sad face, and said, "You've never even given me your phone number."

"I'm sorry, let me call you right now, then it'll be in your phone." I called her number, and when her phone rang, she picked it up and said in her best whiny voice, "Hello, I'm lonely and horny."

I laughed, and she joined me. We kissed again, and then she walked me out the side door of the kitchen. I stopped and said, "Oh no, I forgot. I didn't drive. Can you call me a cab?"

"I will do you better than that. I'll drive you home."

"I couldn't ask you to do that. A taxi will be fine."

"Nonsense. Either I drive you home, or you'll have to stay here."

With a laugh, I said, "As much as I'd like to stay, I do have to get back. If I stayed, I wouldn't have the strength to work tomorrow."

Katrina smiled, and her face transformed into one that only a goddess could have. She was beautiful in an innocent kind of way.

"Then it's settled. I will drive you back to your hotel. I will hear no more about it."

"Well, okay, Ms. Smarty-Pants."

I gently rubbed her behind, and we kissed. "Better stop that or we will never get out the door."

"You're right. It's just so hard to let you go."

We laughed as we went into the four-car garage and climbed into her Buick. She drove me back to the hotel and we talked all the way. It was so easy. We were natural together.

When we arrived at my hotel, I got out and walked around to her side of the car. I leaned into her window and gave her a long, gentle kiss. I said, "Good-bye, sweet thing. We will talk tomorrow."

She smiled and tears filled her eyes. "This is the happiest day of my life. Please come back to me. After today, I couldn't live without you."

I kissed her again and said, "Me either."

As I watched her drive away, I realized my heart was no longer mine. She had stolen it, and I didn't want it back.

CHAPTER TWENTY-EIGHT

• •

S ophia was sitting in a chair in a basement with
no windows and only one light bulb. Her hands
were tied to the back of the chair and her ankles
tied to each front leg. Her face was tear-stained—
not from physical abuse, but from the stress of
being kidnapped.

Ten hours earlier, two hooded men had come
into the store where she was shopping with her
friend, Marcie. They grabbed her and Marcie and
immediately pushed rags in their mouths to prevent them from screaming. Black hoods were put
over their heads.

Apparently, the men tied the store clerk's
hands and told her to lie on the floor behind the
counter. They took the two women out of the back
of the store and brutally shoved them into the
backseat of a car. Sophia thought it must have been

a limo, because when she fell into the car, she could feel that there were two seats facing each other.

The vision of the awful man at the beach who had accosted her a few days earlier came to mind. She felt fear spread throughout her body. The thought of him touching her sent shivers up her spine.

She and Marcie were held face down on the seats, their hands still tied behind their backs. After about ten minutes, they were allowed to sit upright but were told not to move.

The car ride lasted about twenty minutes, with so many turns that Sophia could not keep track of which direction they were going. Once they arrived at their destination, a garage door went up and the car entered. Once the door was down, they were taken from the car and into a house.

Immediately, they were separated. Sophia was taken downstairs and tied to the chair. She had no idea what happened to Marcie. She only hoped she was okay. They removed Sophia's hood and took the rag from her mouth, but told her to stay quiet or they would put it back in to shut her up.

After a few hours, they brought her some water, but nothing to eat. She didn't feel she could have eaten anyway. She had been in the chair and silent for almost ten hours. She felt better if she was alone. The further her captives were from her, the better. However, she did need to use the bathroom—soon—so she started yelling for someone to come to her aid.

After about five minutes, she finally heard the basement door open and the sound of someone walking down the stairs. A man wearing a hood appeared at the bottom of the steps. "What do you want, Ms. Pretty?"

"I need to use the bathroom." She heard him chuckle. It gave her the chills.

"Well, little lady, we wouldn't want you to piss your pants now, would we?"

The voice sounded familiar. Then, it hit her like a brick. It was the man at the beach. All she could do was think about what he had said he would do to her. She felt her hands beginning to shake.

He walked over and untied her ankles. Before he released her hands, he pulled a rag out of his pocket and shoved it in her mouth. Then he reached down and massaged her breasts. Her body tightened. She tried to scream but couldn't. He let go of her breasts and laughed.

"Don't say a word if you want to live past the next two minutes." He untied her hands and led her to a door at the other side of the basement, opened it up, and turned on the light. "You have two minutes. Any longer than that, I'll have to come in to make sure you're not trying to get away."

She went in and locked the door. There were no windows or other doors, so she still felt trapped. The man outside laughed and said, "Do you think that stinking door lock can keep me out? You're mine, bitch, as soon as they give me the OK."

She stayed in as long as she dared, but opened the door to find him still standing there chuckling to himself.

"Back to the chair, little pretty." He grabbed her arm and squeezed, causing her to wince in pain.

"Please stop. You're hurting me." He let go of her arm but shoved her down into the chair. First, he tied her hands behind the chair and then her ankles, but before he was done, he shoved the rag into her mouth again and reached up her skirt. He started rubbing her thighs and then moved up to her panties. She felt his fingers probing, trying to find the spot. She rocked back and forth in the chair until it fell backward. She hit her head on the concrete floor and blacked out for just a moment.

She felt him pull the chair upright. "Don't worry, Ms. Pretty, I didn't do anything . . . yet. But just think about me for a while and know I will have you sometime soon."

Just then, the door to the basement opened, and someone shouted down, "What the hell is taking so long? You better not be messing with her."

"I'm not, boss. She had to go pee. I was just tying her back to the chair." He removed the rag from her mouth and put his index finger to his lips to indicate that she should keep her mouth shut.

"Get your ass up here now." Whoever was upstairs had enough influence to make him jump.

"Coming, boss." He lowered his voice to a whisper and said, "I wish I was coming." He let out a sinister laugh.

Sophia was relieved, but wondered how long it would be before he would come back. She had never been so scared in her entire life. She always thought she was tough, but at that moment, she knew she wasn't tough at all.

Two hours later, the door finally opened, and a woman in a hood came down the stairs carrying a plate of food and a small folding table. She set the food down on the steps and then set up the table. She placed food on the table and said in a soft voice, "You must eat, my dear. It's not much, but it will sustain you for a little while."

She untied Sophia's right hand and stepped back. "I'll be back in a little while. Try to eat." The woman walked up the stairs and shut the door once again.

Sophia looked at the plate and saw a peeled orange, an apple, four types of cheese, and two types of crackers. To her surprise, she realized she was hungry. She started with the orange, and soon, everything was gone.

For the first time since they took her, she felt somewhat alive. The fear seemed to wane after eating. She knew she should drink some more water; she would ask when the woman returned.

They had taken her and Marcie about eleven that morning. She figured it must be after midnight. She was getting tired after all the stress of the day. What would happen to her? Where was Marcie? Was she being treated well? Who did this and why?

The questions were eating at her so much that she started feeling physically sick. The renewal she had felt immediately after eating was instantly replaced with nausea. She felt like she was going to vomit.

Why was she like this? Was she so emotionally weak that she couldn't handle the stress? Another wave of nausea hit her. She bent over and clutched her abdomen until it passed, but then it hit her. She realized why she felt this way—she was pregnant.

The realization instantly gave her a new strength. She had to be strong, not only for herself, but for the baby too. No sooner had the thought hit her, then the basement door opened and the same woman walked down the stairs.

She knew it was the woman, because the sound of her steps was entirely different than those of the huge man who had visited her earlier.

Sophia was still bent over holding her stomach when the woman came near to her. "Is something wrong? Are you ill?"

Sophia looked up at her and said, "I'm not sick. I'm pregnant."

The woman gasped. "Why didn't you tell me? I would have made your stay more comfortable. It doesn't matter now anyway. We're letting you go home."

Sophia could not believe her ears. Was this some kind of trick? "Why are you letting me go when you've only had me for twelve hours? I would have thought you would use me as a bargaining chip against my father."

"I'm not privileged enough to know the family business, but I think they already have."

"What do you mean by that? Whose family are you talking about?"

"I'm sorry, I've already said too much. I'm just supposed to come down and remove your plate. Please don't say anything. I'll be punished if they know I told you anything."

"Does your family beat you if you get out of line?"

She laughed. "No, nothing as drastic as that. My husband will just get real mad at me and force me to stay in my house for a few days. He would never harm me physically. He's a gentle man."

"Doesn't sound like that to me," Sophia replied.

"They will be down to get you in a few minutes. If they send the same man, I will be with him. I don't trust him—he is a vulgar man, and I don't want him to touch you."

Sophia smiled and said, "Thank you very much. He *is* crude and vulgar, like you said. I appreciate your concern."

The hooded woman turned and walked up the stairs without another word. She seemed very nice, and Sophia *was* thankful for her concern.

In about twenty minutes, the woman returned with the vulgar man. He put a hood over Sophia's head and untied her without a word. When she stood, he said, "Put your hands behind your back."

Sophia did as he asked. This time, instead of tying her hands behind her back, he placed hand-cuffs on her. The woman grabbed her elbow and guided her up the stairs.

They loaded her in what seemed like the same car and told her not to move. She wondered where Marcie was and if she was going to be released too.

A few minutes later, the car door opened, and she heard Marcie ask, "Is that you, Sophia?"

"Oh my god, Marcie! I was so worried about you. Are you okay?"

"I'm fine. How about you? Did they hurt you?"

"No, I was treated fine, but I was so scared. I'm so sorry I got you into this. I know it's entirely my fault."

The car door opened, and a deep baritone voice commanded, "Shut up. No talking." The silence was complete. Sophia did not want them to get mad and change their minds, and Marcie was just too scared to say anything.

The ride lasted another twenty minutes. They pulled to a stop, and the car doors were opened. The same baritone voice told them, "Get out of the car. Watch your heads."

The woman who was with Sophia in the base-ment said, "They are going to lead you over to a bench and will uncuff you both. Do not take your hoods off for five minutes. I will give you your per-sonal things, including your cell phones. Call whoever you like, but not for five minutes. We have someone watching over you. If you don't do as we say, they will take you back and put you in the house again."

They did as the woman said, and waited on the bench for five minutes without saying a word. Finally, they removed their hoods and stood holding each other and crying for several minutes.

CHAPTER TWENTY-NINE

Thomas had been sitting in his room since Irish and Jack left. Not eating, talking to no one, and only drinking an occasional cup of coffee. As each hour passed, he became more distraught. What was happening to his wife?

He kept telling himself that nobody was cruel enough to ever hurt a defenseless woman, but he knew the reality of the world. There were cruel, evil people who cared nothing for others—people who would take a life without a second thought.

A little after 1:00 a.m., his phone rang, startling him. He let it ring four times before he emerged from his trance-like state.

Finally, he answered, "Hello, this is Thomas."

It was Sophia. She sounded agitated, as well as excited. "Thomas, it's me. They released us. Oh my god, come and get us quickly. We are at the City of Miami Cemetery. It's on North Miami Avenue." She could see the street sign from the bench where they were let go.

"Oh, Sophia, are you all right? Did they hurt you in any way?" He sounded desperate, almost forlorn, like a lost little boy who had just found his mother.

"We are fine, Thomas. They didn't touch us. We are okay, so please come and get us. We are at the cemetery on corner of North Miami Avenue and NW 19th Street."

"I'm on my way." He hung up the phone, grabbed his car keys, and ran out the door.

Fifteen minutes later, he pulled up to the cemetery and immediately saw Sophia and Marcie. They came running to the car, and he had to slam on the brakes to avoid hitting them. He jumped out of the car and embraced Sophia, not wanting to ever let go. They kissed and then laughed at each other.

"Marcie, are you okay? They didn't hurt you, did they?"

"No, I was just scared to death. I couldn't believe it when they just let us go. They didn't even ask us any questions."

Sophia broke into the conversation, "Marcie, they didn't want anything from us. We were the bait. They wanted something from my father, and apparently, they got it. That's why they let us go. There cannot be any other reason."

Thomas spoke up and said, "Now is not the time to talk about this. We should discuss this later. Get in the car, and let's get the hell out of here."

"Thomas, you don't understand. There's a lot of information that you're not privileged to."

"Sophia, that's enough about this for now. Just get in the car."

Sophia could tell by his voice that she had better take his advice. Without another word, they all got into the car. On the way back to the hotel, Thomas said to Marcie, "Please don't call the police. I want you to trust me on this. There are certain agencies working on this already. I'm sure they will come and talk to you real soon. Try to keep this to yourself for at least the next twenty-four hours. Will you do that for me?"

Marcie looked at Sophia, and Sophia nodded her head yes, so Marcie replied, "I will do as you say and just wait to hear from you. I'm just relieved to be free again. It was very scary. I never thought I would be important enough to have someone want to kidnap me. It was kind of exciting in a weird kind of way."

They dropped Marcie off at her hotel, which was nice, but not on the same scale as the place where Thomas and Sophia were staying. She had come to Miami Beach just to hang out with Sophia.

As soon as Thomas and Sophia were in their room, Sophia started in with the questions. "Tell me what's going on. What do you know about this that I don't? Is my dad in trouble?"

Thomas remembered that he hadn't called Jack or Irish. He told Sophia, "Something very dangerous is going on, so before I get into this, I need to call two people and tell them you're free. I promise I will tell you everything, but I need to get advice from one of them before I do. Please trust me on this."

Sophia gave him a blank stare. "Thomas, you're scaring me. Is my father in trouble? Are you?"

"I will tell you everything, but you have to be patient." Thomas pulled his cell phone out and called me.

I heard the ringing, and finally came out of my stupor to answer the phone. "Hello, this is Irish."

I heard Thomas's excited voice. "Irish, they have released Sophia and Marcie. I have Sophia here in my room. She and Marcie are okay. They never laid a hand on them. They're fine."

Sophia thought about the gruesome man who had put his hands on her breasts and groped her thighs. She shuttered at the thought. Thomas looked at her and frowned.

I asked, "Did you call Jack?"

"No, I called you first."

"What about Marcie? Have you talked to her about keeping this quiet for now?"

"Yes, I did, and she's good with that, at least for now. She's going to hold off calling the police until we get back with her."

"It's late now, so let's hold off until the morning. I will call Jack right now, but if you don't hear from me within the next five minutes, go to bed. We'll call you first thing in the morning."

"Sounds like a plan. How much can I tell Sophia? She wants to know what's going on."

"I guess it's your call. Tell her what you want, but make sure she knows how important it is to keep quiet about everything."

"Will do, Irish. I will talk to you in the morning."

I hung up the phone and immediately called Jack, obviously waking him from a deep sleep. I told him about Thomas's call, and we both agreed to talk in the morning.

After Thomas hung up the phone, he and Sophia told each other their stories. He especially emphasized that her father may have been forced to do the things he had done for the past year, and why.

She told him about the woman at the house where they were taken saying the kidnapping was not about her and Marcie, but about forcing some-one else to do what the "family" needed to have done.

After another hour or so, they finally went to bed, holding each other and talking intimately about the future with their baby.

CHAPTER THIRTY

Joseph Pinata hadn't slept much the previous night. In the morning, he was filled with a happiness he hadn't felt in almost twelve months. *No,* he thought, not twelve months, his entire life. The previous day had been filled with despair followed by relief.

When he learned that Sophia had been kidnapped, he was filled with a rage he thought he would never feel again.

When he first found out that his wife, Angela, had actually been kidnapped instead of running away, he felt the same rage that he had yesterday. She had supposedly left him without a word, just a note in her handwriting that said she was going to commit suicide. Instead, she had been taken in the middle of the day and held captive for the last twelve months.

The previous day had changed everything. The Mafia had sent a messenger, telling him that if he didn't settle the contract for another week, his daughter would be released immediately, followed by his wife a week later.

All he had to do was delay the settlement for seven days. The Mafia family was manipulating the stock market to their advantage and possibly others. Apparently, another week was going to make a big difference to them and whoever else was involved.

As soon as he heard Sophia had been released, he knew he had to tell her about her mother. She deserved to know. Sophia and her mother were close—closer than any mother-daughter relationship he had ever witnessed. He knew he was never there for them, so they clung to each other for support and comfort.

It was eight in the morning, and the time had come for him to talk to his daughter. He called her phone, and Thomas answered on the first ring. "Hello, this is Thomas Sharpe."

"This is Sophia's father. May I speak to her?"

He sounded strange to Thomas, who asked, "Are you all right?"

"For once, I think I am, Thomas."

"Just a moment. She's in the bedroom."

Sophia picked up the phone and said, "Hello, Father, what can I do for you?"

"Are you okay? I couldn't believe it when I found out you'd been kidnapped. I went crazy. I thought I had lost you too."

"I'm fine. Do I owe you thanks for cooperating with whoever it was that kidnapped me, or are you going to deny everything?"

Joey was silent for a moment. His heart was breaking for everything that had happened. He felt he had lost his daughter, all the while thinking he was protecting her. In as gentle a voice as he could muster, he asked, "Can I come and talk to you?"

"You want to come here? You're not summoning me to your luxury suite to meet with the king?"

He could feel the hair rise up on his arms and neck with the realization that he was uncomfortable talking to his own daughter. He swallowed his pride and said, "I want to come to you. This is very important. Please let me see you, even if it's for only a few minutes."

Sophia could feel the sincerity in his voice and was aware of his desperate tone. She let her heart melt a little and finally said, "Dad, if you want to come and see me, I will be here. When are you coming?"

"Right now, if it's good with you."

"Okay, I'll see you in a few minutes." Sophia hung up the phone and turned to Thomas. "My father is coming here in a few minutes to talk with me."

Thomas, sounding surprised, asked, "He's coming here and not demanding you come to his suite?"

"I guess so. Something big must be up. I'm going to go get dressed. Entertain him if he gets here before I get back."

Thomas smiled and asked, "How do you 'entertain' your father?"

"I don't know. Never thought about it. I don't really know what makes my father tick."

She left and Thomas made a new pot of coffee, just in case Mr. Pinata wanted some. In a few minutes, the doorbell rang, and Thomas answered. Sophia's father was standing in the doorway.

His wide frame and bulk took up most of the door frame. He just stood there, looking at Thomas and checking out their suite, saying nothing. His silence was Joey's way of expressing his dominance of the situation.

Thomas looked Joey in the eye, refusing to be intimidated by his lifeless stare. "How are you doing today?"

"I've been better. Today is just another stressful day, like so many I've had lately."

"Well, come on in and have a seat. Would you like a cup of coffee?"

"Sure, why not. But Thomas, do you mind if Sophia and I are alone for a while? I want to talk to her privately."

"Not a problem, though I'm sure she would want me to stay. I'll just go into the bedroom to get something and take my time. I'll give you all the time you need."

"That would be fine. Thank you."

Thomas went into the kitchen and poured Joey and himself a cup of coffee. He handed Joey the cup and said, "I'll go see what's taking her so long."

Thomas went into the bedroom and found Sophia crying on the bed. "What's wrong, Sophia? Are you all right?"

"I was just thinking about my mother. I wish she would come back. I know she didn't run away, but I'll never understand why she's been gone so long. I miss her so."

"Maybe your father can shed some light on why she's been gone. Now, go into the bathroom and wash your face. You don't want him to see that you were crying."

She stood up to give him a kiss and said, "Thank you. I don't know what I would do without you."

Sophia went into the bathroom and washed her face, then walked out to greet her father. Thomas stood just out of sight but within range to be able to hear their conversation.

When Sophia came into the living room, Joey stood up and reached to give her a hug. She hesitated, but gave him a perfunctory one in return. Deep inside, she wanted and needed her father, but their relationship has been so strained since her mother went missing that sincerity seemed distant for both of them.

"Tell me, Father, what is going on."

"Sophia, the last twelve months have been living a nightmare for me for reasons I will try to explain. I want to ask you for forgiveness that I probably don't deserve."

Sophia was shocked at his humble attitude. She had never heard him talk like this, even when she was a child. There must be something very troubling going on. "Why do you need to ask for forgiveness?"

"You see, your mother is alive, and hopefully in good health."

The statement took Sophia's breath away. "What do you mean? Where has she been all this time? Did she really run away?"

"Hold on a minute, Sophia. Your mother was kidnapped by the same people who took you."

"What?!" shouted Sophia. "Why haven't you done anything? Did you call the police, the FBI, anyone?"

"Please understand. They told me that if I called anyone, they would hurt her. I couldn't take the chance, so I held off on trying to find her."

Sophia sat down, shattered, and then started crying. "Oh my poor, poor mother. How could anyone do this to her? She is so gentle and sweet. Daddy, we have got to get her back."

"Sophia, that is exactly what I have been trying to do. They told me they would release you immediately and your mother a week later if I extended the strike for another week."

"Why? What the hell does the strike have to do with her and whoever has her? How can that possibly help them in any way? Why her? What does she have to do with any of this? Daddy, we have to try something."

"Honey, please understand. They are vicious people. They will hurt her if we do anything—maybe even kill her if I don't cooperate. We have to be patient. They told me yesterday they would kill her if I tried in any way to get her free. We cannot risk anything further."

"What do you mean?"

"Shortly after they took her, I hired a private investigator to find her. What I got was . . ." He hesitated because he knew this would be a shock to Sophia. "What I got was her little finger instead."

Sophia felt like she was going to throw up. This news made her physically and emotionally sick. She took deep breaths, trying to calm herself.

"Oh, poor Mama. How could anyone do that to her?" She started to cry again. Joseph Pinata, for the first time in his life, reached over and drew Sophia to him. He held her and whispered, "I promise I will get her back, even if it's the last thing I ever do."

"Have you talked to her?" Sophia asked through her tears.

"Yes, two days ago, they let me speak to her for the first time since she's been gone. I told them I must talk to her before I would agree to any more of their demands. She told me she was in good health and not to worry, they were treating her well. She sounded good."

"Treating her well? Cutting off her finger is not treating her well. How long have you known that she was kidnapped?"

"They contacted me about a month after they took her. It was just before the strike started. Everything that has happened during the strike was orchestrated by them."

"How did you know for sure they had her all this time?"

"They started sending pictures of her holding a newspaper with the date on it right after she went missing. I had each picture analyzed to make sure it wasn't Photoshopped into an updated newspaper. Besides, she wore something different in each picture. I am positive each one was real. They kept promising me they would release her if I didn't settle the strike, but it kept going on and on."

"What makes you think they'll release her this time?"

"They kept their word and released you immediately like they said they would. I thought they would keep you like they did your mother. I was afraid I would lose both of you. Plus, I told them that this was the last time I would agree to do anything for them and that I would go to the FBI if it went one minute past the deadline. I told them I would name names and testify at a grand jury. That's why I increased security for all members of the executive board. I also think they hired someone outside of the family to kill Henry Rodriguez. I believe the FBI has a person who is willing to testify that this Mafia family is behind all of this. So along with my testimony, that would be enough to put them away for years."

"Who exactly are these people that have her?"

"I believe it's all Mafia-related. I'm not exactly sure who they are because they have never identified themselves, but my sources think it may be the Marzetti family. My cousin, Frank Marzetti. That dirty son of a bitch."

"How do they benefit if the strike goes on?"

"I'm not a hundred percent sure, but it must have something to do with money."

"Daddy, this is so scary." As a little girl, she always called him Daddy whenever she was troubled. Now, out of nowhere, it came back naturally. "What are we supposed to do now?"

"You're supposed to do nothing. Everything should be in place. I've done everything they've asked me to do. Now we just have to wait out the next week."

"What about all those poor people who have lost their jobs, their homes, and their marriages? What about their lives?"

"Your mother was all I could think about. Protecting her, and you, was my number one priority. Nothing else mattered. How could I live with myself if I did something and they killed her?"

"Is what you have done illegal? Can the police arrest you for this?"

"At this point, I really don't care. All I want is for your mother to be returned safely, and to keep you both safe for the rest of your lives."

Thomas was listening and could not believe his ears. What Joey had agreed to do was illegal. He could be facing many years in prison for his part in this scheme. Even if he was forced to do something like this, he could still be prosecuted. Thomas knew he had to contact Irish and Jack as soon as possible.

Joey continued trying to persuade Sophia what should be done now that they both knew what was happening with Angela.

"Sophia, you need to be very careful, and you need to stay out of sight for the next week. I cannot risk them coming after you again. I have hired someone to watch over you and Thomas until this is all over. Will you promise me that you will stay here, in this suite, for the next week?"

"Daddy, if you think that's best, I will do as you say. I just want Mama to come home. I miss her so much."

Joey sat upright in his chair, trying to maintain the appearance of the strong, rigid person he was feared to be. He could not let anyone think he was weakening by any means. Just one more week was all he needed to get through. He thought now was the best time to lay a bombshell on Sophia that would surprise her and everyone else in his life.

"Sophia, there is one more thing I have to tell you."

Sophia could tell by his tone and the look on his face that something very important was coming. "What is it, Daddy?"

"As soon as the strike is over, I am going to resign from my position as president. I'm so tired of all the bullshit, the stress, and the heartbreak that

I've caused your mother and you. I cannot only ask for you and your mother's forgiveness. I have to show that I'm really willing to change my life."

These were strong words coming from Joseph Pinata. Sophia was completely taken aback. She could not imagine her father stepping down as president of the union. The union was his entire life. It had always seemed more important to him than either her mother or her. What else was going on with him that he wasn't saying?

"What will you do if you resign? The union is all you've ever done. Is there something more to all of this?"

He hesitated as if thinking about how to say what was on his mind. She waited for him to gather his thoughts.

"I have been diagnosed with a terminal malignant brain tumor. The doctors refuse to say how much time I have, but the way they talk, it doesn't sound like it's very long. I want to spend my last days with you and your mother as much as I can, or as much as you and Thomas will let me."

Tears came rolling down Sophia's face. She didn't know what to say, so she stood up and gave her father a hug. She held him as he grabbed onto her and buried his face into her neck. Then he sobbed.

She could hardly hold him, because he was squeezing her as if holding on to life itself. They cried together. It was the first time she had ever seen her father express such deep emotions, and the first time she had ever felt the love between them that must have been hidden all these years.

"I also have to tell you that as the tumor grows, it causes me to have abrupt personality changes. I go into these rages I can't control. It's part of the disease. So if you hear about me going nuts, it's the cancer and not really me."

Sophia cried freely as she murmured, "Oh, Papa."

After the crying subsided, Joey gave her a kiss on the cheek and said, "I have to go now. I will keep in touch with you every day. I want to be the father and husband I never was. Please, let me try."

He stood up and left without another word. Thomas immediately came out of the bedroom and looked silently at Sophia. She came to him and fell into his arms. She cried for what seemed like five minutes.

Finally, she took a deep breath and smiled up at him, saying, "I love you. I have always loved you, but now for the first time, I love my daddy like I have never loved him before."

Thomas smiled and said, "That's really a good thing. I have always felt sorry for you because you never had a loving father like I had. But now you do."

CHAPTER THIRTY-ONE

· ·

I had been awake for about an hour, sitting in my room drinking coffee, when the phone rang. I picked it up to hear Thomas announce, "Irish, do I have some news for you."

I smiled at his enthusiasm and in a deadpan tone, replied "Okay, tell me what you've got."

"You remember we were talking about how Sophia's mother has been missing for over a year?"

"Yes, but I thought she took off because she'd had enough of Joey and his antics and is in hiding somewhere."

"Not even close. It's just like we talked about, but with a little twist. Mrs. Pinata was kidnapped by a Mafia family to force Joey into stretching the strike for twelve months. Not only that, this family is the one that kidnapped Sophia. The deal they offered is if Joey agreed to keep it going for another seven days, they would immediately release Sophia and then his wife a week later." The excitement in his voice was palpable.

"Can Sophia testify against these guys?"

"Probably not; they all had hoods on their heads, so she didn't get a look at anyone."

I asked, "How did you find all this out?"

"Mr. Pinata came to our suite about fifteen minutes ago. He confessed all of it, but the thing is, he's never seen anyone either. He said they contacted him with pictures of his wife holding newspapers showing the date to prove proof of life."

I thought about this for a moment and said, "I have to get ahold of Jack and have him call you. He needs to hear this from you. Or, do you think Sophia would talk to him?"

"I really doubt it. Her father asked her to stay put in this hotel and to keep a low profile. He said emphatically that neither he nor anyone else can attempt to find Mrs. Pinata or try to set her free and that they are especially not to involve any type of police. About nine months ago, Mr. Pinata hired a private investigator, which made whoever is keeping Mrs. Pinata cut off her small finger. Since then, Mr. Pinata is doing only what they want."

"All right, Thomas, let me go. I have to call Jack."

"Wait, wait, there's more."

"What are you talking about? Let's hear it." My interest was really piqued now.

"Joey told Sophia that he is going to resign as the union's president right after the strike is over."

"What? Are you serious? Why would he do that? He's a king reigning over his servants. There is no way he would resign. He's yanking her chain."

In a serious voice, Thomas said, "No, Irish, he told her he has a terminal brain tumor and the doctors don't think he has much time. He said he wants to spend his last days with his wife and Sophia. He sounded to me like a changed man. I was listening from the bedroom."

"I don't want to sound like a skeptic, but I think he may be stretching things. I don't trust him one bit. Be careful, and you should tell Sophia the same thing."

"I can't do that. She is so overwhelmed with the joy of finally having a relationship with her father. I can't destroy that. I won't say anything to her. It would put questions in her mind, and I don't want to do that."

"Thomas, of course, I wouldn't ask you to say anything if you feel she needs this. Sophia is a smart, wonderful gal, and I know her relationship with her father has always been questionable. I won't be the one to destroy it. Besides, if Joey really has cancer, they need to be totally committed to each other."

"Thanks, Irish. I have to let you go. Sophia will be out of the shower any time now. Keep me posted."

"I will, and you do the same. Remember, Jack may be calling you. One more thing—does Sophia know you're working with Jack and me on this?"

"I haven't confessed that to her yet, but I told her I would tell her everything."

Maybe you should be very diplomatic and not tell her everything, just enough to satisfy her concerns."

"Good idea. I'll do that. Take care. I will talk to you later." He hung up the phone, and I did the same.

I gathered my thoughts before calling Jack. I needed to tell him everything. So I dialed his number, and he answered on the first ring. "Jack, it's Irish. How are you feeling this beautiful morning?"

"I'm better. Today, I only feel like a car ran over me instead of a truck. What's up?"

"Are you sitting down? If you aren't, you better take a seat. I've got some news for you."

"You sound serious, Irish. What the hell happened?"

I told him the same story Thomas told me, and when I was done, Jack said, "We have been aware of Mr. Pinata's medical condition for over a week now, but I didn't think I should reveal it just yet. But this scenario is exactly what we've been talking about. Someone has been pulling Mr. Pinata's chain all along, but I'm not sure where that leaves us in the investigation. If we can get him to testify against the Marzettis, we could make him a deal and he could be off the hook for a lot of bad things—not everything, but some of the most serious crimes."

I asked, "Since we have to be careful and not let them think Mr. Pinata might go to the FBI, what do you think our next move should be?"

"You're right about that. We don't want them killing his wife because we made a bad move. I would really like to bring David Shanahan in for questioning."

"What would be the pretense for bringing him in?"

"You remember the guy Bob Lee killed the other night?"

"Sure, how could I forget? He tried to kill me and your witness, Freddy."

"Well, we thought we were seeing double. Last night, we had two guys following Shanahan, and he had another man in the car with him who looked exactly like the guy Bob killed. As it turns out, the guy riding with Shanahan was the twin of the man Bob shot and killed. So we have the right to bring Shanahan in for questioning about that situation. Why was he with this guy's twin? What's his connection?"

"That sounds like it could be completely separate from Mr. Pinata and the kidnappings. It sounds like a safe bet to me."

"I'm going to go with my men when they pick him up. I want to see his reaction and what his response will be. See if he tips his hand on anything."

"How could he possibly deny involvement if he has the guy's twin in his car? I would think that would be proof enough to arrest him."

"Arrest him on what charge? I can't arrest a man because he knows a hired assassin's twin brother. That's not illegal, but it is questionable. We would pick him up just for questioning."

"Would he have immunity since he works for the National Labor Board?"

"Not with the FBI, he wouldn't. We can bring the director in if we believe he committed a crime."

"Anything you want me to do today?"

"Have you talked to anyone on Pinata's staff who you think you can trust?"

"No, actually, that was on my list for today, but I was hoping you had something else for me to do. I'm not real keen on trusting anyone on his staff other than Thomas Sharpe."

"Can you talk to him and see what his take is on the rest of the staff? Maybe he has some insight on someone he particularly trusts. We have to find out who else on Pinata's staff is involved with this."

"I think Mr. Pinata's gofer Michael Ferrier would be a good one to bring in for questioning. I'm sure he knows almost everything that's going on."

"I thought you and he didn't get along."

"We don't. I was talking about letting me identify myself as an FBI agent and putting some pressure on him. Force him to talk."

Jack started laughing. "You dummy. From what you've told me, you would like that."

"I sure would."

"I will have one of my agents bring him in for questioning. Steve Hill is a great intimidator.

Maybe he can get Ferrier to squeal a little bit. You, on the other hand, are out of the question. I might have to fire you after you're through with him."

"So fire me. Hell, I've been fired by better companies than the FBI." I laughed harder at my own joke than Jack did.

"Let's go after David Shanahan and leave Mr. Pinata alone for now. From what you told me, maybe Mr. Pinata has had a change of heart, and he may do an about face and help us out."

I thought about that, but I certainly was not convinced that Joey had changed, or ever would. "According to Thomas Sharpe, Joey was different in a way he's never seen before. I suppose it's possible that he's changed, but I'm not convinced. Joey is such a jerk. Too much water has passed under the bridge for me to believe that."

Jack laughed and said, "Well, then, like I've told you in the past, I go with my gut, and my gut says go after David Shanahan."

"If that's your decision, you have to leave me out of it. I'm not ready to reveal my alter ego just yet. What about David changing his name and withdrawing his previous name from the Social Security files? Is that against the law?"

"It would be if he hadn't paid his taxes all these years, but legally, he just changed his name and paid his taxes under his new identity. There's nothing wrong with that."

"You know, Jack, there is one person on the staff who might be willing to give us some information. I have dragged my feet because I didn't want to find out that he was in on everything. I like the guy. He has a wife and a kid, and I don't want to see him flushed down with the rest of the dirty water."

"Irish, in this business, you have to be blind to people you know and like. They are the toughest ones to bring in. You don't want to believe they did anything wrong, but in reality, they're still criminals and must be apprehended."

"I don't like it, but I will talk to him and see where it goes. Good luck with David Shanahan."

We said our good-byes and hung up. I looked at the phone and knew what I had to do.

CHAPTER THIRTY-TWO

David Shanahan pulled to a stop in front of the big house. Kit was in the car with him for security purposes. David looked up on the big porch with the large white pillars and saw his personal bodyguard, Carlos, standing in the doorway. He had a puzzled look on his face.

David wondered what was up with Carlos. He and Kit climbed out of the car and up the steps to the porch, where he asked, "What's up, Carlos?"

"We need to talk, boss."

"So go ahead and talk. What's stopping you?"

Carlos glanced at Kit and then back to David and said, "It's personal, boss."

"Very well. Kit you go on inside and grab a bite to eat."

"Sure. I'm starving."

As soon as Kit walked into the house, Carlos grabbed David's elbow and led him off the porch. "We have a problem, boss—a big problem."

"Carlos, you know I don't like any bullshit. Get to the point."

"Kip has been killed."

"What the hell do you mean?" shouted David.

"I just got a call from our source. He said Kip has been lying unidentified in the morgue for the last two days. That's why we couldn't find him. It appears he got into a gunfight with a Miami homicide detective the night he went after Freddy."

"That dumb son of a bitch. I told him to back off if there was any question about making a clean hit. Who was the fucking cop that shot him?"

"A detective named Bob Lee. He works homicide out of Miami's main office. Apparently, he walked up behind Kip and told him to drop his gun, but Kip decided to shoot it out with him. He took two to the chest and was DOA at Miami General."

"Kit is going to go fucking nuts. We can't let him go off half-cocked. I had better tell him before he finds out on the news."

"You might be too late. It was on the six o'clock news just a little while ago."

"Did you leave the TV on?" David asked, sounding angry and frustrated all at once.

"No, I took the cord off the TV, so he couldn't watch it, but you better hurry. You know how much Kit likes to watch that damn tube."

"Come on, you better come with me in case I can't handle him. Get your gun out and shoot him in the leg if you have to."

"Are you serious, boss?"

"No, I'm not serious, you dumb ass. Just stand by me when I tell him."

They walked into the house and made their way to the kitchen. Kit was sitting on a stool next to the counter. He looked at both of them and asked, "What the hell is wrong with you two? You look like you saw a ghost."

"Kit, I'm afraid I have some bad news."

"What happened? Did little Ms. Sharpe wet her pants?" He laughed at his own joke. David and Carlos didn't.

David stayed five feet from him as a protection barrier and said, "You knew that we sent Kip to take care of Freddy for us. You remember that?"

Kit said with a mouth full of ham and cheese on rye, "Sure. Where the hell has he been for the last two days?"

"There was a problem. Kip was shot and killed. A Miami homicide detective got into a shooting match with him, and he was killed."

Kit stopped chewing and just sat there. David and Carlos were waiting for him to explode, but instead Kit slid off the stool onto the floor and began to cry.

Here was a three-hundred-pound killer sitting there, crying like a baby. David was waiting for him to spring up and charge out of the house seeking revenge. Instead, he just cried and cried for twenty minutes.

Finally, he calmly said, "Kip was never too smart. He almost got me killed three times because he didn't use his head. He probably deserved this because he did something stupid. Now I have to kill a cop."

He said it like it was nothing more than swatting a fly on the wall. Now David had another problem to deal with. David had never told anyone, but Kit scared him. He was a cold-blooded killer. He killed without remorse, without feeling, and with no conscience—the perfect makeup for a killer. David shuddered.

Nothing more was said. Kit went back to his sandwich like nothing had happened, and David and Carlos walked into the other room.

Before they could say anything, David's phone rang. He pulled it out of his pocket and said, "Hello, this is David Marks."

"David, this is Jack Casey. How are you doing?"

"I'm doing fine, Jack, just looking into a couple of leads."

"Say, David, do you have a few minutes to talk? I would be happy to meet you somewhere. Just name it."

"There's a little bar off Twenty-Ninth on Twenty-Fourth. It's called T.J.'s Bar. Let's say, in about an hour? Would that work for you?"

"Sounds great. I'll see you then."

The hour would give Jack just enough time to get men stationed around the bar and hotel. He couldn't take any chances because he knew David would do the same.

An hour later, Jack pulled up in front of the hotel in an old Ford and parked. He limped into the lobby, bent over due to the pain. He found the bar on his right and walked straight to a booth in the very back. As usual, he sat with his back to the wall.

David hadn't arrived yet, but Jack's agents were already in place. There was a loving couple holding hands in the first booth off the entrance to the bar—they were both agents, and another one was sitting at the bar. The bartender was also an agent, and there were three others in the lobby and two outside of the hotel. Jack felt safe enough, but where were David's men?

After five minutes, David walked into the bar. He stopped and looked around like he was searching for someone. Jack felt for his nine millimeter in its holster on his right side.

David spotted him and, with a smile, walked over, extending his arm for a handshake. "Jack, it's nice to see you as always. You're looking a little rough. What the hell happened to you? It looks like someone tap danced on your face."

Jack studied David's face for any indication he knew what had happened to him, but saw nothing. "I had a little confrontation with this smart-ass who thought I was over the hill. I guess he proved himself right."

Jack laughed and David joined in, saying, "Hope he at least looks a little worse for wear. So what's up, Jack? Why did you want to see me?"

Jack had already gathered his thoughts before David arrived. He knew the best way to do this was straight on and right to the point.

"David, two nights ago, one of our officers got caught in a confrontation with an alleged hired gun, and when it was over, the hired gun was dead. His name was Kip Gardner."

Jack stopped for a moment to see David's reaction. David didn't move, but his eyes grew wide with surprise and the grin on his face was gone in an instant. Jack had purposely taken the seat facing the entrance, forcing David to have a limited view of the bar. It didn't give him a chance to look around to see if any of his men had arrived unless he was obvious about it.

"One of my men spotted you riding with Kip's twin brother on Seventy-Ninth Street by Hialeah Race Track. Can you tell me why you were with him?"

David's face grew wild with anger. "Have you been watching me, Jack? Who the fuck do you think you are? What I do and who I'm with are none of your fucking business."

His voice grew loud enough for Jack's people in the bar to turn and look. It was enough warning for the agent at the bar to put his hand on his weapon. The couple in the booth had already drawn theirs, but didn't move while concealing them under the table. The bartender had his shotgun in his hands beneath the bar, ready.

In an instant, David pulled his .38 Special and, at the same time, lifted the table and slammed it into Jack's head. He raised his gun and fired two shots through the table, hitting Jack in the chest.

As David turned around, three guns fired simultaneously, striking him in the chest. The bartender turned and guarded the door to the bar in case some of David's men came running in.

David dropped his gun and went down in a heap.

The agent sitting at the bar was the first to get to Jack. He threw the table off him and shouted, "Jack, are you all right? Jack?"

Jack lay there motionless for a moment. Then all of a sudden, a smile crossed his face. "Man, that hurts. Oh my god, am I sore. I think he broke my ribs."

The agent helped Jack get up, but he wavered and almost fell backward. "Sorry about that. It wasn't supposed to go down that fast. Are you sure you're okay?

"I think he gave me another concussion when he slammed the table into me." There was blood coming from his nose, and his forehead had begun to swell. Jack looked down at David and asked the agent checking him, "Craig, how is he?

"He is dead as dead can be."

"Shit! I was hoping we could do this without all this foreplay. Goddamn it. He's no good to us now."

Catherine, the agent playing one half of the couple, said, "We didn't have any other choice, Jack. Shit, he almost killed you. It's a good thing you were wearing your vest, or you would be dead now."

"I'm not blaming anyone. You did what you had to do. There's no question about that. It's just that I wanted a chance to interrogate him. He probably had a lot of the answers we were looking for."

Just then, one of the agents from the lobby came running into the bar and said, "We have two of his men in cuffs outside and one dead on the floor in the lobby. A fourth one hightailed it out of here before we could grab him."

Jack said to Jim Walker, his top assistant, "Please tell me that Kit Gardner is one of the ones you have on the floor in the lobby."

"He was. Now we don't have to worry about him anymore."

"Did you get a license plate on the car?"

"We did, and two of ours are also out trying to chase him down."

"Were there any more of his men who might have gotten away?"

"Not that we are aware of. You never know really who is who."

"Great job, everyone—thanks for saving my ass. Let's get this mess cleaned up and get back into the office. Hey, Jim?"

The agent turned around and asked, "What do you need, Jack?"

"Have you put out an APB on the runner?"

"We have. Every cop in Miami is looking for him."

The FBI had an ambulance standing by out of sight that was just now approaching the hotel. Jack looked up in time to see the driver, who was dressed in plain clothes, open the car door and run like hell across the parking lot.

Quickly, he put two and two together and yelled, "Everybody, down, now!" He ran and dove back into the hotel bar and slid across the floor to the bar just as the bomb exploded.

He felt the crushing blow as the wall toward the street blew in. The blast, strangely enough, pushed him behind the oak bar, saving his life. The glass behind the bar shattered, chairs were blown to pieces, and tables were ripped apart like kindling.

The smoke made it difficult to breathe. He was totally deafened for the first minute after the blast, but still wondered immediately if any of his agents had been killed. His hearing returned suddenly, and all that filled his ears was the screaming of the victims who had survived the blast.

He struggled to his feet and stumbled over the carnage that lay in front of him. He saw two bodies lying face down. The first one he didn't recognize, but the second was that of Catherine, the agent who was the only woman in the bar.

His anger suddenly boiled over. To no one in particular, he yelled, "Oh no, not her!"

He didn't even know her last name. She was just a rookie—young, smart, vibrant, and eager to do her duty.

Now *he* had the duty of telling her parents. How would he be able to do something like that? He had done it many times throughout his career, but never for someone as young as her. He was at a loss for words.

He wandered further into the hotel lobby, at least what was left of it, and saw Steve and Craig.

"How bad was it?" he asked, with blood running down his face and out of his left ear. He suddenly felt weak, and blackness overcame him. He was out before he hit the floor.

Jack came to a few minutes later as he heard the sounds of more police cars and ambulances heading their way. "Man, I screwed the pooch on this one. Henry Sullivan will be pissed when he gets word of this."

Steve Hill was kneeling next to him and said, "Don't worry about Henry Sullivan. This was not your fault. No one could have predicted what would happen here. We took all the normal precautions; it couldn't be helped."

CHAPTER THIRTY-THREE

· ·

I was just about to meet Ken Cloutier, the ITU recording secretary, at a coffee shop on Bayshore Drive, when my phone rang. I picked it up and said, "Hello."

"Irish, this is Bob Lee."

"Hey, Bob, what's shaking?"

"I'm at Miami General, and when I came down to the ER to get some smokes, I saw that an ambulance was bringing Jack Casey in on a stretcher. There were also another six people brought in at the same time."

"No shit? Do you know what happened?"

"I don't know anything yet, but I will find out as soon as they let me in to talk to Dr. Myott or one of the nurses. I think you should get over here as soon as possible."

"I'm just meeting some guy who Jack wants me to talk to. As soon as I'm through, I will come to the hospital. If you get an update, call me at once."

"I will keep you posted."

I hung up the phone and walked into the coffee shop. Ken was already sipping a cup of coffee. I said hello and sat down. The waitress came over, and I ordered a black coffee.

"What's wrong with you? You look like you saw a ghost."

"I think I'm getting the flu or something."

"Bullshit, you're hung over." Ken laughed.

"No, I haven't had a drink for two days. Maybe that's what's wrong," I joked, though I didn't laugh.

There was a television hanging behind the counter, and it showed a scene of a building with the front walls blown out. It was obviously was viewed from a helicopter, as it was an overhead shot.

I asked the waitress to turn up the volume.

The commentator was saying, "Someone set off a bomb in front of TJ's Bar, causing multiple casualties, with two dead and seven injured. It is not clear if this was a terrorist bomb, an accident, or an isolated attack."

"Have you been watching this, Ken?"

"Yeah, I saw it, but the sound wasn't up, so I didn't know what was going on."

The television commentator said, "One thing appears clear, that the FBI is somehow involved. There are many government cars and officials on the scene as we speak. It usually takes more time before this many show up to any possible bombing attack. We will get word to everyone as soon as we know anything at all. This is Linda Collins signing off."

I knew in an instant that Jack was somehow involved with all that I was witnessing on TV. The scene looked incredibly horrible. The entire face of the building was gone, leaving just a pile of rubble. It was amazing that anyone inside survived.

I turned back to Ken and said, "I have some very important things to discuss with you, and I want you to know that what I'm about to ask you may or may not shock you, depending on how involved you've been."

Ken smiled at me and said, "Irish, you sound like some really serious shit is going on. Is this something that you think I'm involved in? Is that why you called me to meet?"

"Nothing I'm accusing you of. I just want to know if you have been involved personally with President Pinata on some illegal activity that has been going on."

"What the hell are you talking about?"

"Let me start over. The FBI has been investigating The International Truckers Union—especially Joseph Pinata—for a number of illegal affairs. Things like murder, extortion, bribery, prostitution, collusion, among other things that are too numerous to mention."

"So you think I'm involved in all of this?" Ken asked angrily.

"No, not exactly. What I want to know is if you are aware of anything illegal that Mr. Pinata is involved with. The FBI is going to bring this union to its knees if we don't do something to save it. There are numerous things that have happened that the FBI think may have come from Joey's orders."

"Like what?" Ken asked, sounding angrier than before.

"Well, let me list a few. Jennifer's hit-and-run, the murder of Henry Rodriguez, me getting beat up, an FBI agent getting beat up, and now that." I pointed to the TV behind the counter. "The report is two dead and six injured. I'm pretty sure that also has some connection, somehow, to Joseph Pinata. What's happening is not only dangerous to all of us personally, but to the ITU particularly."

Ken asked, "How do you know about all of this? What's your involvement?"

Now we were at the breaking point. If I told him the truth and he was deeply involved with Joey and the Mafia, I would put myself in grave danger, but if I lied, I was afraid he would see through it and not trust me.

"Jennifer came to me about three days ago with some accusations against Joey. I told her I would help. One thing led to another, and I have been working with the FBI ever since. I made a deal with them that if I helped, they wouldn't tear our union apart, and if Joey is doing something illegal, they would come only after him."

I tried to read Ken's reaction, but there was no eye or body movement, no sign of anger, nothing. He just sat there silently with a blank stare.

I waited until he finally spoke. "Are you sure you know what you're doing? This sounds like some heady shit. What exactly are you saying? Are you trying to save the union and not destroy it, or are you telling me you have been a spy for the FBI?"

"My only goal is to save our union. I know there are many on our staff who see the crazy things Joey has been doing with this strike, not to mention the intimidation of everyone on the staff and the use of prostitutes, gambling, and favorable contracts with certain companies that he himself has negotiated for relatives and friends. That's illegal. It's called collusion."

"Damn, that is a quite the list of things, Irish. Do you really believe that I would be involved in something like this?"

"No, I do not. I just want to know what you know about all of it."

"Is this a witch hunt for Mr. Pinata?"

"Not on my part, but the FBI has been building a case against him, and if they have to go through the union to nail him, they will. I want to stop them from having to do that. Don't you think it's better to weed out one bad apple instead of throwing the entire basket out? I do not have a personal agenda. I don't want to be president of the union or any other seat on the executive board. I'm just trying to save the union that I love."

"Jesus Christ, Irish, do you know what you're saying? You're putting your entire career on the chopping block if nothing comes of this investigation. As a matter of fact, Mr. Pinata will see to it that you never work for this union or any other union shop for the rest of your life. He will be livid if he finds out you are in bed with the FBI."

"Ken, sometimes, you have to go with your gut. I know this is the right thing to do. Look at the mess Joey has gotten our members into. It's disgraceful what has happened. Our members have lost everything—homes, marriages, and even life itself. We can't let this continue."

"I have to agree with you there. This is quite a mess. Before I tell you what I know, give me the bigger picture of what's happening."

"I will, but first, you have to promise me you will not go back to Mr. Pinata on this. Can I have your word that you will keep this between us?"

"You do," said Ken.

So I told him everything that had happened since the day I talked to Jennifer on the beach. I left nothing out—from the kidnapping of Angela, Sophia and Marcie's abduction, the murder of Henry Rodriguez, the attempted murder of our witness Freddy, my swearing in as an FBI agent, Joey admitting to having brain cancer and his decision to step down as president after the strike is over—up to the bombing at the bar. Ken waited through all this.

When I was done, Ken spoke, "Hell, Irish, that is quite the storyline. It sounds like something from a novel, not a real-life situation. The thing I have to believe is that Mr. Pinata is behind all of this. In reality, it's not hard for me to believe that he could do any of it. My question is what more will he do once the investigation gets further along?"

Ken became quiet, thinking about his options. What would he decide? What had his involvement been?

I said nothing. I just waited until he came to a decision.

He said, "I'm going to go outside to think about this for a couple of minutes. I'm not going anywhere. I just need a moment." He walked outside and just stood by the window of the café.

I watched him closely to see if he made any type of signal to warn someone, or if he used his cell phone. He did neither. I trusted Ken, or I would not have come to him. My gut feeling said he wasn't involved in any of Mr. Pinata's dirty work.

It took about three minutes before he finally came back. "Irish, this is the most difficult decision I have ever had to make in my career. But first, I have to come clean on something to you. That's why I went outside—to decide if I could trust you. So I came back in."

"What is it that you have to come clean about?"

"About a year ago, just after the strike started, I received a call. There was a man on the phone who said that they had kidnapped my wife and they were going to keep her for one day. They said if I went to the police, they would kill her."

I asked, "So what did they want from you?"

"They told me to support Mr. Pinata in the union strike, and if I did, I would be rewarded and many of my union brothers and sisters' lives would improve immensely."

"What did you say to him?"

"I didn't get a chance to say anything. He hung up before I could respond. They released Debra the next morning. I forgot about the reward."

"That sounds like their mode of operation. Threaten the family to get what they want. I can't figure out why Henry Rodriguez was murdered or Jennifer was run over. It seems like two completely different ways of doing business."

"Irish, the reason I hesitated was because I gained financially from all this. You see, about six months ago, I received a large sum of money in my bank account, and I don't even know where it came from. I was given a letter of thanks for my help that said if I didn't cooperate, they would contact the FBI. It also said that there is more coming if I continue to cooperate."

"How much did you receive?"

"One hundred thousand dollars. You tell me what that looks like in the eyes of a judge or jury. It looks like I was bought off, when in reality, I just chose to remain silent and to go along with whatever Mr. Pinata decided he wanted to do. Plus, at the same time, I received a call saying the rules are still in effect—I go to the police, and Debra dies."

"Do you know if Mr. Pinata received any large sums of money?"

"I don't know if he received any, but since I didn't know who else to talk to, I told him about this, and he said to keep my mouth shut and be happy I got the money."

"Didn't that large of a deposit into your bank account throw up some flags to the IRS?"

"It did, but that was taken care of by a letter from an attorney stating I inherited the money from a long lost uncle."

"What exactly have you witnessed that was illegal?"

"I was assigned as the lead negotiator with the eyeglass contract and the safety shoe contract that was agreed upon, but the thing is, I really didn't have anything to do with the negotiation process, but I had to sign the contract. Mr. Pinata negotiated the deals, not me."

"When did that take place?" I asked, even though I knew the answer. I wanted to see if my timeline met Ken's.

"Oh, let me see, that was about two months after the strike started. So I would say about ten months ago."

"Do you know who is really calling the shots?

"Hell, yes, I know. It's the Marzetti Mafia family, and there's another family involved too, but I'm not sure who they are."

"How did you figure that out?"

"During negotiations, we were in a breakout meeting; I was alone in the room adjacent to Mr. Pinata, and the door was ajar. He had the speaker phone on, so I was able to overhear his conversation with Mr. Marzetti. He was giving Mr. Pinata instructions on what he was supposed to do."

"Would you be willing to come aboard and testify about everything you know? Because if you are, I'm sure the Bureau can provide protection for your wife and you. Plus, you need to speak to someone soon about the hundred thousand dollars. You would need to talk to my contact at the FBI. He would be happy to meet with you if he's able."

"Why wouldn't he be able to meet with me?" Ken asked.

I pointed to the continuing coverage of the bombing on the television and said, "That's why. The man heading the investigation might have been involved in that bombing, and I don't know if he made it or not."

"Wow, this looks like it's really gotten out of hand. Are you sure he can protect us? Hell, he couldn't even protect himself."

"I don't know the circumstances with the bombing, but he has been protecting Jennifer for about twelve months."

"Look what happened to her. It doesn't look like he did a real good job protecting her, either."

"Jennifer is hardheaded and doesn't always listen. She was supposed to fly by Jack's rules, but she refused, and it cost her."

"Can I think about it for a few days?"

"We don't have a few days. Besides, what is there to think about? If the FBI takes Mr. Pinata down, they are going to take every one of his staff who is involved down with him, and it looks like you are deeply involved. You are in some deep shit, if you ask me. You could face a long prison sentence if convicted. You know bribery is against the law."

I hated to do it to him, but I think I had just set the hook on Ken. How could he resist testifying against Joey? His life depended on it.

"Well, what's it going to be, Ken?"

"I think you just convinced me that it's in my best interest to climb aboard. Also I want you to know I haven't spent a dime of the money that was put into my account. It's all still there."

"Good. I think you just saved your life and your wife's. I have to get with Jack and tell him about the bribery money and where you stand and what you bring to the table. I think he will be pleased. Now, you have to remember to keep all of this to yourself. You cannot talk to anyone about it. That is extremely important. Do you understand how important it is?"

"Don't worry about that. I'm not running my mouth to anyone."

"You should inform your wife that she should be ready to leave in a moment's notice, but try not to scare her too much."

Ken nodded and said, "I will take care of Debra. She'll understand. She and I have discussed this very thing more than once."

"Good. I have to go now, but someone will contact you real soon. Perhaps Jack Casey, if he's able."

CHAPTER THIRTY-FOUR

I left Ken at the table and headed straight for the hospital. I knew I would catch hell with Dr. Myott. Here I was again, coming to visit someone injured by violence.

When I arrived, there was still an atmosphere of chaos. There were at least half a dozen police cruisers and ambulances, plus another half-dozen federal government cars scattered throughout the emergency room parking lot.

I made my way through the crowd outside and passed through the metal detector into the triage area. To my surprise, Katrina was standing there talking to one of the nurses. She had a very concerned look on her face.

She looked up and saw me looking like a fish out of water. I felt like I didn't fit in, but her smile instantly changed the scene from chaotic to calm.

I couldn't believe I had made love to her just the night before. She hurried over and gave me a hug and said, "Nice to see you. I've been thinking about you all day."

I hated to admit it, but for the last few hours, she hadn't crossed my mind. I was too involved with everything that had happened.

I smiled and whispered, "Katrina, last night was the most incredible night of my life. I've missed you all morning."

I figured it was only a tiny white lie since as soon as I thought about it, I realized that subconsciously, I must have been thinking about her all along.

I asked her, "What is going on with all the victims? Do you know any names or how badly they're hurt?"

Softly she asked, "What do you have to do with all of this? Are you involved somehow?"

I had vowed to never lie to her, so I quickly filled her in on my involvement. I left out a lot of information, but I let her know enough to satisfy her curiosity.

I had to ask her, "Do you have any information on a Jack Casey?"

"He's an FBI agent, isn't he?"

"Yes, he is. So how is he doing?"

"I have been trying to contact some family members, but I haven't been able to. So when I was in getting all of his information, I heard Dr. Myott talking to the neurologist, and they think he may have a serious brain injury. They've taken him to surgery to relieve some pressure in the brain. She said that will hopefully take care of everything, but you never know."

"I heard on the television that there were two people dead. What's the latest update?" I tried to sound composed, but she could tell I was extremely upset.

"From what I've overheard, the number has risen. There are two FBI agents and two civilians who have died. They just brought in four more victims. They were in their apartments across the street from the blast and were not immediately discovered. That brings the total to four dead and eight injured."

"Since Jack doesn't have any family, could I take his personal effects? Just for holding until he gets out of the hospital."

"I think I can arrange that. I was called here because the families should be arriving any time now. I have six of my staff waiting to help too. It's so difficult to be with the families when the doctor tells them about their loved ones."

"I can't imagine anyone better suited for the job than you. They will be fortunate to have you with them."

I looked deep into her eyes and felt the love I had felt the night before. I whispered to her, "You were so completely incredible last night. I can't wait to make love to you again. My god, you're so beautiful."

She came close and gently reached up to pull me down to her for a soft, gentle kiss. It was nothing more than a soft touch of our lips, but it was enough to make me feel the love I had for her.

She suddenly pulled away when she saw a family come running through the door, bypassing the security but not caring whatsoever. Katrina said quickly, "I have to go. I'll see if Dr. Myott can keep us updated on Mr. Casey, but she is extremely busy at the moment. Wait a minute and I'll get his things."

After a few minutes, Katrina returned with a bag of Jack's things, and I joined a packed crowd in the waiting room. I found a single seat in the far corner, sat down, and readied myself for a long wait. Jack's things were in a white plastic bag that was tied at the top. Out of curiosity, I opened the bag and looked inside. All of his clothes were there along with an envelope.

I retrieved the opened envelope from the bag. It felt heavy, as if a flat rock was inside. I immediately saw that my name was on it. I wondered what the hell was inside. I opened it to see an FBI badge with a picture of me and a note that said, "Sean, this is your official badge. Welcome to the club. Remember to keep your head down and your mouth shut. Congrats. Jack." This brought a smile to my face, knowing Jack felt so positive about me joining the FBI.

I waited another two hours until Dr. Myott finally paged me to triage. As I walked in, the nurse looked up and said, "Well, if it isn't Mr. MacSween. How are you today?" It was the same nurse who was there the other times I'd been in the ER. I think she was making fun at my expense.

"I guess I'm as good as I can be under the circumstances."

"Sorry to hear that your friend got hurt again. Is he a troublemaker or just unlucky?"

"He's an FBI agent, but I think he's also a little of both." I smiled, trying to make light of the situation.

Just then, Dr. Myott opened the door behind the triage desk and said, "Mr. MacSween, please come this way."

I followed her through triage down the hall and into another office. She sat down behind the desk and said, "Please have a seat."

I sat down and asked, "How is Jack doing?"

"He's a very lucky man. He has sustained a very severe trauma to the head, but the neurosurgeon was able to stop the bleeding around his brain. Jack had what is called a subdural hematoma. It's a hematoma between the dura mater and arachnoid in the subdural space. When a person has this condition, it may put significant pressure on the cerebral cortex, and in turn cause a neurological deficit."

I asked, "Can you put that in layman's terms?"

"Yes, of course. He has bleeding between his brain and the lining of the brain, which can cause severe brain damage or death if not treated in a timely manner."

"Is he going to pull through this?"

"I don't see why not, as long as the bleeding stops. Dr. Henderson, the neurosurgeon, believes he stopped all the bleeding, so there should be no more pressure on the brain. Jack's recovery should turn out just fine as long as there are no further complications."

"How did he get into the brain area to stop the bleeding? It seems impossible to get there."

"Well, Mr. MacSween, he had to drill holes through Jack's skull. I know it sounds horrible, but it's the only way."

"When can I talk to him?"

"Probably not be until tomorrow at the earliest," Dr. Myott responded.

"Can you tell me who exactly is dead and who's injured, and how bad the injuries are?"

"I'm sorry, but that is confidential, unless you are family to every one of these people, or you're a police officer."

"I see." I thought for only an instant, and then I pulled out the badge Jack was going to give me and showed it to Dr. Myott.

She looked down at my FBI badge with surprise. "You are full of revelations, Mr. MacSween. This explains why you're involved with practically everyone who's been coming into our ER lately."

She told me the names of the dead—two were FBI agents and two were civilians, one by the name of David Shanahan.

I was completely surprised when I heard the name David Shanahan. I knew Jack was meeting him, but I didn't know the circumstances or the outcome of their meeting. Now I just knew the final results.

"There was something particularly interesting with Mr. Shanahan's death—he had four gunshot wounds to his chest. He was evidently not killed by the bomb blast, but our pathologist will confirm that when he does the autopsy."

I chewed on that information for a while before she finally told me they were keeping Jack sedated for the next twelve hours, so I might as well go home.

I left the ER and went upstairs to give Jennifer the bad news. As I got off the elevator, Bob Lee met me outside her room. I gave him a rundown on everything that had happened, and he was glad to hear that Kit Gardner's brother was no longer a threat.

I told him I had to give Jennifer the bad news about David Shanahan. He said he would give us all the privacy we needed. Nobody would get past Bob Lee—that, I was sure of.

Jennifer was sitting up when I entered her room. She smiled at me, and then demanded, "What the hell is wrong?" She must have read my facial expression.

"Jen, I'm afraid I have some very bad news."

I began to tell her the story as it had unfolded, including that David was not who he seemed and the link between him and the Mafia. She found it very difficult to believe he was involved with the intimidation and violence that had been going on for the past few years, and especially, in the last few days.

She took the news hard. I believe she really did have a thing for David. It was too bad—she is such a nice gal and deserved a nice guy, not one like David Shanahan.

I told her about Jack, Mr. Pinata, Thomas and Sophia Sharpe, and Ken Cloutier. I discussed their involvement with all the trouble that had been going on, and what probably lay ahead of us.

She sobbed continuously throughout my explanations. It was difficult for someone as sensitive as Jennifer to understand why people acted the way they did. She wanted nothing more than a nice husband, a family, and a decent job. She thought she had that when she was hired into the International Truckers Union, but so far, it had been nothing but misery.

When I left, she said good-bye through reddened eyes. My heart felt for her.

CHAPTER THIRTY-FIVE

I finally left the hospital and headed over to Thomas and Sophia's place. I thought maybe we could call Ken Cloutier and have him meet us to discuss what was ahead for us and the union. I especially doubted Mr. Pinata was going to resign. I was still skeptical about the idea.

I called Thomas on my cell while in the cab ride over. He said he would be there and that he had told Sophia everything. He said she had special ways of extracting information from him that he couldn't resist, and then he laughed.

When the cab pulled up to the hotel, I saw Ken getting out of Joey's limo.

I thought, *Oh shit, what's this all about?*

I told the cabbie to pull up to the curb but to stay a hundred feet back. I sat in the cab for two or three minutes until Ken, Mr. Pinata, and Frank

Bartolone, the ITU's financial secretary, had walked into the hotel.

I walked directly to the elevator and went to my room before going to see Thomas and Sophia. When I walked into my room, my cell phone rang. I looked at the caller ID and saw that it was Ken.

I hit the green button and said, "Ken, what's up?" I wanted to sound light and breezy, not alarmed by what I had witnessed downstairs.

"Irish, we need to talk right away."

"Why, what's going on?"

"I will tell you when we're together. Do you know where we can meet?"

"Sure do. I was on my way to Thomas Sharpe's room when you called. Let's meet there. Ten minutes."

"Sounds good, I'll see you in a few minutes."

When I got to Thomas and Sophia's room, they let me in immediately when I knocked. They both looked anxious.

"Hey, I just talked to Ken Cloutier, and he's coming here in about ten minutes."

"Why, is there something up?" asked Thomas.

"I really don't know, but when my taxi pulled up in front of the hotel, Ken, Joey, and Frank Bartolone were getting out of Joey's limo. I don't know what that was all about, but I think we are about to find out."

Thomas poured each of us a cup of coffee while we sat at the kitchen table waiting for Ken to arrive. Sophia came out of the bedroom, and I stood up to give her a hug, saying, "It's nice to see you're back home here with Thomas."

"You're not as glad as I am. That was the worse experience of my life. I was never as scared as when they put that black hood over my head."

I asked, "What about your friend? Is she okay?"

"She's fine but she's still shook up like I am."

"Did she go to the police?"

"No, she is staying quiet until this is all over. She's okay with that."

I studied her for a moment, then said, "Sophia, I understand Thomas has told you everything."

"Yes, he has."

"The thing is, nobody knows about the agreement your dad has made with the Mafia. I suspect we are going to talk to Ken about that when he arrives in a few minutes. I don't mind you hearing what we discuss, but I don't know if Ken is aware that you know everything that's going on. I'm not sure where he stands just yet. If he's not with us, it could put you in more danger."

"So you want me to hide in my own bedroom while he's here?"

Yes, that would be best. It's the smart thing to do," I answered emphatically.

Thomas jumped at that and said, "Sophia, listen to him. I think he has a point. Why put yourself out there any more than you have to?" Sophia started to pout, but Thomas didn't buy it. "That's just the way it needs to be, Sophia. Will you do this for me?"

"Okay, Thomas. You're just so protective sometimes. I'll stay in the bedroom like you ask, but it will cost you." She smiled mischievously, which caused Thomas's face to turn red, but there was a big smile on his face as well. I turned away, giving them a moment to enjoy their banter.

I said, "If Ken is still tight with us, then you can come out and join us. I'll let you know when it's okay."

At that moment, Sophia's phone rang, taking the smiles off their faces. Sophia answered, paused a moment, and said, "Hello, Daddy?"

Her face turned ashen as she listened to her father talk. Then, she said, "But, Daddy, I don't want to leave Thomas here alone. I'll be safe with him." It was like she was pleading as if she was still a child.

She listened a short while and then handed the phone to Thomas, saying, "You talk to him." He put the phone on speaker, so we could all listen.

"Mr. Pinata, what is it that you want Sophia to do?"

His voice sounded desperate, but excited at the same time. "I want Sophia to go into hiding at a place that I've prepared for her. It's a place that will ensure her safety."

"Why does she need to do this? Is something going to happen that will put her in danger?"

"Thomas, I am going to do something that I should have done a long time ago. I'm tired of taking orders from these scumbags. They have pushed me too far. I've had enough."

Joey sounded like he wasn't asking, but was telling Sophia and Thomas what to do. Thomas was confused and didn't say anything for a few moments.

Joey broke the silence. "Ken Cloutier is coming to meet with you in a couple of minutes. I've told him what I intend to do. Listen to him, and then, if you agree, Sophia will be taken away like I asked. If you disagree, then Sophia's life is in your hands, Thomas. I pray you make the right decision."

In true fashion, he hung up the phone like he always did when he was through with you. We all stood there staring at each other, not knowing what to say.

Our silence was interrupted by a knock on the door. I glanced at Sophia, and she scurried into the bedroom. Thomas looked through the peephole and opened the door.

Ken Cloutier was standing there with a solemn look on his face. "Can I come in?"

It was as if Thomas was in a trance. "I'm sorry, Ken. Of course, come on in. Can I get you a coffee or something else to drink?

"Do you have any beer?"

"I do. Kind of early though, isn't it?"

"Not when you hear what I have to say."

The tension mounted as we waited for Thomas to get the beer. As he handed it to Ken, he said, "Shall we sit at the kitchen table?"

Thomas and I waited while Ken took a long pull on his beer. Finally, he was ready.

"I just met with Mr. Pinata and Frank Bartolone, and they told me what the hell has been going on and how Mr. Pinata has been blackmailed by the Marzetti family. Not only that, he told me about all the crimes he's committed on their behalf and why he did it."

I asked, "Ken, how did Mr. Pinata seem when he was telling you this? Was he angry or troubled?"

"Not really. Do you know that he has cancer and the doctors don't give him much time?"

"Yes, he told Sophia just yesterday," Thomas admitted.

"So what is his plan that he mentioned? He said you knew everything."

"I don't know if he told me everything, but what he did tell me scared the shit out of me. He got a call last night, apparently from the Marzetti family godfather or whatever the hell they call themselves nowadays. He said that the FBI had gunned down his son, and he is going to get his revenge. He told Mr. Pinata that he was coming after him too. He feels Mr. Pinata was somehow responsible for setting his son up."

Thomas broke in and asked, "What about Mrs. Pinata? Are they going to kill her like they promised?"

"He told me he asked them that, and this godfather character said not right away. He was going to wait so Mr. Pinata can watch."

I let out a deep breath and said, "This has gotten out of hand. Maybe we should contact Jack's boss in Washington before there's a real bloodbath."

"Wait, there's more. Mr. Pinata said he found out where they are keeping his wife, and he is going to go after her. He said he has met with another Mafia family that's fighting the Marzettis, and together, they are going to have an all-out war. Plus Mr. Pinata has hired twelve men of his own. Hired guns are a better name for them."

I asked, "What's the name of the Mafia family that he is bellying up with to go against the Marzettis?"

"It's the Sarduccis. They've been in the news a lot lately. The Feds have been trying to nail them for all sorts of crimes they apparently didn't do. Mr. Pinata said they were innocent of all the accusations, and the illegal things they were being accused of were all manufactured by the Marzettis."

After Ken mentioned the Sarducci Family I said, "Jack told us just yesterday that the Marzettis and the Sarduccis have been in business together for four to five years. Sounds like Frank Marzetti double crossed them.

"It sounds like it's going to be a fucking bloody mess, if you ask me. What the hell can we do to stop something like this?" Thomas asked.

Ken held up his hands and told Thomas, "All Mr. Pinata wants from you is to let him put Sophia somewhere where she will be safe. He is afraid if things go bad, they will come after her."

I looked at Thomas and asked, "Do you think it would be wise to get her to safety? It sounds like a good idea to me, but should it be up to Mr. Pinata or the FBI to assure her safety?"

"I don't know. What do you think, Irish?"

"The trouble with the FBI is that Jack is in the hospital recovering from the blast this morning. The doctor said they would keep him sedated for at least twelve hours, so he's no good to us right now."

Ken said, "It's not my call, but you better do something quick before it's too late."

Thomas turned to face the bedroom and called for Sophia to come out. I saw the surprise on Ken's face, but neither he nor I said anything.

Sophia ran to Thomas's arms. He reached for her and hugged her tight. "What do you think, darling?" Thomas asked her.

"I think I'm scared to death. I can't believe people are actually talking about killing each other. I don't want anything to do with all of this, but I think Daddy's right. I would like to go someplace where I can't be found."

"Then it's settled," said Ken. "There will be three men to come and collect her. They should be here in about an hour. Ask the lead guy what his name is. He should say 'my name is John F.

Kennedy.' Any other name comes out of his mouth, do not open the door. You got that, Thomas?"

Thomas answered, "Sure, not a problem, but I want to know where they're going to take her. I need to know so I can get to her if I have to."

"Mr. Pinata said he doesn't want anyone to know. That way, they can't be tortured and forced to tell them where she is," responded Ken.

"I think that makes sense," I offered.

Sophia asked, "Can Thomas come with me?"

"I'm afraid not. You see, there's still more that your father has planned. He and Frank Bartolone are going to resign tomorrow as president and financial secretary, but before they do that, he is going to have the executive board appoint Irish as the interim president, Thomas as the financial secretary, and me as vice president."

There was complete silence in the room. I saw the shocked look on Thomas's face.

I asked, "He wants me to be president of the International Truckers Union? Are you two good with that?"

Ken smiled and said, "Irish, you are the best person to lead this union; far better than me. I have no problem being your vice president. As a matter of fact, I think the three of us can help patch this union back together again. I really think it can work."

"Thomas, what about you? Are you okay with being financial secretary?"

"Mr. Pinata said you are the most honest person in this union. I think he's right on that notion. All three of us would get the full support of the executive board if Mr. Pinata advised them to support us."

The three of us looked at each other, and finally, Thomas said, "I'm in."

Ken followed with, "You can count on me."

They all looked at me while I was contemplating the offer from Jack to join the FBI. And what about Katrina? I remembered what Jack had told me about getting the union back to the people. This is exactly what he said was supposed to happen. How could I say no?

"How can I say no to an offer like this? The three of us can accomplish a lot of good for our members if we keep our heads on straight and put their needs as our number one priority. I trust both of you, so I'm in too."

We all smiled and shook hands. Thomas got another long hug from Sophia. I wished Katrina was there. I wanted to share this news with her.

CHAPTER THIRTY-SIX

· ·

Ken left shortly after we were through talking. I stayed to talk to my new financial secretary and to make sure Sophia got off in good shape.

As soon as Ken left, Sophia went into the bedroom to pack everything she had brought with her to Miami and everything she'd bought since she had arrived.

Thomas offered a little quip about his wife. "I don't think there are enough suitcases in this hotel to put all her shit in." We both had a good laugh. It helped cut the tension that was filling the room.

Exactly one hour later, there was a knock on the door. To Thomas's surprise, I pulled the gun Jack had given me and stood to the side of the door.

Thomas asked, "Who's there?"

A man answered, "John F. Kennedy. Mr. Pinata sent the three of us to fetch Mrs. Sharpe."

Thomas opened the door slowly and let the three men enter the suite. I stood back from the door and put my gun in the back of my pants.

Thomas walked into the bedroom, and we heard him tell Sophia that the men were here for her. Then there was silence for a couple of minutes. They obviously were saying good-bye.

When they came back into the living room, Sophia's eyes were filled with tears. Thomas said to the men. "There are four suitcases in the bedroom. Can you help carry them for Sophia?"

"Sure, Mr. Sharpe. That's why we're here." Two of them walked into the bedroom, and when they returned, they were each carrying two suitcases. Their jackets were opened, and I could see they were each carrying what looked like .357 Magnums on their left hips. Whatever they were, the pistols were formidable. I felt safer for Sophia with these three thugs caring for her.

Thomas and Sophia hugged once again, and Sophia said, "You still owe me. Don't forget. Take care of yourself, Thomas. We have a child to think about."

"You can count on it," Thomas assured her.

The man who seemed to be in charge said to Sophia, "I'm sorry to tell you this, but you are unable to take your cell phone. It would be easy for our enemies to track your phone and find out where we're hiding you."

Sophia reluctantly gave her cell phone to Thomas. The two men carrying the suitcases went first, followed by Sophia, and then as he left the room, the third man pulled his weapon and brought up the rear. He stopped, turned, and said, "Don't worry about a thing. We will take good care of her. We have two men waiting, one holding the elevator and one in the lobby, plus two more men outside."

Thomas breathed a sigh of relief and said, "Please take great care of her."

The man smiled and said, "I will. She is my entire gig here. There are four of us just to take care of her alone. She will be fine. Don't worry about a thing." He turned around and followed Sophia down the hall to the elevator. Thomas shut the door and asked, "What happens now?"

I wish I knew. I needed to talk to Jack right away, but that didn't seem possible.

CHAPTER THIRTY-SEVEN

．．．．．．．．．．．．．．．．．．．．．．．．．．．．．．．．．

Back at Miami General Hospital, Jack was starting to awaken. He didn't know where he was or what had happened. All he knew was that he had a gigantic headache. It was so bad, it hurt to blink.

He finally struggled enough that his eyes opened, and to his surprise, he could focus. He was in a hospital.

Why am I in a hospital again? he thought. He couldn't pull that information to the front of his mind.

There was a nurse attending to a tube coming out of his nose that looked like it was filled with a mixture of blood and mucus.

What the hell happened to me?

The nurse looked at him and said, "Well, good evening, Mr. Casey. How are you feeling?"

At least now he knew who he was, because a moment ago, he didn't have a clue. He thought to himself, *Now I am Mr. Casey. I wonder what my first name is.*

He cleared his throat, trying to get the tube out of the way so he could speak. In a croaky voice, he asked, "Where am I?"

"You are in Miami General Hospital."

"Who am I?

She smiled gently and replied, "You are FBI agent Jack Casey. You were injured in a bombing this morning. You had surgery right after you arrived here. That's why you are having temporary memory loss."

"What time is it now?" he asked, though he wasn't sure why he wanted to know.

"It's almost nine o'clock in the evening."

"I'm starting to remember some things, but I don't remember a bombing. Was anyone else hurt?"

"I don't think now is the time to talk about that. The doctors want you to stay as quiet as possible. As a matter of fact, it's time for another sedative."

The nurse turned and walked out of the room. Jack wondered why he had to have another sedative. He tried to move his legs, but it was too painful. He did discover he had a catheter running into his penis.

He said to himself, *Oh great, that's just wonderful. I have a splitting headache, and now I have a goddamn tube running in me so I can't even pee for myself.*

The nurse had entered his room without him noticing, and asked, "Mr. Casey, what are you swearing about?"

"It's bad enough I have a headache, so bad that I can't even think for myself, and now you take my manhood away by putting this god blessed tube in me."

She laughed aloud and asked, "Did you have plans for your manhood this evening?"

Sounding grumpy, he said, "With my life, you never know. I always have to be ready."

"You men are such babies. Buck up, buster, and take your medicine."

"I suppose you put this in. You seem the type whose only job in life is to inflict pain on sweet men like me."

"I didn't put it in, but I will rip it out if you keep giving me a rough time." She laughed at her own joke, and as she walked past his bed to get to the IV, she gave a slight tug on his catheter.

"Ouch! You are a sadistic nurse. I've heard about nurses like you. You're just mean. That's what you are."

"I'm not mean. I'm the nicest person you're going to see in the next thirty seconds."

Jack asked, "What do you mean by that?"

He watched as she picked up his IV line and stuck a needle in to forcing more sedative into his veins.

"Nighty night, Mr. Casey."

"Wait, I don't want you to put that—"

He stopped talking as his mind faded to blackness. It would be another four to six hours before he regained consciousness.

Five hours later, I had been sitting outside Jack's door for more than four hours, waiting for him to awake. It did not matter how long I had to wait. I had to talk to him. I was only praying that when he woke he would be able to converse with me.

The nurse came out of his room and stopped. "Mr. MacSween, Jack was awake for a few minutes but was confused, very confused. He didn't know what had happened or why he was here in the hospital. He didn't even know his name. But all things considered, he could talk a little, and that is a very good thing. When he wakes in another six hours, I wouldn't be surprised if he becomes fully aware of everything that happened."

"Did you give him something more to make him sleep?"

"Yes, I did. When I contacted the doctor in charge and told him about Mr. Casey's responses, he ordered more sleep time before anyone can see him. I'm sorry. I knew you wanted to talk to him, but he couldn't have talked to you even if he wanted to."

I let out a big sigh and said, "I fully understand. Do you happen to have a place where I could get a few hours of sleep?

"I sure do. Come with me."

I followed her down the hall and around the corner. She led me to a waiting room with four sofas and said, "There are blankets and fresh pillows on each sofa. I'll turn the lights off, and you should have the entire room to yourself for the rest of the night. There's a bathroom and a shower over there."

She pointed to the far corner where a room was labeled Men's Showers. "There's shampoo and soap in the showers, as well as brand-new underwear of different sizes on the shelf. Please help yourself."

"Is there a place I can get a cup of coffee if I happen to wake up early?"

"Yes, of course. There's a one-cup coffee pot on this counter. Just help yourself."

I said, "Thank you. You are very kind."

She smiled and left the room. I pulled out my cell phone and called Katrina. She answered on the first ring. "Hello, Irish. I have been sitting here waiting for your call. Where are you?"

"I'm still at Miami General."

"Oh my god, Irish, what are you doing back there? Are you hurt?" Her voice sounded awake in an instant.

"Katrina, this has been one of the worst days of my life. I came back to the hospital because I needed to tell Jack something very important, but I have been here for more than four hours waiting for him to wake up. The nurse just told me he wouldn't be awake for at least another six hours. So I guess I'm staying here for the night."

Sounding like a loving mother, she said, "No, you are not. I am going to come and get you. I'll be there in fifteen to twenty minutes."

I started to say *No, don't bother,* but she hung up the phone before I could. I smiled. Spending the night with her had to be better than being in this waiting room by myself.

I walked to the elevator, and when it opened, Bob Lee stepped out.

"Bob, what's going on? Why did you leave Jennifer alone?"

"That's the thing, Irish. About thirty minutes ago, two men came out of the elevator hell bent for Ms. Jenny's room. They didn't see me sitting behind the nurse's counter, so before they made it to her doorway, I put both of them on the floor and called for immediate backup. They would not identify themselves, but a little later we found out they were hit men for the Marzetti Mafia family. What the hell have you boys gotten yourselves into?"

"It's truly a long story, but I think you may hear about all of this in the news in the next few days. That is, if things go like I've heard they will. I know you knew they brought Jack in this morning, but did you know it was a Mafia hit? The Mafia caused all the death and destruction that happened at that little bar this morning."

"Can I give you some advice?"

"Sure, why not."

"You should get your ass out of Miami right now. If they are coming after Mr. Pinata and his men, you may get caught in the crossfire. You are a union man, not an FBI agent. Leave the fight to Mr. Pinata and the FBI."

"You should watch your back also. After all, you killed one of Mr. Marzetti's hit men and now, two more have been arrested. He may not take kindly to that."

Bob responded by saying, "I've always got my back covered."

I asked, "How did Jennifer react when this happened?"

"Great. She didn't even know they were there. She slept through the whole thing. I shut her door and locked it. Plus, I was quiet when I laid the two gentlemen out."

"Bob Lee, you are a very talented man. It has been my pleasure to get to know you. I wish I could stay and work with you for a while. I think some of your tricks would eventually sink in to my thick skull."

"I'm going to get back up to Ms. Jenny. Where are you going to be tonight, just in case I need to get ahold of you?"

"I will be with Katrina Bernetti at her home. She is supposed to pick me up in a few minutes out in front of the ER."

"You have got yourself one beautiful woman, Irish. Don't do her wrong. Her daddy is a powerful man."

"Really? He seemed like such a gentleman. Is he someone I should watch out for?"

"Not unless you cross him or hurt his family. There are lots of stories about Mr. Bernetti. Just take my heed."

"Don't worry about me hurting his daughter. I'm already head over heels in love with her. You know, I think I fell in love with her the moment I saw her. Do you think that really is possible?"

"That's what happened to Darla and me. We fell for each other the first time we were introduced. Been together ever since, twenty-two years."

I was glad to hear another person say love at first sight was possible. It made me feel more normal than I previously thought I was.

We said our good-byes, and Bob went back up to Jennifer's room while I hurried downstairs to meet Katrina.

CHAPTER THIRTY-EIGHT

I t was a little after midnight, and Katrina and I were lying in bed, holding each other. We had made love again, and it was as beautiful as the first night.

We talked about everything that had happened over the previous few days and what lay ahead, when I heard something like a glass breaking.

I sat bolt upright and put my hand gently over Katrina's mouth. I whispered, "Quiet." I sat and listened, and a moment later, I heard it again— more glass breaking, like someone was trying to get into the house.

I whispered again to her and asked, "Does your daddy have an alarm system on the house?"

She nodded her head yes and said, "It's a silent alarm. It goes off directly at the police station."

Even if the police were alerted, it would take a few minutes for someone to get here.

I quietly got out of bed and put my pants on. I grabbed hold of Katrina's hand and led her to the bathroom. I told her to lie in the bathtub and cover her head and ears. I was hoping the cast iron of the tub would be enough to stop a bullet. I really didn't know, but it was the best idea I could come up with. Her hand was shaking when I let it go.

She whispered, "Please be careful."

I kissed her, then walked back into the bedroom and arranged the pillows on the bed to make it look like two people were under the covers. Then I reached for my jacket and got the gun out of the pocket. I checked to see if it was loaded, even though I had checked it before I got into Katrina's car to come out to her house.

I thought the best way for me to protect Katrina was to stay in the bedroom and hide in the walk-in closet. It was on the opposite side from the bathroom, so if there was shooting going on, the bullets would be directed at me and away from Katrina.

I lay down on the floor to make less of a target. I held the gun with both hands for a steadier grip. I heard the bedroom door across the hall open and close. Then the doors on each side of the hall were also opened and closed. My heart was pounding at what seemed like two hundred beats a minute.

The only bedroom left was Katrina's. I could hear the faint sound of a siren, but didn't know if it was coming toward us or not. I didn't have much time to think about it, because the door burst open, and a huge man came barging into the bedroom with his automatic weapon firing directly at the bed and the mounds under the covers.

The sound was deafening, but everything happened so quickly that it was all over in about ten seconds. He was smiling as I nailed him with two rounds, one in his head and one in his chest. He stumbled toward the bed and fell face first onto the floor.

Just then, a second man stepped into the bedroom and sprayed the bed and walls with bullets. He didn't see me as I shot him twice in the head from eight feet away. He went down in a heap, on top of the first guy, dead before he hit the floor.

Once the shooting stopped, it was deathly quiet. My hands had stopped shaking. Memories from the war came back to me in an instant. All of a sudden, I realized that Katrina was screaming her lungs out. I breathed a sigh of relief. If she was screaming, she was alive.

I got up slowly, keeping my weapon aimed at the two victims on the floor and my eyes on the doorway. I stepped around them and checked the hall for anyone else. It was clear. I bent down to the two men on the floor and felt for a pulse. There was no sign of a heartbeat in either of them.

I rushed into the bathroom and grabbed Katrina, holding her until she quieted down. I kissed her cheeks and lips and said, "It's all over, sweetheart. Are you okay?"

Through the sobs, she managed to say she was fine. We turned and looked into the bedroom because we both heard the same sound. I said, "Get back in the tub." But before she could, we heard her papa's voice pleading, "Katrina, are you all right? Oh, my little darling, are you okay?

"Papa, I'm in here!" Katrina yelled.

We walked out into the bedroom just as her daddy came running in. He stopped when he saw the two bodies on the floor.

He had a pistol in his left hand. It was a Smith and Wesson 9 millimeter. I was happy to see that he was armed, as long as he didn't shoot me for being with his daughter in her bedroom at this late hour.

I was still holding Katrina, who was grabbing my shirt as if she was holding on for dear life.

Mr. Bernetti looked up at me and shouted, "What have you brought into my house? You could have gotten my child killed. How dare you."

Katrina held up her hand and said, "Papa, don't judge him so quickly, at least until you hear the story he has to tell."

I could see hate and anger on his face, and I couldn't blame him. He looked directly into my eyes and said, "Sorry, son, I was just so scared that something had happened to Katrina. Are you two injured in any way, my dear?"

"No, Papa, both of us are fine."

I reached into my pocket and pulled out my wallet. I grabbed my FBI identification and showed it to him.

He looked at it and then at me and asked, "Who the hell are you, son? I thought you were a union man."

"I am, sir, but I am also an FBI agent."

"Are you a mole for the Feds?"

"Before I tell you the answer to that, hear my story. I think you would approve of what I'm doing."

"Fair enough," he responded, "but who are these two gentlemen?"

I answered him the best way I could. "Sir, I believe these are hit men from the Mafia. I would like to run everything by you and get your take on things."

"Absolutely. I think that would be a grand idea," he answered wholeheartedly. "But I think the first thing we need to do is to wait for the police to get here. My alarm system has already notified them; they should be here in a few minutes. Let's get the hell out of this bedroom." Looking at Katrina, he said, "You look like you've seen a ghost."

I glanced at her. She had a look of shock on her face as she stared at my FBI badge, and then at me. For the first time since we'd met, there was doubt on her face. She let go of my shirt and my hand. She stood there with a confused look, trying to figure me out.

This was not the way she should have found out that I was involved with the FBI, or that this wasn't my first firefight. I saw that doubt and quickly said, "The same thing goes for you, Katrina. Hear me out. Will you do that for me?"

"I guess so," she squeaked.

It wasn't a complete endorsement of what I was trying to do, but it was a start.

Mr. Bernetti said, "Let's go into the kitchen, and I'll make some coffee and maybe we can calm down a little." The three of us walked to the kitchen in silence.

We had no more gotten seated when we heard the sound of sirens. I looked at Mr. Bernetti, and he said, "We should put this talk on hold until the police are through here."

"I think that would be a good idea," I agreed.

A few minutes later, they knocked on the front door. I put my pistol on the kitchen table so there would be no question of me using it.

Katrina and I followed her father into the living room. The sight of the state police entering reminded me what a serious incident this was. Also, for the first time I realized I had killed two men in self-defense.

There were three officers; two entered the house with guns drawn, while the third one stood guard at the door. I imagined there were probably more men out back.

The commanding officer stepped forward and said, "I am Lieutenant Daniels from the Florida State Police. We received an emergency call that there were shots fired in this house."

Mr. Bernetti answered him straightforwardly, "I am Frank Bernetti, and this is my home. There are two men dead in the last bedroom on the right, down that hallway." He was pointing to the hall off to the left side of the living room.

"Does anyone know the victims?"

I stepped forward and said, "I think know where they came from, but I don't know their names."

"Who did the shooting?"

"That was me, Officer."

"What is your name?"

"Sean MacSween. I work for the International Truckers Union, and I am also a sworn FBI agent." I showed him my FBI badge and my union ID.

The officer looked at his partner and said, "Take Officer Wilmers and check out the situation down the hall. Be careful."

The two officers walked slowly down the hall with their weapons leading the way, checking each bedroom before they passed it.

Lieutenant Daniels asked me, "Would you explain what you meant when you said you know where they came from but not who they are?"

"Sure, but before we do anything, you should also know I put my weapon on the kitchen table."

"Is that the gun you shot the two men with?"

"That is the weapon I defended myself with, yes. When you get to the bedroom, you'll see they sprayed the room with automatic weapons."

"Of course, sir, that is what I meant. Let's stop right here for a moment. I think it would be best if we get you out of here and down to the station. Maybe it will help calm you down some."

In a quieter voice, I said, "I'm calm now. So why don't you and I go down to the bedroom and I can explain to you what actually happened?"

Mr. Bernetti stepped in and said, "I think that's a great idea, and I also think I should come along as a witness so you have someone who can vouch for what is said."

"Thank you, Mr. Bernetti, I appreciate that," the lieutenant responded with a tone of respect.

Just then, the two officers returned, and one of them reported, "The place is clear. There are two bodies lying in the last bedroom on the right. The place has been shot up like a shooting gallery."

Lieutenant Daniels looked at me and asked, "How did you survive without getting shot to pieces?"

"Come on, I'll show everyone what happened." The six of us went down the hall into the bedroom, and I narrated the scene as it had unfolded. I explained where Katrina was and why, and where I had positioned myself as I waited for the perpetrators. The officers had multiple questions and seemed satisfied with my answers.

Officers Daniels asked, "You seemed to have prepared and reacted in a professional manner. Why is that?"

"I spent many months in Iraq and Afghanistan while I was in the Army Rangers. I was trained to react in a professional manner."

Lieutenant Daniels said to me, "Mr. MacSween, I will still need you to come with me to headquarters. You have to fill out a statement in writing saying exactly what happened. I will also have to talk to your superior officer in the FBI. What is his name and phone number?"

I gave him Jack's name and number, and told him where to find him. He was surprised to find out that Jack was in the hospital. He asked, "Who is his supervisor?"

"That would be Henry Sullivan."

He started writing down the name, but then stopped. "Do you mean Henry Sullivan, the director of the FBI?"

"One and the same," I responded.

"Man, you fly in high circles. What's my chance of getting ahold of Mr. Sullivan?"

"Probably slim to none. Can this wait until morning?"

"I suppose so. Why?"

"It would be best to call Jack Casey, but since he is in the hospital, can he testify on my behalf in the morning?"

"Mr. Bernetti, will you vouch for Mr. MacSween?" Mr. Bernetti looked at me for a few seconds and then turned back to Lieutenant Daniels and said, "I sure do; you can trust him."

Daniels replied, "Not a problem, but I would still like you to come with me to headquarters, if you don't mind."

I responded, "Sure, I would be glad to." I turned to Katrina and her father and asked, "Is it okay if I tell my story when I get back?"

Katrina smiled for the first time since we heard the glass breaking. "That would be fine, Irish. Just come back to me."

I shook Mr. Bernetti's hand and gave Katrina a hug and kiss before I left. As I was getting into the police cruiser, I wondered why Lieutenant Daniels had so much confidence in and respect for Mr. Bernetti. It nagged at me, wondering who this Frank Bernetti really was.

CHAPTER THIRTY-NINE

After spending three hours at the State Police headquarters, I called Katrina to tell her I was being released and that I was taking a taxi to her home. She informed me that she was waiting for me in her car right outside the station. That made me feel really good for some reason; I think it's because she had faith enough in me to come there and wait.

When we returned to Katrina's, it was shortly after eight in the morning. When we walked into the house, I immediately smelled bacon. I hadn't had a home-cooked breakfast in over a year.

We went into the kitchen to see Mr. Bernetti standing by the stove with an apron on cooking bacon in one pan and something that looked like goulash in the other.

I walked up to him and asked, "What's in the pan?"

"Why, that's bacon, son. Haven't you ever had bacon before?" He smiled and then laughed heartily. "It's Italian goulash. Our goulash is not like any you've ever eaten. I guarantee you'll love it."

I said, "Smells great. What's in it?"

"It's my mama's secret recipe. But I think I can trust you with it. It has onions, fresh mushrooms, bell peppers, chopped garlic, sweet Italian sausage, ground sirloin, more garlic, and finally, lots of pepper and salt. You have to cook the sauce for three hours. Not a minute less. After three hours you add the angel hair pasta and cook it for another twenty minutes. Finally, you shred lots of fresh parmesan cheese on top so there's at least an inch covering the entire dish and bake it for thirty minutes or until it's brown and crispy on top."

"Is it traditionally a breakfast food?"

"It's eaten whenever you have something to celebrate."

I looked at Katrina, and she smiled. I asked, "What are we celebrating?"

"I was promoted to director of my department today," she replied proudly.

I opened my arms and said, "Well, congratulations. You will make a wonderful director." I went over to her and gave her a kiss on both cheeks. As she wrapped her arms around me and buried her face into my neck, I could tell she was crying.

"Katrina, what's the matter?"

"Nothing. I'm just being silly." She gave me a kiss, the first ever in front of her father.

He bellowed, "Let's eat."

We had a wonderful breakfast—Italian goulash, eggs, bacon, and homemade bread with almond butter. I almost forgot that the world was imploding around us.

When we were finished eating, I offered to give my explanation of how I knew what to do in that terrible situation with the attackers in the bedroom. Both Katrina and her dad were ready to listen.

I thought about it for a moment and finally said, "Between the ages of seventeen and twenty-three, I was in the Army Rangers, where I served three years, six months in Iraq and two and a half years in Afghanistan. When I returned home, I swore to myself I would never hurt another man the rest of my life. It has been extremely difficult for me to live up to that promise. I'm very sorry this happened, but I couldn't let anything happen to you, Katrina. I would have died for you in there if I'd had to."

Katrina asked, "Why haven't you ever told me this part of your life?"

"I've never told anyone. I'm trying to forget about that time in my life. I want you to know I do not normally tell this story I'm about to tell you, but I hope one day soon to be part of this family."

Katrina looked deeply into my eyes as I spoke. I commenced to tell them about my exploits while

I was an Army Ranger. Well, almost everything. I left most of the bloody gore out of the story.

I explained that I was in many firefights, that I had killed men in both Iraq and Afghanistan, and that I had been wounded four times.

I told of some things I was ordered to do, but I also confessed some horrible things I did that I that were not under orders—things war makes you feel you have to do; things I looked back on where I was ashamed to admit it was me who did them. Life in war changes a man forever in that he either becomes more violent when he returns home or dedicates his life to one of peace.

Katrina asked how I knew what to do in a situation like she and I had been in, especially how I had known to put her in the bathtub and to lie on the floor in the opposite closet so they didn't shoot her way.

I told her, "It was just instinct. Everything happened so fast. I just reacted; I didn't have time to think."

She offered me a compliment of sorts when she said, "It just seems like you are such a nice, quiet man who wouldn't have any idea as to what to do in a situation like that."

I said in return, "Ranger training never leaves you, and no matter how hard you try to live peacefully, it doesn't always let you live your life the way you want to."

When I was done, she asked, "Sean, can we talk in private for a few minutes?"

I told her absolutely, but she had never called me Sean before. Why now? We rose from the table and walked back to her portion of the house. As we sat down on her love seat in the living room, I felt nervous that she was going to tell me to get lost because of what she had learned from my confession.

We looked at each other. She grabbed my hand and held it for a few moments before she spoke. "Sean, you just opened your heart to me like no man has ever done before. It was like you bared your soul to reveal your deepest, darkest secrets. There is only one reason a person says those things to another. That reason is love. I believe you love me deeply, with all your heart. Am I right?"

I felt my eyes become moist but didn't try to hide it. I pulled her close and said, "The words came without me even thinking about them. Even I was surprised when I said them. I love you with all my heart. I want you to be a part of my life forever. Will you marry me?" I never thought I would be able to say those words, but they came so easily.

She kissed me softly and said, "You are my soulmate. Of course, I'll marry you. There is no other man in this world for me. I give my heart to you."

We kissed long and gently, and when our lips parted, we knew we had committed ourselves to each other for life.

After a few minutes, we walked back into the kitchen where her father was washing the dishes. "Have you two gotten things worked out?"

"Daddy, Sean asked me to marry him."

He smiled and asked her, "Well, girl, what did you tell him?"

"Of course I said yes. Did you really have to ask that question?"

"No, but I wanted to hear you say it." He turned to me, stuck out his hand, and said, "Welcome to the family, Irish." We shook hands, and then he screamed, "Let's party."

Finally, it seemed that all the stars were lined up in their proper order for the first time in my life. At this instant, life was good. Suddenly, I realized I hadn't told them about my involvement in the union and the FBI. I figured I might as well tell them the truth about that too.

"I hate to break the good mood we're all in, but I need to explain why I'm involved with the FBI."

Mr. Bernetti said, "I was wondering if you were going to get to that. You know it's really not necessary for you to tell me why you're involved; I already feel I know what kind of man you are. I have to admit something, though. I have a friend who has access to military records, and I asked him to check yours. It seems you were the recipient of numerous combat medals and that you personally saved the lives of your men many times. You are good in my book."

"Thank you, but I feel it's important that we not have any secrets, especially between Katrina and me. First of all, I love my union. It's more of a calling from a higher power that instills in me the need to help my fellow workers. I didn't agree to work with the FBI to bring down the International Truckers Union. I did it to save it. That's what Jack Casey offered me, and that is why I accepted. Jack is an honorable man, and I felt I could trust him. And you may not know this, but we just might find out in a very short time whether I was right or not."

Mr. Bernetti held up his hand and said, "Wait a minute. Now that you're family, if there's anything that concerns you, it now concerns all of us. If you need help with anything, just ask. I have many resources I can bring to the table. Don't hesitate. I am here for you."

I felt good hearing that. I guess it was proof of his acceptance.

CHAPTER FORTY

The three of us were just finishing our glasses of champagne when my phone rang. I was afraid to answer the phone for fear of destroying the moment.

As it turns out, I was right.

I answered the phone kind of sheepishly, "Hello, this is Sean."

It was Thomas Sharpe, and he was frantic. "Irish, it's Thomas. Oh my god, I'm glad I reached you."

"Thomas, what's going on? You sound upset."

"Have you seen the news today?"

"No, I've been pretty busy. Why?"

"Matthew Sims and Luke Coletta and two of their bodyguards were gunned down as they came out of a restaurant at three thirty this morning. The police are saying it looks like a Mafia hit. One of the shooters was also shot, and the police have him in custody, but he's not talking."

Matthew Sims and Luke Coletta were two of the vice presidents of the International Truckers Union, and they were big supporters of Joseph Pinata.

"Are they dead?" I asked Thomas.

"They were taken to Miami General. The two bodyguards are dead, Matthew is on life support, and Luke is still in surgery. The doctors are trying to repair his liver that was shot to pieces. From what they told Mrs. Coletta, he's got a fifty-fifty chance of making it. Matthew has more serious injuries. He was shot in the chest and head. The doctors aren't saying what his chances are. They have him in an induced coma. It's wait and see, basically, I guess, on both of them."

Thomas's voice sounded nervous as he explained all that had happened.

"Where is Joey right now? Have you heard from him?"

"Negative. No one knows where he was, but apparently there was a big hit on the Marzetti family home around six thirty this morning, and there is speculation that Joey was involved. The police say they have witnesses who claim they saw him and his wife leaving the scene."

"Did you say his wife, too? That's very interesting."

"Yes, that's what I heard."

"You said that Matthew and Luke were hit at three thirty in the morning?"

"Yes, about that time. Why?"

"It just so happens that two men broke in to my friend's house at about the same time and tried to kill me."

"Are you all right?"

"Yeah, I'm okay, but the two intruders are dead."

"Really? How did you manage that?"

"It's kind of a long story. How about Ken? Have you heard from him?"

"I haven't. Do you suppose that they were trying to hit him as well?"

"I really don't know, but it sounds like it may have been their plan to hit all of us—to coordinate the hits simultaneously. What about you? Did anyone come after you?"

"Nobody knows where I am. I snuck out of the hotel right after you left our suite, and I found a place to stay where it's safe. I didn't tell anybody."

"We have to check on Ken to see if he's okay. Since you're in hiding, I'll try to get ahold of him. I will call him, but if I can't reach him by phone and since I don't know if it's safe for me to go back to the hotel, I can have the police check his suite at the hotel. I know a lieutenant with the Florida State Police who will do that for us."

Thomas asked, "How is Jack doing? Have you talked to him lately?"

"Jack is still in an induced coma. The last time I checked was last night. I haven't checked in on him yet this morning."

"Irish, do you see what's going on here? It looks to me like there has been some kind of war declared between that Mafia family and Joey and his troops. Apparently, we are considered part of Mr. Pinata's army."

I said, "I think you hit the nail on the head. Are you sure the Mafia family that was targeted was the Marzettis?"

"The Miami TV stations are saying it was the Marzetti family, but that has not been confirmed by anyone in a position of authority," Thomas replied.

"If the media is reporting that, you can probably take it to the bank. This sounds like Joey's revenge is in full swing."

"It sure does," said Thomas.

I asked him, "How many people have you heard got hurt in that raid?"

"The Channel Five News hasn't been able to confirm whether anyone was hurt, but it has been reported that a hostage was taken out of the mansion. I'm hoping that hostage is Sophia's mother."

I offered the only hope I could. "We can only pray she was the one freed, for her and Sophia's sake. Mr. Pinata told Sophia that if he tried anything or went to the police, they would kill her."

"Let me go, Irish. I don't want to stay on the phone too long. Someone might be trying to locate me by the phone signal."

"Sounds good, Thomas. You just stay hidden for as long as you can. I will let you know if I find anything out about Ken."

"Irish, I appreciate everything you're doing. Thanks for everything. I will talk to you later." Thomas hung up the phone.

I turned back to Katrina and her father and said, "Sorry about that. It seems things are heating up."

Katrina came up to me and whispered, "You do whatever you have to do. I understand. Don't worry about us."

I looked at her father and asked, "Are you able to take care of Katrina and yourself?"

He laughed and replied, "I don't have any real enemies anymore, and this neighborhood is so peaceful and quiet, I don't think it'll be a problem."

Katrina asked, "Papa, when did you ever have any enemies that you needed protection from?"

He smiled at her and said, "Honey, your papa has had enemies his entire life. Whenever you stand up to people with power, you develop enemies." He gave me a quick glance that said Katrina didn't understand.

I turned to Katrina and said, "Is it possible that you could call off work for a couple days?"

"I have today off and then there's the weekend, so for the next three days I don't have any plans. Why do you ask?"

"I would like both of you to stay here and not go anywhere. I don't know if you're in danger, but I'm not willing to take any chances. I want you to stay out of sight. You're safer here than anywhere else."

I turned back to Mr. Bernetti and said, "You also need to repair the broken window as soon as possible."

"I will take care of that immediately, but tell me, Irish, what exactly happened last night besides our encounter here?"

I didn't want Katrina to hear it, but I had no other choice. "The call I just received was from Thomas Sharpe. He told me that last night, two of the International Truckers Union vice presidents were gunned down along with two of their bodyguards. It seems someone is hell bent on taking Mr. Pinata's entire staff out. Besides that, there was a hit on the Marzetti Mafia family. We don't know how many were killed or injured."

Katrina's mouth was agape as if she was saying "wow" really loud, but she was silent in shock.

Mr. Bernetti stepped up to me and said, "I have friends I can call, friends who I used for protection when I was the union president. It's not a problem—they will come and spend the weekend with us."

"That's great. At least I won't have to worry about you. Another thing I have to ask—Katrina, may I borrow your car?"

Katrina looked at me and smiled and replied, "Everything I have is yours. Of course you can."

Mr. Bernetti smiled at that and said, "That's too much information for a father to hear."

We all shared a welcome laugh.

I told them I had to make some phone calls and then I would have to leave. I walked back into Katrina's part of the house and dialed Ken's number. It rang ten times with no answer and no opportunity to leave a message.

I gave up and dialed the hospital instead. I asked for the nurse in charge of Jack's floor, who answered the phone and asked what I needed. I told her that I was Jack's brother and that I was inquiring about Jack's condition.

She told me Jack was awake and was able to see visitors, but only for a few minutes at a time. I felt a wave of relief wash over me. I hung up the phone and took in a deep breath. Katrina had followed me into her living room and overheard my conversation.

"Is your friend okay?"

"Yes, he is. I can even go see him. Apparently, he's awake and talking. I have to go see him right away, but first I need to take a shower. I don't have any clothes to change into, but a clean body will help."

Katrina smiled at me and said, "Papa and I went shopping yesterday, and he bought some new underwear. Maybe he will give you a pair."

"What are you smiling about?"

"I don't know if they'll fit you." Then she laughed heartily and gave me a kiss.

"You never know. Your papa might be well-endowed."

"Oh my god, that's too much information. I can't even think about it." She blushed a brilliant red.

"You better stop, or I may not make it out of here this morning." I gently pushed her away and said, "Go see if I can borrow a pair, and I will go take my shower, alone."

She gave me that pouty face again, but walked away. I quickly showered and emerged to find a new shirt, pants, and underwear. I dressed quickly. Mr. Bernetti was about my size, so apparently, he had given me some of his new clothes. I liked him better the more I got to know him. It felt good. When I came out of the bathroom, Katrina had a travel mug full of coffee and her car keys. "Please be careful and come back to me."

I kissed her on the lips, and said I hoped to be back later that day. I got into her Buick and went directly to the hospital.

After I parked, I walked in and took the elevator to the ninth floor. When I got off the elevator, I was met by two men with their weapons drawn. One of them demanded, "Hold it right there. Where do you think you're going?"

"I came to see Jack Casey. I've been working with him on his investigation. I heard he was awake."

The taller of the two men said, "Working with him? How come I don't know you? Turn around and put both hands on the wall."

They frisked me and told me to turn around. "What's your name?"

"I'm Sean MacSween. Jack calls me Irish." They looked at each other, and the shorter one asked for my ID. As soon as I took my wallet out, he grabbed it from me and started rifling through each slot until he found my driver's license.

"Isn't that against the law? Aren't you supposed to ask for permission before you go through my wallet?"

"Just shut up. We will tell *you* what's against the law and what isn't."

I said, "Why don't you go ask Jack if it's all right if I come in to see him and stop this hard line bullshit?"

I looked up ahead and could see Jack lying in his bed talking to another man. His head was wrapped in a gauze dressing, but he seemed to be conversing normally.

I yelled before the two men could stop me, "Hey, Jack, can I come in and talk?"

Jack turned and said something to the man standing by his bed. The man strode up to me, stuck out his hand and said, "Irish MacSween, it's a pleasure to finally meet you. I'm Henry Sullivan."

I took his hand and said, "The pleasure is all mine."

He looked at the two men standing by me and said, "It's okay, this is Sean MacSween," like I was someone of importance.

FBI Director Sullivan was a tall man, about six feet four. He was impeccably dressed and groomed. He had a deep voice and pleasant smile on his face.

"Let's go in and see Jack."

I followed him into Jack's room. Jack smiled at me and said, "It's good to see you're still alive. I heard about the attack at your girlfriend's house. I guess the Ranger training is still with you. That was another reason I came after you. With your background in the Army Rangers, you seemed to be thorough enough to do the things we needed to have done. So tell me, what do you know about this war that's going on?"

"First of all, I want you to know that Joseph Pinata is going to resign his position as president of the International Truckers Union. I don't know if this has anything to do with it, but now with Frank Bartolone and Matthew Sims shot to hell, he is also going to appoint Thomas Sharpe to the financial secretary position, Ken Cloutier as vice president, and he wants me to become president."

"No shit. When did you find this out? That's a huge surprise."

"He came to Thomas and Sophia Sharpe's place and told them his plan."

"He's really mixing things up. I wonder why."

"There is one more thing. He told Sophia that he has a tumor in his brain and the doctors are not giving him very much time."

Henry Sullivan said. "We were aware of his medical condition."

"Thomas Sharpe said he was there when he told Sophia and that he felt Mr. Pinata was being completely honest. You knew Mr. Pinata's daughter was kidnapped and then released twelve hours later, didn't you?"

They both nodded their heads and said yes at the same time.

"Good. So now Mr. Pinata has taken Sophia and put her somewhere she can't be found. Apparently, she has four bodyguards with her at all times. He's afraid Mr. Marzetti is going to try to kill her."

Jack said, "So the Marzetti family is behind all of this."

I looked at Mr. Sullivan and said, "Here's the deal. Twelve months ago, just before the strike started, the Marzetti family and certain people on Wall Street made a pact. They needed to figure out how to make Wall Street crash when they were ready and recover when they wanted it to. Their plan was to sell a vast amount of their financial investments, have the ITU strike every trucking company in the United States, and keep the strike going for as long as it takes to get the market to crash to its knees. Once they accomplish that, they'll start buying back everything they sold and then have the ITU settle the strike. Once the strike is settled, the economy and Wall Street will start to grow, and they become filthy rich."

Mr. Sullivan broke in and added, "Which is the basic advice any economist will tell you: sell high and buy low. But the way they did it is very illegal. Hey, Jack, how come we didn't come up with that idea?" Jack just smiled.

I ignored the last statement and said, "Thomas Sharpe is really the one who figured it out. Sell when the economy and Wall Street are reaping profits at a tremendous rate, and then, buy vast amounts of your investments back when the economy and Wall Street are in the shit tank. Then all they have to do is wait for everything to eventually climb back to prestrike levels and rake in incredible profits. It's brilliant."

Henry Sullivan said, "If we can link the two parties together with the plan you laid out, Frank Marzetti and some people on Wall Street will spend many years behind bars."

Jack said, "For some reason, I can't quite remember everything. Are you saying they are getting the union to go along with them just for their own interests? What does the union gain by doing this? They didn't have the money to sell and buy like the Marzetti family or the guys on Wall Street."

"Just a minute, Jack. I'm getting to that. The way they make all of this work is to control the strike parameters. Look what's happened since the strike started. The auto industry is essentially frozen because they cannot get their vehicles to the customers. Their plants are either shut down or producing at levels that are way below what's needed to make a profit. The multinational corporations are losing billions because they can't move their products away from the warehouses and get them to their customers. Imports and exports are at a standstill because, again, there is no way to move them to or away from the docks. Look at the housing market—it's down to its lowest level in over twenty years. Even the farmers are going bankrupt because they can't get their meat and produce to the warehouses, grocery stores, and restaurants. Now, because of all of this, the unemployment rate is the highest it's been in fifteen years. It doesn't take much to figure out that all of this happened because the ITU has been on strike for twelve months. It has affected every sector of our economy, and even the world economy at some point or another. Have you looked at China's stock market lately? It's crashed. All because of this truckers union strike."

Jack said, "This is starting to make sense. Cut off the blood supply and all the organs in the body die. Then you go to surgery and fix the arterial supply lines and all the organs start working again. Wow, that is quite a plan. But I have one question. How do you force the ITU to cooperate? Like we said, the union doesn't have enough money in any market to make this worth their while. I know because I've checked myself."

I smiled, and they looked at me, waiting for the magic answer. Finally, I said, "You kidnap Joseph Pinata's wife and keep her hanging as bait until you get what you want. You threaten to kill her or you start cutting off fingers every time Joseph Pinata doesn't do what he's told."

Jack said, "Are you kidding me? I thought she had just had enough of Mr. Pinata's shit and ran off. What's this about cutting off her fingers?"

"Mr. Pinata said after he hired a private investigator to find her, he received one of her fingers in the mail. He said he didn't have any choice in the matter. He cooperates or his wife dies."

Mr. Sullivan asked, "Did any of the union officers gain monetarily from the strike?"

"Someone started putting money in the union officers' bank accounts to make it look like they are on the take. It happened to Thomas Sharpe and Ken Cloutier, and probably to the other union officers too. The thing is, Ken didn't even know the money was in his account until he happened to go to the bank and make a withdrawal. He couldn't go to the police with this because, quite simply, no one would believe him."

"Did he spend the money?" Jack asked.

"He said he hasn't, and though I have no way to verify he's telling the truth, my gut feeling says he is. I bet if you look at the Marzetti financial records, you would find that a lot of stock, bonds, mutual funds, or whatever they had were sold just before the strike started and that they are presently buying back much of what they sold because the strike will be settled within the next week."

"How do you know that?" asked Henry Sullivan.

"That's what Mr. Pinata was told they needed—one more week."

"The same theory goes for whoever they are partners with. So whoever is in a position to do that sort of thing on Wall Street, their records will probably show they have a nearly identical financial pattern to the Marzetti family."

Henry Sullivan said, "This all makes sense. Who would ever link a union strike with the financial investments of a corporation or a CEO on Wall Street? They are not even remotely related. It's a perfect plan."

Jack laughed and said, "I told you this guy would make a great FBI agent. He has the tenacity to follow things through to the end, and he's even a tiny bit smart."

I smiled at that compliment and said to Jack, "That offer may have to wait a bit. I have to see how this all shakes out. If I truly end up in the president position, I have a big decision to make, so until this is over with, let's just keep everything on hold."

"It's your call, Irish. Just let me know, but I think you just convinced Mr. Sullivan that you are FBI material."

"Thanks, Jack. So what's our next move?"

Without hesitation, Mr. Sullivan took the lead. "First of all, I am going to call back to my office and instruct them to do a financial check on the Marzetti family investments. Then I will have them do a financial search of everyone on Wall Street who may profit from this situation. I am going to bring in Mr. Marzetti and Mr. Pinata for questioning, and if we find any sort of link to Wall

Street, we are going to bring them in too. Jack is going to stay right where he is for quite some time. Irish, may I call you Irish?"

"Absolutely. Call me anything you want. After all, you are my boss."

"Great, thanks. If you are willing, I would like you to follow up any leads you find within the union, anything that may help us in this investigation. Especially if you hear anything from or about Mr. Pinata."

"I have not been able to get ahold of Ken Cloutier this morning. I would like to go over to the hotel to try to find him and make sure he's okay. I would also like to talk to Thomas Sharpe again and see if he's heard anything from Sophia or Mr. Pinata."

Henry Sullivan said, "You are not a trained FBI agent, so I do not want you to do anything that could possibly be dangerous. You are to call me and inform me of what is going on, and I will take the proper action. Do you understand?"

"Yes, sir. I will do everything in my power to avoid whatever danger lurks out there."

Jack looked at me and rolled his eyes.

Henry said, "Here's my card. It has my cell phone and office number. If you can't reach me on my cell, call the office and tell them you need to talk to me. I will instruct them to respond to me instantly if you call. Do you have any questions?"

"Yes, I have one. How do you expect to keep Jack here in bed?"

With a grin, Henry replied, "I will arrest him if he even thinks about leaving here. I already have two men outside the door. They are not here to protect Jack, but to prevent him from leaving."

Jack laughed and said, "Thanks a lot, Henry. I thought you had my best interests at heart."

"You wish," Henry replied.

"Okay, sounds like a plan. I'm going to try to find Ken Cloutier right now, so I will talk to you later." I shook Mr. Sullivan's hand, and when I shook Jack's, he held on to me and said, "Keep me informed about what you're doing. Maybe I can help keep you alive, even from this bed. I want you to take what Henry just told you to heart, and don't do anything stupid. You got it?"

"Yes, Mother," I said with a smile on my face as I walked out the door. I knew Jack was serious and that I would take his warning to heart.

CHAPTER FORTY-ONE

I hopped into Katrina's Buick and headed back to the hotel. On the way, I tried to contact Ken again, but I was unable to reach him.

Once I got to the hotel, I went to Ken's room first. I was hoping it might be something as simple as his phone not working properly.

I knocked on his door and waited a few moments, but no one came to the door. I was about to leave when I heard a noise, possibly a voice, from inside. I listened carefully and realized it truly was a voice, but it was so muffled I couldn't understand what was said. It was a man's voice nonetheless.

I knocked louder and shouted, "Ken, is that you. Are you hurt?" The voice became louder again, but I still couldn't understand. I decided to call down to the desk and get someone up to open the door.

When they answered, I told them someone was obviously hurt inside Ken's room and that I needed help. It was only a couple of minutes before a hotel security officer emerged from the elevator.

He was an affable-looking young fellow, about twenty-five.

"What's going on, sir?"

"I think my friend is inside, and for some reason, he's unable to open the door. There must be something wrong with him."

The guard pounded on the door and yelled, "Is anybody there?" The inaudible voice came back again.

The security officer spoke into the microphone attached to his shirt and told whoever was listening that he was opening the door. He took out his keys and said, "Let's do it."

As soon as the door was opened, the first thing we saw was a lamp lying on the floor with its lampshade crushed. The coffee table was smashed to pieces. The sofa was overturned, and we heard Ken's voice coming from underneath.

We grabbed the sofa and rolled it back. Ken was lying on his stomach with his hands tied behind his back. A rag had been stuffed into his mouth and covered by duct tape.

The security guard untied Ken's hands, and I carefully took the tape off his mouth and pulled the rag out. His face was swollen around his eyes, and his lower lip was twice its normal size, but he smiled and seemed to be in good shape otherwise.

"Ken, what the hell happened?"

He took some deep breaths and said, "A man came to the door and said he was the hotel manager and needed to speak to me immediately. I opened the door, thinking something had happened, and as soon as I did, three men came busting in."

I made a motion with my head and eyes toward the security guard, indicating not to say anything more. He smiled his understanding.

The security guard said, "My name is Miles, and I'm from hotel security. Can you stand up?"

"Sure, give me a hand."

We helped him up, and Miles asked, "Did you know these men?"

"Not actually, but I know who sent them. I was in a poker game last night, and I lost quite a bit of money. I told the guy that I would get the money for him this morning. I guess he got a little impatient."

Miles said, "Sir, I want you to know I am supposed to report this, but I don't think this is something you want me to pursue any further. Am I right?"

"For sure. Besides, I am going to take care of this right away. Just tell your boss I was so drunk I couldn't get up to answer the door. Can you do that for me?"

"Not a problem, sir. I will do whatever you like. This stuff happens all the time."

Ken pulled twenty dollars out of his pocket and offered it to him for keeping his mouth shut, but he just smiled and said, "Sir, that's not necessary. You two have a nice day." He left without taking the money.

After he left, I asked Ken to tell me the real story. He said, "The three men came busting through the door and wanted to know if Mr. Pinata or Mrs. Pinata was here. I told them they weren't here and to get the hell out, but they didn't seem to like my answer. When they were done with me, they shoved a rag in my mouth and taped it shut, then tied me up and slammed the damn sofa on top of me. I've been here like this for about five hours. I didn't think I was ever going to be found."

"Quit complaining. They had Mrs. Pinata for twelve months. What's five hours? That's nothing."

Ken said, "You should try it. Not much fun, especially if you're claustrophobic. You know what this means?" He didn't let me answer the question—he answered it for me. "It means Mrs. Pinata is free and that Mr. Pinata must have been the one who got her out. Now they're looking for both of them."

"We need to talk to Thomas, and I have to let Jack Casey know that Mrs. Pinata is free. Do you need to go to the hospital or are you good enough to come with me?"

"Hell, I don't need a damn hospital. I just need to clean up. I haven't had a shower since yesterday morning. Do we have the time?"

"Why not; a few more minutes won't make any difference."

As Ken walked to the bedroom, I said, "We need to go back to the hospital and talk to Jack. He may have some questions for you. Then we need to call Thomas and see if he'll meet with us."

Ken stopped and asked, with a puzzled look on his face, "Why don't we go down the hall to his suite and talk to him?"

"Thomas went into hiding right after you and I talked to him. He wouldn't even tell me where he was, so he will have to meet us somewhere safe."

Ken said to me, "Let me get this shower and get some clean clothes on. Then we can go."

Ten minutes later, we left the hotel and headed back to the hospital. Jack was sleeping when we arrived. I yelled, "Wake the hell up, you lazy turd."

Jack jumped when I yelled. "What the fuck?" He quickly looked around and brought his pistol out from under the sheet. He smiled and said, "Irish, you asshole, I could have shot you."

"Jack, you're too old and slow. I had the drop on you."

"No, you didn't." He brought a small electronic device out with his other hand. "It's a warning beeper. My two buddies out there guarding me buzz me when the elevator opens up. I had my little buddy here cocked and ready to go." He held up his pistol and grinned. "Now, who do you think had the jump on whom?"

"You are a wise old fart—that, I will give you. Jack, I want to introduce you to Ken Cloutier.

He is the other one working with Thomas Sharpe and me."

Jack held out his hand, and Ken shook it. "It is nice to meet you, Ken."

Ken answered, "Likewise, Jack."

I said, "Listen, Jack, we have some news."

He interrupted me. Looking at Ken, he asked, "What the hell happened to you?"

"That's what Irish was about to tell you."

"Jack, early this morning, three men conned their way into Ken's room. They were looking for Mr. and Mrs. Pinata. So apparently, Mr. Pinata somehow got his wife out. We haven't heard from him. Have you?"

"Not a word," answered Jack.

"I wonder if Sophia or Thomas has heard anything. Hopefully, this could put an end to the war that's started. With Mrs. Pinata safe, the Marzetti family doesn't have a hammer hanging over Mr. Pinata's head anymore. I wonder what his next move is."

Jack said, "I will get ahold of Henry Sullivan and give him this update. Maybe he will give us heads-up on what else is happening. Irish, I think you should follow up with Thomas Sharpe. He may have some answers for us, but make sure you keep me in the loop."

"Will do, Jack."

"One more thing. Ken, if you are working with Irish, you should become one of our FBI gang. I should swear you in as a temporary agent. That way, you don't have to answer any local authority's questions. Just tell them you are an FBI agent and that you are involved with an active federal investigation."

I looked at Ken and said with a smile, "Go ahead—it won't hurt, and besides, Jack is right. You won't have to answer to any local police departments."

Ken nodded his head in agreement and said, "I guess I'm in."

Jack said, "Raise your right hand and repeat after me. I, Ken Cloutier, do solemnly swear to uphold the constitution of the United States of America. I promise to yada yada yada, so help me God."

Ken laughed and repeated exactly what Jack had said. Then Jack said, "Now I order you two to get the hell out of here and let me get some rest. If my nurse comes in here and finds more people talking to me, she said she'll lock my door and give me enough pain medication to knock me out for two days. So get out and goddamn it, be careful. That's an order."

Ken and I headed back to the hotel. I decided to check the phone in my room in case Thomas had left a message. When we got to my room, we saw that the lock had been broken and the door was standing slightly ajar.

I drew my gun and slowly pushed the door open further. It was quiet, and everything seemed to be in order. I only had one room and a bathroom to check, not suites like all the union leaders had.

Nothing seemed to be missing. I said to Ken, "It looks like they were looking for Mr. and Mrs. Pinata here too."

Just then, my phone rang.

"Irish, it's Thomas."

I asked right away, "Where the hell are you?"

"That's not important. What *is* important is that Sophia's mother is free, and we need to get her and Sophia some place where Mr. Marzetti cannot get to them. Mr. Pinata called and told me that when Marzetti was through with him, he was going to kill Sophia, her mother, and me. I just now talked to him; he told me where they are and asked me to get over there as quick as I can to take them somewhere safe."

"Slow down, Thomas. Why do you have to get them? I thought Mr. Pinata was keeping Sophia hidden safely away with those four bodyguards."

"Apparently, Mr. Marzetti found out where he had been keeping her, so he had to move her. But listen, I can't talk over the phone. Can you meet me right away?"

"Sure. Where do you want to meet?"

"Do you remember last summer when our entire staff met at this place for a picnic?"

"Sure, I remember. When?"

"As soon as you can get there. I'm only five minutes away."

"Ken is here with me. We can be there in fifteen minutes, depending on traffic. See you then."

I hung up the phone and asked Ken, "Did you hear all of that conversation?"

"I did, so let's get our asses in gear."

We left immediately, and as I was driving like a mad man to get there, Ken asked, "Where did you get a car?"

"My girlfriend is loaning me her car for a while."

"Girlfriend? Is Riona here?" Ken asked.

"Riona and I broke up. We decided it just wasn't going to work anymore."

"You mean you where cheating on her, right?"

"No, nothing like that, you dummy. She found someone new, and after that, I found someone new. It was a mutual agreement."

"Who is this new girl, and where did you find her?"

"Actually, we met at the hospital. I was there helping Maria Rodriguez after Henry was shot, and she was the social worker."

"Wait a minute. That just happened. How could you fall for someone that quick?"

"I don't know, but it's incredible. She's incredible. Believe it or not, I think I just experienced love at first sight. She feels the same way."

"There's no such thing as love at first sight," Ken countered.

"I beg to differ. I know that it happens because it happened to me."

"Okay, if you say so," Ken replied with a grin.

Nothing more was said about my love life until we arrived at the park Thomas had described.

"You need to be careful with this lady of yours. You two could get hurt," Ken said.

I looked at him and said, "Thanks for the concern, but wait until you meet her. She is incredible."

Thomas's car was backed into a space directly in front of the exit. He got out as soon as we pulled in.

"I'm so glad you came. We need to move quickly. There's no telling how much time we have," Thomas said with urgency.

I asked, "Where do we have to go?"

"Mr. Pinata has them in an apartment north of Boynton Beach on Lantana Road, just west of Haverhill Road. It should take us about fifteen minutes to get there. Anyway, we have to get moving ASAP. Whose car is this?"

"It's my girlfriend's car. Do you want to use it?"

"Did Riona come down to see you?"

"No, she and I broke up. This is someone new."

"Whatever, Irish. Let's get going," Thomas said, seeming not to care if I had a new girlfriend or not.

We all climbed into Katrina's Buick and Thomas gave me directions. After five minutes, he called Sophia and told her we would be there in about ten minutes.

We arrived in front of a large, grey, nondescript warehouse. There were no windows and only one door in the center of the building. The parking lot was full of broken glass and busted asphalt. Urban decay was the main theme of the area surrounding the building.

I drove around the back to park, and Thomas said, "They are supposed to be in an apartment back here somewhere."

As we came close to the door, it opened and out stepped a man carrying a semi-automatic weapon. He waved us to come with him. When we got to him, he said, "My name is John. I'm Mrs. Pinata's bodyguard. They are inside. Follow me."

Even though we didn't know who John was, we followed. However, I pulled out my weapon and carried it behind my right buttock, just in case. Once inside, John took us up some steel steps to what looked like a home inside the warehouse.

We walked in and were greeted by Sophia and her mother. Sophia wrapped her arms around Thomas and gave him a long kiss. "Thomas, I've missed you so much."

"Me too, sweetheart. We are going to get you out of here right away. Hello, Angela."

Angela Pinata was a strikingly beautiful woman. Sophia could have been a clone of her mother, except that Sophia's body was full and firm, like Angela's once might have been. Angela stepped forward and gave Thomas a hug and said, "Thank you for taking such good care of Sophia while I was gone. I was so worried about her. She has told me everything that's happened during my absence. I was worried the whole time I was away, but she has convinced me that was senseless. She was in good hands."

Thomas gave her a squeeze and said, "Thank you, Angela. I had hoped you wouldn't have worry, but somehow they got to her. I'm just thankful that she was returned safely."

I looked around at their home away from home and found it to be a fully furnished apartment. The furnishings were first class, and the place looked very comfortable.

I said, "Thomas, shouldn't we be getting out of here?"

"You're right, Irish. Angela, do you remember these guys? This is Irish MacSween and Ken Cloutier."

"I remember Irish, but I don't know if I ever had the pleasure of meeting Mr. Cloutier."

I interrupted her by asking, "John, are you coming with us?"

"That's my job. Mr. Pinata would shoot me if I abandoned Mrs. Pinata. Where she goes, I go."

I noticed Angela looking longingly at John and wondered if something more was going on. Maybe he was guarding her body and not being her bodyguard.

The six of us gathered our belongings and loaded everything into the Buick. Everyone climbed in except Thomas and me.

He asked me, "Do you have any idea where we can take them that would be safe?"

I thought for a minute and said, "A few months after the strike started, I took a long weekend to do some fishing. I rented a cabin for a couple of days that would be perfect for them. There was lots of room, and each cabin was on the lake. It's real quiet, and the owners are down home-type folks. They keep tabs on everyone who comes around. They even have guard dogs that they let out at night."

Thomas asked, "Is this place pretty secluded? Do the cabins have a wide perimeter around them?"

"Yes, that's the thing. Each cabin is alone but surrounded by about a fifty yard radius of trees."

"That sounds good. Let's get going."

It took us about an hour to reach the cabin resort. Thomas and I got out of the car while everyone else stayed inside. The owners, Jim and Tressa, came out of their cabin to greet us.

We walked up to them, and I said, "Hello Jim, Tressa. Do you remember me? I was here about eight months ago."

They both smiled, and Jim replied, "Sure, we remember you. How have you been, Irish?"

"I've been good. I'd like you to meet a friend of mine. This is Thomas Sharpe. Thomas, this is Jim and Tressa. They own this little piece of paradise."

Thomas stepped up, and the three of them shook hands. Looking at all the people in the cars, Jim asked, "Tell me, Irish, are things really good, or are you in some sort of trouble?"

"Well, I'm pretty good, but we do have a slight problem. I have two women in the car who I need to keep secluded. There are certain unethical people who aim to do them harm. Do you think you would have a place for them to stay for a few days?"

"Sounds kind of serious, Irish, but if you need our help, you can count on us. Do you remember Jeb, our handyman?"

"Sure—we fished for an entire day when I was here before. He had quite the knack for catching the big fish, and left me holding the net." We all laughed.

"Jeb is not just a handyman. He has other skills and responsibilities around here. He used to be a big-city detective back in the day. He came here four years ago to get away from it all, but I'm sure he would be willing to help out and watch over your friends for you."

"I would be willing to pay him if that would help."

"No reason to do that. I already pay him, so no double dipping around here," Jim laughed.

"Thanks so much. Angela Pinata and her daughter, Sophia, are the two we are trying to protect. Sophia's husband—Thomas here—and Mrs. Pinata's bodyguard, John, will also be staying. Maybe Jeb, Thomas, and John can coordinate the protection."

Jim said, "I thought I read that Mrs. Pinata ran off about a year ago. The news reported she left Mr. Pinata of her own volition. Was that true?"

"No, not even close. She was kidnapped over a year ago. The Marzetti Mafia family took her.

Her husband Joseph Pinata managed to get her out yesterday."

"No shit? He's the president of the truckers union, isn't he?"

"One and the same. It's been a long year for all of us."

Jim said, "That strike has affected the entire nation. Hell, it's even had an effect on our business. People stopped coming, saying they couldn't afford vacations anymore. It is a hell of a thing, if you ask me."

Tressa broke in, "Well, let's get them settled. We have a large two bedroom cabin that will be quite comfortable. There are two beds in each bedroom, a remodeled kitchen, and two bathrooms that have been redone. Just drive past our cabin, take an immediate left, and follow the path. It's at the very end, and it's unlocked. We will be there in a few minutes."

We did as they said, and after ten minutes, Jim and Tressa arrived to show everyone around the cabin, which even had a safe room below the kitchen floor. After an hour, Mrs. Pinata, Sophia, Thomas, and John were settled in for the wait. Sophia and Thomas got one bedroom, and Mrs. Pinata got the other one. John would use the sofa, which was fine with him.

Jim said, "The safe room is well-stocked and impenetrable. It may come in handy; one never knows." As he walked by me toward the back door he whispered, "I'll show Thomas and John how the safe room works.

I warned them not to use the computer and to keep their cell phones off unless there was an emergency, and even then, to keep their calls to no longer than one minute. I also told them that we would keep in contact through Jim and Tressa.

After all the good-byes, Ken and I drove back into Miami. I thought it would be best initially to try to locate Mr. Pinata. Thomas had given me his cell phone number and his last location. He said that Mr. Pinata had told him he had a feeling that blood was in the air.

I took a few minutes on our drive back to call Katrina. While we were talking, her father interrupted. Katrina said he needed to speak to me at once.

Before I said anything, I heard him ask Katrina to give him some privacy. I heard her argue for a minute, but then she said, "If you insist, Papa." I could hear her footsteps walking away, and then a door closing.

"Irish, how are things going, my son?"

"So far, so good. Things are a little tense, but that's to be expected in the situation that I'm facing," I replied.

Mr. Bernetti said, "I have been contacting some of my friends and we found out what's happening with the ITU and the Marzetti Mafia family. It sounds like your union may need some help with this situation."

"Mr. Bernetti, I do not want to involve you in any of this. It's a private affair between the two parties. Besides, this could explode any minute. It's a very dangerous situation that I don't think you should be involved in."

"Irish, I'm no fool when it comes to trouble. I've faced many people like this piece of shit Frank Marzetti who's causing you and your union all the problems. I have certain men who are very experienced in dealing with assholes like him."

I was thoroughly surprised by both his reaction and his offer. At his home, he had seemed too passive to have ever been involved with the likes of a Frank Marzetti or even a Joseph Pinata. I find that sometimes people will surprise you. You never know their true past, or what beliefs drive them, or how they will react to protect their world as it is.

I asked, "What exactly do you know?"

He chuckled quietly and said, "Irish, I know everything. I know that Frank Marzetti kidnapped Mrs. Pinata, that he cut off her little finger, and that Joseph Pinata has been handled like a puppet for the last year. I know that Mr. Marzetti and some people on Wall Street are in bed together. I know they plan to get rich at the expense of the ITU and the people of this nation. I know he murdered three of your union officers. We just found out that Mr. Pinata orchestrated an attack on the Marzettis that left four family members dead."

I was amazed. How did he know all of this? It had been a well-kept secret. Not until Mr. Pinata spilled his guts to Thomas and Sophia did anyone know about his wife's kidnapping.

Then it hit me like a brick. "What do you mean three of our members? So far, only Henry Rodriguez has died."

"I'm sorry to have to tell you this, but about thirty minutes ago, Frank Bartolone died on the surgery table. He started bleeding internally, and by the time they got him to surgery, he bled out. Matthew Sims was found dead in his bed. The doctors were really surprised because they thought his surgery went well, and they expected him to pull through. I know it's a great loss for your union and probably to you also."

I was shocked by the news. I kept silent for a few minutes, trying to act like it didn't really bother me, but it did. Then, I said, "Did anyone think about checking on Matthew's death? Maybe he didn't die from his wounds, but had extra help."

"The FBI has ordered an autopsy just to rule out such a scenario."

I asked, "So what do you suggest? I'm kind of flying by the seat of my pants right now."

"I suggest we find Joseph Pinata and stop him from going after Frank Marzetti again. Apparently, he has vowed to kill Marzetti before this is all over, and I know he wants to avenge his wife's kidnapping. He is also really angry that they forced him to cooperate with their scheme. But I'll tell you one thing—if he tries to kill Frank Marzetti, he himself will get killed. Then it'll only be a matter of time before Marzetti comes after his wife and daughter, and I don't believe he will stop there. Rumor has it that he is going to come after Pinata's entire staff. That means you, along with everyone else on his bargaining staff."

"I thought it was unethical for the Mafia to go after families. Families are supposed to be untouchable. Aren't they?"

"Frank Marzetti is a monster. He will do whatever is necessary to please himself. He thinks he is untouchable. Besides, I believe his ultimate goal is to take over the International Truckers Union. If he can control that, it would bring him great dividends."

"What do you think we should do? I'm certainly not going to lie down and let Frank Marzetti take over this union. Do you have any suggestions?"

"We have to kill Frank Marzetti before he kills Joseph Pinata, his family, and his staff."

The frankness in Mr. Bernetti's statement shocked me to the core. It was so out of character for the man I thought I knew. I wondered if Katrina knew this side of her beloved papa.

After a moment, I asked, "How do we go about doing something like that?" I tried to sound casual, like he just said we need to take Marzetti out to dinner and have a nice talk with him man to man. Not that we have to kill him.

"You don't have to do anything. Let me take care of Mr. Marzetti. What you can do is help me find Joseph Pinata. Once you find him, I wish you would let me handle him. I don't want anything happening to my future son-in-law."

I looked at Ken, and he was staring at me, confused by what Mr. Bernetti had just said. "Is he serious?"

"I hope so, Ken. He has seen Katrina and me together. He knows love when he sees it."

Ken smiled but said nothing further.

Trying to sound confident that I could do the job, I said with as much conviction as I could muster, "At least I know Mr. Pinata and I know the place where he was hiding last night. I could start there. I also have his cell phone number. Maybe I could try to reach him before we do anything."

"Irish, are you sure you want to do this? You could get in the middle of a war."

"I'm sorry, Mr. Bernetti, but I insist that whatever happens, I be included." I looked at Ken, and he was pointing to himself to say he wanted to be included too. "I also want Ken Cloutier to come along. He's as much a part of this as I am."

"As you wish, but it might get ugly before it's over."

"It's our union, and it's our job to keep it secure. We also have another problem. What about the FBI? They are waist deep in all of this. Even Henry Sullivan himself is involved. He has insisted that I keep him informed."

Mr. Bernetti surprised me again when he said, "I have already talked to Henry Sullivan. I informed him that I was going to do some looking around. He seemed to accept that without reservation. He knows the situation and he knows me, and I know how best to eliminate smaller problems before they become huge problems."

"Do you mean that he is endorsing your involvement with Mr. Marzetti?"

"Irish, some things are best worked out without FBI involvement. I know you want to play by the rules, but sometimes following the rules is not the best way to go about it, and Henry knows that. If Marzetti is put into prison, he'll still have the ability to come after whoever he wants. We are going to eliminate that possibility. As far as Henry Sullivan is concerned, we never spoke, and the FBI has no knowledge that I am involved. We need to keep it that way. Are you going to have a problem with that?"

Ignoring his question, I asked, "Have you ever handled something like this for him before?"

Mr. Bernetti chuckled again. "During my lifetime, I have always done whatever was necessary to keep myself and our union alive. I didn't stay the president of our union for thirty years without crossing, or at least blurring, the lines once in a while. I did whatever I needed to do. It's called life, Irish. We do what we must, for the benefit of the people who entrust us with their lives."

I listened to what he had to say, and didn't have a problem with any of it. It may seem wrong to some people, but I didn't see it that way. A guy like Frank Marzetti could be a menace to society for many years. Justice could be served in many ways; this was just one of them.

I said, "I'm okay; I don't have a problem with any of this, so what's our next step?"

"Meet me at our international union headquarters. Do you know where that is?"

"Yes, I have been there a couple of times over the last year."

"Can you be there in, let's say, an hour and a half?"

"Sure. We could be there in thirty minutes, if you like."

"No, an hour and a half will be just fine. I have some other business to attend to, so that will give me enough time."

"Mr. Bernetti, why are you getting involved in this? This is not your fight."

"I have been watching all of this for quite some time now, and as of this morning, it *is* my fight. I can't let something happen to you. Katrina just found you—you are now family. We protect our own. It's as simple as that. I think she loves you, so I could never forgive myself if something happened to you."

I didn't know what to say. I had never felt this type of loyalty in my life. I was overcome with emotion realizing that he felt protective of me because of my commitment to his daughter, and her commitment to me.

I hung up the phone and stared at Ken. "I am dumbfounded by that conversation. I didn't realize Mr. Bernetti still had the power to get things done. I thought he was quietly retired and enjoying a mundane life. Man, was I wrong."

I wanted to use the time we had to call Jack Casey, but for some reason, I felt I needed to respect Mr. Bernetti's interest. He had survived thirty years doing things his way. Why should I try to step in and change things?

When we got back to the hotel, I told Ken to get some rest, even if it was only for an hour. I didn't know when we might next get the chance.

CHAPTER FORTY-TWO

I couldn't sleep and felt mentally drained, so I took a shower and changed clothes. I wanted to look renewed even though I didn't feel that way. They say appearances are everything, whoever 'they' are. I could never figure that one out.

After an hour, I woke Ken up. He opened his eyes like he had been asleep for days. I envied him. Some nights I couldn't sleep even if I'd had the blessing of the pope.

We walked out to the parking lot, hopped into the Buick, and headed for Mr. Bernetti's union headquarters.

When we arrived, we were met at the door by two armed guards. Each of them carried semi-automatic rifles. We gave them our names and showed our IDs. They let us pass, but not before they frisked us and took our pistols.

Mr. Bernetti was sitting in an office behind a large desk. There were four other men present. I introduced Ken to Mr. Bernetti. They shook hands and greeted each other cordially. We took the two remaining empty chairs in front of his desk and sat down.

Mr. Bernetti offered us drinks. We said, "No, thank you" in unison.

He countered pleasantly, "You sure you don't want a drink? You might need one after what I have to tell you."

I said, "We better keep our heads clear, especially if decisions have to be made quickly."

"I understand completely. What I have to propose takes a certain type of person who is able to keep things to himself when all hell breaks out. I think I know you, but I know nothing about Mr. Cloutier. So I am going to rely on your opinion about whether he is this type of person or not."

"Mr. Bernetti, I not only endorse him, but I am willing to lay my life on the line for him. He will stand strong whatever happens. You have my word on it."

"What about you, Mr. Cloutier? Are you able to withstand immense pressure from the local police and possibly the Feds?"

"In my previous life, before I came to work with the ITU, I was a border patrol officer in Texas. Every time we had to use force on the illegals, folks from the newspapers, as well as local authorities, would raise all kinds of hell. We were brought before the State of Texas Border Crossing Review Board whenever something unsavory happened. We were treated like the criminals instead of the law enforcement officers. So yeah, I think I can withstand any kind of scrutiny. These people never intimidated me and never will."

Mr. Bernetti looked at me and said, "He sounds good. So are we a go?"

"I don't think this is necessarily my call. If the director of the FBI is not going to stop you, neither am I."

"Of course, Mr. Sullivan does not know of my plan, only that I am going to help out."

Just then, another one of his men walked into the room and handed Mr. Bernetti a note. He read it and then handed it to me. The note read, "Our bee keeper can sting the queen bee this evening."

I looked up at Ken as he read over my shoulder. "What the heck does this mean?"

Mr. Bernetti said, "When I was a kid, my grandfather used to raise bees. The queen bee was like the center of the colony's world. The female bees, other than the queen, do all the work like gathering food, building, and protecting the colony and the queen. The males'—or drones'—only purpose is to fertilize the queen, which they do while she is in flight. Once they mate, they die. The female bees do a dance to tell other females how far away it is to get the food. They do a round dance if the food is close and a waggle dance if the food is far away."

I asked, "What does this have to do with our situation?"

"I'm getting there. My point is, if the queen is destroyed, the rest of the colony is in turmoil. The physical as well as the social structure of the colony are in peril. The colony cannot sustain itself until a new queen takes over. You eliminate the queen—in our case, Mr. Marzetti is the queen—and the rest of the family structure will fall apart."

I said, "So what you're saying is, if Mr. Marzetti is eliminated, the vendetta against Mr. Pinata will go away."

"That is exactly what I'm saying."

I looked at Ken, and he was nodding his head in agreement. I asked, "How is this going to happen?"

Mr. Bernetti gave us a wink, threw up his hands in a gesture of bewilderment, and said, "How would I know?"

Ken and I left it at that.

But then, I asked him. "What about Mr. Pinata? We have to stop him before he takes any further action and gets himself killed. Do you need the info that I have?"

"You said you wanted to be involved. I have decided to let you take the lead on finding him. Do you think you and Ken can do some digging and find out where the hell he's keeping himself and what his plans are?"

"We can try, for sure. I'm just not real positive if he's still where Thomas left him. Thomas suggested I call him and ask him to meet with us before he does anything stupid."

Mr. Bernetti said, "Why don't you go to this last hiding place first. That way, he can't put you off. If you call him, he could run and you'll never find him in time."

"If you think that's best," I replied.

"Make sure you keep me informed about what's happening. If Joey Pinata finds out I am involved, he may refuse to go along with you. He and I haven't gotten along very well since the time when his father was president."

He handed the note to one of his men, who pulled out a lighter and set it aflame. Ken and I stood up, shook his hand, and turned to leave.

As we reached the door, Mr. Bernetti stopped us and said, "I will let you know when the problem is solved."

"Sounds good," I replied.

"There is one more thing, Irish."

"What's that?" I asked.

"Be careful. I don't want anything to happen to you."

I smiled and said, "Neither do I."

CHAPTER FORTY-THREE

Ken and I left Mr. Bernetti's office, retrieved our weapons, and headed for Katrina's Buick. I was not really surprised that Ken had a concealed weapons permit, but I was surprised that he carried a .357 Magnum, which has enough firepower to stop a tank. He was a man of many resources. I read him the address Thomas had given me and told him that there was a GPS in the glove box.

He entered the address, and the GPS showed it would take forty minutes to get there. After he finished, he turned to me and asked, "What do you think of Mr. Bernetti's plan?"

I took my eyes off the road for an instant, looked at him, and asked, "What plan?"

He nodded his head and said nothing.

After a few minutes, I asked him, "Do you have a problem keeping that quiet?"

He looked at me, smiled, and replied, "Keeping what quiet?"

We both laughed.

As we drove, I realized we were going in the same general direction where we were hiding Thomas, Sophia, her mother, and John the bodyguard.

As we drew near their location, we turned off and headed south, farther into the marshy woods. We drove another five miles on a gravel road before the GPS instructed us to turn right, and our address would be on our left.

We couldn't see the house due to the thick moss hanging from the decades-old cypress trees that lined the drive. I drove slowly up the drive, the eerie scene laid out before us like a movie set. I waited for some monster to leap out and swallow the entire car.

As the house came into view, two men stepped out from behind the huge trees; they were each holding semi-automatic rifles. When I saw them, I slammed on the brakes, bringing us to a sudden halt. Our windows were down, so we had no problem hearing their commands.

They trained their weapons on us as they came up to our side windows. "Where the hell do you think you're going? This is private property."

I didn't recognize either of them, so they obviously didn't recognize us. "I am Irish MacSween, and this here is Ken Cloutier. We are on Mr. Pinata's staff. Thomas Sharpe gave us this address because it is imperative that we talk to Mr. Pinata."

The man holding the rifle on Ken stepped away from the car and turned his back to us so we couldn't hear. He pulled out a small two-way radio and spoke into it. After a couple of moments, he said something more, then closed it and walked back to the car. He said something to the other man, who turned back and looked at us.

"Let me see your IDs." Without a word, we pulled out our wallets, removed our licenses, and gave them to him. He checked them, and us, out for an instant, and then handed them back to us. "You may proceed up to the house. Make sure that when you get there, if you have any weapons, leave them on the hood of your car."

For some reason, I said thank you, and we drove ahead as he had directed. As we approached the house, we saw a picture-perfect Southern plantation-style home, with huge white pillars and a large porch with white rocking chairs setting the scene as if it was the 1860s Civil War era.

As we got out of the car and were putting our weapons on the hood, Mr. Pinata emerged from the porch along with four armed men, two on each side of him. He had a large smoking cigar between his lips and stood with both hands on his hips as if he was an original Southern plantation owner. Reality couldn't have been more in opposition.

Ken and I walked halfway up the steps to the porch and stopped.

"What the hell brings you two out here?" he asked in a gravelly voice that sounded like he hadn't slept in days.

I answered, "Mr. Pinata, it is vitally important that we speak with you. There are things that are happening that you should know about. Things that could resolve most, if not all, of our issues."

He looked at us like we were invaders from outer space, studying us as if deciding whether to talk to us or shoot us. I saw Ken standing casually with his hands at his sides. Apparently, he didn't mind four armed men pointing rifles at us. I didn't care for it much myself, but I didn't waver.

"You can come in, but I don't have much time to give you. We are moving in a little over an hour."

Ken and I looked at each other in surprise. What did he have planned now? Whatever it was, we had to stall him or stop him if necessary.

We entered the mansion and walked into a huge office with books lining three of the walls. A large oak desk stood at the far side of the room, with a painting of Robert E. Lee on the wall behind it. Southern charm at its best.

Mr. Pinata sat down behind the desk. "Okay, gentlemen, tell me what plans you have put together."

Before I told him anything, I asked, "Mr. Pinata, what exactly are you planning to do?"

"Irish, before I say anything about my plans, I want to know if you are willing to stand up and fight for our union, or if you're going to stand back and watch it be taken over by a bunch of thugs?"

"You know damn well that I will fight anyone who thinks about destroying the union. I will not sit back and watch it crumble. That's why Ken and I are here. We already have a plan in motion that just might prevent a lot of bloodshed and the destruction of this union."

I watched his reaction when I told him this and saw nothing. He sat staunchly in his chair without so much as a flicker of his eyes. He was not willing to show his hand quite yet.

So I just asked, "Joseph, what do you have planned? It's important that we know." I put emphasis on the *we* so he would know Ken and I were in this together. "Either you have to put your plan on hold, or we have to. But we each have to know what the other is doing."

Mr. Pinata sat motionless for a moment without uttering a word. He obviously was contemplating what I'd said. Then he smiled and said, "You show me yours, and I'll show you mine."

He obviously wasn't going to offer up his plan until I said something.

I couldn't imagine what he had in mind, but whatever it was, he sounded like he was trying to keep us out of the loop, so I broke the silence. "Okay, if you're not going to answer, then I will tell you what *we* have in mind, but first I need to tell you a little story." I was trying to kill as much time as I could, so I repeated the story Mr. Bernetti had told us about the bee colony.

When I was about halfway through the story, he looked at me and said, "Irish, I don't have time for a long drawn-out line of bullshit."

"Just hear me out. It won't take long."

"All right, go ahead, but make it quick. We are on a timetable." He rolled his eyes like this really was a bunch of bullshit.

I continued Mr. Bernetti's story, and when I finished, looking like he was out of patience he yelled, "What the hell does this have to do with our problems?"

So I said, "Here's the thing. Ken and I have hired a sniper to take out Mr. Marzetti. Our sniper is our rival queen bee. He has been watching Mr. Marzetti for the last two days. He knows his routine—when he eats, when he shits, when he comes and where he goes, when he meets with his staff, and when he's alone. Late last night, he learned that Mr. Marzetti will have a meeting in his hotel suite this afternoon around four o'clock. He will take Marzetti out then."

"Where did you find this sniper?" Mr. Pinata asked doubtfully.

"I have a friend who has used him before."

"What's your friend's name?"

"You know how these things work. I can't divulge his name. He said if he found out we were running our mouths, we would be his next target."

Mr. Pinata sat staring at us without blinking, thinking about what I had just told him. He seemed to be weighing all his options. "So you think by killing Marzetti, our troubles will be over?"

"We are sure of it. His family is not that tight; there's a lot of infighting. We don't think there will be anyone strong enough to stand up with his convictions. We know for a fact that not everyone is in bed with him on this vendetta against you and this union of ours. It's a personal thing for him. So we figure if we cut off the head, the body will fall apart."

Ken spoke abruptly, "Our sniper also found out that Marzetti's security is enormous inside the hotel. He has the entire floor reserved for his goons. It's impenetrable, and it would be suicidal for anyone to attempt getting at him in his hotel."

Joey looked at us again with skepticism, trying to figure out if we were running a game on him. "I want to know how and where you found this information. You don't find this kind of thing in the social pages, so either give it up, or my men and I are out of here."

I drew in a deep breath and let it out slowly for effect. "If you would talk to your wife, you could find out a few things. She told us there was constant fighting within the family. His two sons were totally against this vendetta of his. Even his wife begged him to let it go. So if he is no longer running things, the family will get back doing what mob families do."

I was going to continue my litany, but before I could say anything else, Ken spoke up. "Mr. Pinata, what I'm about to tell you must remain between us. This information cannot be made public. I hope I can trust you with this. You see, my brother is sort of in the business of killing queen bees. He was in the Navy SEALs for fifteen years, and for the last five of those, he was the best sniper the SEALs ever had. He has been killing targets for many years, and he doesn't think this will be any more difficult than the targets he's eliminated in the past. As a matter of fact, he thinks this will be even easier than most, because he said that Mr. Marzetti is very lax when it comes to his own security, especially while in his hotel suite. He told us that he's seen it in the past—once you eliminate the queen bee, the other bees will scatter or a new queen will come in and take over. The social bees will immediately protect and feed the new queen and keep feeding the colony, but it's a different social setting."

Mr. Pinata smiled at us and asked, "Are you sure the rest of the family will scatter after Marzetti is dead? If one of his sons takes over, what makes you think the family won't continue on with the same vengeance he sought?"

"It could happen, but we don't think, in this instance, that the same thirst for revenge is there. Besides, his sons do not appear to have the leadership, the loyalty, the close-knit family, or the work ethic that are all necessary to keep the revenge factor alive."

Mr. Pinata asked, "So you think a sniper is the best way to eliminate Mr. Marzetti?"

I answered him, "The only other way is to infiltrate the hotel, which could be difficult and deadly for both parties involved because of the likelihood of getting killed due to all the protection.

"Our guy can sit across the street in another hotel and have a clear, simple shot at Mr. Marzetti's hotel suite. He is absolutely deadly from that distance. Our problem would be solved."

He asked, "So you feel your guy can do this job?"

Ken came back into the conversation. "I'm sure he can handle it without a problem. He started observing Mr. Marzetti two days ago. He's one hundred percent confident he can get the job done."

I felt the tension build inside me because it didn't look like Joey was buying any of this, but I tried to remain calm. I looked at Ken and knew he was feeling the same. We had come up with this story on the fly and knew that if he didn't believe us, blood would flow, and soon. The thing I didn't know was that the earliest blood would be ours.

I looked up at the clock on the wall and saw it was only one o'clock. We had three hours to kill before Mr. Bernetti's man could take his shot. I felt beads of sweat form on my forehead and down my back.

Before I could say anything more, Ken spoke again. "Mr. Pinata, I want to get your solemn vow that you will never repeat this. It's a family matter for me that can never get out to the public—especially to the local authorities or the press."

Mr. Pinata seemed surprised, but he heard the urgency in Ken's voice and saw the intensity in his face. "Ken, whatever is said here will never leave this room. So if you have anything more to add, you'd better do it quickly."

Ken looked nervous and upset—almost afraid to say whatever it was he had come up with. "When my brother got out of the Navy, he was hired by a private firm that did pestilent work for the US government. A few years later, he went to work directly for the CIA."

He paused for a moment to let that info sink in. He looked at me with a serious look on his face, then back at Mr. Pinata. "What I'm trying to say is that my brother is a hit man for the United States government."

Joseph Pinata sat staring at Ken as if he was about to leap on him and rip his head off. His face grew red, and he began clenching his fists as though he was crushing something to death. He stood up quickly, causing his chair to topple over, and said with venom in his voice, "I don't trust government men, so that means I don't trust your brother, and I don't trust you two."

Suddenly, the four men rushed over with their weapons leveled directly at us. Ken and I stood up instantly, and I yelled, "What the hell is going on?"

Mr. Pinata said to the men, "Tie these traitors up and take them to the basement. And make damn sure they stay there."

As the men grabbed our arms, I asked, "Pinata, what the hell are you talking about? We're not traitors. We're on your side."

"Don't give me that shit. You know goddamn well what's going on. You ratted us out to the Feds.

You were their mole, and you gave them everything we had. You're a goddamn snitch, and I hate goddamn snitches. You, and now I see Ken, have turned your backs on this union and all your brothers. You're both a disgrace and not fit to be called union men."

I felt myself get red with anger. I was at my boiling point, but I didn't give a damn. He was going to hear what I had to say. As the men tried to pull my arms behind me I screamed. "Everyone in this union is so sick and tired of your dirty dealing ways, your heavy-handed methods, your own personal interests, and the slow destruction you are causing the organization. We've all had enough of your bullshit, and about enough of you. You've had your way long enough, and if everyone wasn't so afraid of you, they would bring you down and throw your ass out forever."

He was enraged as he shouted, "You insolent bastard! Who do you think you are? You're just a low-life traitor who can be bought and sold. So don't get so highhanded with me. You sold us out and deserve what you're going to get."

I screamed right back at him, "Yes, I was helping the Feds! Not to bring down the union, to rid it of *you*. Joey, you're an infection that has been untreated for a long time, but now your reign of terror is over."

He stood there defiantly as an evil sneer crossed his face. He took three steps toward me and drew his fist back like he was about to shatter my nose into little pieces, but before he could, I grabbed the arms of the men who were holding me and brought my heel up so quickly he didn't have time to react. It landed directly on his chin. His head snapped back and he fell onto the large desk, hitting the back of his head in the process. He slid to the floor like a soft rubber cartoon man.

Before I could do anything else, the two men, obviously pros, slammed me to the floor face-first. I felt the bones in my nose shatter into those little pieces I thought I was protecting myself from when I had kicked Pinata in the face, but obviously that didn't work out too well. My eyes watered, and I could instantly smell and taste my own blood.

I looked to my left and saw that Ken was in a similar position. They twisted my arms behind me and tied them with rope before I could protest. They did the same to Ken. I wondered what was going through his mind now, other than his nose.

The larger of the two men holding me jumped up and went to Mr. Pinata's aid. I could barely see him out of the corner of my blurry eye, but it was enough to know that he was again standing, though very unsteadily. His man was practically holding him up as he led him to the chair I had been sitting in.

After a few minutes, Mr. Pinata rose to his feet and came over to where the guard was holding me to the floor. He said, unemotionally, "I'll deal with you after I deal with Frank Marzetti. I want you to think a while about dying, because that's exactly what's going to happen to you. You're going to die, and you're going to die slowly."

With that, he kicked me in the left side of my chest. I let out a huge gush of air, and I thought I could hear some of my ribs break.

After I regained my breath, I said with a laugh, "Joey, you're such a stupid fool. You don't know what you're running into when you go after Frank Marzetti. He's so heavily guarded you won't get on the same floor as him. He's got more armed men than you will know what to do with. You're heading into a bee's nest, and I hope they blow your fucking head off."

He screamed, "Shut up, you bastard!" He kicked me in the ribs again, and this time, I was sure he broke a couple of them. I couldn't breathe through my mouth because it was too painful, and I couldn't breathe through my nose because it was full of blood. A panic began to roll over me until I took in a slow, deep breath.

Mr. Pinata started his rant again. "I've heard about enough from you. You're lucky I don't shoot your ass right now. Take these traitors away so I don't have to listen to their lies anymore. No, fuck that. I can't wait that long. Maybe you would like to know what it feels like to have a foot slam into your face."

Before I could see what he meant, his boot came crashing down on my face. I felt the bone below my right eye break, and then for a moment, everything faded to black. I came to as they were dragging me down the basement stairs. My head struck each step along the way. My hands were tied behind my back, making it even worse as I slammed into each stair tread. Ken was at the bottom, looking up at me as they threw me onto the floor next to him.

I screamed as my face and ribs exploded with pain. I was getting a little tired of kissing the floor so often; that was going to have to stop. The goons turned around and stomped back up the stairs. I lay there, trying to catch my breath. I could feel my cheek swelling up and my eye starting to shut.

I looked over at Ken and realized we were in deep shit. He rolled over and laid a hand on my shoulder. "Take it easy, pal. Take in some slow, shallow breaths. We have time to think this out. They won't be back for a while, if ever. Maybe we will be lucky enough and Pinata will get his ass shot off."

"We won't be that lucky. They'll be back. We have to get the hell out of here before they return. Can you help me up?"

"Just take it easy for a minute. You just lie there, and I'll see if I can find a way out of this dungeon, but first, we have to get rid of these ropes. Let's lie back to back, and I'll see if I can get yours untied."

We stayed that way for an hour before Ken was finally able to untie my wrists. I struggled to a sitting position and untied Ken's, but not without pain in every movement.

Ken stood up and looked around. There were small windows on three walls, but we couldn't even get a leg through any of them. He went up the stairs and tried the door, but it was locked and secure. He came back down, and I said, "Look in the cupboards and see if there are any tools. Maybe we'll get lucky and find a sledge hammer, and then we can bust our way out."

Ken opened the first four cupboards with no luck. As he opened the fifth door, he whistled and said, "Why, look what I found." He pulled out an electric drill with a large bit and an extension cord. Then he pulled out a hammer. "I guess we found our key to the door."

He looked around for an outlet and found one on the side of the stairwell. He plugged it in and hit the switch. The drill came to life with a sweet humming sound. He walked up the stairs and began to drill around the handle of the door. After he had six holes around it, he gave it a kick and the door flew open.

He came back down and said, "Let's get the hell out of here." He practically carried me up the stairs, I was in such horrible pain. When we reached the top, I began to cough, and before I knew it, I was coughing up blood. That was confirmation that Joey really had broken my ribs.

Ken looked down to see the blood and said, "We need to get you to the hospital."

I whispered, "That will have to wait for a while. We need to stop Joey before he kills half of the people in that hotel."

Ken laughed. "You can't even move. How are you going to stop anyone?"

"I can still think. Besides, I have you to do all the heavy hitting. I'll be the brains, and you can be the brawn."

"Whatever. Let's get the hell out of here."

CHAPTER FORTY-FOUR

The keys we had left on the hood of the car were surprisingly still there. Ken said with a smile, "They must have left through the garage and forgot about our keys."

I said, "See, Mr. Pinata is not as smart as he claims to be." Ken reached over the hood and picked up the keys without letting go of me. Then he put a hand on each of my shoulders and helped me into the car. I sat down with a groan. I noticed my breathing was still labored. I needed to get to a hospital as soon as possible. I was getting waves of panic as breathing became more difficult with each passing minute. Ken walked around the car and climbed into the driver's seat with a smile. He put in the key and turned it, but the engine did not respond. His smile vanished.

He got out and raised the hood. I heard him say, "Son of a bitch." He walked back to my window carrying six spark plug wires. They were all cut in two. He said, "Looks like Mr. Pinata isn't so dumb after all. He cut the fucking wires."

He opened my door and said, "Looks like we walk. Are you going to be able to make it for a while?"

"I'll walk until I can't walk anymore," I answered.

"Good enough."

We started down the driveway and made it to the road, but I had to stop three or four times to catch my breath. "If someone stops to help us, we have to tell them we had an accident of some kind. Let's say I was up in the garage and fell on top of you. My ladder gave way."

"Sounds like a plan. That might explain why we both look like punching bags."

Ken thought that we should try to make it a half mile down to the next cross road. It would give us a better chance to catch a passing car.

So we continued walking, albeit slowly. I felt like screaming with each step I took. After a couple hundred yards, I finally said, "I can't go any further. Why don't you run up to the cross road and try to wave down a passing car. Maybe someone will be nice enough to come and pick me up."

"I'll just sit here until you get back. I'll be okay; just go."

Ken nodded and ran down the road. I tried to sit, but it was impossible. The pain was excruciating. There was a tree a few feet from me, so I leaned against it and then slid down. Although the pain was unbelievable, at least I didn't pass out.

Once I was sitting, I started hacking up more blood, almost choking with each cough. When I spit out a huge amount of blood, I knew I was in real trouble.

I did wait, though, for about forty-five minutes before Ken returned in a police car. The officer got to me first and saw that the front of my shirt was covered with blood.

"Hello, I'm Officer Compton. Your friend here told me what happened. I want you to just sit tight and try not to move. I already called an ambulance. They said they should be here in about twenty minutes. Can you hold on that long?"

"I don't know. I think that may be too late, but I'll try."

He went to his car and pulled out an oxygen tank with a mask out of the trunk, walked back, and put the mask on my face. I felt a little relief as soon as he turned on the oxygen flow.

Ken asked, "Would you feel better if you lie down?"

"No, that makes it worse. It feels like I'm drowning."

The officer said, "You are probably filling a lobe or two of your lungs with blood." He took out a stethoscope and listened to my lungs. He explained, "I'm a trained EMT too, and I'm not getting any sounds from the right side of your lungs. We need to get you to the hospital right away. It's best that you stay as still as possible. By the looks of you, we may not be able to wait for the ambulance. You have to be honest with me. If your breathing is getting worse, you have to tell me. If it is, I am going to put you in the cruiser and take you to the hospital myself."

"Do you think I could borrow your phone? I need to call my wife," I asked breathlessly.

Ken looked at me and almost broke out in a grin. The officer didn't notice Ken's expression as he handed me his phone. He went back to the cruiser to call his post.

I called Jack's cell, and he answered on the first ring.

"Hello?" He said it cautiously, not knowing who was calling.

"Jack, it's Irish."

"Where the hell are you?"

"Right now, I'm lying alongside a country road waiting for an ambulance."

"Jesus Christ, Irish, a bloodbath just happened at Frank Marzetti's hotel. Were you involved in that?"

"No, Ken and I found out where Mr. Pinata was hiding, so we drove out to try to talk him out of going after Marzetti." I could feel myself panting in order to get enough air to talk. I hesitated because my breathing was getting worse with each word I spoke. "He and his thugs beat the hell out of me. I'm sure he crushed my ribs, and now I'm coughing up large amounts of blood. Plus I think he broke some bones in my face. I can't see out of my right eye. I'm a mess. What the hell is going on at the hotel?"

"Apparently, some men burst onto Mr. Marzetti's floor with guns ablaze. Our agents are just now responding, so we don't know anything yet. Preliminary reports indicate there are multiple casualties. Witnesses said they saw two men running out of the building carrying automatic weapons. One of the men they described sounds like Joseph Pinata."

I said, "That goddamn dumbass. What a fool. We tried to tell him not to go."

All of a sudden, Ken pulled the phone from my hand and said to me, "That's enough talking. Jack, this is Ken. Irish shouldn't be talking anymore. We are going to bring him to the hospital as soon as the ambulance gets here. I will keep you posted on how he's doing."

Jack replied, "I will have one of my men in the ER when he arrives. If they admit him, I'll have him placed in my room with me. Tell him we are going to be roomies."

Ken hung up the phone and turned around to hear the officer say, "We are going to take him to the hospital ourselves. It seems the ambulance got waylaid by another important call to some shootout at a hotel in downtown Miami. I don't know what the hell is going on in the world anymore. Can you help me get him into the cruiser? We need to pick him up just like he's sitting. Irish, is it?"

"It is." I knew what was coming. The pain was going to be excruciating.

They gently picked me up, and the pain shot through my chest like a bullet. I blacked out for just an instant, but it helped because when I opened my eyes, I was sitting in the cruiser with Ken at my side, holding me upright.

Ken asked, "How you doing?"

"I feel like I got stabbed with a spear."

Ken smiled at me and said with a laugh, "I have great news for you. If you get admitted, they are going to place you in Jack's room. You two are going to be roomies."

I let out a little chuckle but stopped when it felt like that spear was once again being jammed into my chest. It was a good thing the cop car was a big Chrysler 300, because the ride was smooth.

When we arrived at the hospital, two nurses came out with a gurney and asked me to lie on it. I refused and asked for a wheelchair. They skipped all the preliminary paperwork and took me directly back to one of the ER rooms.

The first person who walked in was Dr. Myott. In a somewhat sarcastic voice, she said, "Well, look at you, Mr. MacSween. Looks like people will have to come and visit you in the hospital for a change. Have your shenanigans finally caught up with you?"

I just smiled and didn't say a word.

"Tell me what happened to you."

"I fell off the top of a garage and landed on a table saw. I think I broke some ribs. I'm having a hard time breathing."

She took the stethoscope from around her neck, pulled my shirt up, and listened to my lungs. She asked me to take in deep breaths and blow them out slowly. I did the best I could, but I knew something was very wrong.

She looked at the scars on my chest and abdomen from the injuries I received while in Afghanistan. "My god, it looks like this is nothing new to you, is it, Mr. MacSween. What the hell have you been doing with your life?"

"If I told you, you wouldn't understand. So let's leave it at that."

"This was not a personal question. I need to know from a medical standpoint what type of injuries you've had."

Gasping for breath, I pointed to my chest and said, "Four large pieces of shrapnel from an exploding rocket;" then to my abdomen, "Two rounds from an AK 47 from an unhappy Afghan;" then to my left shoulder, "Stab wound with a knife. It ripped my shoulder open, thanks to a boy about sixteen." Lastly, I pointed to my right hip area. "Steel fragments from a roadside bomb."

She was totally silent for a moment. Then she asked, "What happened to the sixteen-year-old boy?"

"Is this a personal or professional question?"

"Personal."

Sarcastically, I said, "I killed him with my bare hands. That's what you do when you're at war fighting for your life. I didn't ask him his age before he shoved a knife into me."

The room was totally silent. I could hear the oxygen flowing but nothing else.

Finally, she said, "I am so sorry I asked such a stupid question. Please forgive me." She turned to the nurse who had just come into the room and said, "I need you to have someone call Dr. Hale and tell him we have a severe trauma to the chest, and he needs to come stat. I need you to get an IV started. I'll have Katie call surgery and let them know we have one coming their way."

I didn't even ask why about the surgery. I didn't have the strength and I didn't care. I was pissed.

Dr. Myott said to the nurse on her left, "Have Sherry come in and help get his clothes off and switch him over to the hospital oxygen. Mr. MacSween, we need to get x-rays to see what's going on inside your chest, and we also need to take some x-rays of your face, but we will wait on that until we can properly assess your chest injuries. At this point, the chest is much more important than a busted up face. That is unless you have a skull fracture, which I don't think you do."

I squeaked out an "okay," but otherwise, I just sat there in silence, letting the hospital staff do their thing.

As Dr. Myott turned to leave the room, she looked into my eyes, saying she was sorry about how she had acted. I said, "Hey, Doc, it's okay. You didn't mean any harm."

A nurse came into the room, shut the door, and started cutting my clothes away. She cut off my shirt, had me stand, and then threw a gown over me. Then she removed my pants and underwear. I guessed she must be Sherry. It wasn't the first time a woman had taken off my clothes without me knowing her name. I faintly felt the indignity of having my clothes removed without any foreplay, but didn't really give a damn.

She brought in a stretcher and had me sit on it with my legs stretched out on a pillow. Lying there with nothing but a hospital gown covering me, I thought of Katrina for the first time in a couple of hours. That was the longest time she had been out of my mind since the moment I saw her.

Sherry got the IV going and then took me to radiology for x-rays. I saw from their nametags that the technologists were Ronda and Todd. My eyes pleaded with them to take it easy when they had to move me, but Ronda said that unfortunately, I would have to move and that ideally I should lie face up on the hard-as-rocks x-ray table.

I whispered that I could not possibly lie down. Todd said they would do their best with me sitting up, but I would eventually have to be moved onto the table. When the pain hit, I couldn't breathe. I felt like I was unable to get enough air, and the panic hit me once again. Ronda patted my arm and softly talked my panic away. I could see the compassion in her eyes and felt it in her gentle hand movements.

After the x-ray ordeal, I was taken back to the ER. Two minutes later, Dr. Myott came into my room. "Mr. MacSween, it appears we have a serious problem. The ribs you fractured are still sticking into the middle and lower lobe of your right lung. We need to get you to surgery right away. The thoracic surgeon, Dr. Hale, called; he has just finished up a case in surgery and he is waiting for us to get you there."

Panting with shallow breaths, I asked, "Dr. Myott. I need to get ahold of my fiancée. Can you have someone call her? Her name is Katrina, and her number is at the top of the list of names in my phone."

Sherry, the nurse who had undressed me, said, "I will take care of that personally, Mr. MacSween. Katrina is a lucky lady to have you as her fiancé." Then she blushed.

Dr. Myott looked at Sherry, then turned back to me and asked, "Mr. MacSween, have you been flirting with the nurses even in your condition?"

I cracked a soft smile and nodded my head. Sherry left the room in a hurry. Must be true what people say about nurses. Horny little devils.

"I am going to give you some morphine for the pain, but not too much because of your pending surgery. They will put you out shortly for the surgery. Afterward, you will feel much, much better. Someone from surgery is here to ask you some questions about your medical history."

A few minutes later, Sherry came in and gave me the morphine Dr. Myott had ordered. She put it directly into my IV and I felt an immediate rush when she finished. The pain didn't let up, but I didn't care as much.

The woman from surgery came into the room and asked the routine questions about my medical history and any lung problems I may have had.

Sherry came back and said, "We are going to take you to surgery in about ten minutes, so try to lie perfectly still. The medicine I gave you will keep your pain to a minimum." She turned to leave but stopped and said, "Oh, I almost forgot. I got ahold of your fiancée. She said she would be here in fifteen minutes. If she gets here quick enough, she can see you before you go into surgery."

My breath was coming faster still, but I whispered a thank you as she walked out the door. After five minutes, I felt myself drift off to sleep in spite of my pain. I figured the morphine must be working.

The next thing I knew, there were five people pushing me on a gurney out of my ER room. As we reached the elevators, I suddenly heard a man screaming at the top of his lungs, "MacSween, I'm going to kill you with my bare hands, you son of a bitch."

I looked to my right, and saw Joseph Pinata charging past two security guards with a pistol in his hand, heading my way. All of a sudden, two more guards came crashing down on him. All three of them fell to the floor. By then, the other two guards had regained their footing and were on top of Mr. Pinata and seemed to have him secured.

Then abruptly, with more strength that I have ever seen, Mr. Pinata stood up and threw the guards off him. He punched one of the guards, kicked another, and picked up the third and threw him against a wall. He turned back to me and yelled, "I'm going to kill you! Just remember that, you rotten son of a bitch! You're going to die, and you're going to die very soon!"

He turned and ran out of the hospital. Everyone was stunned. Dr. Myott stood with her mouth agape, looking at me. Our eyes met, and I knew at that moment she didn't believe for a second that I had fallen out of a garage ceiling. Instead, I was caught up in the shenanigans of a crazy man. Joseph Pinata had finally gone nuts right before my eyes. I was so high from the morphine I didn't care.

As the elevator doors opened, I heard Katrina screaming, "Wait, wait, please wait a minute." She rushed over to me, and I registered the shocked look on her face when she saw me. "Oh darling, what did they do to you?" She gently put her hands on my face and the tears started flowing freely. She sobbed as she tried to see me through her tears. She lifted my oxygen mask and, with her soft, warm lips, kissed me and held me for just a moment. It was the most tender moment I had ever known.

Through my panting I whispered to her, "I will be fine. Don't worry; nothing will stop us from being together. I promise. I love you too much."

Then I saw her father gently squeeze her shoulders and say, "Come with me, Katrina. Let the doctors and nurses take care of him. They can't do it here in the elevator. You'll see him when they're through. They will take good care of him. Let them do their jobs."

She let go of my face and stepped away. The gurney was pushed into the elevator and the doors closed. I heard Sherry ask, "That's the Katrina who is your fiancée?"

I smiled and nodded my head as I drifted off to sleep.

CHAPTER FORTY-FIVE

First, I heard sounds. I didn't know what they were, and I didn't know where I was or even really *who* I was. It was like coming out of a dream filled with haze so thick nothing made sense. People were talking, but I couldn't make sense of what they were saying.

Slowly, my sense of being came into focus. I opened my eyes, or I should say my eye, and saw a person in a blue shirt scurrying around the room. I didn't know if the person was a man or a woman. I just knew it was a person.

It's funny when you're in that position. You don't even know what life is. For all I knew, I was waking up in heaven, or even hell for that matter, and the person running around was the gatekeeper for eternity. These thoughts were going through my mind before I knew I had a mind.

Finally, I heard, "Mr. MacSween, can you hear me? Mr. MacSween?" It was like a switch that turned on my awareness of life. I was finally able to focus and saw a nurse in a blue uniform smiling down at me.

"There you are. Welcome back to the land of the living. My name is Carol, and I'm a recovery room nurse. How are you feeling?"

I cleared my throat and said, "I guess I'm okay. I'm alive."

"Are you having any trouble breathing?"

"Not that I'm aware of."

"I would like you to take in a couple of breaths." I then realized that I had a dressing around my chest and that my breathing was somewhat back to normal. However, when I tried to take in a managed breath, the pain once again shot through my chest like that spear probing my lung.

Afterward, when I returned to normal breathing, I did feel a dull ache on the right side of my chest, but it wasn't nearly as bad.

"The doctor had to repair your lung and put two tubes in to allow the fluid to drain. You also broke your right zygoma, which is the bone just below your eye. The doctor had to put a pin in it to stabilize the bone. Once you are more awake, the pain will likely increase in both areas. Don't worry though; the doctor has prescribed plenty of pain medication that will keep you comfortable."

I asked, "What's the name of the doctor who fixed me up?"

"Actually, there were two doctors. Dr. Hale repaired your lung. He's a thoracic surgeon. Dr. Henderson repaired your cheek bone. He's an orthopedic surgeon. Both doctors told me to tell you that you are going to heal just fine. Although you will have a black eye for a couple of weeks and a tube coming out of your chest for the next two to three days, everything should eventually turn out well."

I managed to say, "Thank you very much."

The nurse said, "I was a surgery nurse over in Afghanistan for a year. Is that where you got all those other scars that you wear?"

I looked at her and could see the look that a person gets when living like we did in a war zone.

"Horrible time in our lives, wasn't it?"

"Only people like you and me know what it was like," I answered.

She said, "I tried to explain it several times but understood quickly that you really can't do it. It's too horrible to explain."

I felt myself drift off, and when I woke again, the nurse was gone.

Did I dream that or was it real? I couldn't say for sure. Another nurse said, "Oh, you're finally awake. How are you feeling?"

I felt odd, like I had been dreaming, but at the same time, as if I had been awake. I asked the new nurse, "Was there a nurse named Carol who was working here a little while ago?"

"No, there's nobody named Carol who works in recovery. Why do you ask?"

"Do you have anyone who served in Afghanistan as a surgery nurse?"

"We do have a few, but they are not working today, and none of them are named Carol."

She looked at me like I was crazy. Maybe I was. I drifted in and out for the next couple of hours, and when I was finally able to stay awake, the events of the day came back to me as I lay there thinking about my injuries. It had been a remarkable sequence of events, and as I thought about it, I realized I was lucky to be alive.

I wondered how Ken was doing, and how Katrina was. I wonder if Mr. Bernetti's sniper had completed his mission by killing Mr. Marzetti or if Mr. Pinata had killed him at the hotel. Then I wondered how many of Mr. Pinata's people had been killed at Mr. Marzetti's hotel.

After I was in the recovery room for what seemed like ten minutes, but was actually two hours, I was taken to my hospital room. Just before we left, the nurse gave me a shot of pain medicine in my IV.

The next thing I knew, I heard a familiar voice saying, "Are you going to sleep all day, you lazy bum? You are an FBI agent. Get off your dead ass and onto your dying feet. Break's over."

I opened my eyes, and through the fog that once again engulfed me, I saw Jack Casey standing next to my bed. The sight of him brought a smile to my face.

Jack was staring down at me and said with real concern in his voice, "What the hell did they do to you, son?"

I gathered my thoughts and replied, "Looks like I stood up when I should've shut up."

Jack smiled at my remark. "That's the Irish I have come to know and love. At least that mouth is still working. Although it looks like someone tried to shut you up permanently."

"I think Joseph Pinata has finally gone over the edge. What the hell happened at Mr. Marzetti's hotel? I heard there were a lot of injuries. Did anyone get killed?"

Just then, a nurse came into the room and started yelling at Jack. "Mr. Casey, I have told you four times that you are to stay in bed. You have a very severe concussion, not to mention the small bleed you had on your brain. Now get your butt back in bed."

I laughed as Jack scurried back to his bed and pulled the covers over himself, laughing all the way. "If I catch you out of bed another time, I will have the orderlies remove all your clothes, take away your bed covers, and tie you to the rails so you won't get up until the doctor releases you from the hospital. Do you want everyone who comes into your room to see you lying there butt naked?"

"Only you, Kay."

"You are incorrigible, Mr. Casey.

"You better listen to her, Jack. I don't want to have to lie here and see you butt naked every second of the day. It wouldn't be a pretty sight. I would have to ask for a transfer."

Jack laughed and said, "That wouldn't be too bad. What do you think, Kay?"

The nurse blushed and said, "Jack, stop hitting on me. I'm trying to be professional, but with you, it's impossible."

I noticed the serene, happy look on Jack's face and the same on hers. They were looking deep into each other's eyes. Maybe something was brewing between the two of them.

I broke the silence by saying, "Excuse me, ma'am. Could Jack and I have a few minutes of privacy? We have some important things to talk about."

I saw her take a double look at Jack, and then she smiled and said, "Of course." She walked out of our room and quietly shut the door.

"Thanks, Irish. I have been working on her since I got here and you go and ask her to leave. What a pal."

"Seriously, Jack, I need to know the details of what happened at the hotel, but I want to tell you something. Mr. Pinata broke into the ER and was screaming my name like he was crazy. He had a gun in his hand and was heading my way until four security guards drove him to the floor. But to my surprise, he threw all of them off and I thought he was going to kill me. But then he ran out of the hospital."

"I am aware of what happened in the ER, Irish. We have been trying to locate him for the last six hours. I still have men on it, but so far no luck. We don't know where he went."

"I just wanted to make sure to tell you what happened if you didn't know about it already. So tell me the dirty details about the attack at the hotel."

"More like a massacre. Joseph Pinata and ten of his men came into the hotel through the loading dock. They made their way up the freight elevator and surprised Frank Marzetti's men who were guarding it. The problem was, Pinata and his men thought they could quietly make their way down the hall to Frank's suite."

"Jack, Ken, and I tried to stop him, or at least stall him, but he wouldn't have anything to do with that. He accused us of being traitors to the union. He knew we were working with you and the FBI. He wouldn't listen to what we had to say, so he had his men hold me while he beat me up and kicked in my chest."

Jack nodded and continued, "Once they were halfway down the hall, they got caught in cross-fire. Half of Pinata's men were killed in the initial burst of gunshots. They manage to get four of Mr. Marzetti's men, but everyone except Pinata and another man were killed. Somehow, Mr. Pinata got away. The next thing we know, he's at the hospital and coming after you in the ER. We are sure he would have killed you if the guards hadn't stopped him."

"Fourteen men were killed? Are you kidding me? That's so sad. It could have been prevented, but he wouldn't listen to me. I feel like I failed all those people who lost their lives."

"No, you didn't, Irish. Joseph Pinata killed those men. He was responsible, not you."

"I can't remember, are you aware that he may have a terminal brain tumor?"

"Yes, we have been aware of that for quite some time. We were afraid he may be nuts, knowing he has nothing to lose. The doctors are saying he only has a few months to live. He is on a lot of medication that keeps him going. We don't think he's slept for four or five days."

"So what do we do now?" I asked, knowing full well they were waiting for him to come out of hiding.

"We are going to do nothing. Nurse Kay wants to keep me in bed but doesn't want to join me, and the doctors say you'll be unable to move for at least three or four days. They told us the rib bones tore the hell out of your lung. It will take a little while for that to heal."

The shock of all the killing was heavy on my mind. If Mr. Pinata had listened, all those men would still be alive. I felt like I had failed my duty. I should have done more.

"Have you heard anything about Ken? I never found out how badly he was injured."

"Ken is doing fine. The doctors looked him over and released him. We have him in protective custody. We're afraid Mr. Pinata will come looking for him too."

Just then, the door opened quietly, and Katrina smiled when she saw that I was awake. She approached me like I was a china doll, afraid she might break me with the slightest touch.

I smiled and said, "Hello, beautiful."

She bent down and gave me one of those soft, warm kisses that she was so good at. She whispered, "Are you going to be all right? The doctor wouldn't tell me anything because we are not officially related. Your sweet beautiful face is so swollen. How could anyone ever do that to you?"

"The nurse told me the doctors said I would heal just fine, but I would need a lot of tender loving care. Do you know where I can get some of that?"

She whispered in my ear, "You are going to get that plus a lot more. I won't let you out of my sight for a minute. I'm not going to let one of these nurses even give you a bath. I will take care of that."

I laughed as hard as I was able and said, "I can hardly wait."

She kissed me again, and we held that position for half a minute. When our lips parted, she said, "Papa is already getting things ready at home. I will take care of the rest." She smiled her wonderful smile, and I felt I was already at home. We kissed again.

I heard Jack clear his throat a couple of times and then say, "Excuse me, love birds, but you are not alone here. I'm watching all of this, and I'm jealous."

"Jack, you old fart. Let the kids comfort each other." It was Kay the nurse. She came back with Jack's medication.

"I'm jealous that I don't have someone to cuddle me in my misery." Jack laughed out loud.

Katrina sat down on the left side of the bed and laid her head gently on my shoulder. I put my arm around her and gave her forehead a kiss. I was just about to tell her that she needed to sit up when the door burst open.

To my surprise, I looked and saw Joseph Pinata standing in the doorway holding a gun in his right hand. He screamed, "Now it's your time to die, traitor!" He raised the gun and pointed it at me, and at the same time, I found the strength to push Katrina off the bed onto the floor.

I saw the hatred on his face and the crazy eyes of a madman. I knew it truly was my time to die, and there was nothing I could do about it.

He screamed, "Good-bye, you fucking bastard!"

But as he squeezed off his shot, the roar of a .357 Magnum went off from under Jack's bed covers. The shot hit Mr. Pinata square in the chest and slammed him back out through the doorway he had just burst through. His shot missed my head by inches and tore through the IV bottle hanging at the head of my bed. I was showered with a full bottle of IV fluid.

I heard a quiet *pop, pop* and then it was deathly quiet. Jack jumped out of bed and saw the frightened look on Kay's face as she lay on the floor.

"Stay there, do not get up." Quickly, he ran out the door with his Magnum leading the way. A few seconds later, I heard him say, "He's dead."

The door remained open, and I raised myself up on my left elbow, but not without a lot of pain. I saw Jack stand and turn to the agent next to him and say, "Just where in the hell were you when he came off the elevator?"

"I had to take a piss break, so I locked the elevator down and left for three minutes. He must have come up the stairs."

Jack said, "I thought you had the stairs locked out too."

The agent nodded and said, "I did."

Jack said, "How the hell did he get in here?" They turned and looked at the stairwell door and saw that the latch had been broken away. Problem solved.

Jack yelled at the agent, "Secure this floor. I don't want anyone getting off the elevator or coming from the stairwell unless they are from our office. That includes the local police. This is a federal crime area. I'll call this in to the department and make sure everyone on this floor is okay."

Jack looked at Joseph Pinata lying on the floor with his death mask staring into eternity. He came back into our room and asked, "Is everyone okay?"

Katrina stood up, and we all said yes and nodded our heads.

Kay said, "Jack Casey, what the hell are you doing out of you bed? I told you what I was going to do if I caught you out of bed one more time." She hesitated, then smiled and said, "I guess it can wait until later."

We all laughed except Katrina. She had no idea what Kay was talking about.

Jack walked up to Kay and said, "Not too much later, I hope." He held her as she shook with adrenaline. I could tell Jack was enjoying this.

She said, "Jack Casey, you are incorrigible. Two seconds ago, you shot a man in the chest and now you're flirting with me. Don't you have a conscience?"

"Not when it comes to saving lives and impressing beautiful women."

CHAPTER FORTY-SIX

The scene at the hospital was chaos for the next few hours, with plenty of federal officers arriving, including FBI director Henry Sullivan. I could see Jack out talking to him while standing over Mr. Pinata's body. They both turned to look at me, then talked some more before finally walking into my room.

Henry Sullivan smiled as he walked up to Katrina and me. He stuck out his hand and said, "Mr. MacSween, I want you to know that we could not have gotten Mr. Pinata without your help. I owe you a great deal of thanks for volunteering to do this." He shook my hand and asked, "Who is this lovely lady?"

"This is my fiancée, Katrina Bernetti."

"Pleased to meet you, Ms. Bernetti. Are you related to Frank Bernetti, the former president of the International Auto Workers Union?"

"Yes, he's my father."

"You have yourself one hell of a father there—very brave, very dedicated—and I am very sorry that Irish was beaten so badly. He's a good man too. You take good care of him."

"Don't worry; I won't let him out of my sight. Besides, I already know he's a good man. That's why I fell in love with him."

I expected Katrina to blush, but instead, it was Henry Sullivan who did. He said his good-byes to Jack and then turned and left the room.

"Jack, what does he mean when he said you couldn't have gotten Mr. Pinata without my help?"

With his head down, Jack shuffled his feet nervously like a whore in church, and then said, "We arranged for you to be put in my room because we thought Mr. Pinata might come after you."

"You mean I was the bait?"

"Not exactly. He wasn't supposed to get near you. Then Agent Petrie left his post to go take a leak, and lo and behold, Mr. Pinata ends up in our room. I'm awfully sorry about that. I didn't think you were in any danger whatsoever. We had the stairwell locked out in addition to the elevator, but unfortunately, he got in undetected. It was a total SNAFU on our part."

Katrina looked at me and asked, "What's a SNAFU?"

I laughed and so did Jack. "It's special FBI jargon they use for a massive screw-up."

She looked at me, puzzled, but just shrugged and said, "Okay."

Feeling pissed, I said to Jack, "You could have gotten Katrina killed. Didn't you think of that?"

"I didn't count on her being in the area either. They were not supposed to let her in, but she threatened to punch one of our agents, so he relinquished and let her pass. She's pretty tough- looking."

Katrina flashed a bright, happy smile and said, "I can be tough when I need to be, so you better not forget it."

"I'm sure I won't."

Katrina whispered, "I wish we were home in my bedroom. I would make you forget your pain and feel good instead."

"You're a tease, Katrina, but I hope you keep it up."

"I'll keep something up. You can be sure of that."

Jack cleared his throat and said, "We had to find Mr. Pinata before he hurt anyone else. We didn't think he would go after Frank Marzetti after what happened, and you were the most likely target. That's sometimes the job of an FBI agent."

We had resumed making small talk when one of Jack's agents came rushing into the room carrying a note. "Sorry to break in on you like this, Jack, but this is something I knew you would want to know."

"What the hell's happened now? The agent handed him the note. Jack read it and said, "Well, I'll be goddamned. I thought this was all over."

I asked him, "What is it, Jack? What the hell happened?"

"Well, it seems that Frank Marzetti was shot to death by a sniper. He was in a meeting in his suite, and the sniper shot him from the building across the street. I wonder if it was a hit by one of the other Mafia families. Our informers told us that everything was going to quiet down now, but I think someone didn't get the memo."

I didn't know what to say, so I said nothing. I wasn't going to tip my hat, but I knew where the shooter came from. I looked at Katrina and smiled. I wondered what she would think if she knew her papa had hired a hit man to take out Mr. Marzetti.

Apparently, Mr. Bernetti still thought Marzetti was a serious threat to the union, the staff, and Katrina and me. He was a man of his word, and a powerful one at that.

The dust finally began to settle after they removed Mr. Pinata's body from the area. I noticed it was getting dark by the time the last officer left. I told Katrina that I needed to get some sleep and that she should go home and do the same. She looked awfully tired.

She said, "I was not going to let you out of my sight."

"Katrina, you look beat. I think I will be fine here in the hospital. You go home and get some real rest. You can take care of me when I get home."

"You can count on it." She gave me a big hug and a kiss. She even hugged Jack and gave him a peck on the cheek, saying, "Thanks for saving Irish's life. We'll name our firstborn son after you. Jack

MacSween sounds pretty good to me. How about you, Irish?"

"It's okay with me as long as he's not ugly like Jack."

Katrina laughed and said, "Jack's not ugly. He's handsome in a mature sort of way."

Jack cracked up. Laughing, he said, "Katrina, give me another hug. If your son is going to be my namesake, that makes me part of the family. I will forever be Uncle Jack. Hell, that makes Irish my brother. That okay with you, Irish?"

"If that's what you want Jack. Welcome to the family."

Katrina gave him his hug and said, "I'll leave you two boys alone, but behave."

Kay startled everyone by saying, "Don't worry. I'm working a double shift so I will be here all night. I'll do my best to keep them quiet. It's time for Mr. MacSween's pain medication, so that will put him out for a while. I don't know what I am going to do with Jack, though. Maybe I'll have to drug him too."

Katrina said her final good-byes and left. Kay said she would be back in a few minutes with my medication, but I asked, "Can you give us some extra time?" Jack and I needed to talk before I got too high on the drugs.

She asked, "Can you last an hour without more pain meds? I don't want to let you go too long, or your pain will spike and then it makes it more difficult to deal with."

I said I could, so she left. Jack and I remained quiet for a few minutes. I spoke up, "Jack, I have been thinking about your offer to become an agent with the FBI, and I wanted to know if the offer still stands?"

"Funny you should ask. Henry and I were discussing that very thing before we came back into the room. After your training in Quantico, he wants me to offer you a position here in Miami with our local office. He already was aware of your relationship with Katrina, and he thought that would make it more enticing to you. He really wants you on our staff."

"That's what I was afraid of. I will have some decisions to make in the next few days. I have to have time to talk it over with Katrina, and the two of us will make the decision together."

"I understand, Irish. You'll no longer have just yourself to think about, so there's no rush. We'll give you all the time you need." He laughed again, and then said, "As long as you decide in the next day or so."

"Thanks, Jack. There is one more thing I have to confess to you."

He stopped me in my tracks, saying, "You don't have to. We already know."

"What are you talking about? You have no idea what I was about to say."

"Sure I do. You were going to tell me that Frank Bernetti hired the gun that took Mr. Marzetti out of the picture."

I was flabbergasted. "How the hell did you find out?"

"Find out? Hell, we set the entire thing up. It was our idea, not Frank Bernetti's. He has been working undercover for us for years. Hell, he was brought into the fold twenty-five years ago. He is a very resourceful man, a good man. He would never sacrifice his principles for anything or anyone. I wish I had ten men like him."

"Well, I'll be damned. I never would have thought he was working for you. Is this known to the general public?"

"Hell no. For Christ's sake, the media would crucify him, those vicious bastards. They have no idea how valuable he's become. He has settled more issues for us than any man or woman in our agency, including me. Henry Sullivan thinks you are of the same mold, so if you don't want to work directly for us, perhaps you would like to do more clandestine work."

"Are you saying I could keep a union job and still work for you?"

"That's actually the best possible option for us. But if you are really set on becoming an official agent with the FBI, we will accept that also."

"Could I still be assigned to the Miami area if I worked undercover?"

"For the first two years, for sure. After that, I can't guarantee anything. By then, maybe you will be ready to get out of Miami anyway. Who knows?"

I sat there, stunned by Jack's offer, as my mind raced thinking of the possibilities. "Hey, would this be a paid job if I was undercover, so to speak?"

"Absolutely. We would pay you at the top grade because of the dangerous duties an undercover agent faces. It's standard procedure."

"What are we talking here, money-wise?"

"You would get a hundred and twenty grand to start if you're employed full time. If you work in a lesser capacity, it would be sort of prorated. But at no time would you make less than a hundred grand. This job would not be a freebie. You would be required to be actively available for whatever job we need you to do. But at the same time, we understand that you'll have obligations to the union. So at no time would we require you to compromise your job with the International Truckers Union."

"This sounds pretty damn good to me, but I will still have to run it by Katrina. She may not want my pretty face messed up any further than it already is, and I can't say as I blame her. This is a pretty good-looking face."

Jack said, "For right now, we would like this to be between you, me, and Henry Sullivan. Katrina would be informed on an as-needed basis. It's not that we don't trust her. It's for her own benefit. We will be able to let her know that you are working with us in perhaps a year from now, if it all works out. So why don't we let this lie for a few days, at least until your head is clear enough to make a proper well-thought-out decision? There's no rush."

"Okay, Jack, let's do that. If I can't talk to Katrina about it, I'll let you know my decision in a couple of days. Deal?"

"Deal," Jack responded with a broad smile.

A few minutes later, Kay came back in to give me my pain meds and, once again, put it directly into my IV tube. After a few minutes, I could feel myself drifting off into a deep sleep. I smiled, because for the first time in quite a while I felt safe and free from turmoil.

CHAPTER FORTY-SEVEN

I woke with a start. Someone was vigorously shaking my left big toe.

"What the hell?" I said as I looked up and saw that it was Ken Cloutier. Thomas Sharpe was standing next to him.

Thomas said, "Wake up. It's daylight in the swamp."

I finally brought them into focus. They were smiling like foxes in a hen house. "What are you two smiling about? Looks like you got caught with your hand in the cookie jar and could care less."

Thomas Sharpe spoke first. "I know this must look strange to you, the two of us smiling like this after all that has happened in the last few days, but we are just so relieved now that the union is out of Mr. Pinata's hands, and we don't have to worry about him ever again. We can get back to representing our members like a union is supposed to do."

"How are Sophia and her mother doing after learning about Mr. Pinata's death?"

"Of course Sophia was quite shook up, but she was okay after she had her initial cry, especially since she knew he was terminally ill. He became a raving lunatic at the end. She talked to her doctor this morning and he told her it was probably because of the brain tumor. He said many times it can cause personality changes in people. I think she felt better knowing that about her father. Her mother didn't care that he died. As far as Angela is concerned, she stopped loving him a long time ago. She didn't even shed a tear."

"I'm glad to hear Sophia is doing okay. Now you two can have your baby without being afraid of Mr. Pinata interfering."

"What really tickles my fancy is that we can now give the union back to our members."

I smiled at that thought, and then, it finally hit me. He was right. We could give the union back to our members. All we had to do was get ourselves elected to the positions that would allow us to best serve them.

Ken spoke up next. "Irish, right after Mr. Pinata was killed, we gathered as a group, the members of the staff here in Miami, and we had a heart-to-heart talk about the future of the International Truckers Union. It was the general consensus that we have to involve our members if we expect to save this union and our members' jobs."

Thomas took over at that point. "There was a unanimous decision by those present that you should be our next president. You have shown the leadership, conviction, and dedication that it will take to lead this union back to respectability."

"How many were at this meeting, just you two?"

"No, Irish. We had the entire staff present, at least what's left of them. We even pooled all the regional directors, and they said they would support you one hundred percent. They are all ready to go to work for the union if you agree to be our president."

"Aren't you getting ahead of yourselves? The president needs to be elected. You can't just appoint someone to the presidency. This is a democracy. They have to be elected."

Ken said, "Since when did this union become a democracy? Anyway, you would think someone who may be our next president would know the rules of our constitution. It says that if the president dies or leaves office, he is to be replaced by the first vice president. It also says that if the first vice president is not able to accept the position, the international executive board can appoint someone to fill the position until the next general election, which happens to be in three and a half years."

I lay in my bed, stunned. I looked at Thomas and said, "I know when the three of us talked, we decided that I should be the next president. But are you still good with that idea?"

Thomas smiled. "Am I good with the idea? I *thought* of the idea. It takes more than just brains to be a union president—not that you don't have brains. It takes leadership, dedication, determination, and love for the union. You have all those characteristics. You're a natural."

I responded, "So you say."

Thomas said, "I have agreed to be the financial secretary, and Ken here is going to be the recording secretary. Mary Monroe has accepted the position of first vice president, Jeff Boone has accepted the second vice president position, and Kim Peppin will be the third vice president."

Ken spoke up, "So, what do you say?"

Thomas said, "It's not just me. Everyone feels that way. There wasn't one negative vote. So what do you say?"

I was still trying to come out of my fog. The nurse had come in early to give me another pain med dose, so I was still on the hazy side. I looked up, and all the people Thomas had just mentioned came into my hospital room, clapping and smiling from ear to ear. What could I do?

I looked each person in the eye, smiled, and said, "I accept your nomination to the position of president of the International Truckers Union."

Ken stepped forward with a Bible and said, "Place your hand on the Bible, and Mary Monroe will swear you in."

Mary Monroe was a middle-aged woman who always kept in the background during negotiations. She stayed away from the fray but had the knowledge and the burning desire to help our members. She was always a very dedicated union member and would make a great vice president, and later, a great president. I was really happy to see that she had stepped forward to accept the job

She smiled at me and asked, "Are you ready for this, Irish?"

"I am as long as you stand beside me."

She answered by saying, "I think we will make a great team."

"Me too."

"Repeat after me: I, Sean MacSween, do solemnly swear to uphold the Constitution of the International Truckers Union. I swear that I will dedicate myself to my union, my country, and my family. I will fight for every member no matter how difficult or troubled their situation may be. I will dedicate myself to grow union jobs, to fight to keep the jobs we have, and to improve the working conditions, benefits, and pay of all our members. So help me God."

I repeated the words, and afterwards everyone clapped loud and long. Then I saw Jack Casey, Katrina, and her father standing proudly in the doorway clapping and yelling wildly.

The moment was so overwhelming that tears formed in my eyes and I was overcome with emotion. Katrina rushed to my side and gave me one of her long, soft kisses that drew cheers from every-one. This was truly a moment of happiness.

"What are your first orders as president?" Ken yelled.

"Get me another shot of pain meds in my IV line and let's party."

ABOUT THE AUTHOR

Dennis Seiler has been happily married to his wife Ronda for 44 years. Dennis is a retired local union president as well as a retired Radiologic Technologist. He and his wife have two sons; Andrew, who is a pediatric physician in Ann Arbor, Michigan and Matthew, who is an attorney in Arlington, Virginia. They also have three grandchildren. His first book, *Reprehensible Conduct*, is the completion of a dream he has worked on for over three and a half years. His past experiences provide readers with an inside look at labor unions, the actions of the officers, and the struggles of the men and women they represent.

CPSIA information can be obtained
at www.ICGtesting.com
Printed in the USA
FSOW04n1040140716
22702FS